TΔLΣ

PILGRIM

TALE

BOOK 1 OF THE PILGRIM TRILOGY

TIM MURGATROYD

CLOUD
LODGE
BOOKS

First published in 2019 by:

Cloud Lodge Books (CLB)
51 Holland Street, London W8 7JB
www.cloudlodgebooks.com

ISBN 978-1-9995873-2-1

A CIP catalogue record for this book is available from the British Library.

1 3 5 7 9 10 8 6 4 2

Printed and bound by CPI Group (UK) Ltd, Croydon, CR0 4YY in the United Kingdom

A fasting belly may never be merry.

Medieval English Proverb

Sweetheart, do not love too long:
I loved long and long,
And grew to be out of fashion
Like an old song.

W. B. Yeats

CONTENTS

TALE ONE

THE HUNGRY WINTER

Baytown, North Yorkshire Coast

ΘΠΣ

THE PUZZLE WELL INN

The bartender and owner of the Puzzle Well Inn called above his customers' thirsty clatter: 'One in, one out, Michael.' He referred to the funeral of a neighbour's baby son, a far from uncommon event thereabouts. 'Shame's everywhere, I suppose. The usual?'

The tall, square-shouldered man he addressed replied with a nod. He sported a violin in one hand, empty clay tankard in the other. A broad streak of silver-grey parted his thick black hair. He had recently turned twenty-nine. His name: Michael Pilgrim.

The Puzzle Well itself had seen tides of décor go in and out over three centuries. Much like the waves breaking on the stony beach and quay its porch overlooked. Right now, in the middle years of the twenty-second century, the plaster on the Puzzle's walls was pockmarked, its oak beams weary of paint, furniture repaired once too often. A single electric light fuelled by a rechargeable power-cell glowed dimly behind the bar. Otherwise, shark oil lanterns cast flickering corners of reddish light over tables shiny with varnish.

It being a Saturday night, several dozen folks had gathered, old and young, male and female, to stage what was known in Baytown as 'a bit of a do'. This required coarse local cider and home-brewed beer – not to mention indiscreet line dancing for the young 'uns, to the strains of fiddle, guitar and accordion.

Just then the Puzzle's front door swung open. November gusts set the lanterns flickering. The crowd quietened as a procession of men came in one by one.

DRONES

The length of England away, far beyond the imagination of merrymakers in the Puzzle Well Inn, across a cloudless indigo sky a-glitter with crooked constellations, over lands where few lamps glinted back at the stars, a vast hangar constructed of alloy blazed with arclights.

Two operatives in black plastic overalls bearing heraldic coats-of-arms moved through lines of stationary machines. Dutiful automated trollies followed with tools, equipment, spare parts, ammunition. Scents of oil, bleach, chemicals. Hollow clangs, reverberations.

A bus-sized jump-jet drew the technicians and their trundling servants. Quietly the uniformed men discussed symbols projected by glowing screens. Doors on the side of the drone aircraft lowered to form ramps.

A LONE VIOLIN

As the procession of men entered the inn by the shore, higher up the hill music leaked from a former chapel. Night seemed to pause in its progress towards dawn.

A lone violin confronted the wind's moan, the repetitive crash of waves on the beach, its voice aloof from the jigs and re-invented pop tunes favoured at the Puzzle.

A ginger tomcat padding along the grass-tufted pavement froze. Back went velvet ears.

Still, the brooding melody poured out a lonely, wordless song. You might imagine the violinist's bow sweeping back and forth, a pendulum of sound in a dark, empty room where shadows echoed. Until – necessary release – soft piano chords joined the solitary voice, minor chords heavy with sustain, one upon another like stepping stones across a void.

As if summoned, the tom padded along a pitch-black alley at the side of the chapel. Jumped the high wall into a yard at the rear. Here it lingered, tail swishing, glancing over the cliff at a sea dappled by moonlight. The moon flecked prisms in its amber eyes. So clear and lovely a night, ocean and music and sky and cat's eyes connected by a road of silver moonlight.

With tail raised the crafty old tom mewed like a winsome kitten, head-butting open a cat flap into the chapel. Two women played. The pianist grey-haired, her face lined by life's travails, peering through thick round spectacles at sheet music lit by candlelight. Beside her, a young woman of middling height, slim and porcelain pale, curly masses of auburn hair concealing slender shoulders.

The resolving chord died. The cat meowed. The women smiled uncertainly at one another.

'Oh, it's you, Harry,' said the elder. 'What's driven you in so early?'

BIG JACKO

Michael Pilgrim counted six strangers into the Puzzle Well Inn. Their leader, short and bull-chested, swayed broad shoulders and hips as he walked. His pumpkin head was completely bald. He greeted the Puzzle's proprietor in an accent associated with the mounds of rotting masonry and concrete known as London.

'I'm thirsty!' he cried to the barman. 'Six pints of yer best for me and my boys.'

Talk resumed in the crowded room, cautiously then heedlessly. As Michael turned to rejoin the musicians, a large hand touched his elbow to detain him.

'I'm addressin' Mister Pilgrim?'

Michael knew the big black man by repute as a newcomer. Nothing unusual in that. Or necessarily objectionable. A bad harvest and the roads sprouted hungry people.

'That's right.'

'Call me Jacko,' said the stranger. 'Big Jacko. I hear you're known as *Lieutenant* Pilgrim. Crusader man, I'm guessin'?'

Michael felt a stir of irritation. 'Until my luck changed.'

'I bet you're wondering why I introduced me-self. Am I right?'

He reached out and touched Michael's elbow again.

Michael shrugged. He liberated his elbow with an unhurried movement. It crossed his mind the big man's grin resembled a Greek comic mask.

'It's good to get to know people,' he said.

'Ha! Ha!' boomed Big Jacko. 'The thing is me and my boys and my little adopted family have just moved to these parts.'

Michael waited.

'Well, the thing is, I like the look of that big old house you live in. With your brother, as I understand? I'm told people round here call it Hob Hall.' (His pronunciation was queer to Michael's ears). 'Wouldn't be for sale by any chance?' asked the bald man.

'No chance at all.'

'A shame! If you change your mind, Lieutenant, I'm easy to find.'

'We won't.'

Big Jacko's grin stiffened. It was quite sudden. Michael instinctively stepped back.

'Never say never,' said the stranger. He surveyed the crowd. 'Never say never, friends! A drink for everyone! Big Jacko's treat!'

Motioning to his companions who were smoking fancy cigarettes in a quiet corner, he called out. 'Send me the bill tomorrow, Charlie.'

After they had gone the buzz of conversation in the Puzzle gained intensity. Everyone had opinions about the small gang. The fisher-folk and crofters of Baytown – men and women alike – were tough knots of trees with dense, thorny undergrowth. Comers-in found them hard to penetrate. One or two had even found themselves tossed off the cliff. Still, a free drink was a free drink, and Baytown folk seldom turned up their noses.

The innkeeper, Charlie Gudwallah, grumbled, 'He better bloody well settle up for this little lot.' Before the world's population dwindled to dregs like sand through an hourglass, Charlie's forebears had hailed from Calcutta. All that remained of this noble heritage was a surname, brown skin and a bronze statuette of Ganesh he kept behind the bar for good luck. 'What were all that about?' he wondered. 'Funny way to win friends, badgering one of the oldest families round here about where they live.'

'Demonstration of power,' said Michael. He blinked. Unbidden memories of vehicles massing on desert sands drove him to drain his beer. 'I reckon it's time for more music, Charlie.'

Charlie leaned over the bar. 'Watch that Jacko,' he whispered. 'Seemed a bit too particular about the Hall for my liking. There was summat to it.'

'Birds like him have blown in and out of Baytown before.'

'He brought crates of stuff with him,' said Charlie, 'like he means to hang around.'

But his friend had rejoined the musicians.

A lively jig sparked dancing until Big Jacko was forgotten. Yet the suppressed memory of a desert convoy lingered in shady corners of Lieutenant Pilgrim's mood until drowned by beer.

TWO SISTERS

Up the hill, Harry purred on his mistress's lap. The back of her hand, as she stroked, was waxy, veined, watermarked by age. Her lissom companion perched on a damp sofa, cradling a mug of camomile tea.

'Playing together was like old times, Mhairi,' said the young woman, brightly. Her voice was smooth and soft as her pale skin. 'You always loved Elgar. Time is so strange. It makes us strangers to ourselves.'

They met each other's gaze. Silence lengthened.

'Why exactly have you come here, Helen?' asked the older woman.

Her guest examined steam rising from her mug. Wind rattled the tall, stained glass chapel window.

'Mhairi, do you wish I hadn't? But really it wasn't just because of you. The Museum drew me.' She set down her drink and rose to stretch. 'And I thought, at last, I have a chance to do something useful with my life. That's what you've managed, isn't it?'

Helen impulsively picked up a night light flickering on a saucer and stepped into the dark cave of the chapel. Its glow revealed row upon row of books – hardbacks, paperbacks, crates of magazines.

'You created this library for one thing,' said Helen, 'so the people here could remember how it was before. You're preserving past treasures. Well then, why shouldn't I? You know how Mummy and Daddy always loved visiting the Museum. It feels like my last link to them.'

'Someone else could have been the new Curator,' pointed out Mhairi, 'someone with better qualifications than powerful friends. Have you come here because of Blair?'

Helen laughed uneasily. The saucer she held wobbled. Light danced over the bookshelves.

'Oh, Blair ceased to be ordinary Blair Gover a long time ago. He's *Bertrand du Guesclin* now. They've all taken French names from medieval romances. It's the latest fad.'

Mhairi's eyebrows rose. 'Thirty years ago, before my – let's just call it my *departure* from the City – I seem to remember they were playing Gods and Goddesses on Mount Olympus. Oh, and wearing togas.'

'Well, they're all chevaliers or maidens now,' said Helen. 'Sometimes both at the same time. "To make every precious moment an aesthetic moment" is the mantra. Preferably in Medieval French, *naturellement*.'

A cough of derision from Mhairi. 'What about that nasty little sister of his, Ellie?'

'You refer to *Eloise du Guesclin*? Humble Ellie Gover has also been deleted.'

Helen went over to a bookcase and ran a finger down the dusty spine of a paperback from the last century, printed before the Great Dying.

'You're working very hard to avoid my question, Helen Macdonald,' pointed out Mhairi. 'Assuming you're still a Macdonald. Maybe you've adopted a silly French name as well?'

'Actually, I always use Mummy's maiden name, Devereux. After what happened to you it seemed ... Oh, don't look at me like that, Mhairi! You know I was never brave.'

With a sigh, Mhairi's youthful sister – whose beauty resembled a screen goddess in soft focus from the days of cinema – returned to her chair and tea.

'Actually, I have quarrelled with Bertrand,' admitted Helen. 'Horribly, in fact. It was about...' She struggled to explain herself. 'How wrong they are. How selfish. I can see that now. As for the City, it's a gilded prison. Everyone afraid of everyone. It's all built on fear, you know. Even of the poor, poor people in the countryside. Not that Bertrand or the others consider them people anymore. They are referred to as ur-humans or primitives or unevolved hominids.'

'Did they force you to leave?' Mhairi asked, softly. 'Like they forced me? Is that why you've come here? Tail between your legs?'

'No, I heard about the Curator of the Museum dying and made Bertrand give me the job. He owed me that much. After all, the only reason the Museum still exists is because I made him maintain the place. I came here of my own free will.'

'Well, that's a start, at least,' said her sister, 'making a decision without Blair Gover – please note I refuse now and forever to call him *Bertrand du Guesclin*. Bravo, my dear! You're growing up. Even if you have contrived to never look like it.'

'Oh, please don't be horrible to me,' begged Helen. 'I know I deserve it, but I need you so badly, Mhairi!'

She subsided into her chair. Harry, sensing a new food supply, deserted his mistress's lap and rubbed speculatively against Helen's legs. She reached down and stroked his head.

'Let's see how long your good resolutions last,' said Mhairi. Her smile was brittle.

DRONES

In the hangar's echoing belly the technicians commenced pre-op procedures. Two drones trundled over to the jump-jet carrier on smooth caterpillar tracks. Machines tall as men, wide as doorways, kitted with relevant tools. Chivalric designs painted on their plasti-armour: unicorn and croix d'or, silver grail goblet and lion rampant. After tests, the land drones rolled up the carrier's ramp and disappeared inside.

Once more the black-uniformed operatives consulted handheld screens. Spoke instructions in a jargon of numbers and codes. In a separate corner of the hangar, a third drone came to life. This resembled a giant spider borne aloft by propellers encased in protective steel mesh. It also carried tools. The flying drone rose and joined its fellow machines in the jump-jet carrier's cargo hold.

Stifling a yawn – it was midnight – the senior technician confirmed the operation's status to Control. He muttered, and his screen heard. Symbols flashed. With a high-pitched rumble, the aircraft's engines activated.

BAYTOWN

Baytown, winding and steep-sloped, lay a few miles south of the mouldering port of Whitby. People in Baytown complained: *Daft place to build 'cept for billy goats. Strong legs their reward.* They needed to be strong.

Up from the Puzzle Well, streets of stone and slate-roofed houses climbed at forty-five degrees. Courtyards and terraces, flagged paths and overgrown yards forming a maze of cottages, sheds, boarded shops, snickleways. Granite steps worn by centuries of footwear: leather then plastic, then back to leather. Baytown was old. Half its houses vacant for any taker. A bustling country village in times like these.

MOONSHINE

After midnight Michael Pilgrim stepped out of the Puzzle Well Inn, his head whirling. People wandered home singly or in groups. A volunteer constable chatted affably with Charlie Gudwallah, shotgun slung over her shoulder, spiked club at her belt. Michael served in the same role four times a month.

Despite a lifetime's proximity to the coast, his eyes were automatically drawn to the sea. Quiet elation rose like joy-sap. Such a moon! Gibbous and waxing. Its silvery sheen softened the craggy foreshore. Already the tide had withdrawn to reveal rock pools, the haunt of crabs and sea snails.

Michael left the quay beside the Puzzle Well Inn for the beach. A cold, steady breeze fluttered inland, stirring wave crests to foam. Stooping he took out a torch hung from his belt, playing its beam over a ledge of weed-fringed stone. There he found, as he had been sure to find, a humble snail. Its shell glinted in the torchlight, a tiny replica of a conch. And out of the past, from tangles of childhood, he thought of his grandfather, old Reverend Pilgrim.

It occurred to him his whole family had endured like snails by staying close to their ledge. And why not? Where else was there to go?

He picked a route over slippery rocks and piles of rotting plastic to the surf, breathing in the tang of ozone. Waves broke and fizzed. The cloudless night enveloped his smallness.

For a long while he gazed at sea and stars, inwardly lit by wonder. Gratitude, too, to be granted this passing moment. To be granted the fellowship he had enjoyed that night among neighbours and friends. Even to belong in this forgotten corner of the world beside a cold, heedless sea. A belonging earned by generations of Pilgrims.

We Pilgrims are good people, for all our faults, he assured himself.

But inevitably stifled memories popped open like rotten pomegranates full of black, bitter seeds: a convoy gathering in the desert. Vultures following as gulls shadow a fishing boat. And his elation slackened.

THINGS BEST NOT MENTIONED IN BAYTOWN

The window-rattling breeze having also slackened, Helen and Mhairi ventured into the chapel's backyard and stood by the cliff edge. Helen cried out at such beauty.

'Oh, Mhairi, look! In the City, I almost forgot the stars. Too much pitiless light, one never sees the heavens there. Too much fear of the dark to let them in.'

Mhairi glanced sideways at her sister. For the first time that evening, suspicion left her tired face. She reached out for Helen's hand.

'I wouldn't mention the dear old City of Albion so freely if I were you,' she said. 'People here – and no doubt everywhere outside the limits – harbour resentments. They might not appreciate your peculiar position.'

Helen seemed not to hear. Her delight had focused on the three-quarter moon hung over the bay.

Mhairi smiled wryly. 'Perhaps you should not mention we are sisters either. People round here are rarely fools. They'll take one look at me, one at you. And one and one will not make two. Let's say you are my niece. That should account for any family resemblances.'

'If you like,' said Helen, still distracted. She leaned recklessly over the low wall separating yard from cliff edge. 'We're not the only stargazers out tonight,' she said, pointing downward.

On the beach, an upright shadow faced the retreating tide.

Mhairi, whose instinct was always to investigate, stepped inside, returning with a pair of twentieth-century binoculars.

'Thought so,' she said, focussing. 'That's Michael Pilgrim. His family's land adjoins the Museum grounds. You'll find the Pilgrims lead all sorts of things round here.'

Helen frowned. 'Did you know, my predecessor complained to the Deregulator in Whitby about the Pilgrims? I found a holomail about it on his old screen. You see, they planted oats and barley on the site of the deserted village.'

'Well, they feed a lot of mouths up at the Hall. Half the orphans in Baytown end up there.'

'I'm sure nothing will come of the complaint,' said Helen, though really she had no idea.

Before stepping out into the night, Helen took her sister's pale hands.

'I'm so glad to see you again!' she cried. Her green eyes filled with tears. 'I was such a fool to neglect you all these years! I gave Bertrand such power over me, Mhairi. It's no excuse really.'

Mhairi smiled sadly.

'And just look at you!' continued Helen. 'You defied all they did to break you. I'm sure the people here love you for the way you help them.'

'Cupboard love,' said Mhairi. 'Like furry little Harry's loyalty. I'm the only qualified doctor they're likely to get in a century of Sundays.' She nodded at the dark, empty street. 'Please change your mind and stay the night, Helen. You're not in Albion now. I hear shady types have drifted into Baytown of late.' She smiled. 'No need to look like that, I didn't mean you ... exactly.'

'I cannot live in fear any longer,' declared Helen. 'It has choked and choked me. The Museum is only twenty minutes' walk, and I have a torch.'

Both turned at a sound like scraping feet. No one appeared from the shadows.

LOST

Twenty minutes later Helen had forgotten her enthusiasm for moonlit wandering. Moon and stars had vanished. A thick slab of cloud advanced steadily, blacking out the horizon. Unused to the world's fickle weather except through plastiglass, the speed of the clouds surprised her. As did the darkness they brought. Baytown became a series of dead ends and blind courtyards.

If not for pride she would have returned to the chapel and Mhairi's offer of a bed. Even that possibility vanished after another half hour's confused wandering. She found herself in a street of semi-detached villas built two hundred years earlier, before the second great war of the twentieth century. The road's skein of tarmac humped and riven by tree roots. All its houses had surrendered to vegetation; none were occupied, unless by foxes, adders, insects or rodents.

To add to her discomfort the torch she had taken from the Museum early that evening dimmed. Then it went out.

She stood in the ruined road, paralysed. How stupid to have not listened to Mhairi! A sharp lesson that survival in Baytown demanded swift evolutions.

Torchlight appeared at the end of the abandoned street. Boots crunched. There was a low regular thud on the ground.

FOUND

She took one glance at the light and slipped into the shadows of a tall shrub growing over a brick wall. Perhaps the advancing figure heard her, for the regular thud on the road ceased. A beam swept the ground she had just vacated.

Helen shrank back. Surely, the man – she was sure it must be a man – would hear her breathing. Or the pounding of her heart. The footsteps resumed. Again the low thud, louder now. A few metres away at most.

She peered through bitter-scented leaves as the nightwalker drew parallel. A switch clicked. The torch's beam doubled in intensity, swinging at her like a cyclops' eye. Blinded, she raised a gloved hand to shield her face, half-expecting a blow.

Instead, a loud sniff.

'Rum place to find our new Museum Curator,' mused a youngish-sounding man. His vowels and accent marked him as local. She sensed drink in his voice.

Helen flushed. With the torch no longer directed at her eyes she could see clearly. Tall and broad, he wore a thick woollen coat. He had a strong, lean face and a faintly withdrawn air. A canvas violin case hung on his back. Apart from the torch, he held a four-foot high, steel-knobbed staff – a vicious weapon at need and the source of the low thud as he walked.

'I believe we're neighbours,' he said. 'I'm Michael Pilgrim.'

Helen extracted herself from the bush. She tugged back her headscarf to reveal her face and thick auburn hair. Quite suddenly her fear vanished. She laughed at the absurd figure she cut.

'I believe we are indeed neighbours, Mr Pilgrim,' she said, adding, 'I'd shake your hand except – look here!' A slug had hitched a ride on her glove while she was hiding. She shook it off.

At that moment the roof of thick clouds parted. The moon's glowing face grinned down at their meeting. Once more waves out in the bay glinted a restless silvery sheen.

TWO

THE DISUSED TRACK

Both looked skyward. Glanced down to earth.

Michael thought it rude to stare at the features revealed by the moonlight. Yet felt the urge strongly. Beauty of the Museum Curator's kind rarely wore a human form in Baytown, and he instinctively distrusted it.

'Perhaps I should see you back to the Museum,' he said.

An owl hooted nearby. A gust stirred a tree, and laggard leaves, yellow and wizened, drifted down. Michael pointed his torch at the path ahead, and they set off. The way grew muddy and speckled with leaf litter. His staff left small round indentations behind him. She hurried to match his long strides, glancing sideways occasionally. At the corner of the street, he stopped, pointing down a track surrounded by holly, ivy, thorn bush.

'That's the way to take in future,' he said. 'It's a disused railway track. We clear it each year. It's the most direct way to Baytown from Hob Vale.'

'I see,' she said.

The track was dark as a tunnel. Over-arching vegetation cut out all but puddles of moonlight. Even that faded as the clouds once more closed ranks. Michael sensed the woman beside him feared the dark deeply. Though her material position and privileges in this world were infinitely preferable to his own – indeed, to everyone's in Baytown – he felt an odd pity.

'Why not take my torch,' he said.

'Are you sure?'

'I am.'

She took it gratefully.

As they walked, she flicked the beam this way and that.

'Not far now,' he said, gesturing at a side path.

HOB VALE

Helen followed the tall man down a track intersecting the disused railway. Woodland surrounded them, oak and chestnut and beech. She heard the splash and gurgle of a stream in spate as heavy rain on the moors flowed seaward.

A moment later they emerged from the trees and Helen sighed with relief: at last, she recognised the land's lie. Once more the clouds had parted, providing a moonlit view of Baytown a mile or two to the north. A small herd of deer disappeared into undergrowth, white rumps bobbing. Before them lay Hob Vale.

It was a sheltered, grass-clad valley dotted with young apple and pear trees planted by the Pilgrim family. The dale ran straight down to the cliffs and beach where caves were said to house tiny, bearded sprites with magic to command: capricious hobs after whom the valley took its name.

Helen breathed more easily at the sight of the sea. Most of all, however, she was pleased to see the Museum buildings amidst open fields on the cliff-top – once the site of a prosperous village until the Black Death emptied it eight hundred years earlier. All that survived of the settlement was a stone Norman church with a square tower and a yew-filled graveyard. Alongside that, a rambling house and outbuildings, in fact, the same Hob Hall coveted by Big Jacko that evening in the Puzzle Well Inn, home to the Pilgrim family for generations.

'Well,' she declared, brightly, 'thank you for helping me. Though I'm sure I'd have got here eventually.'

Something about his ironic glance nettled her. Word of tonight's misadventures was sure to reach Mhairi. Perhaps that explained, as they followed the last stretch of track to their respective homes, why Helen said, 'By the way, Mr Pilgrim, I understand there has been a problem with barley and oats on the deserted village site.'

'Oh?'

'You see,' continued Helen, 'my predecessor registered a complaint with the Deregulator in Whitby. I thought it best to let you know.'

She sensed him stiffen.

'The only problem we have with barley and oats is not having enough of either,' he said.

They had drawn level to Holy Innocents Church and Hob Hall. The Museum lay half a mile further along the road.

'Yet it's my duty to pursue the matter.'

'Your concern is for these earthworks?' he said, gesturing at the mounds. 'What remains of a village deserted by its inhabitants long, long ago?'

'Yes.'

'I suspect the people who lived and died in that village would be more in favour of oats and barley.'

'That's beside the point ...'

'No!' It was the first time she had heard his voice raised. It carried deep authority. 'Hunger is never beside the point. Goodnight to you. My torch, if you please. No wild animal will bother you here.'

Helen sheepishly handed it over and watched him leave the road for the path to Hob Hall, unlock its heavy door, and disappear inside.

DRONES

The blast doors of the hangar slid apart to reveal a runway exposed to glaring banks of floodlights. The aircraft whined softly then floated out into the night air. Steam drifted in trickles from its silenced engines. Lights flashed red, yellow, green on its fuselage. For a long moment it hovered – then darted up and off, arching to the north.

No human in the aircraft, pilot and crew snug in Control before rows of screens. And the flying machine knew its work. Halfway to its primary target, it slowed to hover high above the deserted remnants of a town. Cameras sought out a concrete office block below, twelve storeys high, one of the last to be constructed before the Great Dying. Heat sensors picked out faint candlelight winking on its top floor.

Stealthily the drone carrier lost altitude. Now the technicians in Control leaned forward, examining close-ups of the building; a range of scans pinpointed a feeble, residual signal on the top floor, an antiquated screen brought back to life by a rechargeable power cell. One operator focused a camera on a window lit by candles. 'Query,' he said. A child's face had appeared, peering into the night: a girl of ten, maybe younger, wild-haired, clutching a stuffed toy panda and the offending screen.

'Proceed,' ordered his superior.

The carrier adjusted position. Two rockets spurted. The top of the office block exploded. Fire bulged from windows. Slowly the creaking walls collapsed. Dust and debris formed a cloud.

'What data were they accessing?' asked the first technician, trying to sound unconcerned.

His screen responded: a flickering cartoon from an age of innocence, a land of primary colour, of music and mountains, jade bamboo forests and ancient temples.

Meanwhile, the obedient drone carrier had turned towards the coast.

LOCKS AND BOLTS

Michael locked the front door of Hob Hall behind him, bolt upon chain. Two a.m. and nothing stirred in the big old house.

Perhaps a faint scurry of mice at the farthest edge of hearing. The gloomy, discreet tick-tick-tick of the grandfather clock beside an imposing, black-varnished oak staircase. The three hundred years old clock was a youngster compared to the house itself. Hob Hall, in one form or another, had stood beside Holy Innocents Church in the vale for six hundred years.

Michael commenced his nightly patrol to ensure lock and limb slept secure. First, the upper storeys of the hall, torch in hand. Outside his brother's room, he paused: a light still burning. James rarely slept well. Barely slept at all. Still half-drunk, Michael did not care to risk his older brother's silent – and inevitable – disapproval, so he tiptoed down the corridor.

No lights in his teenage nephew and niece's rooms, the twins, Averil and Seth. Yawning, he climbed another staircase to the topmost storey of the hall. The younger children's room ran the entire length of the attic and contained a dozen beds separated by partitions and curtains for warmth and privacy. Opening the door, he peered in. No light, no sound. He padded softly back down to the ground floor to check outside.

Darkness thick upon the vale now. Somewhere a cow lowed. The barn owl nesting in the stone tower of the church hooted. A garrulous hunter but effective: Michael had watched her come and go since he returned half-broken from the Crusades.

Using torch and hand, Michael tested the doors and outhouses at the rear of Hob Hall. The family sheepdogs, Bess and Bob, watched sleepily from their kennel, thoroughly used to his ways.

There had been no significant theft of livestock or food by vagrants for years, not since a flare-up of the bad times. Still, he made certain of stable and byre. That the fat sow was still in her sty, the chickens in their henhouse beside the stable block. He rattled the granary's padlock, the barn doors. Above all, the windowless brick and stone storehouse with its double locks: custodian of supplies needed to carry eighteen folk through the coming winter.

All quiet. Black clouds rolled over the bay; no more moon tonight. He could smell rain coming on.

Then he froze. His senses strained. A low rumble to the south. He knew that rumble. Knew that sound. His fists bunched. He peered up at the sky.

VISITORS

The moment he heard engines Michael Pilgrim hurried into the central yard enclosed by the house, stables, outbuildings. Craned in all directions. Surely nothing to worry about. Why should they? He hastily considered his family's transgressions. None worthy of a drone. Papermaking wasn't illegal in the quantity they produced and traded. No communication devices other than perfectly legal letters. The only machines they possessed were non-electrical apart from the permitted light sources. Nothing. Michael assured himself someone else must be for it.

He recollected the new Museum Curator's warning about oats and barley. Such a transgression could not merit a jet-drone, and a large one by the engine noise.

Yet the roar intensified. Michael's hands trembled. A blinding flash filled the night sky, illuminating Hob Hall and casting long black shadows across Hob Vale from the tower of the church. The ground vibrated.

'Fuck!' he breathed.

The stable door flew open and the Pilgrim family's two regular employees (many more were hired at harvest and sowing time) whose quarters lay on the first floor above the animal stalls, rushed out, pulling on boots and clothes. Amar, his pebble glasses golden discs in the blazing light, and gawky, simple-minded Darren the herd boy.

Amar hurried over to Michael. He carried a shotgun.

'It cannot be…' he began.

But it was. A siren went off, so deafening the three men in the yard reeled, covering their ears, buffeted by waves of sound.

A grating, metallic voice boomed through the bedlam: *You are about to be fined. You have five minutes to clear the buildings. You are about to be fined.*

The blinding light dimmed to reveal a hovering drone carrier descending like a dragon upon Hob Hall. Michael shook Amar by the shoulder. The latter stared up in mingled terror and wonder.

'The kids!' shouted Michael. 'Amar! Get them out by the front entrance and head for the Museum. All of them! Count them out!'

For a moment it seemed Amar was too amazed to move.

'And hide that fucking gun!'

Amar turned, rushed into the house.

You are about to be fined. You have three minutes to clear the buildings. You are about to be fined.

Michael looked around to order Darren out of harm's way. But the herd boy had vanished.

'Darren!' he bellowed, his voice drowned by siren and turbine roar. The carrier was landing a mere fifty feet from the buildings. Dust flew, blades of glass whirled. To Michael's horror, doors opened on the carrier's sides. Ramps lowered.

'No!' he breathed, knowing well what the ramps portended. 'Darren!'

Two drones appeared simultaneously. They moved at exactly the same speed, caterpillar tracks trundling, red lights pulsing.

You are about to be fined. You have one minute to clear the buildings. You are about to be fined.

Michael span round. No sign of the boy. Stupid, stupid boy!

A teenage girl dashed out of the Hall's kitchen door. She, too, peered round in confusion, covering her eyes against the brilliant searchlights. Seeing Michael, she scrambled over to join him.

'Uncle!' she cried. 'Please come! We can't get the children out. Father is trying. Please come! Seth's bolted. We need you.'

'Back inside, Averil! Right now!'

Just then the first drone crashed through a perimeter wall, bricks and dust flying.

Too late to flee, Michael grabbed Averil by her wrists. 'Don't move!' he hissed. 'Not a muscle.' He could feel her quaking, hear her terrified moans. Abruptly, his own fear diminished. He reprised a coolness under fire learned when little more than a boy. One that had granted him life when so many around him lost their own.

'Stay quite still,' he whispered. 'If it had orders to kill us we'd be dead by now. A dozen times over. We mustn't look like combatants.'

'Oh God!' she prayed. 'Mother!'

With a snarl of wheels, the drone trundled into the courtyard. Sensors scanned. A searchlight picked out the frozen figures clutching each other, contemplated them.

Crash. A second drone smashed down the fortified back gate, crunching it to splinters beneath steel tracks. Neither were huge machines, yet they bristled with weapons.

'Whatever happens, don't run,' said Michael.

The drones swung in unison to face the buildings. First, the locked storehouse containing the family's precious winter provisions. Two cannons barked. *Boom boom boom.* Averil screamed, and Michael used the commotion to pull her to the ground. Dust, masonry, slates billowed, landing all around them. The storehouse had been flattened. A flamethrower completed the work, setting the wreckage ablaze with a whoosh.

Now Michael glimpsed the drones' instructions. Next in line: the granary. After that, the stables and byre where Darren would hide instinctively with his precious animals.

'They are not here to kill us,' he hissed at Averil. 'Stay completely still. On your front. Hands on head like so. They're programmed not to run you over.'

He began to crawl across the muddy yard on his belly, low as a lizard, half-expecting a jet of flame or crash of cannon fire to single him out. But the drones were behaving exactly as predicted: logical, methodical, busily blowing up the granary. At the stable door, he glanced back.

Good girl! *Good girl!* Averil lay face down, hands on the back of her head. Darren's turn now. With a wriggle, he was inside.

Strange how the brain selects noises. All he'd heard up to then were sirens, weapons, destruction. Now he became aware of a new source of danger. The Pilgrims owned a fair number of animals: cows, a horse and mule, a sow. Sheep and chickens. All but pig and sheep dwelt in the long stable block. Placid creatures crazed beyond hysteria. Cows leapt and butted, bellowing in distress. Iron-shod hooves crashed against stall doors. Red light flickered from the fires outside. Beams from searchlights flashed. Beasts were colliding, bucking.

'Darren!' shouted Michael.

No use, his voice lost in the bedlam. He glanced back at the drones. A minute. Maybe more. Then they'd line up in front of the stable, scan the building thoroughly before letting rip.

Into the chaos of animals ran Michael Pilgrim. He threw open Baxter the horse's stall. Then Noddy the mule's. He dodged a lunging cow to reach the stable block's rear entrance. There he found Darren, crouched in panic, half-hidden by hay. He reached down. One hand grasped the lad's ear, the other yanked open a bolt. With a boot, the double doors flew open to reveal Hob Vale, sickly yellow from the drone carrier's floodlights.

'Move!' he screamed.

He hauled Darren outside and away from the building. Ten feet. Twenty. Was that enough? Whinnying. Hooves galloping. Maddened animals fled past. Then the long building exploded, hurling them into a muddy ditch that saved their lives. Debris landed all around. A brick stuck Michael's shoulder.

'Oh God,' he murmured. Pain dazed him. But he was alive! Alive!

'No! No!' screeched Darren, leaping up to flee, ducking his head.

A hovering black spider had appeared. Propellers whirled and chattered. Searchlight beams played over their refuge.

'Don't run!' begged Michael.

The boy was edging away.

'Don't run, Darren! Listen to me. Please!'

Darren bolted. Guns swivelled. A red dot appeared on the youth's back as he crashed down the hillside towards the beck. *Crack.* A single cannon shot. Darren's body burst in two. Blood and organs scattered in a spray. Halves of him bounced apart then lay smoking on the grass.

Again the beams appraised Michael. He lay face down, hands on head. His shoulder ached from the brick that had struck him. He could almost feel the sensor reading his gender, heartbeat, temperature, invisibly frisking him for hidden weapons, accumulating electronic impulses that would gather to a pre-ordained point then decide whether he should die. His eyes squeezed shut. Oh, if only he believed in his brother's religion! But his faith had burned away upon desert sands long ago. He awaited a delicate squirt of napalm to set his prone body ablaze.

THRΣΣ

———— ❖ ————

AVERIL PILGRIM

At sixteen years of age, Averil Pilgrim was a habitual counter of blessings. To her, they took human forms.

There was her family, of course, including a dozen waifs and orphans who had found shelter in Hob Hall, and her father, Reverend James Pilgrim, the nearest Baytown possessed to a squire, a man respected for his generosity to folk suffering hard times. No shortage existed in the district. Even Seth, her wayward twin brother, catalyst for concern and exasperation in equal measure, seemed a blessing. Only Uncle Michael was taken for granted – as one does a sturdy roof until it springs a leak.

For the last six months, Averil had been employed as general assistant at the Museum in return for a rechargeable light cell payable once a year and, hence, not yet earned.

A few days after the drones came, she was busy polishing a display cabinet when Helen Devereux drifted over. The girl glanced up expectantly. Every facet of the new Curator fascinated Averil. Her elegance and English rose beauty. Her deep wells of knowledge. Her wit and languid grace. Sometimes, alone before her bedroom mirror, Averil struck poses in imitation of the Curator.

'You were telling me all about that horrid business the other night,' began Helen.

Averil rubbed furiously at the glass. 'Yes, ma'am.' She blew an errant lock of hair from her eyes.

'You mentioned your uncle? Mr Pilgrim?'

'Uncle Michael. Yes, I did.' Averil paused to examine Helen through clear blue eyes. 'He lay in a ditch while one of those *things* hovered over him. That was after they murdered poor Darren. Uncle Michael wouldn't let me look at the body. He said bad dreams would come of it. I managed to crawl into the house. Every other building was flattened. My uncle believes the drones had orders to leave the Hall alone, but it puzzles him why.'

Averil vented her feelings by rubbing the glass until it squeaked.

'One of those *things* hunted all our animals in the Vale. Only the mule and sheepdogs survived. The rest burned up like candles.'

Helen hid her mouth with a hand. Was she complicit in this outrage committed against decent, simple people? No beneficiary of the Five Cities was entirely guiltless.

'Your uncle sounds very brave.'

Averil worked her duster. 'Brave?' she said. 'Braver than any machine with no life to lose!' The girl drew herself up proudly, subsiding into a nervous laugh. 'He risked his own life to save poor Darren. Uncle Michael was in the Crusades, you know.'

'I see,' said Helen. 'Poor man.'

'There are quite a few here in Baytown who wouldn't have come back if not for him.'

'I'm sure.'

'The worst thing is,' said Averil, 'we still don't know why they punished us. Father says it's a test of faith, like in the Bible. Though why God should want *that* is a mystery.'

'A great shame,' muttered the director. 'Averil, after the displays, please dust the reception desk.'

For a moment the girl hesitated. 'Ma'am,' she said, 'you know a drone does the cleaning here. I did suggest to the last Curator that I could, well, help with the objects or displays. I can read and write, and I'm good at sums!'

It was true a single, obsolete service drone crawled patiently over walls, cases, floors, vacuuming and dusting.

'Sometimes a human touch is best,' said Helen. 'Drones are merely mockeries of people. But I will try to find more intelligent work for you, Averil. I can see you are clever. And that you've never been allowed the opportunities you deserve.'

Such praise made her assistant blush a medley of peaches and cream.

THE JEWEL

Once Averil had gone, loneliness settled on Helen. She drifted around the echoing museum. Signs guided visitors who never came to shabby exhibitions: *GEOLOGY AND EXTINCTION … THE DESERTED VILLAGE OF HOB VALE: A LOST WORLD … WORKING THE COAST*. And in pride of place, *THE HOB VALE JEWEL*.

Helen Devereux issued an instruction to her screen, and the reinforced glass shield of the Jewel's display case lifted with a hum. She leaned forward, just as she had as a girl when her family came to Baytown for their annual holidays. That had been in the days when holidays still existed. Her parents and Mhairi and her little brother Owen. Yet the Macdonald family had proved extraordinarily lucky: two out of five survived the successive Dyings, each more vicious than the last. Most families vanished entirely, their genes dissolved like blossom.

Sometimes Helen fancied that the Jewel had a special connection with her. That it, not chance, had saved her. Wasn't that why it had been fashioned in the last great time of plague, the Black Death? A magical talisman to defeat death?

The Jewel, diamond-shaped locket sculpted from pure Indian gold, images engraved on its front in delicate, intricate relief, of mother and child. A flawless blue sapphire set in the centre like a clear, unblinking eye. Yet on the locket's hidden back ugliness lurked: two engraved skeletons in a dance macabre, a grotesque *memento mori*. A reminder of how death grins always behind beauty.

In the dark museum's main hall, lit only by the display case, Helen reached out to touch the blue sapphire.

'Thank you,' she said, 'for letting Mhairi forgive me a little.'

Later, she stepped outside. Spiky cases of horse chestnuts gone brown littered the grass-covered car park where no cars came, along with shreds of half-decayed plastic and streaks of the plastic dust Baytown folk called *tilth*. Leaves from the towering chestnut tree lay in dry, wind-rustled drifts. It occurred to Helen the tree's forebears must have shaded people in lost Hob Vale village.

Leaning on a broom, she surveyed Baytown and the grey surface of the sea. A few cobles were out line-fishing cod.

Turning inland, she examined Hob Hall. Crows and rooks cawed in trees around the big old house. Two men were stolidly clearing the charred debris of an outhouse, salvaging materials for re-use. Michael Pilgrim and a dark-complexioned young man she identified from Averil's guileless talk as a Syrian refugee, Amar, saved from starvation by his current employer.

Then Helen glanced up. The distinctive clatter and chunter of an aircar. It grew from a tiny black dot to hover jauntily over Baytown, pennants streaming. She shielded her eyes. Tourists from the City of Albion or maybe one of the other Five Cities, enjoying the picturesque curve of the bay.

The aircraft angled towards the Museum, its livery of gold, white and green diagonal stripes familiar. Loudspeakers emitted a fanfare of trumpets. Crows, rooks and hedge-birds rose in alarm.

AMAR

Amar Abdoulfattakh rarely used his surname because no one could pronounce it. His own mouth was forgetting the shape of its vowels and consonants.

That winter's afternoon he laboured silently beside Michael Pilgrim.

'Something on your mind?' asked Michael.

Amar lifted a pair of smoke-blackened bricks. By aptitude, he should have been an engineer, scientist, problem-solver through logic and calculation. Hence he had studied every scientific textbook and manual in Dr Macdonald's mildew-scented library in the old chapel at Baytown. A dangerous fascination if he dabbled in forbidden technology.

'Here's a strange thing, *Sharif,*' he said. 'The City builds machines to knock down your house.' He banged the bricks together. 'But we are allowed only bare hands to rebuild. Or they come knock the house down all over again. A game we cannot win.'

Michael kept working. 'I've got a far more pressing game on my mind.'

'What is that?'

'Not starving this winter.'

They picked up a shattered roof beam and carried it to the waste pile.

'How much food is left, *Sharif*?' asked Amar.

'Well, the drones clearly targeted our food supply and storehouses. For what reason, I can't work out. They certainly didn't leave much. On short rations, we've got a few weeks.'

Grim news with so many digestive systems to satisfy. But there was no palming off the orphans or other dependents. No one else could afford to take them. Michael sighed.

'Averil should have finished the kids' lesson by now,' he said, taking off thick cow-hide gloves. 'Get them to help you here, Amar. Pity Seth's decided to vanish again, or he could help too. I'll have a talk with the Reverend. I just saw him heading into the church.'

With that, he disappeared into Holy Innocents Church.

Soon after, the aircar landed outside the Museum. A dozen young children who were assisting Amar ran across the fields for a closer look. Reluctant to miss the splendid machine, Averil and Amar followed.

BERTRAND DU GUESCLIN

Lights on the garishly-painted aircar pulsed as it landed. Helen waited, broom in hand. The vehicle's four adjustable propellers span to a halt.

She knew exactly who lolled within, no doubt lisping commands to the pilot-drone (a lisp much perfected), patting glossy, scented blonde locks with distracted satisfaction. It both excited and alarmed her that he'd left the safety of Albion to seek her out.

The doors slid open, and there he stood, one thumb hooked in his girdle, the other resting on the pommel of a sword: Bertrand Du Guesclin.

Helen felt faint surprise. Not at the fact he was unchanged since their last meeting: Bertrand seldom chose to change. It was the incongruity of his costume in Baytown's decline and grime.

Shoes of red satin with tapering toes eighteen inches long. Spangled crimson tights clinging to taut calf and thigh muscles. An extensive crotch forming its own codpiece. Not to mention a tissue-thin tunic decorated with fleurs-de-lis in gold thread. His hat a simple silk beret to denote the sincerity of a guileless shepherd swain. At his belt, a gilded and be-gemmed knight's sword capable of firing taser bolts that could splay a bull. What surprised her most was actually the beret: normally his hats were chosen to draw the eye heavenwards. For Bertrand Du Guesclin was rather short.

A security drone preceded him, scanning the area. Two clone pages, prepubescent girl and boy in identical red, gold, white and green liveries followed their master down the ramp. The children carried piles of gifts wrapped in silver paper and bunches of orchids from one of the City's huge hothouses. Despite herself, Helen could not help smiling at his extravagance.

Bertrand strolled over, hand steadying his sword. He looked around curiously. Bowed with a flourish she had seen him practise under the strict guidance of a comportment master. When he straightened, his eyes sparkled.

'Will my lady allow a knight errant the boon of her precious time?' He glanced at her broom. 'If I'd known you were playing Cinderella, Helen, I'd have brought a slipper along. *Tant pis!*'

Helen offered no curtsy in return. Her instinct was to apply the broom to his backside. She heard herself asking, just as Mhairi had asked when she landed in Baytown out of nowhere, 'Why exactly have you come here, Bertrand?'

N'EST-CE PAS?

Bertrand smiled wistfully. 'Why have I come? To visit the Museum, of course. Why else?'

'I did have another theory.'

'Let me guess! That I could not keep away from you. That I was drawn like a moth to the flame of your beauty, *n'est-ce pas*? I see my arrow hits the mark!' He leaned forward conspiratorially. 'Actually, I have come to see this Jewel you abandoned me for.'

Helen met his eye. Neither spoke. They knew each other's games too, too well. Yet it occurred to her Bertrand's visit might be of use after all.

'Then let me show you the Jewel,' she said. 'This way!'

They made quite a procession into the concrete and glass museum building. First, the handsome young chevalier. Just behind him, his lovely guide still holding her broom. Next the clone pages, desperately balancing piles of gifts. Finally, a small but capable security drone.

Bertrand listened deferentially as Helen took him from exhibit to exhibit, explaining their history and significance. It pleased her to possess superior knowledge. Bertrand was expert in so many fields she always felt stupid in comparison. Helen found herself relaxing.

'Now to the Jewel,' she said. 'Perhaps you will see why it has fascinated me since I was a girl. Why I persuaded you to keep the Museum open all these years.'

He bowed, 'I did it merely to please you.'

At the Jewel's display case she paused. He stared at the golden pendant revolving slowly. The dancing skeletons on its rear made him look at her sharply.

'Why death?' he murmured. 'Did you not tell me it is a talisman to avert the plague?'

'So it is.'

'Then why flatter hideousness? Does it not mar what would otherwise be perfect?'

'One cannot avoid nature,' she said.

Bertrand laughed lightly. 'So they say. Are we not both living proof that nature's so-called laws were never eternal?'

'That is something I have left behind forever,' she said. 'You know my views.'

He nodded sadly. 'Indeed. And thus I no longer have you by my side. But I would like to hold the Jewel. Is that permitted?'

'If you wear cotton gloves.'

Minutes later she placed it on his outstretched palms. Its sapphire sparkled beneath the lights. The engraved Virgin and child provoked a sigh from him.

'This was all they had to set against death,' he murmured. 'No science, just faith and new birth and magic. Nothing at all.'

Helen felt suddenly afraid for the Jewel. Afraid he might claim it. Seek to use it in his grandiose tussle with time. Already he had consumed so much she loved that she no longer knew where to find herself.

'Let me show you the deserted village site,' she said.

He reluctantly surrendered the Jewel back to her keeping. Smiled roguishly. 'After that, I have a proposal to make.'

HOLY INNOCENTS CHURCH

That winter's afternoon, deep shadows filled Holy Innocents Church except where, by some trick of light or manifestation of divine favour, a feeble beam projected through a stained glass window onto the altar. A gaunt man knelt before it, his cropped hair grey as slate. What did he pray for in the frail beam of winter sunlight? Lost people and things. His brooding soul a battered prayer.

The church around him smelt of mouldy earth. Birds roosted upon the roof joists, their white droppings splashed across the flagstones.

With a creak the heavy door opened. The Reverend did not move. In stepped Michael Pilgrim, work gloves in hand, his usual distracted air replaced by diffidence. Coughing apologetically, he removed his cap.

Something scraped. With a soldier's quick instincts Michael glanced around. No one. He walked up the aisle to the altar, heavy boots clumping on stone. At last, his brother noticed him.

'Shall I come back later?' asked Michael. His breath steamed out tendrils of mist.

'If you were wise you would pray beside me.'

There was an asthmatic wheeze in James Pilgrim's voice.

'You know I was never wise,' said Michael.

'I know.'

Silence between the brothers.

'I've come to talk about food,' said Michael, the younger by over a decade. 'Do you know how many weeks' supplies we still have? Thank God there was a lot of dried stuff stored in the cellar. We've got until Christmas at best.'

If the Reverend cared, he gave no sign.

'We need to think how we'll make it through to the spring crops,' continued Michael. 'Even that'll be tight. There's no way our neighbours can spare much. You know how bad the harvest was, half Baytown's pinched in the cheeks.'

The beam through the stained glass faded slowly, casting the altar into gloom. James Pilgrim coughed into a blood-stained handkerchief.

'All of us capable of work,' insisted Michael, 'you, me, Amar, Seth, Averil and the older kids, need to take whatever jobs we can get and pool the food we earn.'

A hacking, stubborn cough was the Reverend's answer.

'Well, maybe not you,' conceded Michael, 'you're unwell.'

James Pilgrim raised a palm. And not in blessing. He bent his head at the same angle as the statue of Christ crucified upon the altar.

'Man cannot live by bread alone,' he intoned.

Just as Michael knew he would. Again, a scraping echo. Rats perhaps. Poor rats indeed if they had to live off Holy Innocents Church and its congregation of three: Averil Pilgrim who attended each Sunday out of pity for her father; the Reverend himself and a mad old lady who walked over each Sunday from Baytown with six cats on leads.

James whispered, 'I would hope, Michael, you of all people, might look to his sins.'

Michael could guess which one his elder brother had in mind. He sat on a pew while James prayed, remembering how they had played together as boys. Time passed among the shadows.

'I'll be outside if you care to walk back to the Hall with me,' Michael said. 'Let's go together, James, it's what I always like best. Always have.'

His brother did not reply.

SETH PILGRIM

The scrape Michael had heard came from no rat. Seth Pilgrim lolled with hands behind his head on a rug hidden in the organ loft, a sanctuary from farm work, cooking, cleaning and tending the animals. In fact, anything he judged uncongenial. Which included most things. Other sanctuaries existed – Baytown was riddled with empty houses – and even a few hidey-holes within Hob Hall itself.

Thus Seth overheard Michael's proposals to save the family. All he heard was the threat to put him out as a workhorse among strangers. Another black mark on the deeply-scored tally he kept against his uncle.

All his life Seth had noted how his father laboured less to fill his belly than anyone else in Hob Hall. As his father's heir, he expected similar perquisites.

Besides, he had important interests old gits could never get. Especially girls, drink and weed – the latter smoked on the cliffs in fine weather or abandoned houses when the winter rains fell and fell. His principal interest, however, was dreaming of the day he left Hob Hall for good.

Even as he listened with cold outrage to Uncle Michael's threat to make him work like a clown, recent arrivals in Baytown entered his mind. Maybe he didn't need to rely on his crazy family. Big Jacko and his boys were envoys from a wider world. A world waiting for Seth Pilgrim to set it ablaze.

THE DESERTED VILLAGE

'Ah, a stroll among ghosts!' declared Bertrand, following a gravel path dotted with thistles. Since handing back the Jewel, he had been subdued.

Fields reverted by slow degrees to bramble and woodland on all sides. The grass of the deserted village site, however, was kept short. A welcome by-product of the barley crop planted by the Pilgrims, along with their grazing sheep and cattle.

'We are now walking up the main street of the lost village,' she said. 'Imagine the people's amazement at our clothes! Not to mention your aircar and faithful drones. And look! By the stream is – or was – a watermill to ground the corn. Broken querns have been excavated there.'

His brooding gaze followed her pointing finger. She knew open spaces made him uncomfortable. Bertrand stepped back toward the Museum. A crowd of local children had gathered to stare at his aircar.

'I am thinking,' he declared.

Here it comes, thought Helen.

'I am thinking how *unaccountable* your decision to live here is. Where is the beauty? The grace?'

Bertrand turned his attention to the wreckage of Hob Hall's outbuildings. A negligent smile played across his rosebud mouth. He met her eye.

'My, my,' he said.

Instantly Helen knew he had played some part in the drone attack. So well did they read one another no query was needed beyond a single word.

'Why?' she asked.

He bowed. 'For you, my love, so the primitives remember their place and, above all, fear you. I did it to protect you. The local Deregulator registered a complaint concerning your neighbours and was diligent enough to suggest a pre-emptive strike. All very sensible and proper, given your presence here. I insisted on no loss of life unless there was resistance – I know how squeamish you are, my dear – *et voila*! Everyone is happy.'

She stared out at the restless sea. 'Oh, Bertrand.'

Back in the Museum, the clone pages had laid out a feast of delicacies: truffles and caviar, kumquats and lychees, pastes of minced quail and hare, wafer-thin slices of roast boar cured in honey. Ice-cold sparkling wines.

It surprised Helen how gloomy Bertrand remained. False gaiety was his natural milieu.

'Why *have* you come here?' she asked again. 'You always hate to be away from the Five Cities.'

He sighed. Motioned to the clone page-girl for wine. His face, youthful and glowing, for a moment seemed weary.

'I am troubled,' he confessed. 'And I'm glad for a chance to share the reason. Or reasons. Some of them.'

He wandered over to a display case containing sandstone slabs carved with ancient spirals none could decipher.

'You see,' he said, 'I sometimes doubt the thing dearest to me. The prize that drove me and the others to overturn humanity's false definitions of nature.' He laughed as though in wonder. 'Actually, I blame you, Helen. Not angrily! Your decision to leave Albion was like a spot of mildew that spread to corrupt the whole fruit.'

Still, she did not reply. This new, vulnerable Bertrand threatened a power over her that the old one had long ago outworn.

'You see,' he said, quietly, 'I begin to doubt the Beautiful Life.'

FOUR

THE BEAUTIFUL LIFE

Helen stirred. 'Doubt the Beautiful Life, Bertrand? *You*?'

'Will you listen if I explain?'

He drank deeply from the crystal wine goblet. The clone-page scurried to refill it.

'First, let me start with what is self-evident. Namely, without a conscious struggle, disgust and contempt for this world are inescapable. How can it be otherwise when one thinks of the plagues, each polluting the world with yet more putrid, decaying bodies, with stenches and eye sockets alive with maggots? Oh, yes. And how revolting is old age! As for children, only a fool desires to have children.'

He gulped at the wine.

'Ah, Helen, what a miserable species is unimproved mankind! Cruel, capricious, ignorant. If time did away with humanity, the world would cry out in relief!' He chuckled. 'And, of course, that is why I – we – those destined to succeed humanity, the next evolutionary step – conceived the Beautiful Life.'

Helen stifled a yawn. None of this was remotely new. 'You mentioned doubts?'

'Yes, incredible as it seems, I have come to understand something we did not anticipate, I mean, concerning the primitives…'

'You mean *people*,' broke in Helen.

'I mean the unevolved hominids. You see, I have come to understand how much more *alive* they are in their brief, nasty, animal life-zones. Their every moment vivid and significant. Why? Because their sum of moments is compressed. But we, who contemplate a future without end for the ultimate good of our species, we lose that child-like vision. More!'

He waved impatiently at the clones.

'Am I supposed to applaud this great realisation?' she asked. 'It is as old as the Beautiful Life itself.'

'Yes! For you know, I never felt this way before. Not for an instant. But Helen, I intend to turn my doubts to profit.'

'You usually manage that.'

'No, do not mock me! Helen, I have decided to revive myself through my daily, no, hourly devotions to you. Marry me and become my queen, my consort, my princess.'

She regarded him with astonishment. He had told her many times he could never marry because no love lasts forever. Was this proposal his best response to a desperate ennui of his own making? She sensed through instinct rather than reason that far more lay behind it. Unspoken things to do with his position in the City.

He stepped over, took her limp hand.

'Return to Albion with me tonight! Anything you desire shall be yours. Life is so dull without you, Helen, so lonely. Perhaps you will remember all I have done for you. I need a trusted friend by my side right now.'

She shook her head. Withdrew her fingers. Stepped back. 'No, Bertrand. Once I wanted only what you offer, but my life has found a new meaning here, even if the price must be to lose it.'

The intensity of Bertrand's gaze frightened her. She knew too well his ruthlessness when crossed, his genius for getting his own way. And she recalled her complete reliance on him for her existence in the Museum and added, 'Give me time to consider your proposal.'

GRAVES

Michael stepped out into the overgrown churchyard. A dull, familiar ache consumed his spirit. Would James never let go of his grievances? Even now, when the family needed unity so badly; when Michael needed his big brother so badly.

Clambering round bramble-choked graves, he made for a wide-rooted yew. Here the graves were swept and sprigged with evergreens by Averil's hand.

He stood with bowed head before the first headstone. Carved lettering read: *Rev. Oliver Pilgrim, MA OXON, DD. 'Give, and it shall be given unto you'.*

'Hello, Grandad,' murmured Michael. He paused, unsure what message he had for the fiery old man who saved Baytown from barbarism, organising volunteer constables for protection, communal food banks for sustenance. Who had served as teacher and faithful friend whether you shared his faith or not.

How would Grandfather have reacted to the drone attack? The answer was obvious. Yet Michael feared so dangerous a course. Proof, if more were needed, he was a lesser man. Grandfather had been fearless against injustice. He would have visited the Deregulator in Whitby to demand an explanation for the murder of Darren, insist on compensation for their losses. Reckless, horribly dangerous, certainly futile, yet that was what Grandfather would have done.

The next grave was more recent. *Florence Pilgrim, beloved wife of Reverend James Pilgrim,* read the inscription. *May all sins be forgiven when the last trumpet sounds.*

That final phrase restored the faint ache to Michael's heart. Oh, there would be no forgiveness from James! Either for Florrie or himself. His was an angry god. Never mind it had been nothing, nothing at all. A moment of clinging together for comfort. An embrace born from despair...

He had been just nineteen when the drones rounded up the young men of Baytown. Twenty-six youths and men, the future marrow of the community, herded and scanned, forced to wear bracelets on each wrist that exploded if you pried them open, blowing off your whole arm. Then – so generous – each conscript had been granted an hour to return home, pack a few precious things, say farewell.

When he rushed back to Hob Hall, only Florrie was home, and he found her alone in the kitchen.

His beautiful sister-in-law! His friend from whom he kept no secrets of heart and mind except the one he dared not admit: that he worshipped her as only callow youth can. Fantasised at night of having his brother's wife for himself. Watched her avidly when he thought she was not looking. Her hair had been blonde as apple blossom. Sometimes she had put her arms around his shoulder, and he had longed for a closer embrace.

Perhaps Florrie felt something similar. That day, somehow, he did not know how, as they clutched each other and wept – for no one ever, ever came back from conscription – his mouth had found Florrie's. Her soft, sweet mouth. They had kissed, gulped, gasped, clutched one another. A moment, it had been no longer. Then both realised the kitchen door was open. There, like a black shadow, watching his little brother's tongue and hands all over his wife, had stood cold, gaunt Reverend James Pilgrim…

Michael brushed a spider's web from the headstone. When he returned to Baytown years later, Florrie lay in this corner of the churchyard. Ever since, though many an unattached – and attached – female had cast speculative glances his way he barely noticed. Not just because of Florrie. Murky, hot-scented dreams of a wholly different woman – one impossible to idolise, one he feared had spoiled him when it came to love forever – lurked in Michael Pilgrim.

Back in the church porch, he gazed out at Hob Vale, hazy with cold and dank, every tree and contour familiar. James stepped from the church. Cold blue eyes studied Michael until the latter glanced aside.

'I'm thinking of visiting our old friend the Deregulator tomorrow,' said Michael, 'to demand he compensates us. After all, we've done nothing wrong. Should I, James? I'm sure Grandfather would have done that.'

Sorrow crossed his older brother's sickly face. 'It is all the same.'

'I'll go tomorrow,' said Michael, firmly.

After they had gone the church door creaked. A head with tousled black hair poked out.

Seth became aware of an unusual noise, a faint buzz of voices. He ran like a hare down the dirt road, joining the crowd just as the Museum doors swished open.

FANFARES

When Bertrand Du Guesclin left the Museum, he encountered a curious crowd. Half Baytown had conquered their fears and gathered to marvel, even if that meant, for some, peering from behind the shelter of a bush or tree trunk. Not within living memory had City people visited the Museum. Among the onlookers were Big Jacko and Charlie Gudwallah, proprietor of the Puzzle Well Inn, a man who hated to miss out on gossip. And here was a topic of conversation for many winter nights to come.

Security drones scanned as Bertrand Du Guesclin flapped a hand at the primitives. Helen watched from the Museum entrance with arms folded, a wry expression on her fair face.

Then a surprise: the drones came to life, pointed stubby barrels. Warning lights flashed. A barrel-chested, muscle-ball of a man was bowing his way towards the aircar's ramp, waving a white handkerchief in homage. Bertrand Du Guesclin's eyelids fluttered at such presumption.

'My Lord!' bellowed the man in an accent far removed from Baytown's. 'May I take this opp'tunity to thank Your Grace for steppin' upon our ground! Bless you, Lord! Bless you!'

A tiny section of the crowd clapped. Namely the bald man's followers.

Bertrand examined him as one might an unusual beetle.

'Your name?' he lisped, his voice magnified hugely by a microphone in his clothes.

'Jacko, sir!' cried the primitive, on his knees now. 'Mayor of this manor. Or soon to be!'

Bertrand nodded. 'Hear this!' he boomed. 'Especially you, Mayor Jacko. The Museum and Lady Helen are under my special care. Note that. Should the slightest harm or inconvenience come to her, you, Jacko, and this whole village will burn slowly.'

'Thank you, Lord!' cried Jacko. 'I am your mayor, sir!' He turned to the crowd. 'Thank the Lord!' He gestured excitedly. 'He's made me Mayor!'

By now Bertrand Du Guesclin had climbed into the aircar, followed by his page-clones and drones. Ramps lifted. With a whoosh of propellers, the vehicle rose, banners catching the wind, loudspeakers pouring forth a jubilant fanfare. The aircar darted off towards the City of Albion.

MAYOR JACKO

The crowd outside the Museum muttered excitedly. Amar enthused to Averil about the finer points of the wondrous flying machine. They stood for a better view upon a heap of rust and glass in the car park, once a sportscar. Averil nodded occasionally to show she was listening.

Seth Pilgrim stared with undisguised admiration at Jacko. There, he thought, is a man who *does things*. Not on his knees like Father. He edged to the outskirts of Jacko's followers. Their strange accents intrigued him.

'Here goes then,' said their leader. The big man stepped forward to address the crowd before it dispersed.

'Friends!' he called. 'Neighbours! You all 'eard what the Lord commanded. It's an honour I take upon me-self. I *will* obey that Lord. From now on Big Jacko is Mayor of Baytown!'

People listened in silence.

'Anyone 'ave a problem with Lord Bertrand's command?' demanded Jacko.

Charlie Gudwallah stepped out of the crowd to face the newcomer.

'Nice of you to offer, but we don't need no Mayor in Baytown. Nor do folk here want one. Especially a stranger.'

'Aye!' shouted a man in the crowd. 'Bugger off back where you came from!'

Big Jacko glared through narrowed eyes at Charlie. Then he grew affable.

'No point blaming me, friends,' he said, 'it's just what the Lord commanded. "Jacko," he said, "either do my work as Mayor or I'll make Baytown burn." Am I right, boys?'

His boys agreed vocally.

'He said nowt of the kind!' protested Charlie.

'Well, tell you what, friends,' countered Jacko. 'Tomorrow I'll take a little trip to the Deregulator and see how *he* interprets the Lord's words.'

A wary hush greeted this threat. Older folk remembered the current Deregulator as a sullen Baytown lad. Not warm memories by any means. And Jacko seemed to have access to foodstuffs and valuables only available in the Deregulator's warehouse. Nor was it obvious how his gang maintained themselves. None worked at a visible trade, neither did they fish or farm.

Charlie Gudwallah snorted. 'The whole point of the Deregulator is that he's not meant to regulate. We'll have no mayors in Baytown, mister, unless we want one. We're free folk here.'

A broken-nosed bruiser from the would-be mayor's entourage advanced with fists bunched. Big Jacko waved him back.

'I'm going home,' said Charlie. 'And I'd appreciate it if you and your pals trouble us no more at the Puzzle Well.'

With that, he led the crowd back toward Baytown. Likewise, the residents of Hob Hall departed. Only Jacko and his followers remained. All except for a nervous, eager youth: Seth Pilgrim.

'I think you'd make a fine mayor, Mister Jacko,' he said.

The latter stepped over and squeezed Seth's elbow with a meaty palm. The lad flinched.

'Good to see someone round here can sniff how the wind's blowing,' said Jacko. 'You come back with me, son. I'll make sure you get a taste of proper tinned warehouse food, not your farm crap. Play fair by Jacko, and he plays fair by you.'

Seth cast an anxious glance back at Hob Hall. Averil and Amar had halted. His sister was beckoning for him to join them. Big Jacko followed his glance with a long, appraising stare at the girl.

'Thanks,' said Seth, puffing out his chest like the men around him. 'Don't mind if I do.'

His voice bore the faintest inflection of flooded London, lost and glamorous as Xanadu.

HOBS

At the foot of Hob Vale, wooded hillsides narrowed to form a gully through sandstone cliffs. A wide beck gargled and frothed as it flowed onto the beach. Set back above the shoreline stood a jumble of connected buildings, a Victorian mill then youth hostel. Now it hosted spiritual voyagers instead of holidaymakers: a community of Nuagers, worshippers of moon and cloud, tappers of Earth's ley lines to fuel psychic journeys.

Nearby, sea-carved caves wormed into the cliff. Within them lived the clan of hobs giving the Vale its name. Diminutive sprites, pointy-eared and bearded, capricious dealers with mortals ready to curse or bless on a whim. Or so ancient tales maintained, and the Nuagers knew for fact.

MISTER PRIEST MAN

Since boyhood, Michael's habit had been to walk off his fears on the beach. He did so that afternoon, accompanied by Bess the sheepdog.

A fine, blowy day, darkness still a way off. The tide out to reveal miles of stony, weed-littered beach, ribbed by bands of gritty sand and pebbles. Mounds of sea-tilth – decaying plastic trash of every imaginable shape and colour – had been piled against the foot of the cliff by a recent storm. Gulls hung on the wind.

He was admiring this view near the caves of Hob Hole when faint laughter disturbed him.

Michael's hand crept to a long knife strapped to his leg. Again the laughter, though no one was visible. A bearded head poked from one of the dark caves. It wore a battered, misshapen top hat decorated with shark teeth from a Great White caught in the Bay, semi-precious stones, dried willow and thyme. Its owner was known far and wide as Mister Priest Man.

'Been watching you, Michael Pilgrim, from this here hole. Just like the little folk watch us. You're fretting.'

Michael's hand left his knife. 'You gave me a funny turn, Priest Man, appearing like that. I almost took you for a hob.'

The leader of the Nuagers scrambled out of the cave. He wore a long coat of diverse animal pelts, multi-coloured rags and feathers. Flapping nervous hands, he replied: 'You Pilgrims could use a hob's kindness, so I'm told. And so my own eyes tell me.'

No denying that. People were talking of the drone attack on the Hall for many miles around. Michael shrugged.

'The Faery o' the Vale might help you yet,' mused Mister Priest Man. 'I could teach you what gifts please her. She visits the Vale when you Pilgrims have your eyes shut like blind puppies.'

The Nuager laughed. Not cruelly. 'Folk say your bellies will be hollow by Christmas.'

'Before then probably,' admitted Michael, 'but we ask for no man's charity. Not that folk round here can offer much.'

Priest Man produced a pair of spectacles lacking one lens and studied Michael. 'Did you mention my offer to your brother, the Holy Reverend? Did you?'

Michael patted Bess's head. The sheepdog looked from speaker to speaker, sniffing the wind.

'No point after the first time,' said Michael. 'So I didn't.'

Mister Priest Man clenched bony fists. Shook them at an indifferent sky. 'Stubborn! Foolish! If he'd only share the church with us, we'd share our fish and food!'

A deep grievance for the Nuagers. It was their conviction Holy Innocents Church capped a deep well of magical energy, a portal connecting directly to astral planes. Cosmic routes that might carry them, if harnessed properly, far from the miseries of this dunghill world. While not seeking to evict the Christians they had proposed several times to share the building as a place of worship.

'You may as well bargain with yon cliff as my brother,' said Michael. 'Be seeing you, Priest Man.'

He hesitated. 'By the way, I'm off to try my luck for a little justice with the Deregulator tomorrow. Do you think I'm mad?'

Priest Man tugged his filthy beard. 'Take care, Michael Pilgrim. We hear whispers you wouldn't like about the new Deregulator.'

Bess suddenly grew alert, staring fixedly at the bearded man.

'A voice in my head tells me this might be the last time I see you, Pilgrim,' mused Priest Man.

'That's true every time,' pointed out Michael.

'Aye. Let's hope the Faery o' the Vale helps you yet.'

With that, he wandered home to the old youth hostel.

FIVƐ

OF MULES AND MEN

The next morning Michael Pilgrim and Amar caught sight of the Deregulator's compound in Whitby. Rain splashed a counterpoint to choppy harmonies of sea. Noddy the mule – named for his head-dipping gait – crunched jigsaw pieces of tarmac and broken glass beneath his hooves.

The road ran along the top of the West Cliff, flanked on one side by hotels and houses riven by trees and bushes, on the other by a steep, tussocky descent to the sandy beach. Burned, rusted cars lined the way. Michael turned to Amar as the towering grey walls of the compound loomed. Reinforced concrete walls sixty feet high, featureless, steel-gated, guarded by drones; a castle to inspire fear rather than loyalty from the people it monitored.

'Keep an eye on Noddy and wait for me outside,' he said. 'Whatever happens, if I'm not out by dusk, head on home.'

Amar adjusted his cap. 'Leave you in there alone, *Sharif*?' His laugh was incredulous. 'Will you not listen to anyone? Your family, me – even this damn mule is less stubborn!'

It was true the creature was showing signs of skittishness near the compound. Michael didn't blame it.

'The new Deregulator was one of my grandfather's last pupils,' he said, doggedly. 'He owes my family the education that took him to the City. He won't have forgotten that, I'm sure. And I know Grandad would have come here to demand a fair trial.'

By now they were entering a strip of cleared ground moating the compound. Michael itched as sensors played over them. In his case, the sensors would detect instant recognition, both from his military service and the ill-judged appeal he and Doctor Macdonald had made for permission to set up a hospital only a month earlier. Ironically, the failure of that petition fed Michael's hope for justice. The Deregulator could easily have punished them then if he'd wanted.

Michael spotted familiar figures waiting to one side with three ponies. Two of Big Jacko's boys, their weapons concealed.

'See those likely lads?' he said softly. 'Keep out of their way.'

Amar wiped beads of rain from his nose. '*Sharif*,' he said, 'I will make one last try. Do not enter there…'

But Michael was already heading for the blast-proof gates of the building. A war drone on Tyrannosaurus shaped legs stood guard: a model used widely in the Crusades. One with the subtlety of a giant hyena biting off hunks of flesh.

For all sane folk, the close proximity of a war drone inspired a pounding heart and sweating palms and often an overpowering urge to empty one's bladder. Michael edged round the pitiless machine, assuring himself it had no reason to activate. War drones either guarded, destroyed or patrolled. In the latter role, they were programmed to detect forbidden technology and soundly terrify the primitives. No cause then to expect this ugly, towering brute on two legs to snatch him up and de-limb him as a child plucks petals off a daisy. Nevertheless, he sidled past it with a bowed head to a wide, high gateway.

EARLY BIRDS AND LATE WORMS

Neither drone nor man barred Michael Pilgrim's way into the inner courtyard of the compound. Concrete walls formed a wide, square box with an echoing steel roof. On three sides small round windows looked down. Arclights ensured an absence of shadow. Functionality was all that mattered here. The building's purpose was not to woo or placate, merely to admonish.

A few dormant drones and vehicles lined the inner walls. His route across the courtyard, however, avoided them. Red pulsing lights formed a path to yet another steel door. Here he gained access to a fellow human being. Or the voice of one through a loudspeaker.

State your business.

Michael hesitated. Was he talking to a simulation or actual woman?

'I'm here to speak with the Deregulator.'

Then I fear you will be disappointed.

So it was a real woman. Drones rarely managed irony. This gave him hope.

'I'm sure he would talk to me if he heard my name,' he said.

Michael Pilgrim, mused the woman, evidently consulting her screen. *I see you've come here before to make 'An unreasonable petition'.*

'I'm not back for that,' he assured her.

Michael glanced around nervously. His voice was amplified by the cavernous steel and concrete box. He feared a dormant drone would wake.

Why are you here? The woman sounded curious. It occurred to him how dull and predictable the compound's routines must be. And Whitby was hardly a desirable posting for an ambitious City technician: suicidal visitors like himself might even offer a welcome distraction.

'I have come for justice,' he said, as boldly as possible. 'Tell the Deregulator my name. He knows me.'

No reply. No command to wait. He was left standing before the armour-plated door. Minutes passed. Half an hour. He sat on the cold floor. An hour passed. At last the wide door slid open, but instead of a functionary wearing the black plastic overalls of the City, a bulky, bald man confronted him: Big Jacko.

Michael rose. For a long moment, they assessed each other. A grin spread across Jacko's face.

'Well, well,' he said.

Michael stepped aside without replying as Jacko swaggered down the path marked by red floor lights. Halfway across the echoing hall, he stopped.

'Guess what just happened,' he called back.

'I can't.'

'You, my friend, are addressing your new mayor. *Mayor Jacko of Baytown*. All official. And look!' He waved a bulging sack of power and light cells and City boots that would never wear out, precious tinned food believed by many to extend their life expectancy and fend off plague, unsnappable knives. 'Lovely, eh? Even better, the position's a job for life.'

Michael's face betrayed a dark thought.

'Remember that little offer I made for Hob Hall?' called Jacko. 'Well, the new Mayor needs somewhere suitable to live. Am I right?'

With a chuckle, he strolled away. Again Michael lowered himself to the floor, his mind whirling with calculations as slow minutes passed.

Nothing to do with Jacko made the slightest sense. District Deregulators had only two functions that truly mattered: to prevent the existence of any effective government among the primitives and deny them access to technology. His elevation of this stranger and generosity with City goods broke both those policies.

If Michael Pilgrim had been wise, he would have understood Jacko's presence as a grave warning and hurried home to Baytown. But as he had told his brother, he'd never been wise – and was perhaps too old to acquire the habit.

AVERIL'S PROMOTION

A few miles down the coast Helen Devereux called a staff meeting. In practice, that meant sipping camomile tea with Averil Pilgrim. They sat beside a complete ichthyosaur skeleton dug from the cliffs in the balmy twentieth century.

'So there you have it,' concluded Helen. 'I want to give you responsibility for re-cataloguing the exhibits stored in the basement. The museum computer will explain how. See if you can identify common themes. Then together we'll work on a new exhibition. I think we could call it *After the Deluge: Patterns of Survival.* I'd like local people to come and learn about their own histories. Along with visitors from the Five Cities, naturally.'

'Oh, Miss Devereux!' Averil's delight was infectious. 'I don't know what to say!' Her expression fell. 'You know, I needed a bit of good news today.'

Out it gushed. 'You see, Uncle Michael's gone to the Deregulator this morning. He said it's his duty to try for something called *restitution.* It seems his grandfather taught him the word. I begged him not to go. There's no justice for us there. And Father tried to persuade him, but Uncle wouldn't listen.'

Averil brushed tears from her eyes. 'We're afraid he'll never come back.'

'Oh,' said Helen.

They huddled over their tea. Helen thought rapidly. Thin lines lie between courage and foolhardy, vainglorious self-sacrifice. Lines she had always been afraid to cross. Not so, it seemed her neighbour.

Pangs of guilt stirred. Certainly, she had reasons to reproach herself. If nothing else, there was the information she could have shared with Michael Pilgrim. Facts that would have prevented his foolish quest. No one in Baytown except herself knew the Pilgrims' misfortunes stemmed from Bertrand.

Had he not boasted the drone attack was arranged to keep the locals in awe of her through a display of raw power? Perhaps she should send Bertrand a holotext and insist he intervene on behalf of Averil's uncle. Except then he would be back in control.

'I'm sorry,' said Helen.

Averil shrugged. 'Father's gone to the church to pray,' she said. 'There's nothing more we can do now, Miss.'

Shame warmed Helen's cheeks.

THE DEREGULATOR OF WHITBY

How long did Michael sit on the concrete floor of the inner hangar in the Deregulator's Compound? Without the sun he could not guess. No one else came or went after Big Jacko, not even a drone. Yet the building was far from silent. Michael listened to its constant hum and occasional clang with the unease of a ghetto child dumped in a rainforest.

He prepared for what might come next by recalling all he could about the Deregulator. Humble Will Birch had always been the sharpest pupil in the small school Grandfather held each morning at Holy Innocents Church. In those days the City of Albion still staged occasional aptitude tests among the primitives to recruit potential technicians. Fourteen-year-old Will Birch passed with an absurdly high rating. Not once had he returned to Baytown, even when his mother lay dying of diphtheria.

Another hour passed before the steel doors slid open. There, accompanied by a four-legged security drone, stood the object of his thoughts. Michael rose hurriedly.

'Will Birch!' he cried, forgetting to be afraid, though they had scarcely been friends when young.

The plump, short man pursed his lips as though about to speak. The security drone adjusted its position, pointing stubby cannons.

'It is usual to address an official of my rank as *sir*,' Will Birch said. All traces of his Baytown accent had been eradicated by years of service to the City. 'I'm told you came here for...' He hesitated over the word. '*Justice*? Isn't that what you told my assistant?'

'You must know how my family has been harmed,' said Michael. 'All our winter supplies ... I know you will give me a fair hearing.' He smiled disarmingly. 'Frankly, Will, we are desperate.'

The Deregulator sighed. 'You never learn, do you?'

'Grandfather helped you and your Mum when you both had nothing,' pointed out Michael. 'I thought...'

'So you want *a fair hearing*?' interrupted the official. 'Do you know, that sounds like a formal trial. Am I mistaken?'

'Well...'

'Trials are provided for,' conceded the Deregulator, reluctantly. He leaned forward. 'Have you considered what might happen if the verdict goes against you?'

'I'm sure it won't come to that,' said Michael, though every word Will Birch uttered was persuading him otherwise.

'We shall see,' declared the Deregulator. 'Let's to court!'

JUSTICE

A second official in black overalls joined them. They entered a long, plain corridor leading from the hangar. Michael recognised the woman's voice from his initial interview at the door as Will Birch's assistant. There were few representatives of the City in the concrete and steel bunker: a closed, sterile little world. Her face was dumpy, pale.

The four-legged security drone monitored Michael's every twitch. Its steel limbs created a slow, heavy drumbeat on the concrete floor as they approached a permaplastic door.

'Here,' commanded the woman.

Inside, a small computer box stood on a central table. Michael sensed from the smell no one had been in the room for a while.

Plain stools for plaintiffs on one side. Padded swivel chairs on the other for the presiding officials.

The Deregulator and his companion settled, taking up handheld screens. They appeared to be stimulated by the proceedings. Formal trials were both a novelty and technical challenge.

'Let's get started,' said the woman.

The computer projected up a hologram of archaic scales.

'I take it you're the judge?' Michael asked Will Birch.

Grandfather had spoken often of judges and juries, law books and codes. In the old man's youth they regulated human affairs, or so he claimed. Was this room a relic of that strange system?

Turning, Michael discovered the drone's pincers poised inches from his neck.

'Perhaps you are both judges?' he asked the woman, doubtfully.

'Oh no.' She nodded at the computer. 'That's the judge.'

'State your case.' The machine's simulated voice was deep, sonorous, grave.

'I will,' said Michael. And he did. The time and outrageous manner of the drone attack. How there had been no warning and no explanation whatsoever so that even now he was ignorant of the crime his family had committed or why they were threatened with starvation unless someone helped. As he spoke, holograms of the attack flashed above the computer, gathered from the drones' recording facilities. Michael and Averil cowering. His own voice: *Don't move! Darren!* The storehouse exploding in a spray of masonry. Darren fleeing down the hillside until a cannon tore him in two. Sheep blazing, licked into ash by tongues of napalm.

'Nothing can restore that innocent lad's life,' he concluded. 'We ask only that this court awards us enough food to survive until the spring crops. The Deregulator's warehouse is always full. It will cost you nothing and redress, just a little, a terrible wrong.' He paused. 'It is a small thing to ask.'

Michael subsided. He squeezed shaking hands to steady himself, conscious of the drone's pincers hovering.

The Deregulator was examining him in astonishment. 'You risked coming here for *that*?'

The floating hologram changed. Now it showed a close-up satellite image of the Museum site. Michael leaned forward. Rows of oats and barley. It must date from the preceding summer's woeful harvest.

'Guilty of a transgression,' intoned the machine. 'Appeal dismissed.'

Michael's mouth went dry.

'Guilty of a further transgression,' the stern voice continued. 'Wilfully seeking to waste the court's time.' Whomever programmed the voice added an angry tremor. 'Punishment to be determined by local authorities.'

Now the Deregulator and his assistant looked confused. Murmured together.

'What punishment scale applies to this kind of case?' asked the Deregulator

The machine answered with a hologram: *Scale 2c.* The image faded. The computer deactivated. Court dismissed.

'Is that it?' asked Michael.

'Not quite,' said the Deregulator. He spoke into his screen. 'What are the punishment options for Scale 2c?'

For a moment he conferred with the dumpy woman over messages on their screens.

'Well, it seems I must make a choice,' he said. '*Termination. Exemplary amputation. Branding. Pain application from levels four to six* – whatever that entails.' He sighed. 'You see, how would it look if you were *not* punished? We'd be flooded with malcontents and pointless cases. Hardly what I would call deregulation.'

'*Termination* for a field of scrappy oats?' asked Michael. His disbelief turned to ragged anger. 'Poor Darren was murdered for a few bags of oats?'

'It has been proven over and over that unevolved hominids respond best to extreme demonstrations,' pointed out the woman. 'It is engrained in their primitive psychology.'

'The man on your left was a *primitive* not so long back,' said Michael before he could stop himself, 'as I bet you were.'

She stared at him. Michael suddenly remembered his conversation with Helen Devereux beneath the moon. Had she known all along what was coming? Even as they walked and talked beneath bright stars?

'The new Museum Curator did this to us, didn't she?'

'What surprises me,' said the Deregulator, 'is how you are still addicted to seeking the last word at any cost. A family failing, I fear. Your grandfather, old Reverend Pilgrim, possessed it to a fault. Now you have forced me to make a proper example of you. That is my clear duty, you understand, you've left me no choice.'

The woman beside him nodded like a cold-eyed bird.

'A proper example,' she echoed.

THIN LINES

As Averil disappeared into the basement to root among dusty crates, Helen was drawn by the Jewel. Today the glittering blue sapphire in its bed of bright gold stared accusingly up at her.

What, it seemed to say, *is the power to do good if one does not use that power?* She knew very well what she should do. Even now Michael Pilgrim was probably provoking a fatal dose of official displeasure. Half-measures, when it came to managing primitives, were not the deregulatory way.

Helen punched the code to raise the screen protecting the Jewel. It continued to rotate slowly. Her hand trembled as she reached out, touching the flawless sapphire.

Taking out her screen Helen talked hurriedly, holotext appearing simultaneously: 'Address Bertrand Du Guesclin.

Composing. Bertrand, I have a favour to ask. Call it a test of your good will. After all, words and vows are just…' She recollected the style he enjoyed best. 'Syllables blown upon puffs of hot air unless accompanied by gallant deeds. This is what I would like, Bertrand.'

After she had finished Helen re-read the message. 'Send,' she instructed.

It was done. Her green eyes confronted the sapphire's blue.

'Happy now?' she asked.

A PROPER EXAMPLE

The drone delicately took hold of Michael's left arm in its pincers then his right. He felt himself lifted from his stool.

'Please!' His breath laboured. 'For fuck's sake! You heard the computer, Will! You have discretion!'

But the Deregulator had other concerns. It soon became clear he was entirely unfamiliar with the application of Justice Scale 2c. Or any kind of justice at all.

'I do not believe this particular drone is programmed for that level of finesse,' he complained to his assistant.

The woman beside him agreed. 'Let me check the manifest.' She spoke into the screen. 'Ah, thought so. There *is* a specialist drone in storage. I'll send for it.'

Michael closed his eyes. Too late to regret. He tried to remember happy times. Wasn't that what you were meant to do in the moment before drowning or plummeting to your death? Wasn't that what they said? Yet reassuring memories would not come. All he could focus on was the pain in his arms from the drone's pincers.

After long minutes the double doors opened. A stubby black cylinder on caterpillar tracks, four feet high rolled in. Extendable arms bristled. A steel cabinet on wheels followed like a faithful, rectangular dog.

'Here it is!' said the woman.

Michael watched in horror as the mobile tool case on wheels opened to reveal delicate saws, blades, hammers, needles, branding irons.

'Scale 2c,' mused the Deregulator, consulting his screen. 'It says here, *Pain application from four to six*. Not sure what that entails. Do you know?'

'I could find out,' replied the woman official.

'We could always err on the side of lenience and say *four*,' mused Will Birch. 'I don't want to spend all day on this. Ah, *Pain Application 4* means … Goodness! *Exemplary amputations*.'

He shot a startled look at Michael. His assistant licked her lips nervously.

'Of course,' she said. 'Now I must … check the warehouse.'

'Indeed,' agreed the Deregulator. He was a tolerant manager of his underling's squeamishness. She hurried off without meeting Michael Pilgrim's glance of entreaty.

The old schoolmates were alone. A bad man might gloat. Enjoy sadistic frissons. Play a little game with his victim. The Deregulator never considered himself a bad man. He, too, found it hard to look at the prisoner.

'Proceed with Pain Application 4,' he instructed the barrel-shaped drone.

Michael kicked out. 'No!' he shouted. An arm extended delicate pincers to tear down his trousers and reveal his groin. 'Oh God!' moaned Michael. Was this the amputation? Instead, another arm swung out: cold metal touched his testicles. There came a searing electric shock. He writhed like a spirit possessed. His screams ended in hopeless sobbing.

Again the electric probe. Again an agonised dance.

'Enough,' ordered the Deregulator. He had gone very pale, unable to lift his eyes from the screen. 'Next step … proceed to amputations. Nothing more than 2c, note! Understand?'

Yes, intoned the drone.

'Clarify 2c,' said the Deregulator.

Right hand at wrist. Eyes.

'Make sure he's alive at the end,' said the Deregulator, gloomily. 'Every wound clean and disinfected and bandaged.'

'Rest assured,' he told Michael, still not looking at him, 'I shall make sure you are delivered to your family in Baytown afterwards. It's the least I can do. You really should not have come here. You have placed me in a very difficult position.'

The drone rolled over to the toolbox. Blades and cauterisers were selected. Antiseptic sprays and quick-drying bandages.

'For God's sake, Will,' pleaded Michael, 'think what your mother would say! What if she could see you now!'

Will Birch's mother had been a kindly, simple soul, thoroughly dominated by her teenage son until he abandoned her.

The Deregulator blinked unhappily. 'Proceed,' he said. His screen flashed and made a jarring, whooping noise. He glanced down. Read the message once. Twice. 'Stop!' he screeched.

The drone halted a whirring saw inches from Michael's right wrist.

The Deregulator stared at the screen then, with a slow release of breath, settled back in the padded chair. 'Goodness me, what a day! It seems you have friends, Michael Pilgrim.' He laughed awkwardly. 'Can't say I'm not relieved.' He glanced round, aware everything he said or did was recorded. 'Not that I would have hesitated to carry out any sentence imposed by the, ahem, court.'

Michael twitched. His nervous system jangled from the electric shocks. Drool dribbled onto his chin. His eyes rolled to reveal their whites.

'Just brand him,' ordered the Deregulator, 'then release him.'

ON A MULE

Amar led the tired mule by the halter. On its back, a broad-shouldered burden too feeble to walk. Michael Pilgrim clung to Noddy's neck. The slightest jolt against his groin made him wince and quiver. Half his face mottled, purple save for a coin-sized, deeply burned mark: F. Branded forever on his right cheek as a *felon*. The only comfort in their miserable journey home was that the rain lifted as they left Whitby.

On the outskirts of Baytown, the mule brayed in protest. It would go no further.

'*Sharif*,' said Amar, 'can you walk a little way?'

'G-g-g-h,' croaked Michael. His swollen mouth and jaw made talking impossible. Deep rings of black had appeared round his eyes and puffed lids. Laboriously, tenderly, Amar eased his master's leg off Noddy's back. The creature whinnied.

'Here's your staff, *Sharif*,' said Amar. 'Try to lean on it. When we get into Baytown, I'll find people to carry you home. Just a little way further.'

This plea stirred Michael. Pus oozed from the ornate, curlicue brand on his cheek. The after effect of the electric shocks on his nervous system tormented him. Every so often his muscles contracted in agony.

Thus he staggered into Baytown, Amar propping him up. It said much about his persistence he remained upright at all. Those who opposed him should have taken note.

At the top of the village was a cleared area used for football and fairs known as the Commons. As they approached, Amar became aware of loud fiddle music and beating drums. An impromptu celebration was taking place on the green. Tables were covered with free food and drink. Half the population of Baytown milled there. Amar recognised neighbours, friends, a few enemies, too. A porker roasted on a spit, scenting the air. Overseeing the distribution of the meat were Big Jacko and his diminutive, white-faced wife.

'They're celebrating his new position as Mayor,' said Amar.

Among the crowd were Averil Pilgrim and her brother, Seth, as well as Hob Hall's hungry orphans. Only the Reverend Pilgrim kept away.

'G-g-g-h,' croaked Michael Pilgrim.

'*Sharif*, I'll get you to the Puzzle Well. People can help you there.'

But their arrival was too dramatic to go unnoticed. Friends hurried up to question, cry out in sympathy or anger, to offer help. After his wife whispered urgently in his ear, the new mayor strolled over to confront them.

For a long moment, Michael swayed, vision blurring. He felt himself fainting. Strong arms held up limbs refusing to obey his brain's scrambled commands. Averil's face came into focus inches from his own.

'Don't assist that man!' ordered the Mayor. 'Can't you see he's branded? A *felon*, good and proper! Do you fools want drones burning *your* houses and livestock? Burning this whole village? You heard what that Lord said! Look what happened to them Pilgrims!'

A few folk stepped away from Michael – notably, by subtle shifts of crab-like movement, Seth Pilgrim. Most stayed put, led by Lieutenant Pilgrim's boyhood friend and comrade from the Crusades, Tom Higginbottom. And thus a deep division of loyalties in Baytown society commenced.

'We decide who's a *felon* in these parts, mister!' called out Tom. 'Not some Johnny-come-lately!'

'Bugger you, mister!' called out others.

For long moments the Mayor and burly fisherman squared up. Then Big Jacko relaxed. He grinned without warmth and turned to his own supporters.

'Let's not spoil the party, friends. I warned 'em fair and square.'

He addressed the people gathered protectively round the injured man. 'You Higginbottoms better not come expecting favours from Mayor Jacko.' He sniffed as though at a bad odour. 'The Mayor can't be seen to help criminals.'

Between spasms, barely conscious, Michael felt himself carried down Baytown's steep hill to the Puzzle Well Inn where Dr Macdonald was summoned to assist.

SIX

***

DECEMBER

December came to the vale and found Hob Hall ill-prepared. Everyone went to bed hungry, adult and child alike. Only Seth looked sleek. The winter's gloom was deepened by a need to ration lamp oil. With their solar and wind rechargers destroyed by the drones, their few electric lights stayed dim. Evenings became tedious hours of huddling in cold shadows until bedtime.

Wracked by a chest infection, James Pilgrim took to his bed, leaving Averil and Amar to keep household routines afloat; Seth refused all chores, vanishing every night and returning red-eyed the next morning. As for Michael Pilgrim, he worked the fields in dogged silence, his one pleasure long walks on the beach with Bess.

It seemed the Pilgrim clan, once so strong, was falling into ruin like the deserted village their ancient home overlooked.

Helen took a walk in Hob Vale, following a muddy path through leafless orchards and fog tendrils. The sun showed a faint patch of brightness in the occluded sky and gems of dew pooled on grass blades and wilted ferns.

Helen heard the sharp hack of a hatchet. Through a stand of interwoven coppiced larch, she glimpsed her neighbour chopping firewood. His mule grazed nearby beside empty panniers.

She almost ignored him and carried on. Since his return from the Deregulator, she had avoided Michael Pilgrim without positively meaning to. Thus guilt comes to resemble a settled dislike.

Hack. Hack. The hatchet rose and fell.

Helen left the path, pushing through coppiced trees and their bunting of ivy.

'Mister Pilgrim,' she called out, uncertainly.

He straightened. Close up the **F** on his cheek shocked her. In the Five Cities simple renewal would banish the brand in a week; here it would accompany him to the grave. She glanced aside, aware she should ignore the ugly mark. His disfigurement was only skin deep.

Helen patted the mule's neck. Noddy munched stoically at the winter grass.

'I just wanted to say,' she began, 'that Averil keeps me informed how difficult it is for everyone ... I mean, in the Hall this winter. I'm sorry.'

'That's kind of you.'

His ironic smile revealed worn, yellow teeth. The sight repulsed her despite all her good intentions.

Helen fidgeted. 'I want you to know I had nothing to do with what happened. I mean, with the drones. I hope you believe that.'

If eyes are the windows of the soul, he gazed deep. Grew thoughtful at what he found.

'My instincts told me that,' he said. 'For a while, I persuaded myself you were behind it. Then I met the Deregulator and thought better. But I'm glad to hear it from you.'

He returned to his work. The hatchet bit deep into a branch. He wore fingerless gloves against the cold and his breath steamed.

'If there is any way I can help...' Helen's voice trailed, aware the help they really needed, large quantities of food, lay beyond her means.

He started to load firewood into a pannier.

'Averil told me how you tried to seek justice from the Deregulator,' she said. 'That was brave of you.'

She picked up a light branch for him to place in the basket. Held it out gingerly.

'No, the heavy logs get loaded first,' he said, stooping. 'Well, it seemed a good idea at the time. My Grandad taught me to always expect the best of people. Little good it did him. Or now me, it seems.'

He paused. Rubbed his spine speculatively.

'If you really want to help us, you could have the bairns over to the Museum,' he said. 'I know our people aren't allowed in there. But if nothing else, they'll learn something. And it's warm. If you found them a bite or two as well, that'd be grand.'

Helen brightened. 'I know. I'll arrange a Christmas party for the children!'

His grateful look reminded Helen of her youthful assistant – and the girl's dangerously stubborn naivety. She felt a deep, hopeless longing for the world to be better than it was.

DUTY

Up the vale in Hob Hall, Reverend James Pilgrim railed at his only son.

'Wh-what has become of you!' Icy blue eyes flashed. 'I tell you once and for all, you must sever your ties with that man!'

Seth Pilgrim lolled in an armchair with an easy grin learned from new acquaintants. Uncle Michael stood annoyingly by the door, preventing escape.

'Your dearest concern right now must be your family,' continued his father.

Seth cocked his ear at a corner of the room where a rustle indicated mice. 'Did you 'ear that?' he said, in an accent known long ago as Mockney. 'Catch a few of them skirtin' board chickens and yer could 'ave 'em for dinner!'

James Pilgrim listened in astonishment.

'And when it comes to the Mayor,' continued Seth, 'now *he* is a proper man. Not like…' He licked his lips. The unspoken word dangled.

'How dare you speak to me like that!' wheezed his father.

Seth sat up furiously. 'You can't even feed your own family!'

'Enough.' The command came from the doorway. For a moment the youth hesitated. He met Uncle Michael's eye. The latter removed his work gloves and blew on cold fingers.

'James,' said Michael, 'may I be permitted to say a few things?'

As the Reverend was struggling with a cough, he nodded. Michael pulled up a chair to face Seth. The youth's glance flinched from the brand on his uncle's cheek.

'What's pissing me off the most,' said Michael, quietly, 'is this. Your lack of duty forces me to do your chores. I should be concentrating on food, nothing else. Your job is simple: firewood. Enough for winter. That's all. Not a complex job. Everyone is contributing except you, even some of the very little ones. It's the only way we'll make it through. Even then it'll be close.'

Michael added with a touch of good-humour, 'If you did your chores, Seth, I wouldn't mind you hero-worshipping an obvious rogue. You'll see through him in your own good time. We've all been young.'

'I forbid you to see that man!' spluttered James, having gathered breath. 'If you don't work, you'll not eat. You will do your duty, young man!'

Seth looked from face to face. 'Oh, I'll eat,' he cried. 'Better than *you*!'

He scrambled from the chair, as though expecting a strong hand to seize his ear. 'I'm a Mayor's Man now!'

'That man is using and deceiving you,' warned Michael.

Tears filled Seth's eyes. 'He's my friend!' he said in his native accent. 'You're never fair! Averil's always been the favourite. You're never fair to me!'

Then he bolted from Hob Hall.

BECAUSE I WILL IT SO

The evening after Seth stormed from Hob Hall, Michael sat in his room, once the library of the grand old house. Bookshelves crammed with mould-specked volumes still lined the walls. His bed positioned near the fireplace. On a winter's night, it got cold in the big, high-ceilinged room.

For a long while, he brooded before the grate, a book of poetry on his lap. Near midnight he dragged aside a heavy wooden clothes chest and pried up the floorboards beneath. An earthy, rotten smell made him sniff. Groping with an outstretched hand into the dark space under the floor, he touched oilcloth. Pulled out a light bundle and carried it to his desk.

Inside the cloth was a second bag made of duraplastic, its provenance revealed by khaki camouflage. His former captain's name and motto embossed on the side in ornate pink lettering: **Eloise Du Guesclin** *'Because I will it so'*. Michael Pilgrim stepped back warily. Realised he was breathing too fast. Not too late to return the parcel to the dark where it belonged: the cold, forgotten dark.

Seven years since he last unzipped this bag. He glanced round guiltily. What if the children found it? That had always been his fear. Easy to imagine a sliced finger, maybe even a limb. Not to mention the worst danger of all. Michael's eyes widened at the thought. At least his family's troubles would be over quickly. Along with the whole of Hob Hall.

Gingerly he unzipped the case. And there it was, just as he had left it, for such objects never really decayed. A sword hilt protruded from a stiff camouflaged scabbard. Michael took hold of the weapon, drew it slowly. Dull plasti-steel with a special edge. It didn't look much. His officer's sword, awarded as a symbol of rank and for saving his captain's life.

He painted a figure of eight in the air with its tip. So light. Balanced. A blade engineered to cut a man in half with one sideways blow. He returned it to the scabbard.

One more weapon in the bag drew his attention. A stubby metal cylinder, surprisingly heavy, the worst risk of all. A danger that, paradoxically, had become his family's best hope.

SΣVΣΠ

SCARBOROUGH

Few towns survived except as ruins.

Michael Pilgrim approached Scarborough from the north, wearing his old army waterproof cape, Noddy's hooves clomping on the crazed road surface. Rain slanted and bounced. The horizon was as misty as the mule's breath.

Houses closed in as he entered the suburbs, many razed to blackened skeletons. Dismounting, he checked the firing mechanism of his shotgun. Loaded two cartridges filled with double shot for extra damage at close range. One hand held the mule's halter, the other his weapon. No one stirred or showed themselves.

A long, watchful walk followed round North Bay towards Scarborough Castle on its beetling cliffs and headland. All around, hints of a phenomenon he understood only as a concept: extended holidays. Imposing hotels and guest houses, parks where exotic trees and shrubs still flourished against all odds. Ancient barricades of burned out cars told their own story of the Worst Times in Scarborough. Amidst soggy, wind-gathered plastic and tilth, mottled bones and skulls indented with tooth marks littered the roadside.

With this warning in mind, Michael led Noddy down a series of side streets towards the Castle. The last time he came no one had lived round here. Rain dripped and trickled from bare winter branches and shattered roofs trailing plants.

A grating noise made Noddy's ears prick. In one motion Michael cocked the shotgun and dodged behind the animal's rump for cover.

The door of an old lodge near the castle scraped open. He half-expected a barrel to point his way. Instead, a young woman appeared in the doorway. Her hennaed hair fell in long, disordered curls, and she was naturally pale. A pistol butt poked from a belt that flattered her narrow waist. She rested against the lintel to appraise him through soft, hazel eyes, yet he sensed tension for all her relaxed pose. Something about her interest quickened his own.

'Good day,' he said, lowering his gun.

The girl examined the F on his cheek curiously.

'I thought you might be someone else.'

Nearer twenty than twenty-five, he decided, her accent – though broadly Yorkshire – strange round the vowels. It reminded him of Hull.

'Any trouble down in the town?' he asked. 'I'd be grateful to know.'

'There's always that.'

'None for you, I hope.'

She sniffed. 'My man's left me, so I look after myself. I'm good at that.'

'Oh?'

'He turned out bad – like they all do.'

Her defiance revealed her fears.

No denying it. He felt stirrings that brought a giddy relief. Since the electric shocks to his groin, he'd dreaded an end to manhood.

'Watch out for the dogs,' she warned. 'They're almost as bad as the folk round here.'

And he understood that the dogs – whether animal or human – particularly worried her.

'This is a bad town,' she said, pulling her shawl close.

He wondered whether he should ask her about Baxter then thought better of it. 'Depends who you know here,' he said.

'Well, I'm getting out of this place as soon as.' Her tone contained a challenge.

He nodded. 'I'll be back this way. First I have business in town. Thanks for the tip about the dogs.'

She watched him leave, her interest ancient as wide open flowers.

BAXTER

He descended steep streets leading from the Castle, shotgun cradled. Two years earlier this area of terraces had been abandoned, but now he smelt wood smoke and the pervasive stench of a carcase being rendered. Turning a corner revealed a clear view of the harbour below.

Michael's business in Scarborough lay between debt collection and intimidation. Two years earlier a fellow veteran from his unit had appeared at Hob Hall. Throughout the Crusades, Corporal Baxter had complained incessantly and irksomely when not high on *stuff*. His civilian incarnation had made just as unwelcome company. In the end, Michael escorted him to Scarborough with a loan of two fully recharged power cells. It seemed the easiest, cheapest way to pry him out of Hob Hall's larder. Hence Michael's visit to the blighted resort that wet day: Baxter's turn to repay his comrade in arms.

On the seafront, his tension slackened. He stared out at the wave-crests of a high tide.

Rising sea levels had flooded the harbour walls, and on the foreshore, a community of fishermen occupied crumbling amusement arcades, their cobles moored to a stone jetty. Several Baytown fisher families had kin in Scarborough, and Michael calculated mutual acquaintances should keep him safe.

He led his mule through the rain until he came to a vast, decaying edifice built into a hillside: the Royal Hotel. In this relic of Victorian respectability, Baxter had settled, dodging plaster-falls, clouds of mould and insect infestations. His particular calling in life wasn't punishable exactly. No one in the City cared a hoot whether primitives poisoned themselves with chemical concoctions. They did care, however, when drugs or indeed any product at all was manufactured using technology more advanced than a brandy still. *That* was punishable by drones, which explained Baxter's aversion to emerging from the Royal Hotel. Even discounting the paranoia-inducing effects of his wares, no one ever knew if a drone had you on its scanner.

'So,' said Michael, having related the Pilgrim family's losses since the drone strike, 'for once you're in a position to help me, Bax.'

They sat in a high-ceilinged salon near the hotel's pillared entrance. Above them, birds roosted in a dome of stained glass. Rain dripped constantly.

Michael scratched his arms. Then neck. He had felt itchy the moment he entered the Royal. Beetles and cockroaches were everywhere. He was also concerned the ceiling might finally succumb to gravity.

Baxter lolled on a sofa covered with sheepskin, smoking a water bong.

'Gargle?' he offered.

As this would involve sharing the bong's mouthpiece, Michael declined. The mud-coloured water bubbled merrily. Baxter exhaled with infinite satisfaction.

'I could sort you out with some of this stuff,' he offered. 'Help you forget your troubles.'

'I don't need stuff,' said Michael. 'I want those batteries I lent you two years ago. Fully recharged, by the way.'

For a moment Michael thought Baxter might bluster or argue. Maybe he would have, except the wiry little man glanced at the branded F. Rubbed his beard nervously.

'I'm thinking you won't take no for an answer this time,' said Bax.

'I can't afford to.'

Baxter picked at a scab on the back of his hand.

'Okay. Okay.' He cleared his throat and spat a sticky gobbet. 'Things are good with me. I've got fuel cells to spare.'

'Oh?'

'Got a new customer,' said Baxter. 'Over your way. Like I say, things are good with me. Payback time, I reckon.'

'What's your new customer's name?' asked Michael, though he could guess.

'BJ!' chortled Baxter, gurgling at the bong. Smoke drifted from the corners of his mouth. 'You should try this! *Dementia!*'

Dementia was Baxter's highest and last word of praise, though Michael was pretty sure he didn't know what it really meant. Maybe that didn't matter. Words meant whatever you wanted when the world had fallen apart.

'You mentioned our new Mayor?'

'You got me!'

'This Jacko,' said Michael, casually, 'where has he come from? No one seems to know. And how come he's in so deep with the Deregulator?'

Baxter found the question comical. 'You gotta make *connections*, Lieutenant! You should ask where the Deregulator was posted *before* Whitby. Then you'll find out about Jacko.'

'Where was he posted?'

'London. Hey, you're a scholar! Wasn't London the centre of the universe years ago?'

'For some. Centres come and go.'

'*Dementia*,' marvelled Bax.

'So why did the Deregulator leave London?'

'Promotion. I heard he helped important people satisfy *tastes*. And Big Jacko supplied the *materials*. Made himself mighty unpopular down there. So he came here.'

'Oh?'

The bong bubbled. Baxter chuckled. His thin shoulders shook. Something fastened its mandibles into Michael's leg. He scratched furiously.

'Just keep an eye on your kids, Lieutenant,' said Baxter. 'More than that I wouldn't know.'

Michael reached for the bong after all. The drug hit him between the eyes.

'Thanks,' he said. 'By the way, know anyone who might be interested in trading a lot of food, and I mean a fuck of a lot, for a City weapon?'

The scrofulous ex-corporal looked up. He was suddenly serious.

'Thinking of trading your sword?' he asked. Then, of all people, Baxter surprised Michael. He looked genuinely upset. Even hurt. 'Don't do it, Lieutenant. No way. You earned that thing. You wear it for all of us who made it back.'

'No, I don't mean the sword.' Michael leaned forward and spoke very quietly.

Baxter put the bong down, openly afraid. He'd long suspected the City monitored his every movement via robotic mice and rats fitted with hologram recorders. Sometimes through drone seagulls who perched on walls whenever he stepped outside and were uncannily realistic.

'There is someone who might be interested,' he murmured.

Baxter traced the letters of a name in the dust then wiped it away.

'But if I were you, Lieutenant,' he said, 'I'd sooner go hungry. I mean, *dementia!*'

IN THE COURT OF BIG JACKO

On the same squally day that Michal Pilgrim rode to Scarborough, Seth led Averil towards the front steps of Big Jacko's residence.

'I've told you,' he said, 'she's worried about the kids. She wants to help.'

'But why?' asked Averil. 'Her husband hardly acts like a friend to Uncle Michael.'

'You'll see,' said Seth. 'She's not how people paint her. Madame Morrighan wants everyone in Baytown to be friends.'

A sentiment close to Averil's heart, as Seth knew better than most.

Upon the cliffs stood a small area of once grand Edwardian villas, their only tenants ghosts. Each possessed a large back garden reverting to woodland. Though the buildings were barely habitable it was here Big Jacko had established his court in two adjoining houses. Each rose four storeys high, sheltering a bagatelle of vagrants: men accustomed to taking not making, a few women serving Madame Morrighan and her children – adopted by the Mayor as his own – as well as Big Jacko himself.

Two bravos lounged in the doorway when Seth and Averil drew near. At the sight of her, they fell silent.

'Wotcha!' Seth called in his best Mockney.

The elder of the pair winked at his companion.

'Just 'ere to take me sister to Madame Morrighan,' said Seth. 'Is she 'ome?'

'Where else would she be?' asked the elder. 'Nowhere else to go in a shithole like this.'

As he spoke, the ferret-thin man's eyes twinkled at Averil. She pulled her headscarf tight.

Seth led her through musty, dusty rooms to a PVC conservatory. Here they found Big Jacko's wife.

Madame Morrighan was a slender woman in her late twenties, her unusual pallor emphasised by hair dyed deep black. Her eyes were also sloe-black. She wore a long, shiny green skirt made of a manmade material Averil did not recognise. A hand-woven plaid shawl covered her shoulders. She was working with a solar powered calculator at a list of accounts.

Averil stirred anxiously at the sight of forbidden technology. The white-faced woman smiled, revealing absent front teeth.

'Come on right in, me dear!' she cried.

She had a light, lilting voice with an accent alien to Baytown. Not of London like her husband but exotic Ireland.

'So you've come to visit me at last,' said Madame Morrighan.

Seth took Averil's arm and led her forward.

'Oh, you wouldn't believe how hard it was to persuade Avi!' he said. 'I had to mention it tons of times, didn't I, Avi?'

His sister nodded.

'You've done very well,' said Big Jacko's wife. Seth swelled at the praise. 'Now be a good lad and nip to the kitchen for a tin of anything you fancy. I need to have a special girl chat with your lovely sister.'

When he had gone Madame Morrighan patted an empty place on the sofa beside her. Averil sat gingerly.

'I can see you're surprised by this little adding machine,' said Madame Morrighan, holding up the calculator.

'We have one in the Museum,' replied the girl, 'but that's still part of the City. My father says it's better not to take risks with forbidden things.'

'He's quite right,' said Madame Morrighan. 'Only, the Mayor is a very special man. He's allowed things other people aren't.'

Averil met her eye then glanced at an odd statue of a naked woman with a heron's head. It stood on a small round table covered by black cloth.

'People say the Mayor is friendly with the Deregulator,' said Averil, warily.

'The Mayor has powerful friends all over.'

It crossed Averil's mind these powerful friends had failed to provide him with a comfortable home.

'Seth said you wanted to speak to me about something important,' she said. 'Something to help our family.'

'Oh, yes!' Madame Morrighan pointed to a canister by the door. 'Now he told me the poor bairns you look after are having a hungry time of it. I want you to give them the powdered milk over there. You just mix it with a little boiled water and let it cool. It's much, much more nutritious than plain old cow's milk. Only, you mustn't tell your father or uncle or anyone. I don't want word to get around or everyone'll be...'

'I can't do that,' said Averil, quickly. 'Not without telling them.'

Madame Morrighan sighed. 'Neither should I do this, my dear. The Mayor would be very angry with me if he found out. Those foolish men! Always disagreeing instead of getting along fine like sensible folk! If women ruled the world, there'd be a darn sight more kindness and a lot less quarrelling.'

Averil nodded earnestly. She had said the same thing to Seth on many occasions.

'So it would have to be our little secret,' concluded Madame Morrighan.

'The children *do* need milk,' conceded Averil. 'Thank you.'

'Who knows that better than a mother?'

Madame Morrighan shook her head at the lack of milk for motherless bairns in this sorry world.

'And another thing,' she said, 'just a little idea of mine. You see, I get awful bored of an evening here, with only rough men for company. Now I'd like to invite all your girlfriends – we don't need no boys – for a proper little Christmas party. Right here. I'll put out tinned and package stuff, and I do have a few clothes I need to give away.'

Averil listened as Madame Morrighan explained. There did seem something terribly lonely about her position in the crumbling terrace. Averil hated to think badly of anyone, and Seth clearly admired the pale, petite stranger. Judging a woman by her husband was unfair, like judging a daughter by her father. Besides, passing on a simple invitation didn't mean she had to attend herself. Her friends were old enough to decide for themselves.

'Okay,' said Averil.

Big Jacko's wife smiled. 'Bless you! Now I have something to look forward to.' She added in her gentle, lilting voice, 'All this rain makes me feel grey as the sky!'

MANHOOD

Michael retraced his route along the seafront, leading Noddy by the halter. On the mule's back a valuable resource: two fully charged power cells, each tradable for rations. Not to mention a large bag of stuff and a meaty feral mongrel shot fresh that morning, part of a pack troubling the town. The same dogs that had frightened the girl from Hull. As Baxter had promised, payback time.

His head span a little from the drug they'd shared, but no one bothered him as he left the harbour. Still, it rained, trickling down the hill in muddy streams.

At the top, he reached the lodge near the ancient castle and, as though waiting for him, the young woman reappeared in her doorway. He noted her hair had been combed and pinned into a bun. She had washed and wore a long homespun woollen skirt.

For a moment they assessed each other.

'The rain's set in again,' she said, 'and I've lit a fire.'

He reached across the mule's back for the sack lumpy with the dead dog.

'A present for you.'

She stepped out into the muddy road and peered into the sack. Her face brightened. 'I'll have a safer walk to the beach now,' she said. 'Did you do that for me?'

Close up he felt the stirring again.

'Maybe,' he lied.

'I need a proper man for a change.'

She looked round for spies. Came closer.

'What do you want in return?' she asked, huskily.

Both knew. Had known from the moment they set eyes on each other. Since the Great Dying courtships often took blunt, hasty forms.

'It's dry in the house,' she said. 'Come round the back.'

At the rear of the lodge, there was a high-walled yard with locked double doors. She let him in and waited as he tethered the animal.

'Anyone else home?' he asked.

'No.' She reached out and touched the F on his face.

'I'm fond of bad boys,' she said. 'Looks like I never learn.'

For the next hour, she showed just how fond: and Michael Pilgrim was allowed to be as bad as he chose.

ON THE CLIFF

Michael broke his journey home at Ravenscar, a lofty bluff of cliff and rocky foreshore. From this high place, the land fell away, the Bay curving to reveal miles of former pasture overcrept by bracken, furze and copse. Hob Hall and Holy Innocents Church lay three miles distant. The dark rooftops of Baytown jumbled a mile beyond.

He tethered his mule outside the smoke-blackened ruins of a hotel near the cliff edge. Found a seat on moss-covered rubble. Abruptly the rain stopped. A break in the clouds drove a bar of pale sunshine across the land like a lazy searchlight.

Post coitum omne animal triste est. The unfamiliar syllables echoed in his mind. He heard his grandfather's voice. *Did you recognise that as Latin, Michael?* Of course, Grandfather knew Latin. He knew everything. Michael had been all of fourteen, in trouble because Grandad found him naked in bed with Charlie Gudwallah's big sister.

Post coitum omne animal triste est, repeated Grandfather, not angry, more in warning. *Do you know what it means, Michael?*

Of course not! He hadn't studied in the fabled city of knowledge known as Oxford University.

It means, 'after intercourse every animal is sad'. Including humans.

Why had the old man shared so strange a thought? Of course, Michael had been able to guess.

At your age, young man, you should be concentrating on studies useful to mankind's future. Not bedroom arts. It is our duty to preserve, Michael, how many times must I remind you. So the wisdom of the past is saved when our fortunes as a species improve.

Vain hope. Despite his Oxford degree – one of the last ever awarded – clever Oliver Pilgrim blinded himself to the Five

Cities' intentions. How they would continue to repress all the progress he had anticipated as mankind slowly recovered and rebuilt.

Michael thought of the young woman in Scarborough. His groin awoke. Despite the animal enjoyment they had shared perhaps Grandfather was right. Melancholy bowed his head.

Why, he asked his grandfather's ghost, did you prepare me for a world that doesn't want or value your precious knowledge? Your ideals? That wants only to feed and fuck.

Bitter ironies were not lost on him. How Grandfather encouraged him to read poems and novels in which men wooed their ladies with flowers, tender words and feelings, courtesy, respect. How had he wooed in Scarborough? Offering a blood-stained sack of dog meat. Enjoying her greedily front and back: not that she'd complained. Scant kissing because her breath tasted rank. She probably thought the same of his own.

How low he had fallen from Grandfather's ideals!

Michael rose hurriedly. Stretched. Shook his head to clear the memory. Another ray of winter sunshine brushed the land. He watched its progress dim then fade.

ΣIGHT

THE DARKEST NIGHT

A few days before Christmas...

As darkness fell, they passed round a bitter punch of herbs, berries and coarse brandy wine – and things better not named. Gladness and tension of a kind he had never imagined possible swelled in Seth Pilgrim. Finally, he almost belonged, part of a circle comprising Big Jacko and his closest, most important men. The women stayed hidden all day in preparation for the winter solstice.

'What happens at the ceremony?' he asked.

A few laughed at his innocence. Fingered lucky charms to ward off evil. No one answered.

'You'll see,' said Big Jacko.

The barrel-chested man grabbed his elbow and, for once, Seth didn't flinch.

'You're going to be one of me boys after tonight,' said Big Jacko. 'If you pass the test, mind.'

'What's the test?'

'You'll see.'

Seth's head whirled from the punch that stained the drinkers' mouths red, made their pupils shrink to black dots. Stories were swapped of fights and dead companions, enemies and friends. He barely heard, sat round a bonfire in the overgrown back garden of Big Jacko's house. For once the rain had stopped.

The night was mild. Big Jacko tenderly led a chorus of a song new to Seth, *'I'm forever blowin' bubbles ... Pretty bubbles in the air.'* In other circumstances, Seth might have laughed. Not here. Not beneath the stale, overcast sky, the darkest night of the year. He floated on a carpet of earth.

Maybe that was why he almost didn't notice the ceremony had started. He was already chanting a chorus without words. A single guttural outburst answered by a clap. Over and over like the beat of a drum: *Aah!* Clap! *Aah!* Clap! He swayed to its rhythm, eyes closed. Savoured a new elation and power.

When Seth opened his eyes the men were no longer alone. He blinked in the flickering firelight.

The two pock-marked Irish sisters who served the various needs of Big Jacko's men were half-shoving, half-dragging a thin, wizened figure in rags. Seth stared in surprise. Through his pleasant daze, he recognised Old Marley the crazy tramp his father helped out with food and cast-off clothes. Surely, *he* couldn't be joining Big Jacko's men too? Then Seth noticed why the old man stumbled. His legs were bound at the ankles, hands trussed with rope and a gag covered his mouth. The whites of his eyes writhed in terror.

Seth shook with involuntary laughter even as he chanted. Look at Old Marley, he thought through the cushion of a happy cloud, shitting his pants!

Aah! Clap! *Aah!* Clap! The chant continued, faster, more urgent. Seth knew he mustn't lose the rhythm.

He gasped in wonder. A figure stepped slowly from the house. He had seen it before! The statuette in Madame Morrighan's parlour come to life. Naked, pale, crowned by a heron's head. Except the statue had grown to the size of a living woman. The heron's head a long-beaked, feathered mask. And he understood. The statue was a living goddess! In her hand, she carried a long, curved knife.

Aah! Clap! *Aah!* Clap! Faster. Hungrier.

The Heron Goddess came to where Old Marley struggled and squirmed, pinioned by the two brawny women.

A voice emerged from the heron's head, one Seth half-recognised in the midst of his excitement and awe.

'I trade this life-blood with the darkest night! Trade it for another year's life!' cried the Goddess.

Slowly, deliberately she gouged the tip of the knife into Old Marley's flank. Not too far in. Just enough to make him bleed. Now his legs were released, and the old tramp tottered towards Seth, his eyes pleading for recognition. Here was someone he knew! Who knew him! Here was help! A Pilgrim! Here was a last chance!

'Let all who want luck and life give to the dark!' called the Heron Goddess.

The clapping stopped. A deep silence followed. Except the world is never silent. Loudly the bonfire crackled. Shrubs and trees whispered, creaking softly in the breeze that blew inland from the dark, indifferent sea. Old Marley's grunts of fear and pain pierced through his gag.

One by one, taking their time, Big Jacko's men took the knife to gash or gouge Old Marley. Each time, they licked the fresh blood on its blade, daubed their forehead. Last of all, it was Seth's turn.

Even with the bitter punch numbing his thoughts he hesitated. He had seen Old Marley come and go through the kitchen door of Hob Hall all his life. Even stern Father softened at the tramp's rambling tales of wayside and wood, animals and distant settlements. Suddenly Old Marley's face blurred with other faces, all afraid, crying out to him to stop: Averil, Father, Uncle Michael. Stop! *Stop!*

'Become one of me boys!' whispered Big Jacko. 'Finish him.'

The blurred faces were frowning now, disapproving, always disapproving, and none of them understood or loved him, not like his mother who had died because Father made her have a baby, none of them cared what he wanted, saw how big he could become...

With a keening cry, Seth rammed the knife into Marley's chest, its handle and blade sticky with blood, pushing in the blade as deep as it would go. Seth withdrew the blade, panting and elated by horror. It made a sucking noise on the way out. He tasted the iron of blood. Painted it on his forehead.

CHRISTMAS EVE

Two days of sullen downpour followed the solstice. Streams bubbled brown and seeped over their banks. Grass blades wore sodden sheens.

If Averil Pilgrim hadn't promised to pass on Madame Morrighan's invitation to her friends, she would never have gone to the party herself. But a promise was a promise. Even if you regretted it afterward.

Arm-in-arm, six girls picked a cautious route to Big Jacko's house. All had agreed no one should be left alone and that they'd leave after half an hour. Dusk lit the western horizon with a false pink flourish. Derelict terraces and uncurbed bushes narrowed the way.

This time no hungry-eyed men were in evidence, just Seth Pilgrim, a boy well-known to the girls, if little respected. He bowed in mock solemnity, raising a lamp tied to a stick. His eyes were unnaturally bright.

'I've been asked to stan' guard 'ere for you ladies,' he said, 'an' to conduct yer 'ome when the fun's over.'

'Why are you speaking so queer?' demanded Averil's best pal, Miriam Armitage.

Seth flushed.

'This way then,' he muttered in his natural voice.

He led them up the stairs and through a corridor lit by gloomy electric lights – an unheard of luxury. Thence to the large conservatory Madame Morrighan used as her private parlour. Not a single male was visible other than Seth Pilgrim. The girls started to relax.

Several cried out in delight as they entered the room. Coloured lights cast a cheery glow. Their lives were bare, practical, more concerned with the next meal than adornment, but it seemed Averil's promise of free clothes might be true – and not the hardy, plain homespun variety. On a long table lay outfits in materials and colours never seen before: dresses, hats, skirts. Strange-shaped shoes with heels more likely to trip you than hold you up.

Madame Morrighan beamed at their arrival.

'How lovely of you to come, me dears!' she cried. 'Come in! Come in! Looks like I might have myself some *nice* company for a change!'

There was a bustle of fruit drinks and honeyed pastries carried by silent female servants. For most of the girls, it was the first time anyone had served them. They felt like princesses. Averil noticed the statuette of the naked woman with a heron's head was gone. Good, she thought, an ugly thing for Christmas-time.

Sweet punch went round and soon several of the girls' heads span. Madame Morrighan produced a small harp. Its gentle, plangent notes made Averil dreamy, especially when the pale woman sang of missing her homeland across the sea. How hard that must be, thought Averil, to leave one's home forever. Her heart went out to the slender, graceful woman forced to live with the bullish Mayor. Perhaps the fact such a person loved him suggested he wasn't so bad after all. Just then, flush with punch and the elegance around her, no one seemed so bad.

After a decorous hour, Seth appeared at the door to conduct the girls safely back through the village. Miriam Armitage and a few others appealed to stay longer, but Madame Morrighan explained she didn't want their parents to worry.

Before they left, their hostess allowed each girl to choose an item of clothing from the table. Everything so strange and beautiful! A couple of girls burst into tears. Another pair, including Miriam Armitage, hissed at each other over who had seen a pair of plastic shoes first. Averil chose a skirt with pastel pink diamond shapes that Madame Morrighan said suited her complexion.

'You're a fair one,' she murmured, 'and I can see we'll be great friends.'

'Yes,' said Averil, though it felt illogically disloyal.

Perhaps that was why it seemed wise not to mention the party at home. She hated upsetting people for no reason. With this white lie in mind, Averil sailed blithely through the night, carrying her precious new skirt and telling Miriam how you should never judge people by appearances.

CHRISTMAS MORNING

By noon Helen had resigned herself to a Christmas alone. She could hardly complain. Her own choices had driven her from the strained, frantic gaiety of that season in the City of Albion or the other Cities with their satellite pleasure resorts. And she could hardly blame Mhairi for wanting to spend the day with friends, instead of a sister who had neglected her existence for decades.

When Helen saw Mhairi coming across the overgrown car park to the Museum, she hurried out. A large sack was slung over her shoulder.

'You came!' cried Helen. 'I thought you wouldn't.'

'I almost didn't,' said Mhairi.

Helen reached out and took her hand. 'I don't expect you to trust me, not properly, I know what I deserve.' She gestured helplessly. 'I felt so lonely just now. And here you are!'

Mhairi patted the heavy bag on her shoulder. 'I've brought company.'

The uninvited guest turned out to be a huge cod, line-caught that very morning out in the bay and offered in appreciation for the doctor's unpaid services to a dozen fishing families dwelling round the Puzzle Well Inn.

'He's a whopper!' declared Helen.

'*He* is a *she*, I believe, and a grand old *she*,' said Mhairi, adding laconically, 'Rather like you and me.'

'We can't eat all of her,' said Helen. 'There's far too much.'

'I've brought potatoes and greens as well,' said Mhairi.

Helen's eye fell on the screen she'd left out in case Bertrand called. Beneath the Museum's strip lights it reflected blue. Unexpectedly she thought of the Jewel's azure heart; as one thought finds another, she had a vision of an elaborate banquet hostessed by whichever beauty now shared Bertrand's bed. She frowned to erase the image.

Helen sniffed the enormous cod: a clean, salty, watery, fishy odour. Its lifeless eyes mocked her petty jealousies. How many thousands of miles had the old dame swum? How many codlings had she spawned in the cold, dark depths? How much life added to the world? All so two childless spinsters would pick at her flesh while half a mile away a dozen children went hungry.

'I've just had a marvellous idea!' she said, poking the fish with a slender forefinger. Silver-gold scales twinkled on her fingertip as she held it up to the light.

'Probably best to leave the gutting and cooking to me,' advised Mhairi.

'Oh, it's not that,' said Helen. 'I think you might be surprised.'

BARE PLATTERS

Christmas at the Pilgrim's had always been a fine time. Guests and well-stoked hearths, fiddle tunes and noggins, all confirming the Pilgrims' eminence among their neighbours. This year guests were served mint tea instead of mulled cider or pear wine. Some had brought a gift of what little food they could spare, though few thought it necessary. The Pilgrim family's prosperity was so settled an idea among the people of Baytown that their true plight was little known and pride kept family members from complaining in public. It is a far less pleasant thing to receive charity than dish it out.

Michael Pilgrim contemplated bare platters as he summoned the straggling household to the long, wood-panelled hall with its hearth wide enough to roast a sheep.

Christmas dinner that year had consisted of watery 'chicken' broth (actually seagull) poured over a scanty mash of boiled turnip and spud. As a treat, baked pears and apples scrumped from trees growing wild in abandoned gardens. Michael had found a shrivelled maggot in his brown, bruised apple. After a moment's hesitation, he gulped it along with the core.

His after dinner plan: to stage games and music. Looking at the glum population of Hob Hall he almost abandoned the idea. Seth, in particular, seemed unable to meet anyone's eye. He had excused himself before they ate and vanished in the direction of Baytown. No prize for guessing his destination and it grieved Michael deeply. Likewise, James had withdrawn to rest, too exhausted by his ailments for anything resembling good humour. So it would have been easy for Michael to read in his own room and treat himself to a pipe of Baxter's stuff.

Except that he spotted Amar manfully attempting to cheer Averil with amusing stories – she looked tired and pale – and a few of the younger children were excited despite everything, so he dug out his fiddle. With no prospect of more food until Boxing Day it made sense to have fun while there was something in their bellies.

'Who's for a jig?' he called out.

Before he could strike up a scream interrupted him.

One of the smaller girls was pointing up at the top of the Christmas tree. Here a plastic fairy from the early years of the twenty-first century customarily reigned supreme. But Barbie – everyone called her that, without knowing why – had gone. Instead, there hung a grinning wax doll, its limbs grotesquely outspread. Lank, grey hair had been melted into the skull and a dozen nails driven into its body, each black with dried blood. Most obscene of all, what looked like human ears were pinned to the doll's back like angel wings.

Michael reached up and examined the totem. Close up the ears were certainly real. He turned to the circle of horrified faces. All – even the youngest – recognised black magic when they saw it. A few moaned and clutched one another.

'Anyone know about this?' he asked.

Their guileless faces reassured him.

'Oh!' he declared. 'I get it! Someone's playing a Christmas jape on us!'

He jiggled the doll so it danced.

'It was you, wasn't it, Amar?'

The shock on the Syrian's face became comprehension.

'How'd you guess, *Sharif*?' he said, coming over. 'It's, like, tradition in Syria, you know. We go crazy at Christmas!'

'Well I think it's in poor taste,' said Michael, emphatically.

'I guess. Hey, sorry, everyone!' The young man bowed to the circle of children. 'Sorry if I scared you people.'

A hubbub followed. In the confusion, Michael strode outside with the wax figurine. For a long moment, he stood in the backyard. Anyone observing his brooding scowl might have grown wary.

Amar appeared beside him.

'You reacted quickly in there,' said Michael. 'Well done.'

'Do you think they believed me?'

'They want to. That's enough for most of us.'

'By the way, *Sharif*, we got visitors.'

Michael looked at the hideous votive doll one last time before going inside. 'We'll get to the bottom of this,' he said.

'You do realise someone from inside the Hall put it up there,' said Amar, reluctantly.

Michael got no chance to reply, for he was shaking Dr Macdonald's hand and wishing her a happy Christmas while Averil shrieked with delight as the Museum Curator passed over a cod more like a whale and a dozen children gathered excitedly to stare in wonder at a large box of strange, wonderful food packages and other items looking suspiciously like small presents wrapped in paper.

CHRISTMAS NIGHT

With lamps twinkling and hearths blazing, darkness closed on Hob Hall. Two violins played a merry reel in unison, accompanied by rhythmic clapping and whoops as dancers passed up and down the line.

On a long table stood the remains of portioned, battered and fried fish, along with crumbs from outlandish City food none of the children had tasted before: syrupy biscuits and tinned fruit, peculiar sausages served in oddly gooey bread with a ketchup of tomato, sugar and vinegar, salty red salmon spread on crackers, all shared out with punctilious fairness by Averil Pilgrim. Helen Devereux had brought over more tins and freeze-dried packets of her monthly rations than was sensible. Most of which, Averil – who was almost always sensible – spirited away for future use. Even so, there was plenty for tonight. Enough for exhilaration and faith in the coming year.

A cask of cloudy cider had also appeared, courtesy of Charlie Gudwallah and the Puzzle Well Inn. Though it had been a lean few months, he delivered the gift in person early that evening, expecting to find the Hall in gloom. Soon as he sniffed a party, Charlie sent out messengers to summon his own extended family to hurry over with extra supplies. Even the Reverend James Pilgrim emerged from his sickbed to say a long, rambling prayer and bless the proceedings.

While Helen Devereux and Michael Pilgrim sawed away at their fiddles, Amar persuaded Averil to teach him a new dance. They made a smartish couple, the young Syrian's partner swishing a voluminous new skirt patterned with pink diamond shapes.

Dr Macdonald talked gravely with Reverend Pilgrim by the fire. As for the dozen orphans of Hob Hall, they capered and hopped or slept on settles amidst blankets thoughtfully brought downstairs by Averil, some with contented thumbs wedged in their mouths.

Outside, cloudbanks gathered, and wind licked the cliffs of Baytown. The sea churned and frothed. Copses and shrubs shivered according to the wind's whim and the planet revolved slowly towards dawn.

The screen Helen Devereux left in the Museum glowed urgently a dozen times while she was away at Hob Hall that afternoon and evening. Then the Museum's antiquated security system was infiltrated; its closed circuit hologram recorders inspected all the rooms and found them empty. Towards midnight a small, dark shape descended quietly through the swirling maze of clouds: a spy-drone on stealth. First, it flew round the exterior of the dark, silent museum buildings, scanning the ground. Then over to Hob Hall where it hovered silently, powerful lenses and microphones zooming on a particular window. Inside, the Baytown Museum Curator, her eyes shiny with cider and firelight, long hair loose in fetching disarray, played a slow, tender, mournful ballad on her violin to loud applause. A moment later the drone whooshed upward and far away.

Christmas night a dreary, wind-gnawed night in Hob Vale save for the island of light and warmth where people danced, drank, joked, gossiped, laughed. One lone traveller enjoyed a feast of its own: the barn owl from Holy Innocents Church tearing with little delicacy the entrails of a young rat.

Another traveller appeared in the Vale not long after the drone left. A watchful, intent shadow on the outskirts of a copse overlooking Hob Hall. Whether male or female, young or old, only the owl with her sharp eyes saw. After a pensive half hour serenaded by gusts of song from the house, wind-moans through the thorny furze, the figure turned in the direction of Baytown and vanished into the dark.

ΠΙΠΣ

THE PUZZLE WELL INN

'The question, I suppose,' said Charlie Gudwallah, 'is whose ears they are.'

'*Were*,' corrected Dr Macdonald.

A New Year council beside the peat fire in the Puzzle's taproom: Michael Pilgrim, Charlie, Tom Higginbottom, Mhairi Macdonald and Mister Priest Man. The gathering select because no one quite knew who to trust in Baytown anymore.

On the table an ugly, blood-stained wax doll decorated with human hair, nails and a pair of ears masquerading as wings. Dr Macdonald examined it closely.

'I'd say the ears belong to someone in their sixties, maybe older. A very sharp knife used to saw them off – you can see by these marks – the left one removed quickly and messily. I'd say they slowed down for the right ear, it's in better shape.'

'An old man without ears.'

Everyone turned to hear Mister Priest Man speak. The size of the Nuager community in Baytown gave him influence, though he seldom used it except to mutter incomprehensibly. 'I'm thinking blood-spells,' he said. 'Aye! Black teats and blacker milk.'

Dr Macdonald rolled her eyes.

'What do you mean?' asked Michael Pilgrim.

'Sacrifice,' whispered the Nuager. 'The dark forgotten gods woke from their long sleep with the plague and found they were hungry.'

'By heck,' said Tom Higginbottom, 'I believe he's right! Though we haven't seen sacrifices round here for donkey's years.'

'Your grandfather put a stop to that,' said Charlie, addressing Michael. 'Folk did queer things back then. Thankfully good sense has a habit of finding its feet.'

They settled back to looking at the doll.

'Do we have any idea who's responsible?' asked Mhairi Macdonald.

Michael stirred. 'I have an inkling who placed it on our Christmas tree.'

'Aye?' said Tom Higginbottom.

'My nephew,' said Michael. 'Though he denies it. If I'm right, it means our ugly little pal there.' He nodded at the doll. 'Came from Seth's ugly *big* pal, the Mayor.'

Mayor Jacko was much on all their minds. For decades volunteer constables had patrolled the streets of Baytown at night, armed with shotguns and other weapons kept secure in a communal armoury beside the Puzzle Well. A system involving all able-bodied men and women by rota. At dawn on New Year's Day, while Baytown slept off the night before, the Mayor and his men sneaked down the hill and carried off the whole arsenal: guns, ammunition, crossbows and quarrels, pikes, clubs and spiked maces. Weapons that had deterred large bands of wandering vagrants in the Worst Times.

Tom Higginbottom said, 'I reckon we should gather all the folk and march on his house. Demand he give back what's ours.'

Michael Pilgrim considered the suggestion. Charlie nodded vigorously.

'I'm not so sure, Tom,' said Mhairi Macdonald. 'The harvest was very bad, and the Mayor's won a lot of support by handing out free food. Seems he has no end of a supply. And half the houses in Baytown turn out to belong to Big Jacko if you believe the certificates he's been given by the Deregulator. Seeing the certificates are so shiny and official-looking, many won't risk losing their homes.'

'We're the people here!' protested Tom.

'Maybe,' continued Mhairi, 'but the Mayor has support now. He's even recruited a few bravos from Scarborough. And he's claiming the volunteer constables are the Mayor's Constables now.'

Charlie exchanged glances with Michael and Tom Higginbottom. 'It's not like we don't know how to sort out unwanted folk, is it?'

All three looked shifty. The pause was long.

'Is that what we really want in Baytown?' asked Michael. 'The kind of things we got up to over there? Not me. *Not me.* I'd sooner have never come back.' He flushed angrily. 'I tell you, I'd sooner cut off my own hands!'

Tom lowered his head.

Charlie sighed. 'No one wants that.'

'Let's wait and see,' said Michael. 'We need to learn Jacko's game with the Deregulator.'

Tom Higginbottom laughed harshly. 'Wait too long, and we'll have nowt left to wait for.'

THE LARK ASCENDING

Life went on, no holding it back by the ankle. January started out warm and dry. Unique blends of colour at dawn and sunset passed with barely a notice: Baytown folk worked the earth and sea, not sky.

But some creatures granted legs by nature long for wings. Just such a one was Helen Devereux.

Weeks earlier, she had been invited to play solo violin for Baytown's ragtag orchestra under the baton of Dr Mhairi Macdonald, its founder and director.

'An orchestra here?' Helen had asked incredulously. 'How remarkable.'

Mhairi's reply had been tart. 'Didn't you beautiful ones in the City realise? Prohibiting broadcasts has driven people to make their own music. People always need entertainment. And the best players gain a lot of respect in the community. But we aren't grand, more a collection of squeaks, scrapes and bangs. And conducting helps to keep me sane.'

The solo piece Helen chose was a rhapsody beloved since her youth, *The Lark Ascending*.

Long ago, when she first staggered into the newly-created City, fleeing chaos and senseless violence, her shoes and clothes torn, precious violin strapped to her back, they had asked at the gates: *What can you offer us? Prove it!* Only people with a talent that Blair Gover or the other founders considered worth preserving were allowed entry. Fortunately, they lacked professional musicians, though engineers and scientists were much preferred. Her solo performance of *The Lark Ascending* had made Blair Gover misty-eyed; and thus its lone, soaring song saved her life. And her sister's, too, until Mhairi protested against the City's cruel trajectory and was exiled.

In the heart of the Museum, Helen's screen swiftly re-arranged the original score. Out went the traditional orchestra envisaged by the composer. In came simplified parts for treble and tenor recorders, tuba, triangle, four guitars, two cellos and three violins, oboe, bassoon, penny whistles, flute, trombone, trumpet, double bass and a virtuosic ukulele.

She projected a hologram of the soloist's score. Readied her bow. Could she still play with the yearning of her youth? She attempted the first trills of the flitting lark. So long since she had sought to fly! Then, as one breathes by habit, her fingers and bow traced eddies of sound, aches of desire, while her screen created a harmony like currents of air beneath the flutter of her flight.

REHEARSAL

With the New Year, fresh energy entered the musical life of Baytown. Twangs and blares sounded in courtyards, bedrooms, kitchens.

At the first rehearsal of the year, Helen sat beside Michael Pilgrim in the old chapel. A stand fashioned from scrap metal held up their music. Their last meeting had been Christmas night. Then, warmed by cider and applauded by a circle of flushed, happy faces she had felt at ease with the aloof stranger. Even his grotesque F had been forgotten.

He frowned over the violin part he had been handed. 'I understand from Dr Macdonald we're to thank you for this little lot,' he said.

Helen had printed off individual parts for each instrument and performer.

'I did suggest *The Lark Ascending,*' she conceded. 'Do you disapprove?'

'There's some controversy about whether it mightn't be a bit *hard* for us.'

Helen realised the people around them were listening.

'Oh, we'll manage,' she said. 'Do *you* find it a bit hard?'

He considered. 'No one likes a racket.'

Before she could reply Mhairi took her place at the front. Though the concert wasn't due for months, they had much to rehearse. Intense concentration entered the old chapel. The rehearsals were the highlight of many of an amateur musician's week. Starved of culture and higher feelings by the pressures of bed and board, drabbed by necessity, they gulped music.

Mhairi conducted as the players faltered and advanced: Helen reflected she should be bored by such slow progress. Yet watching their lamp-lit faces brought her a quiet elation. No ennui here! And though she had to concede Michael Pilgrim was right to predict a racket, she sensed promise.

Two hours passed, waves clapping against the foot of the cliff in perfect time to a rhythm set by the moon. And as he played, Michael Pilgrim remembered his grandfather urging him to *preserve, preserve, preserve*; and felt hopes stir among the people around him, that they might yet rise.

ΤΣΠ

PRESERVE, PRESERVE, PRESERVE

Frosts set in, the first that winter, dusting grass blades, cobwebs, leaf-silhouettes. Michael and Amar's breath steamed as they re-built the barn in anticipation of crops yet to peek through crumbs of earth.

'The hours of daylight are lengthening,' Michael remarked to his companion. 'So long as we make it to spring!'

At night Michael Pilgrim retreated to his room, filled an armchair by the fire, cocooned himself in blankets. Unable to spend Saturday evenings at the Puzzle Well for lack of a means to buy a drink – and too haughty to cadge – he sucked a pipe of Baxter's stuff and dreamed before glowing, sparking logs in the grate.

In that large room full of shadows and musty books, loosened by drugs and hunger, his mind drifted where it least wished to go…

A dusky plain by the sea. A sky bluer than he'd imagined possible when reading of Egypt as a lad, gawping at mould-flecked pictures of pyramids, animal-headed gods. His unit of fifty men and women lined up behind the drones and war-car of Captain Eloise Du Guesclin. Her peevish voice boomed from loudspeakers.

'Conscripts!' A speech coming on. Probably broadcast to admirers back home in the City of Albion, maybe all the Cities forming the coalition of Crusaders. 'The future of our continent rests with us today! Even, to a small degree, with you.'

The rest was familiar: that no healthy tree invites parasites to settle and breed beneath its outspread branches. In time they will devour its roots, bark, leaves until the tree withers and dies. Nor would the Five Cities allow such a catastrophe to befall Europa. Science had pitted a new, perfected humanity against failed genetic strains, just as Homo sapiens once replaced Neanderthals...

As he listened, a hot, steady breeze whirled stinging flecks of grit and dust. He could see many companies of drones deploying, flown to the Nile from all over the world. In the distance were the ruins of Cairo. Banners fluttered, gay with dazzling patterns and symbols. For the Baytown conscripts, a red cross on white, the flag of Albion. He wore the same Crusader cross on a permaplastic tabard so the drones wouldn't mistake him for a Locust. That was the big fear among the Baytown lads and lasses. No one trusted the drones. Or Captain Eloise Du Guesclin, for that matter, when she warmed up her napalm thrower.

'I expect you conscripts to do *exactly* as I order,' concluded their leader as if they didn't know. 'Any who disobey shall learn I have a long reach.'

Electric charges from the plasti-steel bracelets locked round Michael's wrist made him hop and yelp, along with the rest of the company. Captain Eloise Du Guesclin's far away audience no doubt appreciated her wit.

Little wonder she seldom showed her pretty young face. A conscript might decide his arms were a price worth paying for a clear shot at her...

Michael stirred in his blankets. The fire in the grate smouldered. The old library of Hob Hall felt very dark. Lines of book spines on the shelves just as the Crusader army had lined up, a few thousand set against a turbulent dust cloud approaching, camels braying, ancient car horns blaring, massed voices chanting words with one essential meaning: *Let us through so we might live...*

His first battle: butchery a more apt word. His trousers reeking of urine after he wet himself early on. The stench of those around him suggested worse bodily discharges. Dust blocked the sky, limiting vision to ten, twenty metres. Drone cannons thudding and blasting, explosions and the whoosh of flamethrowers. Bullets whizzed, whistled. Michael clutched his rifle, urging the Baytown lads to hold fire.

Jets rumbled. Waves of concussion buffeted. Shit! Too close! As conscripts they weren't even meant to fight, that was the drones' job. Just clear up the leftovers, carry, dig, cook, labour like ants.

By his side stood Charlie Gudwallah and Tom Higginbottom and a cowering Baxter off his head on stuff moaning, 'Are we winning? Are we winning?'

It had seemed to Michael no one won. He had watched the column of Locusts approach all morning, drawn together by a treacherous promise of safe passage to Europa if they entered the continent en masse. Small parties or individuals were to be ruthlessly hunted, they had been told. They must gather to be processed before being re-settled in specially-prepared safe zones. How many Locusts? Some said two hundred thousand had heeded the call, others far more: men, women, children, grey with dust and famine. Folk willing to risk everything for a last desperate rush to the sea. At their head an antique battle tank on rusty caterpillar tracks. Hundreds of salvaged trucks and cars full of soldiers. How many souls marching beside the Nile towards the coast? Too many, always too many.

The battle raged a whole afternoon. For a while, few Locusts got near. Air-drones circled, and walker-drones on tyrannosaurus legs stomped and fired. When they ran out of ammunition, the machines used steel pincers to grab Locusts and tear them in two. Occasionally he saw Captain Du Guesclin's flying war-car, guns flashing, her plastic banners grimed by smoke and blood. The slaughter out there in the fog of dust barely imaginable.

'Fuck!' cried Charlie.

Michael, too, stared in panic. Despite all odds, scores of Locusts were getting through the drones, some crawling on their bellies to avoid sweeps of fire.

No one had prepared the conscripts for this. A few fired blindly, tracer winging out. An urge to flee gripped them.

'Stop!' bellowed Michael, herding the men, forcing down rifle barrels. 'Cease fire!'

Ever afterwards he would wonder where the instinct to lead came from. Perhaps Grandfather, perhaps tales of war and valour devoured in Hob Hall's library during dull, cold winter nights. Somehow he gathered the men, rifle-butting one who tried to run, and marshalled a perimeter round the company's transporter vehicles to establish clear fields of fire. Any Locusts coming near were picked off or sprayed by volleys.

Then it happened. An accident that changed his life. Captain Du Guesclin's aircar appeared through the dust, its right engine ablaze, hit by wildfire from her own side. With a bang, it crash-landed a hundred yards from the company vehicles. The hatch flew open. She did not emerge. Smoke billowed, and Michael knew the vehicle would blow.

'We've got to get her!' he cried.

'Leave the bitch!' urged Charlie.

But Michael was running, firing from the hip when a Locust bobbed up with a sword or just to plead for mercy, lunging through the chaos of dust and smoke. A girl in a headscarf aimed an ancient revolver at him. Fired. Nothing happened. A click. Michael's own gun blew off half her head.

Somehow he reached the Captain's aircar and was dragging her slim, light, unconscious body through the dirt. Before passing out, she had managed to remove her helmet, perhaps gasping for air. Close up he marvelled at her youth and beauty. How could so lovely a mouth order a man's bracelets to blow? Yet he'd witnessed it several times and for no reason at all.

A strange notion settled in his mind as he carried her, adrenalin and fury lending impossible strength: that he could save the beautiful captain from her badness, that he could teach her the conscripts were human … Then her aircar exploded, throwing him to the ground. When he regained his feet, he almost tripped on the girl whose head he had just shot away.

Back at the transport vehicles, an airbulance descended to collect the unconscious Eloise Du Guesclin. None of the wounded conscripts were offered medical treatment. Drones returned. When the smoke cleared the wide plain by the Nile was revealed once more, pyramids still in the distance, just like in the picture books he'd read as a lad.

Except the desert had bloomed a strange crop. Bodies in every contortion and condition stretched to the horizon's limits. The steep banks of the river were topped by an embankment of corpses. Black, melted piles of flesh where families clutched each other in terror before a fireball struck them. Some of the bodies spilled organs. Others had been dismembered. How many souls? So many, always too many. Already a butcher's stench of rotting flesh filled the plain beneath the merciless sun. Already clouds of black flies were arriving…

COASTAL DEFENCE

A year after the first battle. By then the Locusts had learned new tactics to escape the waterless, irradiated wastes of Africa. No longer did they march in packed columns easy to bomb and strafe. Now they sought the temperate climes of Europa by stealth, in small groups harder to detect. And sometimes they came by boat…

He was Lieutenant Pilgrim by then, wore a sword by his side, promoted for saving Captain Eloise Du Guesclin – among other dubious exploits. Their company transferred to the coast of Southern France for recuperation, a sun-scorched, barren region where few people lingered.

They were stationed in a district of rubble once called Monte Carlo. At some point in the last century, it had been razed by war, and the sea lapped deep inland over its promenade, reminding the Baytown conscripts of Scarborough.

One spring day Eloise Du Guesclin's high-pitched, querulous voice stirred the soldiers from tents where they dozed and sprayed flies with repellent.

'To the beach! Quickly!'

All scurried and hurried. It was understood the heat made her irritable. Besides, a wager with a rival Captain was going badly. The first to bag a thousand Locusts would be declared winner; and if the company knew one thing about their leader, it was that she hated to lose.

Lieutenant Pilgrim selected five men and drove to the nearby beach. There he discovered a testament to human ingenuity – or desperation. A clan of Locusts had constructed a solar-powered catamaran from plastic barrels and wood to carry them across the Mediterranean. A kilometre from the coast its engine failed. The ragged gathering of Baytown conscripts watched as the tide ground the makeshift craft's double keel onto the sandy beach.

'Fuck's sake,' muttered Charlie Gudwallah, 'I can't stand much more of this.'

That day he voiced the thought of them all. Twenty dehydrated, shivering people struggled ashore, skins welted by sunburn and sea salt. Several of the women nursed babies. Half the refugees were children with wide, pleading eyes. A tall, dignified African strode through the surf, calling out: 'We are your friends! We are your friends!'

Michael turned to the glowering squad behind him.

'Do you know,' he said, quietly, 'I don't care if I lose my arms. I'm not doing this no more.'

Silence brooded in the company. None were fanatical Crusaders. None understood why Europa's depopulated lands could not accommodate more people. The best among the conscripts had committed suicide early on by refusing to kill or by turning their weapons against the Captains. Some had lost their arms for feeding wretched families with their own rations. Only the cowards or those without decency remained. Of the original fifty, just half survived: mainly thanks to their Lieutenant.

Captain Du Guesclin's aircar appeared.

'Get rid of them!' she boomed over the loudspeaker. 'I count nineteen, no, twenty. Do you hear that, Manfred?' She was obviously addressing the rival captain. 'Add another twenty to my tally!'

Michael slung his rifle on his back. The rest of the company followed suit.

'You're taking too long,' boomed their Captain, icy now. Michael could picture her brown eyes tight with irritation. He laughed scornfully. To think he had hoped to save her from the wickedness they were perpetrating! He was too cowardly to even save himself. The exhausted soldiers exchanged glances, stiff with fear, their fists clenched. Any moment *crack, crack, crack*, arms flying, shoulder sockets spraying blood onto the sand.

'Oh, I see! My goodness! A little mutiny, is it?' Captain Du Guesclin sounded positively amused. 'I didn't think you had it in you, Pilgrim. Yes, I'm sure this must be your idea. Bravo!'

Bang. Bang. Bang. The cannon on her aircar flashed. Machine guns rattled for good measure. Michael hung his head, awaiting his own turn. When he looked up the sea was dark with blood. Not a single Locust left alive on the beach. She had bagged her twenty points.

Crack. A conscript from Baytown, burly Paul Mason, wailed as he stared at short stumps protruding from his shoulders.

'Well, Pilgrim,' said Eloise Du Guesclin, 'the kind thing to do to an animal in pain is end its misery. If you don't, I'll press the button on another one of your friends. And I'll do that until you're the last one left.'

Shaking, he unslung his rifle. Fired. The maimed man stopped moving.

Michael tensed as the aircar flew near, hovering just feet away. His hair stirred from the wind in its engines.

'Pilgrim!' The loudspeaker was deafening. 'You shall come to my quarters tonight and explain your impudence. Back to your duties! All of you!'

The aircar rose and flew off.

Charlie Gudwallah laughed hysterically, throwing himself to his knees. 'I reckon she fancies you, Michael,' he said.

'Bitch!' spat Tom Higginbottom. 'Fucking bitch!'

A TOY

The embers of the log in the grate pulsed; small flames danced. Michael Pilgrim felt the chemicals of Baxter's *stuff* glow in his brain. Memories more deeply suppressed than even his sorry part as a genocidal butcher surfaced. Assumptions of worthlessness that only love might hope to smother like a warm blanket over long, comforting years. Always the sense a dozen lifetimes would be necessary to cleanse what happened beneath the merciless glare of the sun.

Michael fed more stuff into his pipe and sent himself wild and high. Coherence gave way to scenes and memories jumbling, jostling. How appropriate! She had always affected him that way: turning him inside out for her pleasure…

Their trysts had occurred in a zone forbidden to less-favoured conscripts.

'Just give her what she wants,' urged Charlie.

Tom Higginbottom nodded vigorously. 'It can't be worse than anything else you've had to do.'

Captain Eloise Du Guesclin's eye had fallen on other lads and lasses before Michael Pilgrim. Only one was ever foolish enough to reveal what went on in the windowless, bulletproof caravan guarded by drones and electric fences: and his arms had been blown off in mid-boast.

With heart beating furiously, palms sweating, Michael would approach her domain and strip naked. A dwarf-clone kept as a pet hurried out to hose him clean and inject him in accordance with her fancies for the evening. From the dwarf's grin, Michael guessed that the strange little creature watched what followed. There couldn't have been many other diversions in its short existence: the very sturdiest of clones never saw a third decade...

Time swirled. Lazy sparks floated from the burning log. Strange he could picture her so exactly. There, on the bed that seemed to fill half her caravan, splendidly naked, satiated, for now, both of them slippery with sweat. Whatever she suggested he did, his will stupefied by the injection as his body raged to possess her, so that sometimes he heard himself begging ... Oh, she had liked that.

Once, afterwards, she surprised him by sobbing, 'You wouldn't have wanted me so badly when I was fat little Ellie!' Her lovely face had stiffened in a way that scared him. 'But you primitives are too crude to understand. Too *stupid*.'

Other times her weakness was vicious, beating him with an electrified whip, his cries encouraging her to up the voltage. Though a small part of him always calculated his chances of snatching the whip and throttling her with its thongs, the drugs kept him passive. Unless, as she sometimes taunted, he was indeed a natural slave.

Oh, Eloise Du Guesclin liked a slave! *Needed* a slave. He sensed it was the only relationship with her fellow humans – not that he counted as human – she could manage comfortably. Yet how she would talk and boast when buzzed by her own chosen chemicals. His role had been that of adoring audience.

'I often think,' she said, 'we should breed a new species designed entirely for our individual pleasures. *Bespoke creatures*, my friend Dr Guy de Prie-Dieu calls them – he is *so* clever! – even cleverer than my brother Bertrand. Guy says we could measure our exact physiognomy then design a whole new species for our personal satisfaction. Imagine!' She had chuckled and played with his constantly erect penis until he groaned. 'Guy says it's perfectly feasible even if it's not allowed. You see, certain small-minded people – I'm thinking of my dear brother – call it a step too far.'

In his armchair, before the fire, Michael Pilgrim grimaced. How Eloise Du Guesclin had tormented him. Sex the least of it. Yet he had glimpsed her isolation and sullen moods and fearful hunger to be important and deciphered from her ramblings how she was afraid of her brother while always resenting his superiority. How absurdly power had corrupted her weak, impressionable mind. Michael knew with utter certainty his grandfather would have pitied her moral failings.

And then, after all that, she grew awkward with him and found new toys. No announcement or explanation. Other lads and lasses were summoned to be hosed and injected by the dwarf-clone. At least his arms weren't detonated from his shoulders.

'She likes you, Pilgrim,' sniggered Baxter, kiting high on stuff. 'You see, I see what you will never see. D'you see? De-men-tia!'

'Shut the fuck up,' muttered Tom Higginbottom. 'I'll give you fucking dementia.'

'She's got plans for you, Pilgrim,' Baxter had chortled. 'You'll see.'

DEATH MARCH

Eventually, it dawned on the Crusaders that ancient ways could be just as effective as scientific wonders. To rid yourself of Homo sapiens one might learn from its own bloody history.

By then Michael's qualms on the beach at Monte Carlo had diminished to coiled adders of despair. Whenever a snake's fangs bit he took a few more pills. Tried not to think at all. The original fifty conscripts down to eighteen. At first, losses in the company had been replaced, but as conscripted primitives proved unreliable, the Crusaders relied increasingly on drones and City technicians.

One occasion of many haunted him.

Deep in Syria – he called the land Syria though it might easily have been any other lost nation in that region – the column of struggling, footsore people they were herding halted for the night. They were on a motorway of blistered tarmac lined by burned out, sand-scoured vehicles. Some built for wars whose victor no one recalled. What drew Michael's eye were stone ruins a mile or so from the road, high on a lone hill in the scrubby, featureless desert.

Once the column of Locusts had been herded into an exhausted mass by drones, the conscripts set up camp and prepared food for the Captains and technicians. Cries of despair serenaded their work. Most prisoners had not eaten or drunk for two days now. Tomorrow would silence those voices forever. Michael found their noise unnerving. Eschewing a pill, he hurried away from the camp up a steep, rocky slope to the ruins.

His torch revealed an engraved metal sign in Arabic and English script: *Beauvoir Castle*. And then he almost laughed. For the broken stone walls that lay in rectangles and squares over the hilltop had belonged to a Crusader castle long, long ago. He sat heavily, surveying the circle of lights trained on the Locusts. A large trawl: three, four hundred. Tears surprised him. He had almost forgotten how to weep. They stung his sunburned cheeks.

Then Michael flinched. Eloise Du Guesclin might summon him again tonight. He noted with bleak self-loathing that a part of him hoped she would.

Only the cowards are still alive, he reminded himself.

It is time, he murmured, reaching out for his rifle.

Picking it up, he put the barrel in his mouth. It tasted of iron. How easy to close his eyes, squeeze the trigger, do no more harm. Forever sleep in the ruins of the Crusader castle.

Yet it was up there, on the wind-picked hilltop, he decided not to sleep just yet. One task remained. He would bring home the handful of conscripts from Baytown who had survived:

Charlie Gudwallah and Tom Higginbottom, that crazy bastard Baxter, psycho Aggie Brown from Pickering, half a dozen others, all witnesses to the City's crimes and their own.

Maybe it had just been more cowardice, a feeble attempt to justify his part in the ritualised slaughter that would commence when the sun rose. Maybe he had been no better than the Captains and technicians, few of whom, it must be said, savoured their work. Maybe he would have blown his brains out if the horrors had dragged on much longer. Instead, a miracle occurred.

Two days after that last massacre his company drove to a harbour of shiny metal piers jutting into the Mediterranean. He had hurried straight to Captain Du Guesclin's caravan.

'Captain!' he had called to the metal walls.

A tired voice answered through loudspeakers.

'Well, Pilgrim?'

'Why are we here, Captain?' He did not dare to hope. Could not help it.

For a moment she paused. 'Tell the conscripts our time here is over. They are going home.'

'How can that be?' he asked.

Truly, the prospect seemed impossible, like returning to Eden after the Fall. Was this some new game?

'We are ordered home, Michael Pilgrim,' she said. 'You are going home.'

Whitby was their demobilisation point. Of six hundred men and women conscripted in North Yorkshire less than forty returned. Sickness, sniper-fire, stampedes – a thousand ways to die out there. Sheer neglect by some Captains who herded their own primitives into killing zones intended for Locusts.

Yet Baytown, Malton and Pickering fared well. Of their conscripts, a full eighteen had come back, led by Lieutenant Michael Pilgrim as they staggered out of the transport drone into a downpour.

He lowered himself to his knees, tears joining the rain. Kissed the oil-impregnated tarmac outside the Deregulator's compound. Scraped his cheek against the ground to confirm home was real. Dizzy, faint, he felt that he might keel over and die. Sobs and moans from the other conscripts. A shadow fell across him as he grovelled. When Michael looked up he met almond eyes in a pale, pettish face, a rosebud mouth pursed into a superior smile.

She rode a drone with four legs like a metal horse, for once unconcealed by a plasti-steel viewing bubble. Her long hair dripped with rain like his own. For a moment he thought the sweet, clean rain of home might wash the stains from their souls. A wistful, hopeless moment.

'Did I not lead you well?' she asked, triumphantly. 'Are you not grateful?'

Michael rose and stood tall beside the four-legged drone. He held out his wrists, proffering the bracelets.

'Do these come off now, Captain?'

He became aware the other survivors were watching. Her war drone shifted, steam hissing from its vents.

'Yes,' she said.

Captain Eloise Du Guesclin pressed a button. The hated bracelets opened. Fell to the ground all around. A great ragged cheer rose from the conscripts. They danced, hugged, wept afresh. A few bared hairy backsides at the drones. Michael Pilgrim remained facing her, terrible sadness burrowed deep in his soul.

'Come to the City of Albion with me, Michael Pilgrim,' said Eloise Du Guesclin, uncertainly. 'I want you as my souvenir. You ... you please me.'

'To be your slave?'

'It is a great honour,' she said, in surprise. 'Any fool can see that.'

He turned away, picking up the kitbag in which he'd hidden his sword and a few other mementoes, and took the path along the West Cliff that would take him home. He expected a spiteful cannon shot from her drone. Didn't care. Didn't care.

'Wait! Wait!' shouted Charlie Gudwallah.

Tom Higginbottom and the other Baytown conscripts chased after him.

Thus they had straggled home through a downpour, their uniforms wet as sponges, and the whole of Baytown cried and celebrated for days and nights together.

ΣLΣVΣΠ

IN THE BASEMENT

It rained for days and nights, and a terrible storm assaulted the Yorkshire coast. Rumours reached Baytown of riverside communities swept away, but Helen avoided the village and concentrated on her new exhibition, *After the Deluge,* the first innovation in the Museum for decades. Her predecessor, a lowly technician, had been content to receive his monthly stipend of provisions for decades without bothersome changes. Not so Helen.

'Well, Averil, what do you think?'

They were down in the basement examining her proposals. The girl fiddled with a pencil.

'Averil!'

'Ma'am?' The girl started in her seat.

'Is everything all right?' asked Helen.

Averil's guileless face puckered. Tears found her eyes. 'I'm sorry.'

'Perhaps I can help? I wish to know what's troubling my most valued staff member.'

Only staff member, she might have added, apart from the caretaker drone.

Then – as with Averil it tended to – the story tumbled out. How she'd passed on an invitation to the Mayor's wife's Christmas party and now several of her friends – ex-friends, as they were turning out – kept going round to see Madame Morrighan, the Mayor's wife, and how they were given tins of food and pills that made them happy and were becoming the girlfriends of the Mayor's men, at least, a couple were, including her closest friend, Miriam – or ex-closest friend – and how when Miriam's father – Mr Armitage, that is, the blacksmith – went round to complain that his daughter was too young and that, in any case, he objected to her boyfriend as a rogue, he got kicked up the backside for his pains and Miriam refused to come home – and people in Baytown were muttering about it and saying it was all Averil's fault, especially Ben Higginbottom who had been Miriam's fiancé, or as good as.

Helen examined her pasty-faced, malnourished assistant. No doubt the other residents of Hob Hall were just as thin. Yet the first spring crops were still months away.

'You must ignore people's gossip, Averil,' she said. 'Remember, I will help in any way I can. Come, let me make you some soup.'

Later, Helen glimpsed a long, weary procession of people and ponies approaching Hob Hall and Holy Innocents Church. All were drenched and covered in mud. In their hands, a few bundles of possessions and agricultural tools.

'What has happened?' she asked Michael Pilgrim, hurrying up. Rain spattered and splashed.

He turned to her. 'These folks say their hamlet's been washed away by the floods. They were lucky to escape with their lives. They came here because Baytown folk have a reputation for helping others in need, but the Mayor's men beat them off with clubs. One lad who fought back got shot in the leg. Seems the Mayor told them to come to Hob Hall. Said we had food and shelter to spare.'

She stared at the bedraggled group. Two dozen, no, a few more. The implications of helping so many were clear when the Pilgrims could barely feed themselves. Helen watched as Reverend James Pilgrim led the refugees into the church, urging them to take up residence within and promising a hot meal would be provided.

'I told James we had to say no this time, but he wouldn't listen,' said Michael Pilgrim. Rain dripped from his nose. 'He never listens to me! Never! This'll finish us, I reckon. No, I'm sure of it.'

Helen did not know what to say. She bowed and splashed back to the warmth and comfort of the Museum. Not once did it cross her mind to offer the refugees shelter there.

THIN LINES

Amar knew well the thin line between short rations and famine. In childhood, he had strayed back and forth across that border as a way of life.

January became February, and he noted symptoms of real hunger in the swollen population of Hob Hall: hair without body or shine, eyes dry and pale, creeping apathy of spirit. Hungriest of all were the flood victims camping out in Holy Innocents Church. So desperate was their need that Reverend James Pilgrim insisted half the household's meagre stores were diverted their way.

One morning Amar walked to the old chapel in Baytown for a consultation with Dr Macdonald. She heard his tales of Hob Hall and sighed.

'Things go only a little better for most families in Bay,' she said. 'Especially now the Mayor demands rent payments for their homes that he, somehow, miraculously owns.'

'Rent?' asked Amar. The concept was strange to him.

When Dr Macdonald explained, he nodded knowingly. 'Ah, a new kind of banditry, I think.'

'Actually a very old kind,' she said. 'Some would say the natural order is reviving. I've noticed how often the Deregulator sends aerial drones to fly slowly round Baytown and spy in windows. More than he used to. No wonder people are too frightened to protest.'

Amar could tell she was afraid herself.

Dr Macdonald accompanied him back to Hob Hall to examine a child with spongy, bleeding gums, and Michael Pilgrim met her by the gate.

'Good of you to come,' he said. He lowered his voice confidentially. 'I'm sure you've heard how low we're brought.' He nodded at a group of listless flood-refugees clearing rubble from the shattered courtyard.

'We reckon there's just a fortnight's food left,' added Amar. 'After that?' He held out empty palms.

'Desperate days,' said Michael, 'call for desperate measures. I'm going away for a while to trade something dangerous but very valuable. If I don't make it back, I've asked Amar to work with you to look after Averil and the children.'

Mhairi Macdonald shook her head helplessly. 'There's little I can do, but I'll try.'

'With luck, you won't need to,' he said.

ACROSS THE MOORS

The next dawn Michael departed. He did not travel alone. Aside from his mule, a familiar shadow nosed the ground ahead: Bess, his sheepdog.

Amar saw him off, lantern in hand, a chill wind making the flame flicker. The sun's rising was obscured by thick, grey-black clouds charged with luminescence. Neither man liked such a sky. Or felt Michael had any choice but to chance it.

'Expect me back in six days at most,' said Michael, checking sword, shotgun and a vicious, stubby blunderbuss. He also carried a carefully honed axe. 'I'm hoping for a heavy load on the way home.'

'*Inshallah*,' muttered Amar, the phrase surfacing like a half-forgotten charm.

A creak made them glance up: Seth's bedroom window had opened a crack.

Michael led the mule away from Hob Hall, heading inland across the moors. His destination bore a dangerous name in the region: the flooded city of York.

TO LEAVE HOME BEHIND

Michael Pilgrim took a crooked track from Hob Hall, over valleys and riggs known since boyhood, to Fylingdales Moor. Wild upbursts of vegetation had reclaimed fields and arable land, but the moor was its ancient self, a boggy region of dark, peaty soil. He was entering a world deep-rooted as earth, mankind's traces already cloaked by moss and humus. *Amen to us,* he thought, as he crossed the old Scarborough to Whitby road travelled by few now but peddlers and vagrants. *Amen to home.*

Michael glanced back at snow-laden clouds pursuing him inland as icy winds whipped his cheeks.

Then he got lucky.

A nibbling muntjac deer, part of a small herd, bounded from behind a thicket of brambles. Michael's shotgun was in his hand and instinct jerked it up. He fired. Echo and smoke whisked away in the wind. But there it lay, enough meat for his journey to York and back.

Slinging the small animal on Noddy's back, Michael stepped forward with a fresh will. Already his mouth watered. He would beat the snow clouds to a place where the deer might not give up its life in vain.

Jagger Howe Moor, Burn Home Rigg, Little Rigg. Michael had learned the names during a long hike taken with his grandfather who had been teaching him the art of map-reading with a dog-eared Ordnance Survey sadly lost in the years since. No great loss, perhaps, seeing the land it depicted had changed in dramatic ways: woodland expanding, houses tottering, roads vanishing beneath turf. It had been summer then, the heather and furze of the moor dotted with saplings. Now the saplings were young trees, and Michael was glad. They might offer shelter from hostile eyes.

By midday, he had reached a large, brutally functional complex of buildings surrounded by fallen wire mesh fences: the old RAF radar base at Fylingdales. At its heart, a tall concrete pyramid rose from the moorland, ugly, menacing, brooding. Michael glanced nervously at the sky: snow flurries were starting down.

RAF FYLINGDALES

Michael had to think hard to remember what the acronym *RAF* signified. His reading had alerted him to the tradition of an English monarchy, so the *Royal* was clear. As for the *Air Force*, he knew that meant human-operated killing machines as opposed to the City's flying drones. Proof, if more was needed, power ever loves its toys.

Whatever force once existed here had long worn away. Broken cars and military vehicles housed thorny shrubs, and the only commanding voice he heard belonged to the wind. Still, he proceeded cautiously, though he could not imagine people dwelling in the looted, burned-out buildings. After tethering the mule, he walked from ruin to ruin, shotgun ready. All were deserted, just bare rooms and broken down doors and traces of fire. In one bunker, a mound of tangled human bones.

That left the radar installation to inspect.

The imposing pyramid had frightened him as a boy and still made him uneasy. Its shape reminded him of the Pharaohs' tombs he had seen in the Crusades, places of death and nightmare. Yet he knew it would be dangerous to sleep in the base without checking for company.

Snow quickened and danced as Michael approached the towering pyramid. It rested on a high, plinth-like building of reinforced concrete with windowless sheer walls. He remembered heavy blast doors standing open in Grandfather's day and a maze of dark corridors and rooms beyond. Folk in Baytown said dead souls were drawn to the pyramid like iron to a magnet.

As he approached, Michael wondered if he had misremembered, for the steel doors were sealed tight. Not only that, a large padlock secured them, a piece of engineering possible only in the City.

His instinct was to retreat – and fast. Still, nothing moved; the only sound came from his boots squelching. He walked round the large exterior of the building. The ground revealed no vehicle or drone tracks: horse's hooves, yes, nothing more sinister. Moor ponies maybe, though the hoof prints were shod.

A mystery then ... All he knew for sure was that the City wished to keep out visitors and people on horses came here. Maybe travellers like him, passing through; maybe folk on more peculiar business.

Michael shivered. The snow was heavy now. Without shelter, it would be a grim night out on the moor. Returning to a bunkhouse on the outskirts of the base that retained its roof and doors, he used his officer's sword to skin and butcher the doe. Burning an office desk and chairs, he roasted strips and hunks of bloody meat while snow fluttered outside.

Wrapped in blankets and gorged on meat, he slept deeply and awoke to an unsettling calm.

INNOCENCE

Michael listened. Wind sighs, a faint skeetering sound. The fire had burned out. Noddy was still tethered near the door, a steaming pile of manure on the concrete floor. Daylight lined the metal door he had wedged shut.

It took little time to pack the cooked meat, roll up his bedding, check weapons. When he emerged, the world smelt of clean water and a low winter sun smouldered.

Michael shielded his eyes. The snow must have come down all night in heavy flakes for the harsh moor was transformed. Pure white sheets coated thorny saplings and heather. He thought of white paper, truths yet to be written. His heart, wearied by a lifetime's sorrows, swelled with hope. So innocent a world that day, even if for an eye-blink! If he died tomorrow, at least he would have had this moment.

In this mood, he scanned the horizon – and froze. Three riders were rising from a distant contour of Snod Hill.

Michael dodged back inside. Thought furiously. They were too far off to have spotted him unless he was unlucky. Half an hour until they reached Fylingdales, maybe longer, given the heavy going. With luck, they were travellers, traders, hunters, nothing to do with Big Jacko. Perhaps they would ride past; after all, his tracks were concealed by fresh snow. Somehow he doubted it. Perhaps he should try to gain a head start, but on ponies, they would soon catch him and out in the open, without cover come a fight.

Michael led Noddy to another room in the concrete bunker. It faced west, the direction he must take to reach the long road to York. There he prepared.

Fylingdales is a relic of the Cold War, Grandfather had told him as a boy, a kind of war that confused him then. It seemed the cold war in Fylingdales was about to warm up.

Outside he scattered a few sticks of freshly burned wood, scraps of skin and bone from the deer. Enough to draw the riders' attention to a particular spot. He took up position so anyone examining the bait would have their backs to a window, its metal shutter hanging askew. Then he waited, peering through a tiny crack at the bloody remains of the doe.

JOHNNY SAWDON

The three riders came boldly, as Michael knew they would, confident in numbers. He heard voices and hooves clopping round the perimeter of the building where he hid. Using the gap in the rusted metal shutter, he watched them trot into view. All carried guns.

Two of the riders weren't Baytown men: the disreputable style of Scarborough or Geordieland, maybe even Jockland, clung to them. The third, Johnny Sawdon, was Baytown to his bones, a hard man with quick fists and one of the first to sign up as a Mayor's Man. Even out here he wore the gaudy yellow armband. Michael had never trusted him and did not now.

No mystery as to Johnny's presence on the moor: track then finish off an awkward enemy when his allies weren't to hand. Michael remembered Seth's window scraping open, how the lad overheard his destination and watched him depart from Hob Hall. So that was it. His own kin.

Johnny Sawdon leaned down from his horse to examine the firewood and bits of butchered doe Michael had left out. He stood in his stirrups. A breezy, handsome man, Sawdon addressed the dark rooms of the blockhouse.

'We know you're in there, Pilgrim,' he called, 'we saw you earlier. Come out, and we'll take you back to the Mayor. He wants a friendly word.'

Michael waited, and Sawdon glanced significantly at his companions. One reached for a stubby musket in a saddle holster, but his leader mouthed *not yet*. The man nodded, settled back, a hand resting on the butt of his gun.

'I know you're a man of peace, Pilgrim,' called Sawdon. 'You hate a quarrel as much as I do. So does the Mayor. Come out, man! Let's talk this whole mess over. We've known each other since we were bairns, after all.'

Michael crept from the window to a metal door cratered by bullet holes. He stepped outside onto the soft snow. A few silent tiptoes positioned him behind the horsemen, who were whispering urgently.

'Don't turn or move a muscle,' he called to them. 'Put your hands on your heads.'

Sawdon began to turn.

With a dramatic click, Michael cocked and aimed his shotgun.

'Last chance, Johnny.'

The three men stared down from their horses into two barrels and noted the blunderbuss hooked to Michael's belt.

At this range, he wouldn't miss. One by one they put their hands on their heads.

'No need to be so unfriendly like,' sniffed Sawdon.

Michael closed on the mounted men. All carried blades in addition to their muskets.

'Weapons on the ground,' he told their backs. 'Guns first, held by the butts. Then the blades.'

Again they exchanged glances. Sawdon hesitated before gingerly lowering his musket, so it fell in the snow.

'Do as he says,' he ordered his companions.

Guns then swords and a spiked mace were tossed obligingly to the ground. Michael looked over the horses. Sawdon's was biggest and strongest – and rather familiar.

'Dismount very slow,' he ordered the Baytown man. 'Yes, just you, Johnny. Hands stay on heads, all of you! Just you get off your horse, Johnny.'

At this command, Sawdon baulked. 'We've come in peace, Lieutenant, we're messengers, that's all. I'd never have guessed you for a horse thief.'

'You came here to kill me one way or another,' said Michael, reasonably. 'And I recognise that mare as belonging to Armitage, the blacksmith by rights. I'd be surprised if you came by her honestly. So why not get off the horse as I say, Johnny, and lie on the ground with hands on your head.'

After more grumbling, Sawdon obliged until Michael was in control of the mount.

'Okay, Johnny, go over to yon pal of yours and get on his horse with him,' he ordered, taking careful aim with his shotgun.

After a nervous scrabble two men sat uncomfortably on the one pony.

'Now ride back to Baytown and tell the Mayor not to trouble honest men.'

Johnny Sawdon glared at him, half scornful, half afraid. 'You'll pay with your life for this, Pilgrim.'

'Maybe. By the way, I'm just borrowing this horse. If it's rightly yours, you'll get it back.'

Michael watched them trot across Fylingdales Moor, back the way they'd come. It occurred to him killing all three would have been wiser in every possible way. Now word of his location would travel. Worse, far worse, next time they wouldn't underestimate him. Michael hid their weapons deep in the blockhouse, and a shiver unrelated to the wind made him tighten his scarf.

TWƎLVƎ

---◦⊱⊰◦---

REAPING

Over in Baytown, Helen Devereux intended to reap a neglected harvest, one planted and nurtured by disasters unimaginable in the snug and smug years of the early twenty-first century. Her fellow reaper would be Averil Pilgrim, their scythes a handheld hologram recorder and a polite manner.

At first, people were afraid to open up, even with Averil's reassuring presence. Curator and assistant trailed from door to shabby door, targeting Baytown's older residents, some of whom had survived several virulent Dyings.

Interviewing these treasure houses of memories involved negotiations with younger relatives, their protectors. Most folk 'getting on a bit', as it was tactfully put, were infirm and spent their days before peat fires. Heads were shaken, doors shut in the Curator's face, and she began to despair.

Her breakthrough came with the Higginbottom clan.

Blood being thicker than water held true with the Higginbottoms. A tight lot in every way. Well over forty lived in houses round the Puzzle Well, sharing a flotilla of fishing cobles and invisible nets of kinship through hearth and home.

'I expect they won't like the sight of me,' said Averil. She was thinking of young Ben Higginbottom's disappointment with Miriam Armitage, as Helen swiftly guessed.

'Let's try them anyway,' she said. 'After all, Ben has no logical reason to blame you.'

As if logic ever held sway over heartbreak.

Because it was a choppy day, the men were ashore mending line and net. They wore oiled woollen gansey jumpers knitted in the Baytown herringbone pattern. Thus, if a man drowned and was washed ashore, his home village would be obvious. The family smokehouse trailed scents of charcoal and salty cod in the morning air. The women were engaged in a communal wash, their hands raw and chapped as they soaped and pounded the cloth. As they worked, the younger wives sang softly together.

At first, Helen felt afraid. Benign theories about people dismissed as primitives by Bertrand and the City were one thing, actual dialogue with them on their own terms quite another. Certainly, their conceptions were limited. Yet these fisher-folk achieved complex lives through simple means – even if they were regressing steadily to modes of living centuries-old. In that sense, Helen had to concede Bertrand was right, the Higginbottoms *were* primitive. She also recollected his warning she was reverting to savagery.

A gaggle of children played a skipping game near the Puzzle Well Inn and Helen's fears melted into wistful mourning. Bright-eyed, bonny faces! Voices squealing with guileless laughter, all to win a simple contest of strength versus gravity. She watched the children's mothers and grandmothers: most had aged young. Yet for all her youthful beauty and privilege Helen Devereux felt a surge of jealousy – and shame at her pettiness.

'Look,' whispered Averil, 'there's Uncle Michael's old pal, Tom.'

'Well, I'm going to ask him,' declared Helen. 'Mr Higginbottom! Could I have a word?'

Tom Higginbottom came over, a big-boned man with a steady gaze. He scanned the sky suspiciously, and Helen could tell he was afraid of drones. That very morning a small one had flown round the village hovering by windows: folk whispered it was spying for the Mayor and casting the evil eye.

'Mr Higginbottom,' she said, 'I have a request.'

'Oh, aye?'

Within an hour – after repeated assurances that both Dr Macdonald and Michael Pilgrim saw no harm in the Curator's plan – she and Averil sat among a dozen women, hologramming tales of the Worst Times. A display was forming in Helen's mind, one family's survival. She could exhibit their hand-knitted jumpers with the village's special herringbone pattern, homemade furniture and toys, maybe a coble. Snatches of interview could be projected as holograms. That would be one in the eye for City visitors. Watch the ur-humans speak and learn they are uncomfortably like one's Beautiful self.

Her interviews revealed facets of the Great Dying rarely considered in the Five Cities. How intensely primitives could mourn, how they organised systems for the disposal of bodies, how doctors and nurses sacrificed themselves to bring a little comfort to doomed patients. She learned how food was produced and shared in the teeth of terrible privations. Often the name of Pilgrim cropped up in the accounts recorded on her screen: the Reverend Oliver, of course, but also his grandson, Lieutenant Michael Pilgrim.

TO YORK

Mounted on the pony he had 'borrowed' from Johnny Sawdon, his tethered mule trotting behind, Michael followed the ancient Pickering road. He hastened past Dalby Forest where dark shadows beneath the trees harboured a tribe gone wild, so folk said, peaceable enough if you didn't trouble them; cannibals if you did.

The winding highway led south. Snow on grass stems and bare branches melted as the sun brightened. He spied a herd of feral cattle not far from the Hole of Horcum and the shaggy beasts lowed in warning at the sight of man and dog, their fat-rumped bull staring menacingly.

'Steady, girl!' he told Bess.

The wise old sheepdog padded near his stirrup, sniffing the air.

By the forenoon, he was trotting through Pickering. Though the Pilgrims had friends in the town he didn't linger, eager to approach York before nightfall.

At last, he glimpsed the outskirts of Malton rising through trees and a grass-cloaked dual carriageway heading south-west. Michael kept to the wider road, passing tangles of abandoned vehicles. He noted smoke trails in the distance indicating settlements. Agriculture was reviving in the fallow lands around Pickering and Malton; indeed Tom Higginbottom spoke of establishing a regular trade in smoked fish. A comrade from the Crusades, Aggie Brown, was said to have large herds and lands near Malton, and she owed Michael plenty of favours. But Aggie's predilections had always made him nervous; he was too squeamish to get in such a person's debt or abide her company for long.

Onward the road curved, and he reached a crossroads where the wreckage of a large airliner lay scattered. Perhaps the pilot had tried to crash-land here. Sheets of plastic and metal lay among brambles; reedy pools filled impact craters from the crash. Spongy bones and skulls, green with mould, littered the ground.

With darkness coming on he turned off the road and spent the night in an abandoned pub overlooking the ruins of Kirkham Abbey, dreaming of monks and mists and a jet-liner crammed with faceless people. All night the River Derwent flowed towards the sea. Foxes barked. Owls hooted. His mule and newly-acquired horse shuffled restlessly through their own dreams.

THE MODIFIED MAN

York turned out to be an island besieged by swampy ground, willow, thick grass and bulrushes.

Michael rode past a miserable settlement on his way through silent suburbs. Barefoot children played in the dirt, and a chained up dog snarled at Bess. Soon he glimpsed York Minster's twin towers rising from the floodplain. A formation of honking geese flew over, heading for the river.

For the first time, he despaired of this winter journey. Why had he come to doomed York? Baxter had pointed him here, but Baxter was reliable as moonshine. Still, only a madman would trade large quantities of food for what he had to offer, and York was the one place said to harbour such a person.

Michael entered the ancient city from the north, following street patterns littered with the usual vehicles and shrubs. Soft layers of silt suggested previous floods, but the roads were solid beneath the pony's hooves, and he made swift progress.

The medieval city walls came in sight, including a high gatehouse, its sheer face dotted with arrow slits. Michael dismounted to check his weapons. He had expected the antique city gates to be barricaded, but the way lay open. And menacingly quiet. He led his pony into a large, clear area outside a roofless art gallery. Oh, he made a nice fat target out here.

Pigeons could be heard cooing in the grand old buildings. He examined the silt on the road: many boot prints, deer hooves, traces of birds. At least the boot marks suggested some degree of civilisation.

'Fuck it,' he muttered, leading his animals through the dark gatehouse to the street beyond. No one challenged. Nothing moved. It seemed the ancient city, settled for two thousand years, had gone the way of Babylon.

Outside the cathedral, Michael gazed up in awe. What giants constructed this marvel? Ornate carvings and designs and gargoyles cut from living stone; arts learned with the slow craft of centuries now lost to mankind. How low humanity was sinking, year after year, how hard the road back.

Something moved in the enormous cathedral porch. He slowly slung his shotgun over his shoulder. The last thing he needed was a shootout.

'I've come to trade,' he called to the figure hidden in the doorway. 'I've got something the Modified Man might want.'

No reply. Michael's heart beat painfully. If they were going to open fire, now would be their time.

Then a young woman wearing a thick veil stepped out of the Minster. Several armed men followed. Michael heard a noise, turned. More men left the ruins of a grand hotel bearing crossbows, a blunderbuss, shotguns, muskets. Several wore crude body armour fashioned from car bonnets.

Michael bowed. 'I take it the Modified Man is home?'

THE MODIFIED MAN (2)

They led him into the high, shadowy cathedral. Michael's eyes adjusted to the gloom of the long vaulted nave. A few stained glass windows glowed; most were as broken as the Bible stories they depicted. A layer of mud on the flagstones told him even the massive church had flooded recently: no holding back water or time.

He turned to the young woman who seemed in charge. The tightly wound scarf concealed her face.

'Will my horse and mule be safe out there?' he asked. 'I'm rather fond of them.'

Her eyes were soft, large, a hazel-flecked brown, beautiful eyes he must admit. She pointed at his weapons then at a stone bench set into the wall. Armed men surrounded them.

Michael hesitated. 'All?'

His question echoed in the empty space. She pointed more urgently.

'Very well,' he said, having little choice. Shotgun, blunderbuss, knife, sword formed a pile on the bench.

The veiled woman waved to indicate he should follow, and he caught a whiff of her breath through the cloth, acrid and strange.

Michael stared in wonder at stone effigies of kings and archangels, knights and bishops. On the wall, inscriptions commemorated dead worthies: a lieutenant killed in a forgotten colonial war, his name preserved in marble; beloved wives and children snatched early by God.

The veiled woman waved him on, and four guards followed. They reached a space enclosed by ornately carved wooden screens and stalls for choristers, all miraculously intact. At the far end, upon a raised dais, were ancient thrones bearing ornate crosses. One chair had its back to him. All Michael could see was the rear of its occupant's lumpy head covered with warts and wispy grey hair. The old man sat before a vast stained glass window, its leaded pictures busy with people, animals, drama.

'Look up!' called the seated man without turning. 'Look up and behold Creation!' His voice was hoarse, bitter. 'See! Perched upon a cloud, no less, our generous Creator! Do you think he's pleased with his work?'

The question echoed. Somewhere a pigeon cooed.

'Sir!' called out Michael, 'I think you are the one they call the Modified Man.'

'And I think you're the one they call Michael Pilgrim.'

Michael blinked. He had heard the Modified Man possessed strange powers.

'May I take it then,' said Michael, addressing the back of the man's head, 'you know why I've come?'

'Because you desire something from me,' replied the Modified Man. 'Why else?'

Michael glanced round. None of the guards had moved. His sense of danger intensified.

'My family needs food,' he said. 'Much food. I have brought something to trade.'

For long minutes the man on the throne stared up at the stained glass window. The coloured glass was dulled by a layer of dust like a bright light dimming. Finally, the old man sighed, struggled to his feet, turned to face his visitor.

Some moments of revelation are replayed over and over in dreams. So it was for Michael Pilgrim with the Modified Man.

His instinct was to cry out in horror. Step back. Were his eyes playing tricks in the dim light? But no, what could not be, *should not be*, was very much before him. Instead of a man's face, features resembling a grey-faced toad's. Pink, piggy eyes and a small, flaccid elephant's trunk for a nose.

The Modified Man's mouth opened in a horrible, toothless smile.

'How?' Michael stuttered.

'Do you *really* wish to know how I came to look this way, Michael Pilgrim?'

'Yes,' he heard himself saying. 'Yes.'

'*They* did this to me as a punishment. The Five Cities did this. For seeking to stop their abominations against nature, their crimes, long before you were born. I was a warning to others who might oppose the Beautiful Life.'

'I do not understand,' whispered Michael. 'Only God can inflict such punishments.'

The Modified Man's trunk twitched. Mucus glistened at its tip. 'But my dear boy, some men aspire to be God! I'm thinking of one scientist in particular, a doctor. You wouldn't like to be treated by him, Michael Pilgrim, believe me.' He turned to the girl. 'Take our guest to Clifford's Tower and let him rest there tonight. Return his weapons and feed him well. I believe him to be a man of honour like his grandfather.'

With that, the vile face turned back to contemplate the stained glass window.

BARGAINS

Next morning, Michael walked the battlements of a medieval keep, Clifford's Tower, a high fortification on a mound of grassy earth. Dull grey waters lapped all around, fed by the swollen river. Gulls and ducks bobbed. He had breakfasted in a communal dining hall on trout and barley bread after tending his animals. Plenty of folk to be seen. Clearly, the Modified Man was not short of followers, and York was recovering well under his rule.

At noon, he was summoned. The veiled woman remained silent, watching him through her wide, delicate, long-lashed brown eyes. Eyes that made him think of Scheherazade, an allusion no doubt lost to just about every soul in York. Stories decayed and returned to the earth like fallen branches, yet Michael suspected the Modified Man could tell a few interesting tales – and knew how to turn them to his advantage.

He wore his sword as they walked down streets choked with mud, grass, plastic and collapsed masonry. Rats scurried. A persistent cawing of rooks came from trees round the river.

She led him into a large building littered with collapsed metal shelves. Faded lettering above the entrance read *Marks and Spencer*.

The Modified Man sat near the line of tills, their open bellies caked with green, tarnished coins. He was poring over a map laid upon a crude table. The sight of his hideous elephant's trunk so soon after breakfast set Michael's stomach churning.

'I like it here,' declared the creature, wheezing. 'I remember coming here with my mother. Her coat was brown and smelt of perfume. *Chanel No. 5*, it was called. Perfumes had special names then. Her coat was made of a material no one makes anymore, cashmere. This place was a department store.'

The only real shops Michael Pilgrim knew were the Puzzle Well Inn and a few petty Baytown and Pickering merchants. He examined the multi-storey building with its frozen escalators. 'There must have been much to sell when you were a boy.'

'It came at a dear price for mankind,' said the Modified Man. He smiled slyly. 'Does it surprise you I am so old?'

Michael shrugged. 'So you tell me.'

'Oh, I am old. You see I, too, once lived the Beautiful Life.'

Michael risked a glance into the piggy pink eyes. Looked hastily away.

'But even my time draws to an end,' said the Modified Man. 'Without regular treatment the Beautiful Life cannot be sustained.'

'That is the third time you've used the phrase,' said Michael. 'What is this Beautiful Life?'

The only life he'd known was ugly – hardship, sorrow and struggle – yet beauty, too, running like a network of veins through everything.

'It means the Five Cities, Michael Pilgrim, it means why they exist. Why they are sworn to utter ruthlessness so they, at least, can enjoy the Beautiful Life.'

'I see,' said Michael, though he didn't. 'Why hasn't the City sent drones here? Surely, they're aware of your presence in York. They know everything.'

The Modified Man's moon-like face quivered. 'Because they – or *he* – he who humbled me, the doctor I mentioned to you yesterday, if you had the wit to pay attention – in short, Dr Guy de Prie-Dieu, though his name was plainer when I knew him – prefers me to live on and suffer.' His eyes narrowed into slits. 'Remember his name and fear it. He has big plans for you primitives, every last one of you.'

Michael's memory did stir. He *had* heard the outlandish name before. When, exactly, he could not say.

'So you want revenge,' he said. 'Is that true of you all here?' He looked quizzically at Scheherazade. Her soulful eyes met his own.

'You're wondering why she never shows her face, aren't you?' said the Modified Man. 'I can see you have a romantic soul. Considering that you find it impossible to look at me for more than two seconds, I'd advise you not to ask her to remove that veil. But to answer your question, we all want revenge, though I prefer to call it justice. Don't you, Michael Pilgrim? For the brand burned across your cheek? For what they made you do in the Crusades?'

Michael didn't like how much they knew about him.

'You're very well-informed.'

'Perhaps we have mutual acquaintances in Baytown,' said the Modified Man.

At first, Michael thought of Mister Priest Man then glanced up sharply. 'You mean Dr Macdonald, don't you?'

For long moments neither spoke.

'Revenge,' said Michael, 'requires a suitable weapon.'

He reached into his pocket and produced a dull silver cylinder, twenty centimetres long, ten wide. A hefty little device. 'Do you recognise it?' he asked.

The creature's eyes devoured the thing.

'It's powerful enough,' said Michael, 'to blow this building into a pile of dust.'

An excited hiss escaped the Modified Man's toad-mouth. 'I can think of better things to destroy than Marks and Spencer,' chuckled the monster. 'Do you know, I'm beginning to almost like you, Michael Pilgrim. Let us go for a walk round the city walls. It would do you good to learn a few things about the City of Albion. I suspect you have a role to play in the future neither of us can guess. Just as your grandfather played his role. Yes, yes, come with me, Pilgrim.'

THE CITY WALLS

York's ancient walls had not only survived but had been repaired and strengthened under the Modified Man's rule. Medieval swamps had been systematically undrained to create a defensive morass round the city and houses pulled down to allow fields of fire. That cold, overcast morning the slumped, hunchbacked figure led Michael Pilgrim up a steep flight of worn stone steps to the battlements.

'Earlier, you marvelled when I hinted at my age,' wheezed the Modified Man, his steel-shod stick clacking against the paving stones. 'I have been a witness to more than you can imagine.'

'Do you truly remember the time before the plagues?' Michael said. 'Surely that is impossible.'

The Modified Man leered. 'Oh, we've learned the impossible is a concept open to adjustment. But yes, I remember those years in the first half of the last century.'

'My grandfather said that after his youth all sense of coherence in the world faded,' said Michael. 'That one's perspective narrowed to simple survival. But he didn't talk much about the time before everything went bad, except to call it a time of justice and freedom and plenty.'

'Ha!' snorted the Modified Man. 'Fables to instruct and inspire children! So you think life was splendid before the plagues? A paradise, eh?' He snuffled. 'I fear your grandfather lied. Let me disabuse you. The world was a place of war and famine and drought caused by mankind's folly. The nuclear accidents and uncontrolled pollution did not help either. So much plastic, Pilgrim! So much oil pumped from the earth to burn and shape into plastic. All to allow a few – it was never more than a very few – to bloat themselves with the whole world's wealth. Actually, Pilgrim, I was one of those very few. We called it the natural order.'

The Modified Man sniffed at what he had once been so that his trunk wobbled.

'Britain itself was a nation of poverty riddled with gated, guarded islands where our privileged caste lived. Oh yes, even the City of Albion existed as a gated town by the time of the first plagues, albeit in a small way. It was a great centre of technology and science. Huntingdon was its name then, an old, old name for a community that despised the past. Science, Pilgrim, ruthless progress! Those were the gods we worshipped. And some still do, I might add.'

They proceeded wordlessly to a corner tower overlooking row after row of terrace houses with trees growing through their roofs and walls hidden by ivy.

'Nor was Huntingdon alone,' continued the Modified Man, 'all over the world there were similar communities dedicated to science and its darkest possibilities. Few such places, admittedly, five in total, but more than enough to rule when the world emptied itself of people.'

'The Five Cities,' mused Michael, 'Grandfather called them, *five gateways to Hell.*'

'Yes, yes. Just five.'

The Modified Man paused like a teacher allowing a pupil time to prepare dutiful questions. Michael's brow furrowed. 'This Huntingdon, did it have drones?'

'Oh, yes! Primitive ones compared to today, horse and carts compared to an aircar but deadly enough. Governments used them routinely against their own people even before the pandemic.' The Modified Man leaned forward so that Michael was forced to lean back. 'They have no conscience, you see, no sense of morality. They'll do anything you ask and fear no evil.'

'I know what drones will do,' said Michael, thinking of the Crusades. 'But they are just tools. Behind them lie men who should have consciences.'

'No doubt, no doubt. Where was I? Yes, the communities that were dedicated to science like Huntingdon possessed far more than mere drones. They could call on limitless energy. You will not grasp what I mean by the term *fusion* so I won't bother to explain. And they had successfully begun the renewal of living cells and bone and sinew decades before the first plagues. *That* secret was out of nature's bag. Oh, yes. And there was to be no stuffing it back out of sight.'

'Then the plagues came,' said Michael, 'didn't they? Washing away mankind like waves lapping a sandcastle when the tide comes in.'

'Ah, I suspect you're not just a romantic but a poet, Pilgrim,' wheezed the Modified Man. 'A delightful simile! Mankind as a sandcastle and each of us a grain of sand. One year ten per cent of humanity washed away, the next another ten, wave after wave … Nowhere on Earth was immune.'

'Except this Huntingdon and the other science cities you mention?' suggested Michael.

The Modified Man's trunk-like nose twitched. 'What a clever boy we are! Of course, they made sure of that. Complete quarantine and sealed environments gave them a breathing space in the early years. Between ourselves, they developed a partial cure within months, all very hush, hush, as you may imagine. Within a few years, they had nothing at all to fear.'

'A cure! But that means…'

'Yes, yes, they let everyone die. Whole cultures and civilisations. Ancient cities and wondrous places. Traditions and religions. Even the holovision channels simple souls loved to gawp at. Even the trashy food and cheap drugs they gorged upon to become obese and passive. All the Five Cities need do was wait behind their walls while nature did the rest.'

'But why?' gasped Michael. He could not grasp the enormity of what he had heard. Had Grandfather known this? It would have broken his heart.

'To live forever, Pilgrim, isn't that worth a few sacrifices? What they call the Beautiful Life.'

'My grandfather said we may only live forever through God.'

The Modified Man sniffed. 'A quaint notion. The evidence points in other directions.'

'I still don't…'

But the Modified Man seemed to lose interest. He yawned, a sullen, melancholy look clouding his grotesque face. 'You don't need to understand, Pilgrim, not now. One day, perhaps.' He looked with narrow intensity at Michael Pilgrim as though assessing his worthiness. 'They are monstrously arrogant in the Five Cities, utterly sure of their power. One day that hubris might bring their test tubes and beloved devices crashing down upon their heads.'

Michael Pilgrim's affable face had acquired a cold, dangerous expression.

'Who is their leader?' he asked, quietly. 'Do they have a king?'

The Modified Man smiled. 'Like to kill him, Pilgrim? Get your revenge? Well, you'd have to destroy them all. They are led not by a king but by a committee of their greatest scientists and engineers and doctors. One gains influence in Albion and its sister cities around the world by inventing new ways to further the Beautiful Life.' He sighed. 'You will never destroy them, Pilgrim. No one can. Not yet, at least.'

Still, Michael clenched his fists angrily.

'What of the Deregulators? Why place them among us so-called *primitives*? They do not rule us. They just sit in their little hives like wasps and prevent mankind from making anything of itself. The Deregulators merely want us to travel backwards.'

'True, true,' mused the Modified Man. 'Perhaps you primitives should feel flattered they pay you *that* much notice.'

CURIOUS

'One more question,' said Michael Pilgrim, 'one that concerns me closely. Why the Crusades?'

'My, we are curious! Good. More of you people should ask *why*. I will not try to explain the subtleties of climate change as it would be quite beyond you. However, Africa suffered nuclear accidents as well as shrivelling in the heat. A great migration towards Europe was detected. Locusts in a swarm, the cities called them, so off they went to war. If you ask me they did it because they were bored and wanted to play with their toys. In the end, boredom is their greatest enemy, I suspect. It is the thing that will set them at each other's throats.'

Michael hung his head as he recalled scenes no man should witness. Still, he hungered to know more.

'One last thing,' he said, raising his head to meet the Modified man's pink eyes. 'Who is this Jacko plaguing Baytown? He seems to have some power over the Deregulator.'

A blob of mucus dripped from the Modified Man's trunk, landing on his distended belly where it dribbled down.

'Power? I doubt that, Pilgrim. I believe this Jacko provides a service to people far more powerful than a minor functionary like the Deregulator of Whitby. A clandestine service kept secret from those who control Albion. They will drop him as soon as his usefulness comes to an end. My advice, Pilgrim, is to kill Jacko when there are no drones around to see you do it.' The toad-like mouth broadened into a mocking grin. 'After all, he wouldn't be the first person you've murdered in cold blood, Lieutenant, would he now?'

At dawn the next day, Michael left York on Johnny Sawdon's horse. His mule followed, laden with sacks of dried beans, oil, flour and meat. A second pack pony bore yet more supplies. Enough, if they ate the horses, to see the Pilgrims and maybe even the flood-refugees through to late spring. All he need do was transport the provisions through fifty hostile miles where armed enemies waited in unknown numbers. That was all.

THIRTΣΣΠ

---❖---

GRACE

'*Our Father, who art in heaven, hallowed be thy name; thy kingdom come...*'

'Fuck's sake, Father!'

Reverend James Pilgrim's prayer ground to a halt. He had already said grace for the meal and was throwing in the Lord's Prayer as an extra sprinkle of salt. Perhaps he hoped it would take everyone's mind off the watery slop on their plate.

'You expect us to be grateful for *this*?' Seth shook his head pityingly.

He lolled in Uncle Michael's vacant chair at the long dining table of Hob Hall. His outfit was fancy by Baytown standards, and he knew it. A black nylon jacket shiny from use but unquestionably manmade and therefore superior to wool, cotton or linen. A bright yellow Mayor's Man armband. Round his neck a crude pendant depicting a naked woman with a heron's head.

His father peered closely at the pendant. Fingered a large crucifix attached to a silver chain round his own neck.

The children at the table looked with awe upon sleek, well-fed Seth: his curved knife and one-shot pistol, his brazen disrespect for their benefactor. Some of the older children cringed to hear the Reverend hectored by his only son. Everyone knew he never dared talk that way when his uncle was around, but Michael Pilgrim had been swallowed whole by the boggy moors. Wisdom in Baytown, spread by the Mayor's Men, claimed he would never return.

Seth pretended to taste the watery gruel that constituted their nutrition for the day then let his spoon fall with a clatter.

'Father,' he said, winking at an adoring orphan to his left, 'I wouldn't give this to a hungry pig.'

A fresh frisson of alarm at the table. James Pilgrim squeezed his brow into tight ridges.

'Seth!' whispered Averil. 'Stop it! Are you drunk?'

His answer was to turn over his bowl. Watery fingers reached across the table.

'I ain't drunk,' leered Seth in his best Mockney. His whole manner suggested the opposite. 'I'm free!' He laughed with an edge of hysteria. 'I'm *me*! *Me*! Do you know how good that feels?'

The long table of faces stared. For all his defiance Seth grew nervous. He rose abruptly and his chair fell to the ground behind him. He checked the knife and gun at his belt as though afraid they were no longer there.

'This is it, Father,' he said, hoarsely, in his natural voice. 'You've left me no choice.'

He began a tirade rehearsed mentally for weeks. 'I'm leaving home forever. This place don't even rightly belong to you, Father, it belongs to the Mayor.'

Everyone froze except his father who was coughing painfully.

'Yes, the Mayor showed me a certificate from the Deregulator,' continued Seth. 'He told me he offered to pay you for Hob Hall, but Uncle Michael wouldn't listen. It's all *his* fault. You can't blame Mayor Jacko.'

Reverend Pilgrim gained mastery of his windpipe. 'Do not heed the lies of the serpent,' he wheezed. 'That man is an agent of Satan.'

Seth's face darkened with sulky rage.

'Let us finish grace,' continued his father. 'Seth, be seated. *Give us this day our daily bread. And forgive us our trespasses, as we forgive those who trespass against us…*' Here he shot his son a reproachful glance.

Lips fixed in a mirthless grin, Seth watched him recite until, with a snort of derision, he stormed from the dining room. The front door of Hob Hall slammed.

Reverend Pilgrim's voice continued to intone. A few of the orphans were on the verge of sobbing and Averil sat bolt upright, dabbing her eyes. Amar's spoon hovered over his bowl of gruel, waiting for the grace to end. When it did, he announced cheerily, 'Good news!'

Everyone turned in surprise. It was hard to imagine good news with Michael Pilgrim lost and now Seth. Savouring a spoonful of gruel like the sweetest of delicacies, Amar waited, a knowing smile on his pinched, swarthy face.

'What is it, Amar?' asked a lad broaching his teens.

'Looks like we're getting new neighbours.'

He turned respectfully to Reverend James Pilgrim. 'We need to thank you for this good news, *Sharif*,' he said. 'Only you had the wisdom to see how helping those poor people would end up helping us.'

He explained that the people still sheltering in Holy Innocents Church had decided to repair nearby farmhouses and renew spare land in Hob Vale instead of returning to their flooded village. Silence greeted this revelation. Then one of the older boys speculated about work in harvest time. Averil wiped her tears with brusque fingers and urged the children to listen carefully because good neighbours are a blessing. Even her father stirred from his sepulchral gloom.

'The land's fertile and fallow,' said Amar. 'If we help them plough and plant they'll help us with our own crops this year.' Again he spoke diffidently to Reverend Pilgrim. 'And they're grateful to you, *Sharif*, very grateful. Plenty of food for us by autumn, they promise big crops all round.'

Unexpected hope seasoned the vile gruel and spoons rattled with a will. Averil shot Amar a curious glance as though she was seeing him for the first time.

FIFTY MILES

Michael Pilgrim's laden pack animals trotted behind Johnny Sawdon's pony. It was the hour before dawn. Faint promises of light to the east, the direction he must take. Stars lingered in the cold black sky.

His plan: make a dash for Pickering and use some of his newfound wealth and the goodwill of friends to recruit an escort back to Hob Hall. He felt sure Big Jacko would try to intercept him before he got home. A suitable force might make him think twice.

Once more he followed the old dual carriageway from York. The steady clip-clop of the animals mingled with birdsong as the sun rose. Bess ran ahead, scanning through her nose.

By late afternoon Michael topped a low rise and Pickering came into view. Already he planned a few choice tales about the Modified Man over mulled cider in the Black Bull Inn ... Then he reined in, so sharply his horse bucked.

Between his present position and that haven lay a stretch of road edged with young woodland. Moving his way along it, maybe a mile distant, rode a posse of six, no, seven horsemen.

He whipped out his binoculars and recognised a burly figure with a yellow armband at the head of the riders.

'You bastard, Sawdon,' muttered Michael. 'Want your horse back?'

He looked round. A grassy track forked from the main road beside a moss-streaked signpost: *Thornton-le-Dale*. Fading maps came to mind. Thornton was the southern gateway to Dalby Forest, a place no one sensible entered.

'Yah!' he called to his train of pack animals, before cantering down the track towards Dalby.

NOT SHOOTING STRAIGHT

He raced into the ghost town of Thornton-le-Dale with seven riders haring after him on shaggy moor ponies. They weren't underestimating him this time, not with three men disarmed and sent packing on Fylingdales Moor. He should have left three corpses for the crows to peck. Now he had nothing to rely on but flight – and his animals bore heavy burdens. Michael suspected he was done for. But at the central crossroads of Thornton-le-Dale, a small market town burned to the rafters decades earlier, he was offered a last chance.

Back in the Worst Times a high barricade of cars and trucks had been built at one end of the crossroads, leaving only a narrow passage that led to Dalby Forest.

Leading his ponies and mule through the gap in the barricade, he tethered them to the remnants of an ambulance. From Thornton a grassy road climbed into dense thickets and woodland: Dalby. Plenty of shelter from murderous riders beneath the trees. He could stage an ambush in there then melt into the undergrowth. First he needed to slow his enemies, win time to reach the protection of the forest.

A minute later he took up position on the floor of a bus carcase, peering through jagged bullet holes. Beetles crawled near his face; every gun he possessed lay to hand.

His palms grew moist, and he dared hardly breathe. Then the riders cantered up to the crossroads. Reining in, they surveyed the barricade of twisted, rusting vehicles. All the riders were strangers, probably from Scarborough or half savage Geordieland, except for Johnny Sawdon who seemed in charge and carried an enormous blunderbuss.

Michael Pilgrim was an expert in fear. He had learned every shade of trepidation in the Crusades. Close up he read unwarranted fear in the riders' faces and that puzzled him. Weren't the odds overwhelmingly in their favour? Then he understood. To lads hired by the day, even if well-rewarded for their trouble, dying for a little pay was a bad bargain. And Jonny had put them at terrible risk if their enemy started shooting. They were surrounded by hiding places and lacked any cover of their own.

'Go on then!' Sawdon urged his men. 'Find the bugger!'

Sawdon pointed at the same dark gap in the barricade Michael had taken.

'Look! Fresh hoof prints,' he said. 'He's gone through there. At him, lads!'

'You fucking go!' replied a grizzled rider.

'That alley's a death trap!' called out another. 'He'll pick us off like rabbits running from a warren.'

Michael knew he must settle the argument before they did. Knew exactly how. His life depended on it, maybe the lives of dozens of starving people in Hob Hall and Holy Innocents Church. Yet once he started, once he broke his vow of never taking another human life, of never again playing the role of heartless killer, he dreaded what pitiless efficiency might control him. He seemed to hear the Modified Man's mocking voice in his head: *After all, he wouldn't be the first person you've murdered in cold blood, Lieutenant, would he now?*

'Fuck this!' he breathed.

Then he took an insane risk.

He rose to aim carefully above Johnny Sawdon's head. Fired. Fired again. Ducking down, he reloaded. The cross-roads echoed with muskets banging, gunpowder igniting. A lead ball punched a hole through the metal panel beside him. Sawdon's blunderbuss went off like a cannon, shot ripping the roof of the bus open, spraying flakes of dust and rust. Cordite and sulphur scented the air.

He rose to fire again, this time not in warning, but for real – and cried out in relief.

Sawdon's posse – to the last man jack and hairy nag of 'em – was racing back the way it had come. And Johnny-boy led the rout. Michael whooped and jeered.

It didn't take long for his triumph to fade. Oh, they'd be back, and bolder next time. He kept glancing behind him as he led his train of animals into the shadows of Dalby Forest.

DALBY FOREST

Dusk transformed Dalby Forest from a featureless maze of tree trunks, thickets, bogs and deer tracks to something worse: viscous darkness. Already Michael Pilgrim had found and lost several disused roads, one showing traces of tarmac, usually a sign of civilisation. But it petered out at the rotting skeleton of a wooden visitor centre, children's play area and car park besieged by young pines.

As darkness fell any relic of mankind seemed a positive oasis. Yet he hadn't the slightest idea how to return to the wooden hulk.

The horses were unusually nervous. He'd heard tales of wolves in Dalby and big cats whose ancestors once lived in a zoo called Flamingo Land, of enormous boars with long, razor-sharp tusks and shorter tempers. Only Bess remained stoical, her nose sweeping the night like radar.

'We'll stay here,' he told the dog, tying up the horses in a dell. 'Better not risk a fire, girl.'

Animals weren't the only menace rumoured to dwell among the trees: savages making their homes from mud and green branches, feasters on raw squirrel, birds, roots and nuts – when they couldn't catch unwary travellers. Wild folk who came to Baytown every few years, trading deer hides for knives and iron pots. Mister Priest Man was believed to visit the forest folk, but that seemed little reassurance.

Michael kept the horses saddled and settled with his back against a tree, shotgun across his knees. Neither moon nor stars were visible through the dense canopy. All around him complex scents of pine needles, moss, earth. With Bess on guard he fell into a light sleep.

Nigh on midnight a noise woke him. At once he was on his feet, shotgun swivelling to rake the darkness. The horses nickered at his sudden alarm.

Michael Pilgrim listened to the night. Was that chanting in the distance, maybe a drum? For a moment he considered seeking the sound's source, but blundering through the confusion of trees was a sure route to injury. He drowsed, weapons ready, until dawn brought birdsong.

THE BRIDESTONES

At first light, Michael fed the horses with oats bartered from the Modified Man. York felt an age away. During the night he'd dreamt of insect mandibles hidden beneath the veil of Scheherazade as she served her freakish leader. Exactly how she served him was an uncomfortable thought even in his dream.

Today only one thing mattered – escaping Dalby Forest. Michael felt sure Johnny Sawdon's posse, maybe reinforced, would be waiting if he crossed Fylingdales Moor. His best chance lay in traversing twenty miles of pathless valleys tangled with trees and marshes then emerging at the forest's easternmost border, not far from the coast. Without a guide he feared wandering among the trees for days.

Not long after setting off he came across a clear path. Examining the mud revealed traces of bare feet.

Thus Michael Pilgrim entered a steep-sided valley and stared in awe. Its slopes were clear of trees and contorted sandstone pillars rose from the hillside in weird, wind-carved columns. Between the standing stones were wattle and daub huts. Fires scented the air with wood smoke. Children in rags screamed out warnings as he trotted into the vale, fording a boggy stream. Bedraggled women in woollen shifts and sheepskins grabbed their children and a dozen men emerged from huts carrying bows, spears and crude axes.

Michael hastily stowed his shotgun back in its holster.

He'd heard tales of this place, the Bridestones haunted by women's ghosts, their sorrows older than memory, weeping women turned to stone so they might grieve without relief.

Several of the hide-clad men notched arrows to their bows and took casual aim. Michael froze on his pony, beads of sweat on his forehead despite the cold.

'I've come to trade,' he called out. 'I've come in friendship. See!'

Holding out two open palms he gestured at the spare pack-horse laden with sacks.

The wind sighed through the bleak valley. No one spoke or moved. Still, the archers aimed their shafts.

FOURTEEN

SETH COMES HOME

Big Jacko gathered his men in the foggy early morning, everyone capable of bearing arms. Seth marvelled at their numbers. The Mayor's constant supply of City goods from the Deregulator and food-taxes from the Baytown area had attracted many down at heel followers and guns-for-hire.

They marched behind His Honour's chariot, a two-wheeled lash up of car parts and wood, pulled along the muddy lane by a carthorse.

Today was when the Mayor took his due, that was how Jacko put it, addressing his men: 'I'm taking me due, boys, and we'll all be gainers by it.'

Part of Seth ached with shame and anger for his father's weakness, but he had to consider it fair, knew it was natural for Big Jacko to make his move while Uncle Michael was far away. Still, he sidled up to the Mayor as they neared Hob Vale.

'Boss,' he called, 'can I ask something?'

The big, round face turned to examine his young follower.

'Boss,' said Seth, 'can you make sure my sister doesn't get...' He gestured at the men behind. 'You *know*. And my father, he's crazy and sick, boss!'

Big Jacko nodded.

'I'm going to do it clean, Seth,' he said. 'No bloodshed. No pain. And I'm trusting you to persuade your father to go without trouble. None of us want that. You can do that for Jacko, son, can't you? Remember what I promised.'

Seth felt proud then, despite the sick feeling in his gut at what he must do.

'Yes,' he said, 'I can do that.'

The procession led by Big Jacko's chariot left Baytown singing the Mayor's favourite song, *I'm forever blowin' bubbles*, their lusty voices tugged by the wind. A raw lump filled Seth's throat as Hob Hall rose from a fold in the land.

'Giddy up!' called Jacko, twitching the reins.

No one expected a fight. Seth had promised the Mayor that only Amar was capable of resistance. Secretly he hoped Amar would fight back and get a good kicking. He'd always been jealous of the respect shown by his father and uncle to the upstart Syrian.

At the gates of Hob Hall, Big Jacko climbed from his chariot and stretched luxuriously. He waved Seth forward.

'Now you tell 'em like I said,' ordered the Mayor, 'and remember I'm trusting you.'

'Yes, boss!'

They waited as Reverend James Pilgrim and Averil came out of the house.

'Seth! Thank goodness you're home!' called Father, looking and sounding sicker than ever. 'Ah, Mayor! Have you brought my son back? I thank you, sir.'

Big Jacko stared haughtily out to sea, and Seth's mouth went dry.

'Father,' he said, 'we've come because Big ... I mean, His Honour, wants to move into his new house. That is, like, er, today.'

Reverend Pilgrim looked at him without understanding.

'I mean, Hob Hall,' Seth added, his voice hardening as though addressing an idiot. 'You must admit you don't deserve so big a place no more, Father! And the Mayor's got a certificate from the Deregulator saying it's his now. There's loads of empty houses in Baytown. You could even move into the Mayor's old place. He told me that himself.'

Averil cried out in shock. 'Seth!' She couldn't manage more.

'You've got an hour to pack what you like,' said the Mayor. 'No one can say Jacko isn't fair.'

Seth could not meet his father's eye.

'B-but this is our home,' stuttered James Pilgrim. 'We have lived here for generations!'

'You've got to leave nicely,' Seth whispered to Averil, 'otherwise, these men will just throw you out.' He struggled for something to soften the blow and his face brightened. 'Anyway, there'll still be a Pilgrim here. The Mayor has promised me Uncle Michael's room.'

Oh yes, first he'd get rid of the piles and shelves of fucking books, use them to keep the place warm in winter or wipe his arse, then he'd make everything just how he liked it.

'Seth!' moaned Averil. 'What have you done?'

A frantic hour followed under the gun barrels of the Mayor's small army. Bags were stuffed with clothes, bedding, pots and pans. Big Jacko's men laughed and drank apple brandy as Amar and Averil and the orphans rushed from room to room. Many of the Baytown recruits watched shamefaced, but they said nothing.

Seth paced up and down in the front garden, one hand resting on his pistol butt. He felt everyone was judging him, that he mustn't look soft. Somehow he didn't dare give orders to Averil or even Amar. He knew they'd meet his eyes where tears lurked. Bag by sack by frantic box his childhood home became another man's property. But it was only natural: the strong take what the weak can't hold, Big Jacko had taught him that. Look at birds, how the heron gulps its fish while an eagle is given the strength to tear off a heron's head for sheer fun if it wants. Seth had to believe it was fair.

The hour was almost up when a slender figure pushed through the crowd of armed men in the lane, right up to the front door of Hob Hall.

'Get back!' Seth ordered the Curator of the Baytown Museum.

Averil rushed over, crying, 'Miss Devereux! Please! Look what they're doing to us!'

The young woman listened gravely as Averil explained they had been allowed a single hour to pack all their possessions and leave with nowhere else to go.

'I wondered why so many people were gathered here,' she said, laying a hand on the girl's trembling arm. 'I was curious.'

Slowly she looked round, her eye falling on the Mayor, who had climbed from his chariot and stood with hands on hips. Perhaps he recollected the visitor from the City who had graced the woman before him, accompanied by terrifying war drones. Certainly, his expression was wary. Silence descended. Crows squabbled in a nearby copse and the faint noise of a stream reached them.

Seth noticed the Curator's flawless beauty had gone terribly cold. He found it hard to look at her.

'What *is* going on here?' she asked.

All eyes were on the Mayor. Seth waited for him to set her straight, send her back to her collection of junk in the Museum, but Big Jacko flushed uncomfortably – and not with anger. To his amazement the Mayor bowed low.

'Just concluding a little business deal, Ma'am,' he said. 'This is my new house, bought fair and square. I didn't realise you'd be interested or I'd have let you know.'

The Curator turned to Averil.

'Is this true? Have you sold Hob Hall to this man? I can see a lot of guns on display.' Her mouth pursed. 'And where is your uncle, Averil? I haven't seen him for days. Has he agreed to this sale?'

'We haven't sold *anything*!' wailed the girl. 'They're stealing Hob Hall while Uncle Michael isn't here to stop them! And we have nowhere else to go, not even the Church, because they want to use that for their new stable!'

The breeze tugged the Curator's shiny auburn hair. She folded slender arms and considered Big Jacko from boots to brow. The Mayor's bloodshot brown eyes assessed her back then he bowed once more.

'Are you a thief?' she asked.

For once he had nothing to say.

'Perhaps you are unaware I have befriended this family,' she said.

Helen Devereux drew herself to her full height and held up her screen.

'Prepare an urgent message for Lord Bertrand du Guesclin,' she instructed the machine.

Even in daylight its glow lit her neck and jaw from below. Several of Jacko's men murmured in fear at this City wizardry.

'Now what shall my message be?' she mused, barely concealing her anger. 'Lord Bertrand *does* like to find his own punishments for uppity primitives.' She pointed at the Mayor. 'Like *you*.'

Breaths hissed round the circle of Big Jacko's men; a few stepped away from the brightly glowing screen.

She added, 'I'd leave now if I were you. All of you. And don't come back until you are invited.'

For a moment Big Jacko hesitated. The Mayor's London boys waited for the inevitable explosion. A few gripped their weapons though this was a fight with one possible victor, a fight no sane man would undertake. Easy to kill the young woman with the menacing screen, impossible to escape the consequences.

Instead of arguing or raising a meaty hand to slap his frail opponent, Big Jacko stepped backwards, bowing laconically as he went. He seemed to have trouble swallowing and did not take his eyes off her face. With terrible dignity he climbed back into his chariot. The lashed up vehicle suddenly seemed pitiful, a mockery of power not its true symbol. Seth felt tears start to his eyes.

'Come on, boys!' cried Big Jacko, yanking the reins of the sleepy horse. 'We'll come back when we're invited, like the lady says.'

The chariot turned in the road then he was trundling back the way he'd come, his men following in a confused mob. Some glanced back fearfully at the slender woman who had clicked her fingers to make the Mayor run. No one sang *I'm forever blowin' bubbles* now.

A LITTLE TIME

The occupants of Hob Hall were still carrying packed bags and boxes back into the house when a rider appeared. His hair and face begrimed, clothes torn and filthy. Sacks were tied to his horse, and he led a mule laden with more. He did not come alone: fifteen men in animal skins and homespun woollen clothes accompanied him. They carried bows and boar spears and slouched with the ease of hunters used to hard journeys.

At the end of the lane they halted. The rider dismounted and nodded solemnly to his escort, clasping the hand of a hairy giant as though to seal a bargain. Without a further word the wild men melted into a nearby copse like tree spirits.

A few of the children shrieked, pointed, jumped up and down. Others ran inside to fetch Averil and Amar, for the Reverend had retreated to his bedroom to rest. Leading his horse and mule, the rider trudged the last stretch to Hob Hall.

Soon the lane filled with people calling out as Michael Pilgrim tethered the animals. Black rings surrounded his eyes.

After the embraces and tears subsided, after the jubilation over sacks of beans and flour and salt pork and casks of oil – enough food to keep the occupants of Hob Hall upright for weeks and buy precious time – he asked, 'Why was all this stuff taken outside? Has there been a fire?'

Amar explained about Big Jacko and the Curator's intervention.

'So she saved us,' said Michael, 'just as the wild folk in the forest saved me, though they got paid a horse in return. I wonder what she expects as payment from us.'

The younger man laughed. 'Nothing, *Sharif*! Why aren't you more pleased? She ground the Mayor between her finger and thumb like so!' He demonstrated. 'We have a powerful ally against that pig. He won't dare attack us now.'

'Only for as long as she stays in Bay,' pointed out Michael. 'But I'm grateful. She's won us a little time until these supplies give out.'

Wearied as he was and troubled at heart, it seemed a long time indeed until the first spring crops freed them from hunger; and he knew there were more ways than brute force for the Mayor to attack his enemies. He remembered the Modified Man's advice concerning Big Jacko and shivered at the thought of cold-blooded murder.

'I'm frozen to my bones,' he said. 'Let's go in.'

FIFTΣΣΠ

———— ◦✕◦ ————

THE FAERY O' THE VALE

Two days after Michael Pilgrim's return he took a muddy track down to Hob Hole for a stroll on the beach. He found Mister Priest Man leaning over the handrail of the footbridge that led to the old youth hostel, staring into the fast-flowing beck. His battered top hat was in his hand.

'Ah, Pilgrim!' cried the Nuager. 'I'm thinking the Faery o' the Vale led you here.'

Michael smiled. 'What you doing, Priest Man?'

'Gifts for her ladyship. See!' He reached into his hat and produced a sprig of ivy. 'This I give her.' It was tossed into the bubbling beck. 'And this.' A green bird's egg from last spring, a reminder of spring to come. 'Last of all, this.' He pulled out a floppy dead lizard, its limbs dancing as he dropped it in the stream.

The shaggy man held up a warning finger. 'Listen,' he hissed, 'the Faery's come for her gifts.'

Michael did as he was bid. Afterwards, though it made no sense, he remembered time slowing like a sluggish river, chiming birdsong and a shimmer in the trees, one world clasping hands with another. Then he came to with a start.

Priest Man's cunning eyes were upon him.

'You felt her, didn't you?'

Michael looked round. Nobody, just a feeling they were watched.

161

'Aye, the hobs are waking,' said Priest Man. 'They've slept these ages past. Now they will help or harm as they see fit.'

He hustled Michael down to the beach so they stood near the caves where the little magical folk were supposed to dwell. A useful opportunity to glean news of a more worldly kind.

'Out at Fylingdales,' Michael said, 'I found the radar pyramid has been sealed with padlocks. City work, it seemed to me. I asked your pals, the wild men out in Dalby Forest, if they had seen things on the moor, lights, riders, anything strange, but they wouldn't answer. But from the way they looked at each other I knew they had seen things. I could tell they were afraid to talk, at least to me. It made no sense.'

'Aye, no sense at all,' agreed Priest Man, 'except if it does.'

'Meaning?'

Mister Priest Man tapped his hairy ears. 'These hear things Pilgrims never hear. Young 'uns going missing in Saltburn and Runswick, aye, and other places far, far further west and north.'

'Why?'

'Bodies, Pilgrim! What use is a body? A sheaf for a soul? It's that, right enough, if you haven't sold your soul to the devil in exchange for an extra ladle of life. A body can be a cauldron of chemicals some learn how to sup.' He folded his arms. 'Every soup needs ingredients, Pilgrim.'

Michael wondered if he should introduce the Nuager to the Modified Man in York. They'd have fun bamboozling each other.

Priest Man sniffed. 'I've got an offer for you,' he said, 'same one as before. We're stuck here, Pilgrim. My people are dying here when there's a portal to another planet ten minutes up the road. Aye, in Holy Innocents Church. I tell you we could escape this soup! All I need do is puzzle out the key to the portal.' He leaned forward eagerly. 'What if we offered to take you with us when we go?'

Before he could receive an answer the sea delivered one of its own.

The tide was running in fast towards Hob Hole, breakers casting up spray, rumbling, roaring. Priest Man pointed at the surf. 'Look!'

They hurried over. A body had washed ashore, a man naked as a new born babe, youngish but not young. From the state of his skin he hadn't been in the sea long. What made Michael flinch was the lack of a head. The neck gaped black and revolting. He turned the body over with his foot. Aside from a deep gash in the corpse's hairy chest everything seemed intact.

'Stabbed in the heart first, I reckon, then off came his head,' said Michael. He examined Priest Man shrewdly. 'Peculiar you talk of bodies then one appears.'

The Nuager tugged his beard. 'Maybe the Faery o' the Vale is giving us a sign in return for my gifts.' His eyes opened wide. 'Don't forget to speak to your brother about the Church, Pilgrim! Tell him it might be his last chance, nay, *everyone's* last chance before the soup boils us to bare bones!'

Michael watched him amble off. He wondered who might be next to lose his head.

LIBERTIES

Seth Pilgrim blamed the witch in the Museum for his not being one of Big Jacko's close boys. If she hadn't butted in he'd be in Uncle Michael's room by now, lounging by the fire. Instead, he had been banished to a box room in a terraced house adjoining the Mayor's place, back among the local recruits, their quarters munched by woodlice and reeking of mould.

Big Jacko's closest boys got to share the same house as their leader. Got to have women to clean and cook and fuck – or so Stu boasted – he was Seth's special mate and currently banging Miriam Armitage. They ate proper tinned food while the Baytown recruits ate farm crap: potatoes, swedes, meat, fish, anything raised as taxes.

It didn't stop there. Big Jacko's best boys went on secret missions into the countryside on ponies. *Foraging* it was called, though Seth never saw them bring anything back. Loose whispers from Stu mentioned a secret place out on the moors. Seth longed to forage. He hung round whenever the boys rode out, led by Big Jacko himself.

The Baytown lads serving the Mayor kept very quiet after what happened to Johnny Sawdon. Even Seth – who approved all his leader's decisions – felt a twinge for Johnny.

The day after his humiliation at Hob Hall, Big Jacko had gathered all his men in the same overgrown back garden where the tramp, Old Marley, was sacrificed to the Heron Goddess in exchange for more life.

For a long moment, Big Jacko had glared at the large circle of men, examining every face for weakness or disloyalty. A curved knife dangled in his hand, wickedly sharp. Seth recognised it from the winter solstice: he had been allowed to use it then, forcing the blade deep into Old Marley's thin chest while the boys chanted and urged him on. Now he was only allowed to watch, not hold the knife.

'I don't like being made to look a monkey,' growled the Mayor. He scanned the anxious faces.

'One of my own men came to a little business arrangement behind my back. Know what I think? I call that taking liberties.' He grinned. 'Bring him out!'

Seth made himself small as possible as he stood in the thick grass. He was afraid Big Jacko blamed him, too, and that his family's stubborn resistance was somehow his fault. Johnny Sawdon was dragged out, bare chested, hands and legs tied.

'It's not true, boss!' he cried. 'I've done no wrong!'

'*Liberties,*' whispered Big Jacko.

Seth was proud he hadn't looked away like most of the Baytown lot when Sawdon got his due, the knife entering his heart. He'd even helped sling the decapitated corpse over the cliff, though it made him retch. Big Jacko had noticed him then and met Seth's eye. For once he hadn't flinched but looked straight back. And the boss had nodded as though liking what he saw. Seth treasured that moment and prayed to be back in favour. He just needed a chance to prove himself.

BIG JACKO'S GENEROSITY

It was no longer about living in Hob Hall for the Mayor: there were other large empty houses with grounds and pastureland in the area. What mattered was sheer pride – Seth admired that determination about the Mayor – and Johnny Sawdon's fate showed how far the boss would pursue a slight.

Seth and Big Jacko strolled up to the big house in Hob Vale on a rainy afternoon. No armed gang with them this time, not a weapon visible. They rapped the heavy brass knocker of the front door and were shown by Amar into the high-ceilinged hall. Reverend James Pilgrim and Uncle Michael waited for them.

At the sight of their pinched faces, over-bright eyes and pasty skin, Seth grew nervous. Everyone in the house was starving by different degrees, despite the rations Uncle Michael had traded in York.

Big Jacko opened negotiations. 'Sensible of you to meet me, Reverend,' he said. Seth noted the Mayor ignored his uncle. 'First off, I want to apologise for the little misunderstanding we had a while back. Seems I got the wrong end of the stick off someone I trusted. We all make mistakes.'

'Was that someone Johnny Sawdon, by any chance?' asked Uncle Michael.

Big Jacko waved aside poor Johnny and returned to Reverend Pilgrim.

'You know my offer, sir,' he said. 'Set down in writin', fair and square. Enough food to keep you all going until the next harvest. An' help with finding a new place to settle in Baytown. Or elsewhere, if that's your game. Let's face it, Reverend, as a generous man meself, I admire how you help those waifs an' strays. I was an orphan kid myself as a boy. I remember that.

Yeah.' Sadness touched his big, round face. 'And the kids here would starve if it weren't for you. That's why you should seize this offer with both hands, sir, for their sake.'

A flicker crossed James Pilgrim's face. How sick he looked, thought Seth, grey and bloodless, his stubble a shade of ash.

'That's the point, Father,' pressed the lad earnestly. 'It's selfish to let all those innocent children suffer. Didn't you teach me that Our Saviour said, "Let the little kiddies come unto me?" And that Pride is a deadly sin. The deadliest! Sacrificing those orphans for pride would be a terrible sin. And what about the people who came to you for help after their village got flooded?' Seth sniffed. 'You see, Father, I haven't forgotten your lessons.'

Big Jacko nodded approvingly.

Reverend Pilgrim licked pale lips. 'All you say is true,' he murmured. 'Of course, I have considered that.'

'An' let me add,' said Big Jacko, 'because I can afford to be generous, I promise to repair that old church as part of the deal. I'll put it in writing, sir! That church will remain a place of Christian worship.' He bowed as though making a vow to the Almighty, and James Pilgrim fingered the heavy crucifix round his neck. Seth felt proud it was he who had suggested they offer to repair the church.

For a moment, it felt everything hung in the balance.

'Good lord, what a pantomime!' cried Uncle Michael.

Seth could have slapped him, just when Father was weakening.

'But I am puzzled why you want this place so badly.'

Big Jacko shot Uncle Michael a dark look. 'Progress, Pilgrim! In my old age I want to leave me mark on the world. Baytown's falling apart, we can all see that. I want to build a new town where the deserted village used to stand, a town with my name. A town called Jackoville.'

'And Hob Hall will be your castle, I take it?' asked Uncle Michael. 'And you become a sort of feudal lord. No, more than that, a king. In fact, why not an emperor?'

'Every manor needs a master,' said the Mayor. 'Ain't that the truth, Lieutenant?'

Reverend Pilgrim swayed: he seemed to be having a dizzy spell.

'The Curator won't like your plans for the deserted village,' pointed out Michael. 'Growing crops there brought terrible trouble upon this family.'

Big Jacko leaned forward as though to touch Michael's arm then thought better of it. Both were big men. Even reduced by hunger, Michael Pilgrim was formidable.

'I ain't worried,' said the Mayor. 'Maybe I've got friends too. Maybe the Curator won't be around forever.'

'No one is,' said Michael Pilgrim. 'Well, that seems to conclude negotiations.' He turned his blue eyes on Seth. 'Before you leave with this *lord*, I want you to consider something. Come home where you belong, Seth, and we'll never mention the past. Your father longs for that more than anything, don't you, James?'

Were those tears in Father's eyes? Seth cringed with embarrassment.

'If you agree to the Mayor's offer, I'll come back home, Father!' he said, quickly. 'That's a promise.'

'So the boy would,' sighed the Mayor. 'I'm a generous man, as I say.'

'What a handsome offer from you both,' said Uncle Michael.

Seth blushed. 'It's a promise! I'll move back to look after Father if he gives up the Hall. I swear on Mother's grave!'

Tears glittered on the wearied face of his sick father. Even Uncle Michael looked beaten and forlorn.

TEARS

There are countless shades of laughter, so with tears. Michael sat with his arm round his older brother. Sobs, bitter wrenchings of soul, gasps for breath shook James Pilgrim. Michael, too, felt like weeping, his grief provoked by Seth's parting words, sworn upon poor, beautiful, vivacious Florence's grave. Somehow that meaningless oath compounded a thousand losses.

Before breaking down, James had said he thought they should accept Big Jacko's offer. That the welfare of the orphans and Averil must come first. Michael knew only too well the food he'd brought from York was almost gone. It would take a miracle to satisfy so many mouths before the first spring crop of scallions, carrots, beet and broccoli. Even hunting for rabbits and deer, the main source of protein since the drone attack nearly six months earlier, was a challenge. Precious gunpowder to make cartridges was running out: he had little to barter for more.

His plan – if so desperate a measure deserved the name – was to survive by trading anything possible for food. Furniture. Clothes. Pots. Pans. Anything someone might value. Even that would have to be conducted in secret. The Mayor had made it known in Baytown that people caught helping the Pilgrims faced extra taxes and eviction. With more and more armed Mayor's Men in Baytown few were inclined to take the risk.

It hurt Michael how old friends tried not to be seen talking to him. They had their own families to protect, he reasoned. Of course, the Gudwallahs and Higginbottoms brazenly paraded their loyalty to the Pilgrim clan, but they were also hard pressed. He had even considered appealing to other Crusader comrades for assistance, except he no longer knew where most could be found. Some of them he preferred to keep that way.

It occurred to Michael the Curator might help. Yet her means were limited, and it was good of her to share with Averil the preserved rations delivered by the City each month. No assistance from that quarter then. Enough of a blessing that fear of Helen Devereux held back Big Jacko from naked murder – for now.

Michael squeezed his brother's shoulder. Were they to be the last Pilgrims in Hob Hall? Maybe he had brought this upon them as punishment for his sins in the Crusades.

'I … I am sorry,' sniffed James, his sobs subsiding. 'At least Seth is promising to come home if we surrender the Hall. Florence would be glad of that.'

'Do you trust him?' asked Michael.

'He is my son. I must.'

They sat in silence.

'You really think we should give in, don't you?' said Michael, at last.

'Yes.' The word was a murmur. 'It is God's will. To humble our family's pride. Seth was right about that.'

Michael sighed. 'Let us wait a few more weeks. We can just about last that long. And I'll visit Seth to persuade him to come home. It's clearly in his mind or he wouldn't mention it.'

Thin, pale fingers clutched his hand. 'Thank you! I would go myself, but he hates me. Florence's boy, our lovely boy, hates me.'

'Leave it to me,' said Michael, 'I'll find the good in that lad and lead him home.'

SIXTΣΣΠ

---❖---

A FRIENDLY VISIT

Three men climbed the steep hill to a street of plant-infested Edwardian villas near the top of Baytown. The sky pale and cloudless, all around tiny hedge birds twitting and skipping between thickets. A morning for daffodils and lingering snowdrops and purple crocuses.

'Not too late to turn back,' advised Charlie.

'Aye,' said Tom Higginbottom, 'no one would think less of you.'

'There's some who'd think a damn sight more,' muttered Charlie.

Michael Pilgrim frowned. He had tried hard to dissuade his friends from accompanying him. The danger he was courting belonged to his family alone.

'It's you who should turn back,' he said. 'Even if Jacko's afraid to throw me off the cliff because of the Curator, her protection doesn't extend to you.'

He knew very well his friends considered Seth a lost cause. But he had promised James, and like a bright sun sinking behind hazy hills he remembered Florence. How she would have wanted him to lead home her erring son.

'Well that's that,' said Charlie, gloomily.

They approached the barricade of cars and rubble blocking the way to the Mayor's house. Yellow flags fluttered from high poles, and a brace of Baytown lads stood guard, teenagers well-known as work-shy trouble. The elder, a youth of eighteen, wore two yellow armbands to show his rank.

'I'm calling on my nephew,' announced Michael.

He pushed through a gap in the barricade before they could react; Tom and Charlie followed.

They found Seth basking in spring sunshine upon brick stairs leading up to the Mayor's house. He, too, was apparently on guard duty. At the sight of his uncle he scrambled to his feet.

'What you doing here?' he cried, glancing fearfully back at the house. An eager thought occurred to him. 'You've agreed to the Mayor's offer?'

Michael waved Tom and Charlie back so they could talk alone – just in time to intercept the two skinny guards hurrying over from the barricade. 'Whoa there,' said Tom, laying a plate-like hand on the elder youth's chest. 'Wait a bit. Let the Lieutenant have a word with his nephew.'

Such was the burly fisherman's reputation as a veteran Crusader that they hung back sheepishly.

'I've come to bring you home,' Michael told Seth. 'Your father asked me to fetch you. He's weakening fast, and Dr Macdonald believes he's dying. Not this minute, true, but soon. That gives you a chance to make your peace with him.'

His nephew stiffened. 'We all die!'

'You only get one father,' said Michael. 'Come now. Do you want to think back in years ahead how you abandoned him? And when he needed you most?'

'Father has never needed me!'

Michael shook his head. 'Perhaps he rarely allowed himself to show his love. You know his conception of love is a stern one, like his angry God's. But don't break his heart at the end, come home with me.'

A high-pitched snort escaped from Seth. 'Home? Is that what you call it? Anyway, I promised. If you give up Hob Hall like the Mayor says then I'll visit Father. Tell him *that*! It's not my fault.'

Michael was glad Florence did not hear those words. Perhaps death brought some blessings.

The front door banged open. Two men carrying guns spilled out. Another pair rushed round the side of the house. Finally Big Jacko himself, a half-empty bottle of pear wine in his hand. At the sight of Michael he grinned.

'Come to agree to my little prop'sition, Pilgrim?' he said. 'An' you brought a couple of chums to witness the deal, I see.'

His grin extended to Charlie and Tom.

In the silence that followed, Michael heard finches and sparrows chirruping. He ignored the Mayor.

'Well, Seth,' he said, 'now you must decide. Home's where you belong. This ...' He flapped a dismissive hand at Big Jacko. 'This *stranger* is no one much. Not in the long run. Family is the most important thing in a man's life.'

A nasty leer lit the Mayor's face. He gulped a swig of wine, his Adam's apple working.

'You want to go home with this hungry tramp, Seth?'

The lad shook his head. 'I never asked him to come here, boss!'

'Who the fuck would?'

The Mayor's Men roared with laughter. A calculating expression drained all affability from Jacko's face. His blank gaze passed from Michael to Seth then back to Michael. He took another pull at the bottle.

'I can see you never do things the easy way, Pilgrim,' he said. 'Looks like we'll have to starve you out of that damn house. Well, I can wait. Could be a nasty accident might happen to all those crops you planted. There'll be no spring crop for you, Pilgrim, so don't pin no hopes on it. And any animals you come by might suddenly die.'

He turned to his men. 'By rights, the Lieutenant should take flying lessons over the cliff, boys. Lucky for him he's got a powerful friend. So we'll do him proper instead. Just keep him alive and leave his pretty face alone. Got that? Nothing visible on his face, eh, boys?'

They needed no encouragement. Guns were jabbed into Charlie and Tom's necks, forcing them to watch. Three of the Mayor's strongest jumped Michael, dragging him to the floor in a tangle of limbs and the kicking began. He managed a few strong blows of his own, even breaking a nose, until a circle of grunting men formed round him, Jacko roaring encouragement and warnings not to kill the cunt. Charlie and Tom watched helplessly: it was obvious the Mayor wanted them to intervene.

'Fuckin' cowards, that's what all you Yorkie scum are!' he taunted.

Soon enough, however, he called a halt. Michael lay on the ground, his breath heaving and whooping, eyes screwed tight in pain. Big Jacko yawned as he swaggered down to where Seth stood shaking and put a paternal hand on his shoulder.

'I've saved the last for you,' he said.

Seth clenched his teeth. With a cry, he booted his uncle's prone body. Once. Twice. Three times. The circle of panting men watched. Some called out *Go on, give it to 'im*! Those native to Baytown watched the betrayal in deep silence.

'That'll do!' Big Jacko hauled back Seth.

With that,Michael Pilgrim was carried down the hill by his friends to Dr Macdonald for yet another patch up.

SPRING IN HOB VALE

Spring came in its own good time: a shiver of warmth shaking new life through a sieve of the old. Winter had been hard, rain and cold worsened by a meagre harvest. But it was behind Hob Vale now. Bud-break unfurled spring's bunting and honey bees dispatched scouts in anticipation of pollen.

The vale rediscovered lush shades of green: its pear and plum and apple trees answered with pink and white as though for a wedding. When clouds parted like swirling curtains to show the sun, water glittered, whether standing or flowing.

Birds and beasts commenced rituals verified by instinct. Each sought its own kind. The humblest weed became the centre of the universe, a hub around which cosmic wheels turned and intersected, all so a dandelion might enact its stages, all so a tadpole might grow legs.

And Hob Hall itself, bruised bitterly by the malice of mankind and the winter just spent, stirred likewise. Hope or dismay hung in the balance.

BREAKFAST

Each hour Michael Pilgrim lay abed was not squandered by his body, that tiny sliver of universe. He breathed; his blood bubbled. Cells renewed and crushed capillaries reconnected.

Twilight then darkness in his room, feeble dawns and sunny afternoons. His long windows insulated by layers of glass and algae glowed a faint green. By that token he sensed spring's impatience for summer. There were other signs. Flowers Averil brought with his morning gruel and the tweet and flutter of sparrows round the eaves.

He lay abed while livid bruises bloomed and slowly faded. As beatings went, it had been relatively restrained, its aim to break his spirit rather than incapacitate him. Often Michael considered killing Big Jacko as the Modified Man had advised. But to kill the stranger would be to condemn himself to a lifetime of self-disgust. Nor would it put a single crumb on the table; he was sure the Deregulator in Whitby would see to that, although Will Birch's connection with Jacko remained a mystery. And even if he killed Jacko, his dozens of followers would remain alive and would no doubt exact a terrible retribution on the whole Pilgrim clan, perhaps even on the Pilgrims' friends.

A fortnight after his beating, Michael Pilgrim arose before dawn, wearied of rest. He dressed in the quarter-light and felt strength return.

Through a sunrise fanfared by birdsong, he walked from Hob Hall, aided by his tall, steel-knobbed staff, accompanied by faithful Bess. Out into a dawn-glow where crickets serenaded copse and wild hedgerow. He sniffed. The earth smelled good. Kneeling, he took up a pinch of soil, crumbling it to dust between his fingers.

What a thing to be alive!

He felt that quiet acceptance of life, which is a form of exultation. Beneath it all, like an underground stream, flowed the knowledge his stay on earth didn't matter overmuch, that trading a mere house for the means to win more life was a bargain indeed. The trick of joy: accept what you're granted.

He joined the beach at Hob Hole and sat for a long while beside the hob caves in the sediment-layered cliff, watching waves lap the land and hearing their song, until a grumbling in his stomach demanded breakfast. A grumble he was determined to satisfy henceforth.

FORTUNE'S WHEEL

'Can things really be so bad?'

Helen Devereux stood beside her assistant as Averil slurped hungrily at a bowl of rehydrated soup. The girl forced herself to slow down for decorum's sake.

'Father says we must set aside vainglory and pride and bow to the Lord's will,' said Averil.

'But is it really *necessary*?'

The girl looked regretfully at the empty bowl.

'Even Uncle Michael seems to think so,' she said. 'You see, the Mayor's threatened to destroy the spring crop, and it was our only hope.'

Helen decided it would be cruel to ask more. Besides, she knew enough already. How a month earlier messages had been sent to the Mayor agreeing to trade the Hall for food and livestock on the first day of April, now a mere week from today. How houses had been identified near the Puzzle Well, small, damp cottages with low ceilings and cramped yards at the rear. She did not know how the Pilgrims could bear such a rotation of fortune's wheel.

As for herself, Helen knew her exile in the Museum would be less pleasant with the loathsome Mayor as her neighbour. It crossed her mind Bertrand would be pleased by the change, along with anything that made her unlikely to find Baytown attractive, anything to get his own precious way. She had sent him a hologram pleading for food and protection to help a local family from starvation: silence his reply.

She tried not to think too hard about the Pilgrims. Averil would stay on as her assistant, and Helen planned to offer her a room in the Museum. It would be good to have company, and the girl could visit her family every day if she chose.

'It feels like Baytown's emptying out,' Averil said. 'Uncle Michael's old comrades argued with him like cat and dog not to surrender the Hall. It's no use, he said, not this time. But here's a strange thing…'

Averil grew distracted by a shred of rehydrated cabbage on the rim of her soup bowl.

'What's the strange thing?'

'Well, Charlie has disappeared. Uncle Michael's afraid Mayor Jacko helped him disappear. He's been gone for three weeks now and not even his family knows where. We're all worried. You see, he went with Uncle Michael to visit the Mayor that day he got beaten up … Oh, you must be sick of our troubles! I'll say no more.'

Helen knew Mhairi relied on Charlie Gudwallah and Tom Higginbottom to maintain her own position in Bay. If they vanished, Big Jacko's sway would be complete.

'Let's hope Charlie returns soon,' she said.

Averil's gloomy expression gave little encouragement.

FIRST OF APRIL

Never had there been a sunnier start to April. Baytown folk greeted the new day from their doorsteps. Many woke with a heavy heart. This April Fool's Day marked the end of a certainty in their lives, that there would always be Pilgrims over in Hob Vale, folk respected and relied upon through plague and famine.

Thus, venerable buildings collapse in an earthquake, at first causing shock and regret, maybe sorrow; then as years pass they are recalled with indifference, forgetfulness, wonder such things were once upon the Earth and stand no more. What of it? Was not history a parade of fading fortunes, dynasties both large and petty that rose and vanished?

It had been agreed Big Jacko would receive the keys to Hob Hall at noon. For days loyal friends of the Pilgrims had carted furniture and bedding to the hastily repaired cottages overlooking the Puzzle Well. Much had been left behind for lack of space in their new homes. This grieved Michael despite his resolution to face the future boldly.

At least the books in the library had been boxed and carried by dray to Dr Macdonald's chapel. He comforted himself much had been saved – most importantly their lives. Oh, they would dine well tonight, even if the food choked them!

The price for Hob Hall and Hob Vale required Jacko to deliver four months' supplies for sixteen people. It had amazed Michael how readily the Mayor agreed such generous terms. Two months' food in advance: grain and cheeses and oil and plenty of meat still on the hoof, to be pastured with a farming relative of Tom Higginbottom's and slaughtered whenever the Pilgrims chose. After that, another two months' provisions, enough to grow fat as lardy cake until autumn delivered a new harvest. By losing their land they lost the spring crops they had planted, but there was plenty of fallow ground near Baytown. In time they would have many new acres under cultivation.

James, Amar, and Michael waited by the gate as noon approached.

'At least let's go with dignity,' said Michael. 'Heads high.'

His brother muttered a prayer, but Amar scowled, arms crossed across his chest like a malevolent genii, shotgun slung on his shoulder.

'The bastard's coming early,' he said.

Sure enough, Big Jacko was approaching on his chariot constructed of dismembered car parts, accompanied by a half dozen bravos, all armed with gun and blade. Amongst them, a pale Seth Pilgrim.

The proximity of the man who had beaten him and the false nephew who kicked him when he was down made Michael flare. But he must be calm. For everyone's sake put aside his instincts. Yet when the Mayor climbed from his carriage, Michael almost snatched out his razor-sharp sword to slice off the smug, grinning head of his enemy.

'You're early,' he glowered.

'What's an hour among pals?' asked the Mayor. 'Didn't expect you'd be waiting outside though. And armed, too. Taking liberties, I call that, Pilgrim.'

'Where's the food you promised?' Michael looked suspiciously at the empty chariot.

Big Jacko's grin widened. 'Oh that? I'll send it along later.'

'No keys without the provisions,' said Michael. 'And I mean to take an inventory of every single item we agreed.'

His hand strayed to his sword. Suddenly Big Jacko had drawn a large pistol. A clicking filled the lane as guns were cocked. Michael realised the bravos were the Mayor's toughest, most ruthless boys, ones he'd brought from London. Amar hesitated before unslinging his shotgun.

'What is this?' gasped Reverend James Pilgrim, leaning on his stick. 'I don't understand!'

'You didn't really believe I'd keep that deal?' said Jacko. He seemed genuinely astonished. 'A deal with a weakling who hides behind a cross and a man who lets me piss all over him. If I were you, I'd leave before I get angry. You'll have whatever I can spare.'

Later, when the moment had passed, Michael didn't care to think what could have happened next. Would he have tried to fight? Such odds were frightening to contemplate.

But a distant rumble of wheels, thud of hooves, and a hubbub of voices saved them. The mooing of cattle and bleat of sheep saved them.

A long procession had appeared at the far end of the lane, men leading packhorses, a large hay wain followed by three smaller drays. Horsemen were herding a bevy of cattle; shepherds, and their dogs drove a small flock. In the drays: barrels, sacks, cages for chickens, tools and bags of nails.

The group outside Hob Hall watched in wonder as the convoy approached. At its head, Charlie Gudwallah and others who Michael had led beneath the pitiless suns of the Crusades: Baxter from Scarborough, Aggie Brown from over Malton way, brawnier than ever, a wrestler of a woman, her thews strong as her thighs. He'd heard incredible rumours that Aggie lived like a tyrannical queen with animals and grain to spare: now he discovered they were true.

Other former comrades had come, too, gathered at no small danger to himself by Charlie Gudwallah, who had ridden far and wide in his three-week absence from Baytown. Some of the veterans he called upon came with nothing more than their strength or skill to rebuild the rubble of Hob Hall's outbuildings. Some, wearing the rags of their old uniforms as a kind of tribute, came to bury Lieutenant Pilgrim's enemies. Still, they had come. All to repay a man who had led a bunch of murderers safely home when they expected nothing but death; when they deserved nothing but death – assuming a man deserves the same pitiless cruelty he serves his victims.

'*Sharif*, look!' cried Amar.

Streaming along another track were Tom Higginbottom and Mister Priest Man, accompanied by scores and scores of local folk, a great many of whom carried weapons freshly seized from the Mayor's Men left in Baytown. It seemed they had discovered the courage to defy the Mayor after all. In their arms and on handcarts were possessions removed from Hob Hall a few days earlier, not least the ancient grandfather clock that never kept reliable time. Dr Macdonald led a wagon filled with boxes of Michael's musty, precious books.

Armitage the blacksmith drove a cart containing a temporary forge to help the building work. Everyone knew he hated the Mayor's Men for stealing away his beloved daughter Miriam. Now he could spite his tormenters. Many others came, too, desiring to satisfy their own grievances against the Mayor. Some of them carried noosed ropes ready for a lynching.

'We have a deal, Pilgrim!' warned Big Jacko, looking round to escape.

'One you broke,' said Michael.

His Crusader comrades were close now, pulling out guns and swords as they rode. Even if all his boys had been gathered to protect him, Mayor Jacko was outnumbered badly.

'Drop your weapons if you hope to live,' warned Michael Pilgrim. 'And a word of advice, Jacko, see yon fat woman with the big shiny knives and rifle? I'd sooner blow my brains out than let her start work on me. Aggie takes a long time to finish a man, as I've seen.'

Big Jacko's eyes darted around furiously, but all his calculations came to a single conclusion. Slowly, he dropped his pistols to the ground.

'Do it, boys.'

Weapons clattered.

Michael drew his razor-edged sword. Time to finish Jacko for good when he had too few men to resist. Chop him in two. Display the head as a warning to other would-be mayors. No one would blame him; they'd applaud the deed. But he remembered lives beyond count he'd taken to preserve his own. Carcases left to rot in the heat and dust to feed a generation of maggots. He remembered the vow he'd made to never kill another man until the day he died. So the opportunity passed. One he would remember later amidst bitter tears.

'If I were you,' he said, 'I'd leave now and be out of Baytown before nightfall. Or you'll go over the cliff.' His mouth twitched. 'As I suspect happened to Old Marley and Johnny Sawdon. You're finished here forever.'

The Mayor was quick to follow his advice, abandoning his chariot and making off into the vale on foot, followed by his men.

For a blissful hour, people bellowed and embraced, Tom Higginbottom muttering delightedly, 'Tight as a ferret's behind! A ferret's behind!'

'You know those plans I showed you for rebuilding the out-buildings, *Sharif*?' Amar said to Michael. 'Shall I get them out?'

For a wonderful moment, Michael had a vision of new granaries and stables and storehouses, all planned and possible, all far better than the ones destroyed by the drones – anything seemed possible.

'Sure!' he cried. 'Sure!'

TALE TWO

THE THIRSTY SUMMER

ΘΠΣ

---❖---

WHITBY

Seth Pilgrim had rarely felt more miserable – or alive – as he climbed Whitby's famous steps overlooking the harbour. A blue, cloudless sky met horizons of sea. A steady breeze carried tantalising scents of salt and adventure, the restlessness of oceans.

At the top, he perched on a gravestone to smoke. His hangover not half so bad as he'd hoped it would be. The Mayor's birthday revels had been subdued, liquor in short supply, proof the Deregulator was still displeased with Big Jacko, as he had been ever since Uncle Michael's Crusader chums appeared from nowhere. When Jacko appealed to the Deregulator, he always left deflated, tight-lipped. Seth had never imagined the Boss so quiet: he might almost have called him afraid.

Just yesterday Seth had accompanied his leader to the towering concrete fortress guarded by drones, hopeful because it was Big Jacko's birthday.

'Any luck, boss?' he whispered when the ex-Mayor of Baytown emerged.

The big man had gripped Seth's arm with tense fingers.

'You're a smart lad,' he said. 'Educated, not like the rest of me boys. You must see how it is. One fuckin' drone! Just one drone and I could rule these Yorkies from Whitby to Hull, Pharaoh

Jacko, Lord o' the North! If I could only get me enough City stuff together, I'd hire me an army of Jocks and Reivers and take everything I want.'

Seth had nodded eagerly as the hand closed tighter on his arm. But none of it made sense. No drone would help them. There were no more power cells or tins of City food plentiful as corncobs. Nor were there further 'foraging' expeditions into the countryside.

Seth still hadn't learned exactly what used to be foraged. Clues came his way – that Big Jacko had been 'harvesting', a word muttered by Stu, and that the work had dried up. He longed to know more.

For weeks, lads had deserted in dribs and drabs, walking home to Scarborough, Geordieland, even back to Baytown, until the Mayor's few followers rattled round a large hotel on the edge of town, sharing it with mice, rats and cockroaches.

That afternoon, perched on a gravestone that had witnessed generations of wanderers sail from the harbour below, some to conquer, others to drown, Seth grieved over the injustice of this world. The Deregulator's black, rectangular compound rose like a dark castle on the cliff top across the harbour mouth. Sometimes Seth feared he would die in Whitby.

WHITBY (2)

An unlikely teacher taught Seth pony-racing along the miles of beach that led to the fishing hamlet of Sandsend. Despite describing himself in his strange London accent as a *city boy to me whitehalls* (whatever they were), Stu understood horses. Better, he conceded, than he understood women. Miriam Armitage's swelling stomach promised a Christmas baby and Stu felt keenly the pressures of fatherhood.

'She's a good gal,' he told Seth, 'only I gotta go where the Boss tells me. Even if that means 'ome to London.' He laughed. Since fleeing Baytown, all the boys' laughter had an uncomfortable edge.

'What was it like in London?' asked Seth.

They were riding shaggy ponies on the beach over wet ridges of sand. Gulls rose and cried as they trotted through the surf.

'London,' said Stu, dreamily, 'was a sight more int'resting than this craphole.'

'How was that?'

Seth sensed a revelation coming. Maybe even the big secret of what had brought Big Jacko to Baytown.

Stu halted his horse. Patted its neck.

'We lived like pharaohs down there,' he said, 'like nobs. Jacko was the only man that really mattered in all West End. 'Course, you could say that didn't mean much. Hardly anyone lived there 'cept a few crazy fuckers farming the parks and raising a few pigs and chickens in back gardens. Whole place was collapsing. You could hear buildings crash down sometimes. The Broadways had burned down long before I was born, and whole estates and rows of shops were just rubble from fighting back in the day. Don't ask me when exactly.' He sniffed. 'Never saw the point of the past.'

'Me neither,' agreed Seth. 'Go on, so what made Jacko so big?'

Stu shot him a grin.

'Not sure I should be telling you that, my son.'

'Go on! If you do, I won't tell Miriam how you chatted up that fisherman's daughter.'

His handsome companion laughed. 'Nice tits on her! Well, I'll tell yer.' He glanced round conspiratorially though only the gulls could hear. 'Jacko struck a deal, see, with the Deregulator of London himself. Same feller living here.' Stu nodded at the Deregulator's compound up on the cliffs. 'It was all a big secret. Big Jacko provided things some people in the City wanted but wasn't allowed.'

Seth frowned at this. He could imagine nothing the City folk did not possess. Nothing they would want from the ruins of London. 'What do you mean?'

'You see,' said Stu, 'even *they* have rules.' He shook his head as he reminisced. 'Our gang was the biggest in all West End. We taxed what we wanted, we had who we wanted. Over a hundred and fifty people livin' in Jacko's court by the end – that's what he called it, a court, because he lived like a pharaoh. Slaves and free boys like us, bitches and lots of proper wives. Kids everywhere, and people coming from all over to trade. Never a dull moment.'

Seth listened, spellbound.

'We lived in a palace – well the half of it not burned down – called Buck Palace. Fancier place you Yorkies couldn't imagine. Jacko chose it deliberately 'cos it was royal.'

'So what happened?' pressed Seth. 'Did you get forced out? Like from Baytown?'

'What do you mean, Yorkie boy?'

'Why did Big Jacko…?' Seth struggled for neutral words. 'Trade being a *pharaoh* for this?' He gestured at shabby, forsaken Whitby.

Stu muttered. 'Things change, mate. Shit always bobs to the surface. You ask too many questions.' He spurred his horse and shouted over his shoulder, 'If you mention what I told you to anyone, I'll eat yer in a pie!'

BIG JACKO'S PYRAMID

At moments of doubt, Miriam Armitage touched her swelling belly for comfort as one might a talisman. Her boy – from the way he kicked, she was sure of a son – would settle all her uncertainties. Many times Stu had promised her a large farm in Baytown, back among the people she knew. He'd be a big man and their son equally big. The Mayor's bad luck – how that man's bloodshot eyes scared Miriam! – was only temporary.

'Just you wait,' boasted Stu, 'the Boss'll own that big house Seth's family live in. He'll build a whole new town there like he plans. Jackoville! You'll see.'

His faith swept Miriam along.

Right now she perched with the other women behind the driver of a wagon as it jolted on a rutted tarmac road from Whitby. Only a week earlier the Deregulator had relented, summoning Big Jacko for business, and already Stu had ridden out on secret journeys with the other London boys. Miriam didn't care to think what her man did when he cantered away. His face looked hard and cold after he came back. Sometimes he smelt of sulphur, and that meant gunpowder. Once she found blood spots on his coat.

The way from Sleights to the moors was steep as any Baytown road. All the women except Madame Morrighan and the Mayor's bairns were ordered to dismount and push. Slowly, with whip cracking, the mules and horses dragged the heavy dray up the hill and out onto rolling moorland.

Miriam glanced back at Whitby and the hazy sea. She liked living near the sea, it reminded her of home.

Once more the fighting men took up position: a grim crowd, quick with fists and heartless, taunting asides. Stu scouted ahead, musket across his knees, sharp eyes darting over heather and hill. At such moments, with him in the distance, Miriam feared she didn't know the father of her child. That he would spur his horse and dwindle into a dot on the horizon.

On they rolled and rattled. Bright sunshine beat on the saplings and heather reconquering the moor. Miriam nodded off as the wagon jolted until a hiss of alarm made her look up. Madame Morrighan had risen, shading her eyes with a thin, pale hand to see clearer.

'Pull up! Ho, there!' cried the lead riders.

Then the Boss's voice, calm as ever: 'Off the road now. No need to worry. Let 'em pass nice.'

Miriam peered ahead. She'd always been short-sighted. A cloud of dust headed their way, tall white banners emerging. Was that the Crusader cross? The scarlet cross of Albion?

The wagons pulled up at the side of the road, and the boys fanned out to protect them, guns ready. A mare deposited her load of dung on the dusty verge of the road, a gift for beetles.

Like Madame Morrighan, Miriam shaded her eyes with a palm.

Flagellants! She recognised them now. What they called *floggers* in Baytown. A long procession making a pilgrimage from one Deregulator's compound to the next. People in the communities they passed through gave them food and rough shelter, partly out of fear, partly because the floggers were said to bring luck and prevent another dying. Even the City granted them magic pills – that had to mean something.

The dust cloud became people. All were on foot, a Master and two lieutenants bearing the banners, faces hidden beneath long black cowls, eyes downcast to contemplate the hungry earth. Their ragged clothes dark except for splashes of scarlet Crusader crosses to appease the almighty City. Over their shoulders or hanging from their belts, whips with wooden handles, scourges, sticks to beat out a tattoo of pain to mollify the plague-gods.

'Steady, boys!' commanded Big Jacko.

The floggers shuffled past the stationary wagons. No one spoke a greeting. First came the male floggers all dressed alike in robe and cowl, enough to overpower the Mayor's party with ease, then a straggle of women. Some walked bare-foot as a penance. Miriam saw no children: it was whispered pious floggers sacrificed their bairns to the City before eating them.

Then the procession had passed, bound for the Deregulator's compound in Whitby, where they would be rewarded with tins of food, their ceremonies spreading ripples of hysteria through the district.

A few hours later Miriam caught her first glance of the pyramid on the moor. In Baytown, it was well-known vengeful spirits haunted Fylingdales and that even looking upon the place was unlucky. She turned to find Stu, but he had ridden ahead to scout the site. Miriam sensed sloe-black eyes examining her, Madame Morrighan's lifeless eyes.

'There,' said the strange woman, her voice high and lilting, a languid finger pointing at the pyramid, 'that place will make me Queen!'

Her laughter tinkled, and Miriam thought it wise to curtsy.

LIKE A PILGRIM

Using keys provided by the Deregulator, Big Jacko threw wide Fylingdales' padlocked blast doors and occupied the dark building.

The concrete pyramid cast long shadows across the moorland. Seth had never seen Big Jacko so intent: this was his chance to win back the Deregulator's favour. They were to go foraging again and harvest as many bodies as possible in utmost secrecy. That required a safe place to store them while the boys were out catching more, and *that* meant Stu being given the keys. His job was to ensure all the *materials* stayed fresh and secure.

Materials was how Big Jacko ordered his followers to refer to the frightened lads and lasses they captured – unspoilt, healthy, prime, as per the Deregulator's requirements. 'The customer's always right,' growled the Boss. 'So don't lay a bleedin' finger on 'em!'

What Stu failed to grasp was how to keep the *materials* fresh in a tomb like Fylingdales. Currently, they were locked in a filthy, lightless hole beneath the radar station amongst rusting generators that leaked diesel fumes.

One morning in late July, Seth kept guard with Stu on the flat roof of the pyramid, a hundred feet above the moor.

Heather and young trees stretched in all directions. A symphony of birds chattered and trilled. Easy to sneak up with so much ground cover. Which was why Stu insisted on padlocking the blast doors from the inside.

'You know,' said Seth, 'you really should let 'em out for some fresh air. At least once a day.'

Stu regarded him lazily.

'Nah,' he said.

'They'll spoil,' warned Seth. 'Look, you let the horses graze outside and only lock 'em in at night. Those *materials* –' Seth liked the feel of the word. It made him sound like the Boss. '– are far more valuable than horses.'

'Nah,' said Stu.

'They'll spoil,' insisted Seth. 'Why not let me keep 'em clean and healthy while you do the guarding.'

Finally, the older youth relented.

Seth took a torch to light his way through a maze of concrete staircases and corridors. Dark as a mineshaft down there: water trickled and dripped, pooling in places. The only living things seemed to be white centipedes and beetles. He came to a padlocked metal door and heard sobbing in the room beyond and a low, murmuring voice. *Poor fuckers*, he thought, wrinkling his nose at the pervasive stink of urine, shit and stale bodies.

He opened padlock and door, his blunderbuss levelled. The beam of his torch played round the concrete cavern. Risky to speak with the prisoners alone, he was badly outnumbered, but he knew it would help win their trust.

Seven young people sat alone or in huddles on the cold, damp floor. They blinked in the torchlight. All were too dispirited to jump him. Hungry and thirsty, too. Stu wasn't over-generous with the rations.

'I want to make things better for you lot,' Seth announced in his native accent, 'especially as you won't be kept here much longer.' (A lie, he had no idea when or whether they would be released). 'If you play nice I can help. If not ...' He let the threat hang. 'First off, who'd like some fresh air?'

Moans and sobs answered him, appeals for water, food, blankets. A handsome girl in homespun clothes begged, 'Please, sir! Me sister's poorly!'

Seth tutted sympathetically. 'That's why I want to help.'

For a dislocating moment, he glimpsed how Father would approve what he was doing. How Uncle Michael would say he was at last behaving like a proper Pilgrim.

An hour later the prisoners, wrists bound with plasti-steel cuffs provided by the Deregulator, lay or stretched or wandered in the sunshine. Seth passed round buckets of fresh water and pans of food. Nearby a couple of ponies cropped the grass. Butterflies flitted between wildflowers.

He had gathered what spare blankets he could and shared them out.

'If you're good boys and girls,' he told them, 'you can exercise out here every day. Just make sure you don't piss off Uncle Seth, eh?'

He heard a noise and turned to discover Madame Morrighan watching. Her peculiar, jet-black eyes assessed the situation. She lived with her children and women on the second storey of the building, rarely stepping outside. Since coming to Fylingdales, she looked paler than ever. He feared she would think him weak for helping the prisoners, maybe even report him to the Boss.

'You're cleverer than the others,' said Madame Morrighan, 'I'd forgotten that. It's wise keeping 'em in prime condition.'

Seth pinked with pride.

Waving a slender hand, she summoned him over, whispering so only he might hear. 'Them City folk don't want rotten steaks, do they now?'

He glanced at the miserable *materials* on the grass and nodded nervously. All the while butterflies of white and dappled red fluttered round the open blast doors of the radar station.

POWER

Big Jacko approved of Seth's husbandry and, as weeks passed, the need for it grew. Each foraging added fresh bodies to the store; some in a condition more prime than others.

Frissons of anticipation circulated the concrete fortress on the bleak, sun-baked moor. Whispers and rambling speculations about good times ahead – and dark ceremonies led by Madame Morrighan.

When the foragers captured a cripple by mistake, she used an attempted escape by two brothers from Reeth as an excuse. The boys were too valuable to damage or waste, so she found another victim. 'An example needs setting,' she confided to Seth, after giving him special instructions. Her eyes held an odd intensity, her thoughts impossible to guess.

One summer twilight, with clouds massing in the west, she appeared at the top of the pyramid in black robes and heron mask. Big Jacko's entire entourage gazed up expectantly at her dark outline. The Boss's throne-like wooden armchair had been placed on a wagon, so he looked down upon his people. Led by Seth, the prisoners were shoved out of the radar station at gunpoint.

'Shut up!' he hissed at them. 'If you know what's good for you.'

Silence fell save for the wind ruffling leaves and grass. The assembled people stared up at the heron-headed woman. Big Jacko licked his plump lips, fingering an amulet. Then the priestess raised her knife, a signal Seth had been told to look for.

He began a quiet chant. *Aah.* Clap. *Aah.* Clap. Slowly. Gently. Intently. Big Jacko's people joined in. The kneeling young prisoners blinked up at the masked figure with her knife held aloft while Madame Morrighan's lilting voice sang out to the sunset.

'Trádáil mé an bronntanas na beatha do bronntanas cumhachta! I trade this life!'

Aah. Clap. *Aah.* Clap.

Louder. Louder.

Seth felt forces swirl around the pyramid, ghosts, spirits, ancient gods and goddesses, an invisible lattice of energy, just as the pyramid had cast out radar pulses across space in the old time, before the Dyings, before the darkness.

Aah. Clap. *Aah.* Clap.

The priestess's two women servants appeared, bare-chested, their dugs smeared with ashes, dragging out the crippled youth. He was quite naked, his hands tied behind his back. Madame Morrighan's black robes fell to the ground, revealing a slim, naked silhouette against the sunset, topped by the long-beaked heron's head. With sudden fury, the knife flashed, pretending to stab, withdrawing before it touched the cripple's breast.

Aah. Clap. *Aah.* Clap.

Some prisoners moaned in terror, others clutched each other for comfort. The blade dipped and feinted like a cat playing with an injured bird.

Abruptly Madame Morrighan sawed at the cripple's throat. Something dark spurted down the pyramid's steep sides. The bare-chested women shoved the youth into space. He fell, clawing at his slit throat, suffocating even as his body bounced and twisted down to the ground, landing a few yards from the wagon where Big Jacko sat immobile. A life offered to him like a stick laid by a dog at its master's feet. The chant abruptly ceased.

Seth stared in awe at the pharaoh on his high throne, his broad face set hard, grim. A face behind which emotions crawled like restless maggots. Then Seth understood: Big Jacko was mad. He felt it, too, grand schemes and dreams and ambition veined by divine madness. Did he not feel the same pant of excitement? Seth understood it was time to find out what the Boss's face concealed. For the sake of *his own* power, it was high time.

HOW PHARAOHS FALL

That midnight Seth and Stu guarded the silent radar station, pacing the rectangle of its flat roof. Constellations glittered in an inky sky, and a half-moon lent a faint glow to the moors. Brown stains were visible on the concrete roof. Stu reached down to daub his cheeks and forehead with the lucky blood, muttering a charm.

A low rumble in the sky interrupted him, and Stu raised his gun fearfully – though what use it might be against jet or drone Seth could not guess.

'You never told me why Big Jacko left London,' he said. 'Was it something to do with drones?'

Over the last few weeks, Stu had turned from leader to follower when it came to Seth Pilgrim. He puffed at his clay pipe.

'Yeah,' he said.

'What happened?'

Stu spat into the void surrounding the pyramid.

'Something went wrong is all.' He stirred. 'Like I told you, we lived like kings down there. The Boss had a deal with the Deregulator, and everything looked pinky.'

'What was the deal?' asked Seth.

At long last, it seemed Stu was willing to open up.

'Same as here,' said Stu. '*Materials*. Only more of it. A fuck of a lot more. Like I told you, we guessed it wasn't allowed by the City. Everything had to be kept proper quiet. Maybe word got out. Unless Big Jacko got too big for the City's liking. Maybe that's why it happened.'

'What?'

Stu tensed. 'What do you think?'

'I don't think anything.'

It seemed Stu might not explain. Then he sighed. 'One night all our people was asleep in that big old palace, a hundred fifty, maybe more. Like I said Buck Palace had plenty of rooms. Then they came.'

'Who?'

'Drones. Big cunt drones. Two or three. The person who told me didn't know exactly 'cause it all happened so fast. Took less time than it takes to boil an egg. One minute the Boss was king then nothing! He only survived because he was visiting the Deregulator. That saved about a dozen of us, including most of the London boys you see here. I was with him that night, thank God.'

Seth remembered his own terror when the drones attacked Hob Hall.

Stu grimaced. 'The Deregulator was as surprised as the rest of us, shitting bricks he was. Funny thing is, he got transferred up here a week later. Someone in the City was trying to protect him, the Boss said.'

'So that's why Big Jacko followed him here,' said Seth.

'Yeah. The Boss has plenty of enemies in London ready to eat him alive.'

For a long while they patrolled the pyramid's high roof in silence.

'How did Madame Morrighan and the Boss's kids make it out?' asked Seth. 'Were they with him when he visited the Deregulator the night the drones came?'

'Nah,' said Stu.

'Were they away from home?'

'None of his wives made it. He had three on the go back in London. None of his kids either. And he had plenty of those. All blown to dust.'

'Then who the fuck is *she* if she wasn't his wife in London?' whispered Seth, nodding below in the general direction of Madame Morrighan's quarters.

'*She* took up with the Boss after he lost his wives. Those kids aren't his. They're totally white, ain't they, stupid! He protects 'em in exchange for the power she's giving him. She came to him out of nowhere when he had nothing. Just said she was his woman now and that the Old Gods had sent her to help him.'

'Fuck,' breathed Seth.

Finally, he understood Big Jacko's madness. The determination on his face as the cripple's body bounced down the pyramid to land at his feet. Big Jacko feared that if he didn't grasp his destiny, the next cripple would be himself.

TWO☉

THE LIGHTEST DAY

The summer solstice came late with grasshoppers creaking in shimmers of baked air. Snakes basked upon rocks hot enough to scorch bare feet. Winter's torrents shrank to trickles, and everywhere you looked flocks of birds fattened on seeds and grubs and insects.

In fact, the whole district ate well. Cod, lobster and herrings developed a suicidal instinct to nourish mankind, nets bulged, and crabs fought to trap themselves in pots. Salmon ran in absurd numbers and the Higginbottoms' smokehouse worked day and night.

Crops grew hardily, forced up by alternating sun and evening showers and skilful irrigation from specially maintained ponds. The spring crop had proved a bumper that year, and autumn boded an exceptional harvest.

With the scattering of the Mayor's Men, volunteer constables patrolled Baytown once again – except with a difference. No longer would they take their community's security for granted. Lieutenant Pilgrim organised weekly drills, and everyone capable of bearing arms was enlisted.

In this mood, Baytown prepared to celebrate its midsummer revels with a sheaf of blessings.

MUMMERS

Fifty years earlier, Reverend Oliver Pilgrim had hit upon a fine notion. Always he sought to unite the community round his prejudices. Hence his revival of a custom dating back – or so he claimed – a thousand years. His aim was to divert a clan of neo-pagans from sacrificing a virgin to mark the summer solstice.

As years passed, folk swore there'd always been mummers on the longest day of the year; always been a performance of St George and the Hob to bring good fortune to Baytown. None knew Reverend Oliver had written the play himself, basing its rhymes on a tatty paperback of the York Mystery Plays.

'Welcome!' cried Michael Pilgrim. 'Come in, everyone! Wet your whistles!'

A hot day for thirsty business. A day when the thinnest ribbon of shade was welcome. Thankfully Hob Hall had plenty of recently-constructed walls to cast a shadow.

Thirty men and women of all ages trooped through the new gatehouse and into the wide yard envisaged by Amar and now a reality. Stone and brick outhouses, their plaster and mortar still drying, formed an enclosed rectangle with the Hall itself filling one wall. Despite the buildings' newness, their layout felt settled and proper. Nor were they deserted: a dozen folk dwelt there in exchange for labour duties on the land. People saved from starvation by James Pilgrim's generosity when their whole village had been washed away in a winter flood. A good turn that sprouted flourishing offshoots.

The visitors to Hob Hall were a motley, outlandish crew. A few wore armour made of grey cloth and carried wooden swords and shields decorated with the white rose of Yorkshire; others were crimson devils sporting yellow armbands (an innovation that year), led by Satan himself, specially chosen for his baldness and ability to speak in a passable Mockney accent.

Set against the forces of evil were three wise virgins led by Averil Pilgrim and a chorus of nagging women; and St George himself, bearing a long sword to counter Satan's scimitar. Young Ben Higginbottom played the gallant George. It was lucky his main role was smiting the wicked as he struggled in rehearsals to remember half his lines.

A table was laid out in the farmyard for the mummers: freshly pressed cherry and lemon juice, raspberry cordial, all grown in the vale, small ale and watery cider. Not too much of the latter. Easy to forget your lines if fuddled, though a little Dutch courage never harmed a performer, or so most reasoned.

Refreshed, they marched down Hob Vale, Amar beating a drum at the head of Michael Pilgrim and a dozen others from the Baytown Orchestra carrying their instruments. Yet again St George would save a wise virgin from sacrifice. All of Baytown – and folk from as far away as Sandsend, Malton, Whitby, Saltburn, Scarborough and even Pickering – would cheer him on.

ST GEORGE AND THE HOB

Several hundred folk sat round the hob holes in the cliff wall, children near the front, booing and hissing when Satan and his devils came on the makeshift stage of swept sand. The adults sat further back, remembering how they, too, had roared at the Devil.

In places of honour – low wooden stools – perched Dr Macdonald and the Curator of the Baytown Museum. Mister Priest Man sat with them, as well as Tom Higginbottom and Charlie Gudwallah and other local worthies. A stool had been left vacant in honour of Reverend James Pilgrim, too ill to attend for the first time in his life. Meanwhile, Satan snarled, and the children squealed in mock terror:

'I tell thee this, thou fickle folk!
I'll eat thee! Both thy shell and yolk!
Like eggs to be broken thou shalt be to me.

And you'll weep on't. Wait and see!
But first a virgin girl I'll sacrifice,
Promising thee it will bring good fortune. Lies!
Ha! Lies! Sacrifice away, foolish folk, and be accursed!
Then I'll laugh right heartily for thou'll feel the worst!'

At this, Averil Pilgrim was dragged out of a hob hole while Satan waved his sword. The devils danced a lively jig to fiddle and flute.

The hubbub died. Various attempts to rescue the virgin took place. First, a group of soldiers bearing the badge of the White Rose fought the devils but were driven back. Now her fate seemed certain. Except when St George rode into the fray on a hobbyhorse, just as Satan concluded yet another lengthy, gloating speech about the madness of people who believe sacrifices bring anything except punishment and woe.

The children cheered the burly hero. This was more like it! A few jumped up until dragged down by their parents. St George cried out:

'I am that mickle mighty George! Look upon me
Thou serpent-creature that leads folk astray!
Look at this sword!'

(He hefted a whopper and people cheered).

'Meant for thy head, worm!
It'll teach thee, Satan, to learn pure dismay!'

Back and forth St George and Satan fought. Now the crowd fell silent. It seemed their hero was outmatched. His sword was knocked from his hand. How could that be?

'Alas!' he cried. *'I fear to be undone!*
What sorrow will befall us all if this battle's not won?'

Instantly a small, bearded man scurried out of the dark cave entrance in the cliff. Mad staring eyes, a straggly beard, his motley coat of many colours. A hob!

Satan froze, his sword raised to slay the gallant St George. Time itself froze. In this space the little hob crept through the crowd on stealthy tiptoes, tossing out handfuls of roasted hazelnuts like a sower broadcasting seed, all the while giggling and pointing at the hapless St George.

'Tee hee!' he cried, voice high-pitched as a crone's. 'A hob I am from yon hole! Whether I choose to help or hinder nobody knows. Not even me. Tee hee! Tee hee! What is it to be? Help yon knight or let him die in the fight?'

The children and folk roared out the answer: *Help him! Help him!*

For all his magical powers the hob appeared to be a trifle deaf. He cleaned out his ear with a long finger. Cocked his mischievous head to one side. 'What? *Hinder* did ye say? Oh, very well, if ye say so.'

Help him! Help him! urged the crowd.

'Oh, I heard ye right clear! Hinder!'

At last, he got the message. Sneaked over to St George's sword and placed it – after more toing and froing – into the knight's hand. The battle resumed: except this time St George gained ground and, with a final injunction to never sacrifice virgins, smote down the fiend. A loud bang of gunpowder. Smoke billowed from the hob hole then a howling Satan was carried back to Hell by his minions while the crowd jeered.

Afterwards, Helen sought Michael Pilgrim. He had fattened out that summer, regained strength and colour. Even the **F** on his cheek was less vivid beneath a healthy tan. As Averil Pilgrim had told her, *Uncle Michael has a knack for bouncing back.*

'Enjoy the show?' he asked.

'How could I not? Though it was a close thing for the virgin. I was afraid I'd need a new assistant.'

'Oh, Saint George always wins,' he said. 'If only real life favoured the same happy endings.'

They watched the crowd straggling in groups along the beach towards Baytown, parents holding the hands of their hopping children, older kids running after noisy dogs into the surf.

'There'll be dancing and a bonfire by the Puzzle Well Inn tonight,' he said. 'Perhaps you'll …' He let the rest dangle.

'Is that an invitation, Mr Pilgrim?'

'Bring your fiddle,' he said. 'We can always use another in the band.'

She felt a warm rush, just for a moment. As though she was young again and parties and dancing meant something, as though a blur of pleasure might lead to many more. As though she might truly come to belong here.

'I will come, Michael,' she said. 'It sounds jolly. Exactly what I need. Thank you.'

DANCING

A driftwood bonfire burned high on the beach, casting up sparks and glowing wisps. Above, crooked constellations lit a night sky reluctant to relinquish day, a darkness more blue than black. The tide, not due to turn until dawn, frothed gentle luminescence.

Nature might be calm, not so the drunken revellers that Midsummer Eve. They were dancing a favourite from the Worst Times, the *danse macabre*, pronounced *dance mack-a-bee* in those parts, learned step by step as plague winnowed the population. A wild, heedless dance to flatter and defy Death. Skeleton masks of papier-mâché concealed the dancers' faces, so all looked alike as they circled and clapped. They formed long, inter-weaving rings, the musicians blowing, strumming, sawing fiddle bows, banging tambourine or drum, defying night's silence with humanity's blare.

Round the Puzzle Well Inn, older folk conferred over tankard and pipe. Stalls with fancy goods from across the region and beyond attracted late-night hagglers.

Out on the beach, the *danse macabre* ended as it must: people falling to the ground in exaggerated, hilarious deaths, a few clowns rolling and writhing on the sand before expiring with a final thrash of limbs. The musicians mopped their brows and headed for the taproom of the Puzzle. Their pay for the night's music took a liquid form.

Michael Pilgrim, in an embroidered waistcoat with shiny brass buttons, escorted Mhairi Macdonald and Helen Devereux to a bench near the sea wall. Perspiring from the music, they shared a large jug of cool pear cider poured into bowls.

'I'm too old for this,' moaned Dr Macdonald, watching a group of young people begin yet another dance to the voice of a lone guitar. It seemed they could never contain their urge to cavort in one another's arms; they reached out to be loved as breath draws in and out.

'I'm for bed!' she declared. 'And I'll feel all the better for it tomorrow morning. Join me when you're ready, Helen, I've made up a bed up for you.' She smiled wryly. 'Though I'm sure a youthful slip of a thing like you belongs down here with the other young people, eh?' She chuckled. The lissom Curator flushed in a way Michael Pilgrim did not understand.

'I shall join you soon,' promised Helen.

She fanned herself with her hat while he refilled the clay bowls. For a while, they sat quietly beneath blazing stars. He turned to her cautiously.

'Do you know, I don't even know your age?'

He let the question hang. She did not answer. He sensed the topic made her uneasy.

'In fact, I know almost nothing about you,' he said, 'whereas I suspect you've learned more about me than I – or you – might wish. So let me begin by asking your age. I'm thirty this year, by the way.'

'What an unpleasant topic to discuss on a night like this!' she declared. 'We never discuss a person's age in the City. Especially a lady's! It's considered shocking manners. Time is too horrid to talk about.'

He shrugged. 'Time is our natural sea, just as the water yonder –' He nodded at the line of surf. '– is the proper home for fishes and seals and plankton. It seems strange to consider mentioning time as rude.'

She pulled at the cider. Held out her cup for more. There was something reckless in her mood. Something he sensed lay always close to the surface with her.

'I'm thirsty tonight! More please!' she said. '*Never enough* was the motto in the City!'

'Apart from mentioning your age,' he said, smiling.

She fell silent again, and he wondered if he had offended her. Clearly, she regretted having revealed even so little to him. Yet he tried again.

'I don't know much about the City,' he said, 'but I cannot care for the cruel way it keeps our people from regaining what we lost. The way it keeps us in backwardness, as though our progress must somehow hamper their own. A great injustice, I'm sure you'll agree?'

Helen sighed. 'Now you're spoiling a perfect evening with politics!'

He stiffened. It occurred to him she found Baytown folk, *his* folk, probably even himself, quaint and picturesque. Amusing rustics, reminiscent of the birds and beasts, at one with nature. At best, noble savages. Perhaps she found seriousness or signs of intelligence on his part impertinent, a stepping beyond what was permitted for one of his kind. *That* was what she meant by politics: stay where you've been put and be grateful we don't send drones to flatten whatever buildings you raise.

He rose and bowed. 'Thank you for helping our *danse macabre*,' he said, emphasising the pronunciation *dance mack-a-bee*. 'But there are old acquaintances I really mustn't neglect further. Good night to you.'

With that, he left her to the half-empty cider jug. He did not notice her flush as he passed through the crowd, people greeting him and clapping his shoulder. No one approached the Curator, for all her perfect beauty. Soon she climbed the hill to join her sister in the dusty chapel.

BERTRAND ANGRY

The next morning Bertrand appeared via a hologram while Helen nursed a hangover. One look at the stiff jut of his lower lip indicated his mood.

'So,' he snapped, 'you finally return to your duties as Curator after gallivanting all night and risking every kind of infection.'

She folded her arms.

'To what do you refer?'

'Refer? I refer to playing your violin while our coastal primitives caper and hop. Yes! It did not escape my attention! And side by side with a buck ur-human who – do not look so surprised and innocent – bears a brand marking him as a felon.' He waved his hand as she tried to speak. 'No, for once I will be heard! A criminal, I say, with whom you seem to spend an inordinate amount of time.'

Helen laughed incredulously. 'Yet again you spy on me, Bertrand! Can you really be jealous?'

The question appeared to tickle him. 'Of an ape? I think not, my dear.'

She stared at the projection of a man hovering above her bedroom floor. Bertrand's anger was never to be taken lightly. For the first time it occurred to her what consequences his jealousy might trigger for Michael Pilgrim and his whole family. Despite his genius as a scientist, maybe because of it, there was a dangerously spoilt, wilful child inside Bertrand. A child with absolute power to get his way.

'I'm relieved,' she said. 'For you to be jealous would be too, too absurd. Besides, it would be an insult to my taste. One I would find very hard to forgive. Even from you.'

His glowering softened a little.

'Yet you sit next to him in that ragtag orchestra you attend with your ridiculous sister. Oh, don't worry, we keep an eye on *her*, I can tell you, though she is careful not to overstep the mark.'

Now Helen paled. 'If you harm Mhairi,' she cried, 'I'll ... Is this how you woo me? Threatening my own sister? Is this your love? How very gallant!'

She was relieved to note confusion on his face.

'What am I to think?' he protested. 'Do you imagine I have forgotten how once you played *The Lark Ascending* to please *me*. Now you perform for a veritable zoo of primitives. And you have no idea how delicate my position has become in Albion. You make me look a fool!'

His mean, hard look returned. Alarmed, Helen heard herself reassuring him, suggesting he come to the concert where she would perform the *Lark*, promising him its song would be dedicated to her oldest, best friend in the world and then he would see the people she lived among were people indeed, that the City's judgement of them was erroneous, blind.

Bertrand listened haughtily. He shuddered. 'Do not go native on me, Helen, I beg you. Please do not! For everyone's sake, including your sister's. But I shall consider your proposition.'

The hologram vanished, leaving Helen to ponder his warnings about Mhairi and Michael Pilgrim.

THRΣΣ

———— ❖ ————

SENSE

A fortnight before the summer concert of the Baytown Orchestra, Reverend James Pilgrim summoned Dr Macdonald. She arrived at Hob Hall with scant hope and departed with none. His cancer was reaching its crisis; all she could offer was home-brewed laudanum. The rest belonged to nature.

Michael stood by the window after she left. James's wasted body confirmed her prediction, but the laudanum gave him false energy, and he managed a smile.

'Michael,' he whispered, 'sit by me.'

For a while, they sat in a silence not uncomfortable but familiar. So often there had been nothing to say between them, just wary tolerance.

'I must make sense of things,' murmured James. 'Must settle things.'

His little brother's big strong fingers enclosed his own. 'I'm here.'

'Michael?'

'Aye?'

'Will you forgive me?'

Michael stirred. Were there things he must forgive? Always there are things to forgive between people, even the closest chafe and grate as they love.

Forgiveness was a word that haunted him, after all, though not because of wrongs inflicted by James. The cruelties lay on his own side: thoughtlessness and indifference to others' suffering. There could be no forgiveness for a Crusader, the best he could earn was forgetting.

'I can't think of a single wrong you've done me, James.'

The ashen man drifting from life lifted a bony hand. 'You know,' he whispered. 'We both know.'

Michael knew then he must say it: for James's sake, he must name her. Yet he hesitated, as though her two plain syllables would release a last flood of resentment.

James sighed in his weariness. 'I've been a fool.'

Still, Michael did not dare speak her name though it filled the room.

'A jealous fool,' breathed James.

They could hear the children playing cricket outside, and Michael remembered how, once they were grown up, he beat his big brother at nearly every game: quicker, nimbler, stronger; sharp as a bright, shiny pin in comparison.

'You've done nothing in your life to warrant forgiveness,' he said. 'You have lived as a good man should, James, and Grandad would have been proud of you. As I am proud to have such a brother.'

Outside, cheering started as someone was bowled out or caught or hit the ball for a whopping six.

'Let's make a deal,' said Michael, 'I'll forgive you if you forgive me. And if you acknowledge how dear you are to me. And will be forever.'

A bluebottle landed on the sick man's forehead to drink his salty sweat. Michael waved it away. The fly buzzed angrily to a corner of the window.

Tears started to his big brother's eyes.

After more laudanum James revived and said, 'Promise me one thing, Mikey, you'll save Seth if you can.'

'I promise.'

'Another thing,' said James. 'Fetch someone. Yes, today.'

'Who?'

James murmured a name and sank back on his pillow.

An hour later Michael led a shambling, raggedy figure into the sick room: Mister Priest Man, top hat in hand.

What the two holy men discussed he did not hear because James waved him from the room. Truth to tell, Michael preferred the fresh summer air with its scents and warmth, the guileless excitement of the children as he joined their cricket game and allowed them to bowl him out for a golden duck.

THE LAST VICAR

Averil helped her father down the aisle of Holy Innocents Church. Once he had hoped to walk his daughter that same way on her wedding day. It turned out the nuptial ceremony was a divorce. All his expectations in life had confounded themselves.

The pews of the ancient church were full for the first time in years. Bitterest irony to her father, Averil could tell, despite his stiff, haughty expression masking pain of body and soul.

There had been a big turnout to witness the end of an era. For a millennium, Holy Innocents Church had overlooked Hob Vale, even after its Black Death-shriven village was abandoned and reverted to pasture. Though the church would stand, it was not to worship a risen Christ.

The building's new tenants whispered excitedly; at their head a new vicar, if such a title applied to Mister Priest Man. Scores of Nuagers had gathered from all over the district to take possession of the church already known to them as Holy Innocents Portal. Bright eyes and flushed faces. There'd be wild celebrations in the churchyard that night, carousing and coupling.

Averil stepped proudly beside her father to the lectern at the front. She left him propped against the wooden stand alone, his cheeks grey, breath rasping. Many drops of laudanum had been required to get him here.

Lines of faces watched the dying priest intone almost inaudibly to the restless crowd: *For everything there is a season and a time … a time to plant and a time to pluck up … a time to keep and a time to cast away…*

Upright he stayed until half-carried back to his sickbed in Hob Hall.

'I have failed the Lord,' he whispered to his daughter. 'I have given His house to strangers. Can I be allowed to join your mother in Heaven now?'

Averil did not know what to say. Heaven seemed as likely to her as the Nuagers' cosmic journey to a distant galaxy.

PEACE

No Reverend now. No title to hide behind. Just a man stretched upon a sagging, horsehair sofa, his emaciated body as weary as the soul it had carried through the world.

He faced the open window, his senses registering summer even as they withdrew. So blue a sky. He might have been eleven or twelve again, an anxious boy for once gleeful as he played with his toddling brother and friends on the beach. Such moments had been real, had existed in time. Then they had gone. How strange! How wonderful.

The decaying man remembered Florrie, above all, as though confirming his faith in their love was what mattered in the end. When a breeze cooled his hot forehead, he felt the brush of her soft palm across his face. Would he join her soon? Sweet, kind Florrie. What a fool he had been to simmer with jealousy, anger, betrayal after she comforted poor Michael that day they dragged him away. What time wasted! If only he could meet her again and explain, find her waiting when he stepped from this hazy room to the room always waiting.

Long hours on the sofa. Averil and Michael came and went. He was aware they sat nearby, unobtrusive, simply there.

Sometimes he worried as all his life he had troubled himself over little, unimportant things. Except now, long-buried fears pushed up like tangled, thorny briars from the black earth of his dying.

Would he truly wake to find Florrie waiting? And Grandfather? And Father and Mother, who he never really knew. So many, many others. That fear hurt more than anything. It was to doubt God, a last mockery of his life's work.

But when it came – it was dawn, sparrows waking in the eaves of Hob Hall, birds all over the vale singing out for morning – death cleared James Pilgrim like sunshine when clouds part. He dreamt – or felt – or knew, yes *knew* – he had stepped out of himself and gazed down on the lifeless mass of cells and veins in their sack of skin. He looked for a long while at gentle Averil asleep nearby, her long vigil soon to be over.

James was glad his window faced east. There! There was the sun rising! He left the room he'd known since boyhood with its heavy furniture and temporary possessions and was outside in the herb garden at the back of Hob Hall.

No scents now, no sensations except in his deepest self. James realised the sun no longer blinded him. He could see deep into its brilliant heart. And up he flew, Hob Hall falling behind like road dust, up into the white flare of a sun that did not burn but shone forever, where Florrie and Grandfather and so many, many others waited to welcome him home.

THE PUZZLE WELL INN

Amar wasn't a drinking man, but after they buried Reverend James Pilgrim in a mossy corner of the churchyard, he drank.

They say, in wine is truth. Tom Higginbottom put it another way: never trust a man who won't sup with you. Amar knew he could be trusted, and alcohol lent him confidence when inside he felt a stranger. No one in Baytown except Averil and a man with a special knack for getting into trouble knew more than the surface layers of his soul.

'I say,' he told an equally bleary Charlie and Tom, 'I say to him, "*Sharif*, now your brother is dead, you must marry. Have children. Heirs, don't you know. Bam! Bam! Bam! Son! Son! Daughter!"'

Michael Pilgrim's oldest pals nodded at this wisdom.

The taproom of the Puzzle was busy that Saturday night. The prosperous spring and summer had provoked a rash of barter. Few emulated wise squirrels when winter seemed so far away.

'He'd do right *not* to heed that advice,' declared Armitage the blacksmith, earwigging at the bar with a huge mug of cider. 'I could warn him,' he muttered. His eyes moistened.

'Don't take Miriam's going away so hard!' counselled Tom Higginbottom. 'She'll be back sooner or later.'

'And consider your other bairns,' added Charlie. 'They do you proud. Here, let me top you!'

Armitage's grief at his precious daughter fleeing Baytown with the Mayor's entourage was not so easily diluted. Still, he offered his mug manfully.

'Nay, she's gone bad.'

'She wouldn't be the first,' pointed out Tom.

'Such a pretty un' as a lass,' sighed the blacksmith. 'Her little face would light up the morning like a buttercup. The prettiest lass in Bay by a long road!'

Amar's sense of justice stirred at this assertion. 'Not so pretty as Averil, I think.'

Luckily Armitage chose not to hear, and Amar found a more neutral topic.

'A tinker came by Hob Hall yesterday,' he said, 'with a bad story.'

'Oh?' said Tom, glad to move on from Miriam. His eldest son still moped for the wayward lass, and he felt a special protectiveness towards Ben. He'd sired him at the foolish but randy age of sixteen: in fact, the lad precipitated his early marriage. The shame was that he'd got conscripted while the boy was still small and missed half his childhood. Tom grieved for those stolen years. 'Who was the tinker?' he asked.

'Red Moody,' said Amar. 'He told us he travelled far west as the Colne Valley last week and heard rumours of a fresh dying. Among the Welshies, he told us, and in Liverpool by the west sea.'

Charlie snorted. 'Sounds a right tinker's tale. Scousers would find it too much like hard work to catch the plague.'

'Lazy, thieving bastards,' agreed Tom.

He and Charlie had brushed with a company of Scouser conscripts in the Crusades; the dislike had been mutual. In fact, the Yorkies had been accused of exactly the same faults by the Liverpudlians.

'I mentioned what Moody told us to Dr Macdonald,' said Amar, 'and she didn't look happy. I think she's afraid of a dying here. She sent for Red Moody to question him.'

Tom Higginbottom nodded sagely. His respect for Dr Macdonald bordered on the idolatrous, and he liked to think of himself as deep in her counsels.

'She would be concerned all right,' he explained, 'that lady blames herself if she can't cure a single body of its sickness. I honour her for that.'

'Aye,' said Charlie.

'But wise as she is,' continued Tom, 'even the daftest might tell her there's no medicine for a good dying.'

A croaky laugh escaped from the blacksmith, and everyone looked round in surprise.

'Nor for a child's ingratitude and scorn,' muttered Armitage.

He held out his mug to Charlie for more medicine, however ineffective.

FOUR

---◆---

LARK SONG (1)

The summer concert traditionally took place outside the Museum before a picnicking audience on blankets or portable chairs. The prospect of Bertrand joining the good people of Baytown with his aircars, private airbulance, fanfares, lackeys and security drones made Helen's heart race. Mhairi would never forgive her. Not only did her sister loathe Bertrand, but the orchestra was sure to lose its nerve. He would certainly insist that infectious primitives – which was all of them – were banished a safe distance. In short, months of ambition and achievement would be destroyed.

As Helen walked in Hob Vale on the afternoon before the concert, she saw with her ears: melodies of birdsong and slow, patient harmonies of surf breaking on the beach.

Scarlet poppies and guileless buttercups littered the vale. Now was their hour, a time for bees and flies, grasshoppers and aphids. Grass quivered not from fear but a rhythm shared with the breeze.

Joy gripped her. The petty fears of her life melted before summer's music and, most of all, the constant trilling of the larks. Thus, she sensed what to share through her violin that evening.

LARK SONG (2)

The concert was billed on handwritten posters as *Free Music*, its theme chosen by the Baytown Orchestra's conductor to defy the Five Cities: Elgar's *Nimrod*, a suite of English folk songs and dances, *Greensleeves*, and some simpler, community sing-a-long pieces, including *On Ilkley Moor Baht 'At*.

The Lark was the concert's grand finale.

A fine evening for it. Long trails of folk in their best clothes converged on the site of the deserted village, its grassy humps and earthworks serving as balcony or stall. Children ran ahead of the adults, whooping and swooping their arms; drowsy stillness filled the valley, even as the birds – and larks especially – sang their fugues.

The audience formed a semi-circle around the orchestra and names were called out in greeting. Folk in Baytown were proud of their orchestra. Where else in Yorkshire could boast such a relic of past glories? Folk travelled from as far as Malton and Pickering and Scarborough to hear it, often visiting kin at the same time. Besides, the summer concert was a perfect excuse for 'a bit of a do'. Picnics emerged from baskets, fruit juice and beer, bread and cheese, cold meats, home-baked pies, slabs of seedcake. The evening might have proceeded as it did every year except for a vibration in the air.

Those with sensitive ears first became aware of it. One by one folk fell silent. Necks craned, looking this way and that. Still, the noise grew until the swelling vibration dragged people to their feet.

A drone! Yes, surely a drone coming in low. Now people looked instinctively round for places to hide, anywhere less exposed. Even calm Dr Macdonald was staring up, a hand shielding her eyes.

Helen heard the sound and dreaded Bertrand's arrival. She could picture his cortege sweeping into view, the palatial aircars escorted by fighter drones circling as they scanned. But the drone that appeared had nothing to do with Bertrand Du

Guesclin, just a smallish spydrone that had buzzed over Baytown all summer, sent out by the Deregulator of Whitby. It hovered thirty feet above the orchestra, lights flashing, engines humming.

'Please stay!' pleaded Helen as an extended family grabbed its picnic. Others conferred, ready to bolt.

Were these poor, harried people to be allowed nothing at all? Not even a little music on a summer evening? Driven by outrage, she rushed over to where the drone hovered, menacingly waving her screen at it as one might flap a book at an annoying wasp. She could see its sensors train on her. The downdraft of its propellers disordered her hair.

Very well, she thought, activating her screen.

'Holomail. Urgent priority. Whitby Deregulator,' she commanded. 'Message. If you ruin this concert I have worked so hard for, I will make sure Bertrand Du Guesclin never forgets your name. *Ever*. This concert is dedicated to him. Send.'

Still, the drone hovered. She looked small and frail set against the powerful machine, its red lights like spiteful eyes. Would the Deregulator take the threat seriously? Helen turned to nearby families with blankets clutched in their arms.

'Please stay!' she urged. 'It will go away, I promise!'

Her appeal might have been in vain. But a tall, trusted figure rose from the cowering orchestra, violin in hand. A silver streak divided his dark hair, an ugly F branded his cheek; a man with more reason to fear the City and its drones than anyone. When he spoke, it was with a voice accustomed to command.

'Friends!' he called. 'Listen to this woman! I urge you, listen! Do not go!'

As if on cue, the drone ascended. Its lights dimmed as it swept back north towards the Deregulator's compound in Whitby. Within minutes, traces of its engines had faded, and people were discussing excitedly what had occurred. Helen realised Mhairi was looking at her with new respect.

'Perhaps we should start with *On Ilkley Moor Baht 'At*,' whispered the prima violinist. 'To lighten the mood.'

LISTEN

Helen played with a freedom she had believed lost during the long, trapped decades in the City. She played as the larks sang in Hob Vale.

The orchestra behind her was sometimes too hesitant, at other times rushing, once or twice plain discordant; none of that mattered. As the loving chords of *The Lark* summoned her to sing, chords swelled by poverty's instruments – treble and tenor recorders, tuba, triangle, four guitars, two cellos and three violins, oboe, bassoon, penny whistles, flute, trombone, trumpet, double bass and a virtuosic ukulele – she loosed the silver chain of sound.

Soon no one looked up to check the drone had not returned. The music – glorious, strange, soul-consuming for people forbidden recordings – provoked extreme reactions. Tears and frantic embraces. Strange solo dances. One woman rocked back and forth as she wept silently, unguessable sorrows and hopes released. But the lark! Oh, all knew that song! It numbed the folk of Baytown, eased open their souls with claws no sharper than dreams. *Listen,* the lark seemed to sing, *we shall be better than this. You shall live better, for the world is beautiful even in its melancholy and will grow green forever.*

As the dying notes faded, few did not wipe their eyes.

A deep, reverent silence followed. For long moments, Helen's bow hovered above the strings. She exhaled and stepped back, instrument loose by her side.

She blinked at the audience. Intensity muted them like swans. Then a lone voice broke the spell. It belonged to Mister Priest Man.

'The Faery o' the Vale has blessed us! Heed her! Heed her!'

Only then did the crowd cheer and bellow and clap and laugh – as did the Baytown orchestra. Mhairi Macdonald stood quivering, her hand squeezing Helen's until the soloist's sensitive fingers ached. An extravagant bouquet of wildflowers was presented by village children: cinquefoil, silverweed, betony, bittersweet, lily and asphodel.

Why didn't Bertrand come to witness her triumph? Helen wondered, involuntarily. She would have loved even a grudged sign of his admiration. Perhaps he had lost interest in her. Yet she sensed motivations she could not explain and remembered him saying, *You have no idea how delicate my position has become in Albion.*

Amidst the enthusiasm, no one noticed a pair of volunteer constables hurry over to whisper in Michael Pilgrim's ear. They had been guarding the toll gate when travellers appeared with fresh word of the plague predicted by Red Moody – it was a single day's walk from Baytown.

FIVΣ

A LITTLE DYING

Averil Pilgrim was too young to remember a dying, whether great or little. There had been plenty of the latter over the previous century, enough to haunt and shape every subconscious. Enough to fill pits and roadside graves; improvised charnel houses in suburban garages, abandoned schools or restaurants. Enough for Averil to fear doing her duty.

But when the call came, she answered. Every family is sustained by its own myths, few more so than the public-spirited Pilgrims.

Word of plague in Harrogate, Knaresborough and Ripon reached Baytown before the disease itself: a lucky happenstance. Oh, she was proud of her family then! Ever since Big Jacko's inglorious reign, Uncle Michael had taken a leading role in the pettiest community matter. At his insistence, a large meeting was held and decisions made. Close the borders to Baytown with checkpoints manned by volunteer constables. Set up quarantine centres in barns near the checkpoints providing food, blankets, fuel for fires, clean water and medical help supervised by Dr Macdonald.

After explaining the arrangements to her employer at the Museum, Averil expected approval.

'I'm to serve with Dr Macdonald at the main west road until it passes,' she concluded.

Helen Devereux's high cheekbones flushed with emotions the girl could not read.

'Have you any idea what *it* consists of?' said Helen. 'What *it* looks like? You mention the plague too casually.'

Averil had to admit she did not know. Not exactly. She thought Miss Devereux was angry at having to do the museum work alone. 'I could come back in the evenings to help here?'

The Curator seemed to have difficulty meeting her eye.

'Do you imagine I would want you here?' she asked. 'Your very breath perhaps spreading what you refer to as *it*?' Helen's restless fingers plucked at the cloth of her trousers. 'No, thank you. As of today, this place is sealed until further notice.'

For the first time, Averil wondered if the perfect City lady was quite flawless. There occurred in her young mind a shift of understanding of the kind that accumulates into what is termed 'growing up'. Her instinct was to apologise for no fault of her own. She sensed Helen's terrible fear of fear.

The first plague-wanderers arrived late that day. Fleeing an epidemic was standard, though it broadcast the harmful bacilli, or so Dr Macdonald told Averil. The enemy was in the very air exhaled by the carrier, she advised, but there was good news. Catch it and nineteen times out of twenty you died. So that gave you a five per cent chance. Better still, so deadly were the bacilli that anyone surviving four full days was in the clear. Almost certainly. It was the *almost* Averil didn't care for.

'There are many strains of the disease,' said Dr Macdonald. 'Its genius is that, like humanity, it evolves with astonishing rapidity. Hence the cycles of fresh plagues over the years. From questioning travellers and hearing their reports, I believe we may be fortunate this time. Thank goodness birds and insects don't seem to be carriers as they have been in the past. A less virulent bacillus may have mutated, quite possibly connected to the recent hot weather. Nor does it seem to affect all mammals as the Great Dyings did.' Dr Macdonald smiled grimly. 'Our species should be flattered. This strain has a taste for human tissue alone.'

Averil almost imagined the old doctor was relishing a chance to confront a hated enemy.

'Where does the plague come from?' she asked. 'My father believed it was a curse sent by God.'

Dr Macdonald's eyebrows rose. 'Diseases are natural as health. My belief is that the plague mutated in a reaction to poisons of our own making.'

They were stood on the West Road, and the doctor stooped to pick up a rotting plastic bottle.

'I believe,' she said, 'the plague is connected to this stuff. Especially the dust you call *tilth*.'

'Tilth?' said Averil. 'But how?'

Yet she recalled a saying among the old folk of Baytown: *When tilth blows, the plague grows.*

'I don't know,' replied Dr Macdonald. 'Even in the Five Cities, they don't really know, despite developing a cure. At least, they didn't when I left there three decades ago. But we may be absolutely certain of one thing: they will not share their medicine with primitives. Not willingly. It gives them great power.'

Averil was to ponder these revelations; years later Dr Macdonald's words came back to her in a strange place and grew stranger wings.

'Today our concern is containment,' said the old woman, briskly. 'We must isolate potential carriers using different phases of quarantine to be sure they are not infected. Then we may safely allow them access to Baytown. Although, I would prefer a temporary camp, perhaps at the old caravan park near Roger's farm. That's yet to be decided.'

Uncle Michael happened to ride up to inspect their checkpoint when the first weary group bearing bags and bundles trudged into view. Twenty-five, thirty, a whole hamlet. The system's first test. He unslung his shotgun, fired a shot into the air.

Smoke drifted. The report echoed.

'No further!'

Five volunteer constables waited at the barrier, all armed. The frightened plague-wanderers halted in the lane.

'See the barn over in yon field?' he called. 'Inside you'll find food, water and shelter. We'll send over a doctor and nurses to help if they can. Beyond that we offer nothing.'

Everyone knew it was many, many times more than most communities.

No one spoke. Strangers and gun barrels surveyed each other. Uncle Michael reloaded his weapon with leisurely assurance.

'What's it to be?' he called out. 'Follow our rules or fight us?'

The wandering band drifted to the big stone barn, and Uncle Michael winked at Averil from his horse.

'Glad of that,' he muttered. 'If they'd rushed us we couldn't have held them back easily.'

Doctor Macdonald handed out masks, goggles, other items reeking of home-brewed disinfectant to the two nurses assisting her: Averil and a gloomy widow.

'Now our work truly begins,' she said.

STRONG

A few swift words to her screen and the museum building stirred, the rattly cleaning droid taking up position near the entrance. Helen activated its secondary function, and a stubby taser appeared from its plastic belly. Not much in the way of security, but something. A steel sheet slid across the Jewel's display case like a tombstone.

Let them come! They'd find her ready.

Helen joined the drone at the entrance. Nothing moved outside. Her heart quickened at the prospect. Had she not seen it? Witnessed what plague did to the beast lurking in the kindest heart.

She had been a fool to leave the City, imagining the pandemic was over at long last, lulled by years when it had lain dormant. Perhaps she was a fool, too, to forsake the Beautiful Life. Helen felt her chest heave until adrenalin spent itself.

Her instinct was to persuade Mhairi to join her in the sanctuary of the Museum, but she knew it was pointless. Clearly, her sister craved a heroic ending, beloved by the community that took her in when the Five Cities so casually slung her out. What nonsense! What vanity!

Helen awaited the coming of night. No hordes appeared. Not yet.

Do not lower your guard, she told herself, be strong. Just as when she'd pushed Mhairi's unconscious body to the outskirts of the newly-established City in a rusty shopping trolley through corpse-littered streets, fields strewn with putrid cattle, their bloated bodies an illusion of writhing, dancing life as clouds of flies swirled and armies of maggots feasted. Then the frantic crowds beyond the perimeter of Albion, throwing themselves at the drones for a quick end. Many gave up hope within sight of the City, huddling quietly to perish from starvation and disease, their bones left where they lay, a warning to other primitives to come no closer. Some hid. Some abandoned family and friends, others stayed faithful to their loves right into the grave. Some stopped work in despair and ruined the next harvest, adding famine to sickness. Some rutted like drunken beasts to forget their fears. Some – the most vicious – tore apart anyone weaker or slightly different from themselves.

The earth itself sickened of humanity! And it did not matter how good or capable or strong you were, the best went the same way as the worst, virtue and wickedness punished just the same...

Night brought one last memory dredged from the night. Of her dear brother, little Owen who made everyone smile, shivering on the filthy carpet of a shoe shop. Shoes of all sizes and kinds had been scattered like fallen acorns all around. His face grey, cheeks shrunken to coarse, deflated leather bags, buboes on his neck large as crab apples, reeking sweat, shit, black piss, every pore and orifice discharging in time to a hacking, wheezing cough, the stench unbearable...

No, Helen decided, whatever killed her in the end, it must never be the plague.

THE PRICE

Averil hated the price she paid to win Dr Macdonald's trust, a fee of horrors. She loved paying it, too. The quiet, methodical old woman seemed the bravest, cleverest person in the world.

Fickleness it might be, but her worship of Helen Devereux dwindled then faded as word reached the quarantine barn how the Curator locked herself away. Many Baytown folk risked their all during those hot July days. One nurse died. Another miraculously recovered – a five percenter, as Dr Macdonald declared, beaming.

Not all the plague-wanderers proved compliant. Whipped up by a shaggy-haired demagogue of a shepherd, twenty or so charged the checkpoint, halting at a warning volley over their heads from the volunteer constables before coming on once more. Uncle Michael leapt the barrier alone, blunderbuss in one hand, sword in the other, bringing them to a desperate halt. The blade's razor-sharp tip tickled the shepherd's throat.

'Stop, lads!' begged the shepherd, frozen in terror.

His flock promptly fled back to the barn.

At last, as July drew to a close, Averil discovered Dr Macdonald still abed late one morning although it was her habit to work from dawn to midnight.

'Don't come near,' gasped the woman. 'Look!'

A black, putrid bubo was beginning to swell on her neck.

'Another in my groin,' managed the doctor. 'Stay away.'

Averil shrank back in horror. It seemed impossible! Dr Macdonald was immune. Deserved to be immune. And they had been so careful.

'Tell my sister,' whispered the old woman.

Clearly, the doctor's mind was rambling. 'Your sister?'

'The Museum ... Helen ... sister ... tell her to come.'

Her head fell back on the pillow. She closed her eyes, working furiously to breathe. Not long before the true pain began and her body became its own torturer.

Averil Pilgrim ran with the fleetness of sixteen years over field and ditch, through copses and streams. She reached the Museum and banged furiously on the doors.

The cleaning drone scanned her through the Plexiglass until Helen herself appeared, hair dishevelled. To Averil's surprise, she did not open the sliding doors.

'Please!' cried Averil, still panting from her run. 'I have a message. From your sister. I mean, Dr Macdonald. She's caught it! She caught it tending ... it doesn't matter how. She wants you to come.'

Still, the door did not hiss open. Helen Devereux's wide green eyes met Averil's. She turned and walked back into the shadows of the Museum.

In vain the girl banged on the unbreakable glass and spoke into the intercom: at first pleading then angry. Exhausted, she stopped, unaware the object of her scorn watched via a screen, a horrified knuckle pressed into her mouth.

THE LADY OF MISTS

Averil sat as close to Dr Macdonald's cot as she dared. Sunrise brought a golden glow to the ivy-clad hovel that served as doctor's surgery and nursing station. How cruel is fortune's wheel, she thought, how heedless of virtue. Thoughts without words, a pervading disillusion; the sad, fatalistic music she had heard all her life: Baytown's white noise.

The irony was that Dr Macdonald seemed the last victim. For five days not a single symptom in the quarantine barn. Scouts reported no crowds on the roads heading their way except for a single tinker – Red Moody, back on his rounds – who reported the epidemic was vanishing whence it came. A summer flowering only. A little dying indeed.

Averil sighed and stepped outside. There she removed mask and goggles, gloves and cap, tossing them into a steel kitchen sink filled with disinfectant. She watched a billowing wall of mist drift her way from the sea, over the fields and through trees, a sea-fret tangy with salt.

A guilty joy washed over her as the mist closed in; a survivor's joy as she lingered in the dew. Complex aromas still rose from the smoking funeral pyre and lime pit. Averil sniffed. Wrinkled her nose. Within days that foul smell would be a memory fading.

She squinted into the rolling mist and was surprised by a cloaked figure hurrying her way.

'You came!' cried Averil.

Helen Devereux threw back the hood of her cloak. The lovely face seemed to have aged in the day since Averil appeared outside the Museum's doors.

'Where is she?' asked Helen.

Averil pointed into the derelict cottage. 'You mustn't go in. You'll catch it too. She hasn't long left.'

Helen pushed past her and Averil followed as far as the doorway, hanging back with her mouth and nose covered by a clean cloth. She watched Helen kneel by the old woman, and Averil suddenly saw the likeness. Yes, they were sisters! How had she not noticed before? Yet how could it be with so great a gap of years between them? It seemed like something from the faery tales she read to the orphans in the attic of Hob Hall.

'Oh, Mhairi,' said Helen, 'I am sorry I took so long.'

From the doorway, Averil heard a rumble of engines in the sky. Searchlights played through the mist, illuminating the trampled grass round the pyre and lime pit as a long aircar landed with a heavy crump on the wet grass. Doors opened, and two drones rolled out. Men followed – she thought they were men – in white suits and helmets, consulting handheld screens.

Averil gawped. Then she fled through the fog to Baytown and never looked back to see the cloaked, hooded lady carrying her sister through the mist, delivering her to the medicnicians and drones and shiny machines in the airbulance.

GRAVES

Day's sun melted the morning mist. Averil stood in the grave-yard of Holy Innocents Church and stared down. A tall elm cast welcome shade over the three graves she truly cared about: Mother, Grandfather, and a fresh one where sprigs of weed already sprouted from the bare earth. Its hand-painted marker read simply: *Reverend James Pilgrim. 'Abide with me'*.

When Averil tried to enter the Museum after the Curator's sudden flight, she found its steel shutters down, security devices activated. Helen had gone for good. Who knew when another Curator would be appointed? Averil feared the Museum would rot into ruin like everything fine in this world.

Averil rubbed her eyes. When she looked up, a slim figure bobbed up from behind a tombstone. For a moment she stared then shrieked with delight.

'Seth! You've come home!'

His black Mayor's Man uniform was faded and patched. No yellow armband now. She rushed round the graves to embrace him.

'Oh, Seth! You heard about Father then! I wondered if you knew.'

He was leaner than the last time they hugged. Averil realised he was a young man, his childhood cast off like an old coat.

'I had to see his grave,' he said. He looked round. 'Uncle Michael mustn't catch me. Or Amar. They'd hurt me, Avi!'

She squeezed him tighter. 'No they would not. They never would.'

Hob Vale stirred in the wind. Trees heavy with summer leaves whispered and sighed. Tears were in both their eyes now. Perched on a dry stone wall, Averil gushed out the Baytown news even as the trees exhaled their leaf-song. Of the plague and Dr Macdonald flown away by the Curator, never to return. How the storehouses and outbuildings of Hob Hall had been rebuilt, as he could see for himself – stronger, better, more prosperous than before the drones came in the dark of winter. How Amar was proving a genius at practical matters so that hunger of the kind they had endured would never trouble them again.

'So you see, Seth,' she concluded, 'you must come home now. Everything's alright. You can be free forever of that dreadful man.'

Seth's expression stiffened.

'Free to be what?' he demanded. 'Hated by everyone? To be inferior to Amar, an upstart stealing my rightful place?'

'No,' she said, 'you're taking what happened too hard. Amar is a good man, you'll see.'

'Folk round here have long memories, Avi. Can you imagine me walking through Bay, everyone muttering and sneering, "Look, it's Seth Pilgrim. The only reason he's not been whipped over the cliff is that his family are too soft." Do you think I want to be mocked and jibed? Or have to toil in the fields day and night to make up for doing nothing wrong.'

'It wouldn't be that way!'

'Wouldn't it? And what about Uncle Michael? Whatever you say, he'll never forgive me. But he's the one who should be begging *my* forgiveness. And one day he will! Fuck me, yes! Sooner than anyone guesses.'

A sly look she didn't like crossed his face. He whistled. 'You say that witch the Curator has gone for good. That *is* news.'

He rose. 'You won't tell anyone you saw me?' he asked. 'Do you promise?'

'I promise. But only if you come back soon.'

She rose with him.

'Aye,' he said, 'I'll come back soon. Whatever happens, Avi, I'll make sure you're alright. I'll always make sure of that.'

She frowned. 'I don't understand.'

They heard a voice calling her name. It belonged to Amar. With a hastily waved hand, Seth slipped out of sight into the copse adjoining the graveyard.

SIX

DONE GOOD

'So you see, boss,' concluded Seth, 'the whole place is knackered by dealing with the plague for a month. They've stood down the constables. I reckon they'll have neglected a lot of the harvest work, so everyone'll be out in the fields or out at sea. It's a perfect time.'

Big Jacko sat in his throne of an armchair; Seth stood anxiously before him. The big man rubbed an itchy crotch.

'You're sure the City woman's flown home?'

'Like a bird.'

'And she ain't coming back?'

'The Museum's closed for good, boss.'

For a long while, the Mayor sat in thought. The other men grew restless, but Seth waited patiently. Finally, Big Jacko met his eye.

'You know the kind of people I mean to buy in,' he said. 'Aren't you worried they'll run havoc? This is your home ground we're talkin' about here, ain't it?'

A test Seth had anticipated. 'No, boss, because I know you'll promise me one thing.'

Big Jacko still looked suspicious. 'What's that?'

'To make sure my sister is safe.'

'That all?'

'And I still want my uncle's room. Oh, and all his personal stuff. And me Dad's stuff.'

The Mayor chuckled. 'I like your style. You done good, Seth Pilgrim. You remind me of me! Right now you're lookin' like my best boy.' He glared at his other followers. Most shifted their feet. 'There's other boys of mine here who could learn off you, boys who might be lettin' me down. Liberties, I call that. Am I right?'

Everyone remembered what happened to Johnny Sawdon when he took liberties.

An hour later messengers were galloping frantically up the overgrown railway mainline north.

DELIVERY

The child inside Miriam Armitage grew. As summer days shortened, the anxious community in the pyramid also prepared for a delivery. Heat intensified; heavy, brooding, baking the bunker's concrete walls. Flies rose in clouds from the ponies' and the people's dung. The sacrificed cripple rotted and stank like a grisly banner wired to the pyramid roof.

No more foraging now. Big Jacko and his best boys waited and waited, ready at a moment's notice to trade their harvest.

Twilight. A hush across the moor. Few birds sang. Big Jacko sat on his wooden armchair with a restless huddle of armed men around his throne, smoking and talking quietly.

When the aircar descended, it took them by surprise, its engines set to silent. The doors slid open and out stepped a short, plump man, pale from days spent before screens: the Deregulator, accompanied by two security drones. He wore body armour, and a large pistol hung from his belt. His face wrinkled in distaste at the unwashed men before him.

'Mis-ter Birch, sir!' cried Big Jacko. 'Sit, sir! I have a seat here specially for you.'

He swept imaginary dust from the wooden armchair, but the Deregulator ignored him. Both wheeled to face south. A large, dark carrierjet was descending. As it drew near, the downdraft set dust and grit dancing.

Big Jacko snapped impatient fingers at his men. 'Quick now!'

The carrierjet settled with a thump that shook the ground and crushed several saplings. No lights flashed. Vents and engines hissed.

A wide ramp on its side lowered, and a jaunty young man strode out. Despite the rough ground, he wore extravagant shoes with long curled toes. He, too, was accompanied by a pair of battledrones, tall and laden with guns, flamethrowers, pincers. The Deregulator bowed low as he approached. Big Jacko and his fellow primitives literally grovelled.

The young man had unsettling eyes, one brown, the other a brilliant blue. Both eyes inspected the radar station with undisguised interest.

'I remember reading about this place when I was young.' He cocked his head in the direction of the Deregulator. 'Did you know, William, I wanted to be an astronaut as a boy?'

Protesting voices reached them from inside the concrete building. A procession emerged, herded by Big Jacko's men, including Seth, a sorry procession indeed, bedraggled and weary. Four dozen teenage boys and girls, all chosen for their looks or physical strength.

The young man studied them critically then smiled at the Deregulator. 'You have done well, William. Keep it up! We get through a lot, you know.'

Will Birch stirred. 'It's risky to take too many, doctor,' he said. 'The natives will grow incensed.'

'I'd imagine so.'

'With respect, sir,' continued Will Birch, 'does it not increase the danger of *others* noticing what we do? Rather dangerous *others*?'

'Of course,' said the foppish young man. 'But I shouldn't worry about them if I were you.' His different coloured eyes focused on the Deregulator. 'Those holding us back will be dealt with very soon.'

The Deregulator bowed, 'Thank you, Dr Guy de Prie-Dieu.'

But the young man was already strolling back to the carrierjet.

A terrible wail arose as the youths were prodded and shoved towards the aircraft's ramp. One boy tried to run but was clubbed down.

A girl beseeched Seth. She was younger than him, her accent like his own. 'Please! Seth Pilgrim, you promised us! Please!'

It was the girl with a poorly sister, among the first *materials* to be harvested and imprisoned beneath Fylingdales. It had flattered his vanity, somehow, to ladle the pair extra rations when no one was looking. Certainly, they had been grateful enough. He'd learned a little about her family during the last weeks: that they bore the surname of Lyons and farmed the ruins of Fountains Abbey off to the west; that she had an older brother, Jojo, who all the world respected, and who the girl believed would never rest until the family was reunited. Too late for that now. Too late for anything. He blinked in confusion.

'You promised we'd be safe!' she screamed. 'You promised, Seth Pilgrim! You promised!'

And indeed he had promised, just to keep her quiet and appreciative. He had promised.

Then she, too, was shoved into the custody of the drones. With them no appeal was possible. Once all were loaded the ramp rose, as did the carrierjet. The Deregulator turned to Big Jacko.

'You've kept your side of the bargain,' he beamed. 'Now I'll keep mine.' He paused. 'Only be careful what you wish for, Jacko. Those Pilgrims – yes, and Baytown itself – have more lives between them than a cat.'

VERSAILLES

Big Jacko's party of riders trotted into the railway junction. They had ridden north in strength, the boys' numbers bulked by lads hired specially from Scarborough and Whitby. Big Jacko was laden with tradables from the Deregulator since the foppish young man with different coloured eyes carried off his harvest of youth. Seth sometimes dreamt – hunted, sweating dreams – of being herded by drones onto the carrierjet himself.

The delivery of *materials* meant Big Jacko could look to his own business. And he wasted no time. Perhaps he sensed summer peaking. How quickly it must wane.

The railway junction's rusty tracks were overrun by weeds and purple buddleia: butterflies of every pattern and shade flitted round slowly nodding flower heads; bees foraged lazily from bloom to bloom, and a rich, sickly perfume filled the air. Wagons wreathed by ivy and vines stood like a migration of dinosaurs frozen for eternity. Except their eternity was proving brief: several had rotted and collapsed, food for beetles and lice. The junction was hymned by chirruping medleys of birdsong, a slow summer sigh of leaves stirring with the hazy breeze.

Big Jacko held up a hand. The horsemen halted behind him. Some rose in their stirrups, afraid of ambush. Seth detected movement in a burned out signal box near the station, a coloured cloth waving.

'Look!' he cried.

'I seen 'em,' grunted Stu. 'There's more on top of that building.'

Seth hadn't spotted those.

'I want this done nice an' friendly,' announced Big Jacko. He wore new clothes and jewellery. 'Shooters stay in holsters and not in hands. Got that?'

Unease passed through the riders, but no one felt inclined to argue. This meeting had required a dangerous seventy-mile journey along the old railway to Scotland. Success obsessed the Boss.

'Righty-o,' said Big Jacko.

A wide grin plastered across his round face, he led them deeper into the railway junction. The glass and cast iron roof of the station had long ago fallen, but a train complete with carriages waited patiently for passengers – as it had waited for nearly a century. Beside it, a group of men in shaggy, homespun clothes and furs: Reivers, rough and ready land pirates with little taste for regular farming. They left that kind of work to women and slaves. He counted ten, all heavily-armed, a similar number guarded their horses in a car park.

'Wait here,' ordered Big Jacko, dismounting.

Hoisting a saddlebag of gifts – power-cells and a shiny City-forged knife – he swaggered down the concourse, his meaty palms on show.

A burly man left the group of Reivers, his own palms facing upwards. The two leaders disappeared into one of the carriages for a conference.

For a long time, nothing stirred except plant or bird in the railway junction. Seth unexpectedly recalled one of Uncle Michael's dull history lessons. After some twentieth-century war best forgotten (it had involved terrible poems his uncle found embarrassingly moving), there had been a conference in a railway carriage. Like today. A single word surfaced: *Versailles*. That was it. Nothing else remained with Seth of the lesson, just *Versailles*. That and a vague memory the peace conference led to a far bloodier, nastier war than the first.

PHARAOH AND QUEEN

Miriam Armitage kept well away from the strange men camped around the pyramid at Fylingdales. Fires twinkled at night illuminating dark shapes. She knew from Stu it had taken longer than Big Jacko wanted to gather the Reivers and sundry bravos available for hire. The Boss had paced and raged over every delay. Even now, not one of the hired men had been told where or who they were to attack. And especially not when. False rumours had been spread they were heading south to York.

All the while, Baby grew in Miriam's womb, and she felt his kicks.

'Soon we'll have that farm I promised,' Stu whispered as they lay together in their damp, windowless room within the concrete pyramid. Miriam dared not ask who he would take it from.

'We'll have the best stud of horses on the bleedin' coast,' he promised. 'And you'll have servants. Many as you want. We'll need lots for the farm.'

Soon. Soon.

But Miriam fretted. The men camped around the pyramid were wild and cruel as stoats. Madame Morrighan's two women whispered they took slaves for raping and fieldwork. Would Miriam's own family be enslaved, irons clamped to their legs, carried off north to hellish places from which no one ever returned? Oh, a big fat farm was a fine thing! Every girl in Baytown would envy her. But Miriam feared being hated by the folk she'd grown up alongside. Poverty might turn out preferable to that kind of loneliness.

Finally, it was time. Stu dressed in a leather coat, taking out an ancient, dented motorcycle helmet. A broad sabre hung by his side, knife thrust into his belt. In a holster, a two-barrelled pistol. Slung on his back, a wide-bore musket and cartridges.

Miriam shook as she kissed him.

'Don't stand at the front,' she said. 'Don't be a hero. Think of Baby!'

He gently disentangled himself from her arms.

With the grey dawn, the little army gathered at the foot of the pyramid. On its roof stood a sun king. He wore a shiny chainmail coat. His head bore a yellow crown modelled on a pharaoh's headdress, flowing over his shoulders like a lion's mane, the dyed cloth blessed by Madame Morrighan's magic to ward off bullets and blades. Other talismans hung from his armour, soaked in the blood of the cripple sacrificed to the Heron Goddess. His hour of revenge and victory had come.

'The good days are coming back,' Stu had assured Miriam before he left her to take his place. All the boys knew Big Jacko was invincible now.

Madame Morrighan stood proudly beside her lord, gazing down at the lines of horsemen and foot soldiers below. Her hand reached out and touched the hem of his chainmail coat. Pharaoh and Queen. Miriam felt an urge to hide from their gaze.

'Remember boys!' bellowed Big Jacko. His voice drifted through the morning air, competing with the dawn chorus. Not a single bird on the moor paid a whistle of attention. 'I don't want no burning. No massacre. And Big Jacko decides who gets slaved or set free.' He paused. 'And no one touches the Museum or the big house near it. They belong to Jacko!'

He drew a knife from his belt and held it high. The same knife used for sacrificing to Madame Morrighan's hungry gods.

'Apart from that, boys, Baytown is yours for the day.' He paused. Scanned the faces below. A horse neighed and pawed. 'Make 'em squeal!'

Seth Pilgrim stepped proudly forward, and Miriam stared as he produced a power-cell charged foghorn salvaged from a pleasure cruiser.

Bo-o-o-o-m. The long, mournful note rang out across the moor. Now the birds fell silent. Now all nature took note. Fox and wildcat, moor pony and kestrel. Snuffling boar and weasel, mouse in the heather, grass snake sensing strange vibrations.

Ranks of men waved spears, guns, clubs, sundry blades. Shouted oaths. Cheered wildly. Clenched their fists.

Bo-o-o-o-m urged the foghorn.

SΣVΣΠ

---⊰◆⊱---

TO THE CITY

The airbulance vibrated as its jets surged. Helen gripped the arms of her seat. Nearby, two meditechs in white biohazard suits were already scanning Mhairi, taking blood samples, sedating her, their movements unhurried.

Helen picked nervously at the fabric of her sleeve.

Why had she delayed calling Bertrand? Vanity. Stupid pride. Now her sister, her last connection to a kinder world, was almost lost. A fitting punishment to be forever cast out among strangers with erratic, infuriating Bertrand Du Guesclin – or whatever he chose to call himself in the future – for her only friend.

A meditech approached. His plastic face mask caught the light, blurring his features.

'We will arrive in the City of Albion within twenty minutes,' he said. 'You will be isolated there. In case you are infectious, you understand.'

She blinked up at him. 'Can you save her?'

He produced a hypo. 'You are agitated,' he said. 'It would be better if you relaxed.'

'I asked if you can save her!' cried Helen. Her fists bunched. She wanted to tear off his mask, expose him to the rest of humanity's woes and diseases. 'Tell me, please!'

His reply was to pull up her sleeve and inject the drug. Within moments her heartbeat slowed. Anxiety shrank to a dull throb. Through this haze she watched Albion fill the window.

Nine months since her last glimpse of that hated place except in dreams. There it had been an endless labyrinth of tunnels, glass, bone-pale concrete, bustle and motion. Yet as Helen stared, it seemed more like a quiet, modern country town than vast a metropolis: especially compared to the ruined sprawl of Birmingham they had flown over, the interminable webs of roads and abandoned industry.

In fact, Albion had every incentive to never expand. It was a strict policy that each of the Five Cities, whether in Europa or elsewhere across the earth, kept its population of Beautifuls stable at one hundred thousand. As Bertrand liked to say, too many people living the Beautiful Life would turn ugly indeed.

No, it wasn't Albion that had changed. Baytown *had* infected her.

The airbulance swept over the East Anglian fenlands and woods then a cultivated ring of fields and farms where drones laboured to feed the City's small population. Onwards, over reservoirs and natural lakes used for fish and pleasure excursions, over factories and metallurgy plants, chemical works and fusion stations, a practical buffer round the core where the Beautiful Life's rituals and requirements were enacted.

The morning sun glittered on windows as the airbulance descended. Helen's mouth hung open stupidly. What drug had they given her? She tried to rise. Found she couldn't.

'Mhairi,' she whispered, 'we're back...'

Her head lolled before she could utter the word *prison*.

PRISON

Are our very cells prisons? Is prison the space within our skulls? Helen had plenty of time for questions and answers: mostly paradoxical. Her quarantine cube adjoined Mhairi's, and they could view each other through a shared plastiglass wall. If her sister hadn't been attached to tubes and monitors, they might have rubbed noses against the glass. But Mhairi slept almost constantly, too sick to rise.

Is time itself our prison? Wondered Helen. There was speculation! Especially in the City, so terrified of time. Time had its walls, true, and cell doors: births and deaths. The Beautiful Life claimed to level time's walls forever, to banish the current of minutes and hours that washed away all lives in the end, whether human, plant, animal. Helen considered such optimism premature. After all, the Beautiful Life's immortality had existed for as many decades as she possessed fingers.

She caught glimpses of Beautifuls through the window of her quarantine room. How could she not? Few contemplated stepping beyond the City's security fence, afraid of the savagery and sickness beyond. Helen watched them come and go on the street below, all apparently young, all oddly alike in their surgical perfection. Among them, conspicuous because of their unimproved ugliness, black-uniformed contestants for the Beautiful Life, working, scheming, hungering to be elevated to the elect while they still had time. That was how the City functioned. Maybe Bertrand was right to believe it would work forever.

From her window, she watched a pair of Beautifuls stroll gaily by, a loving couple, as she and Bertrand had been, wholly absorbed by their happiness – except for a constant eye out for who might not admire them, who should be courted. Perhaps people had always been that way. Learning how to renew organs and cells, reeling back decay, would never change human nature.

Two clones of the couple followed, a winsome little boy and girl in matching pink outfits: perfect accessories. The nearest the pair would get to children of their own. Neither child would live longer than a pet poodle, ageing at many times the pace of the primitives beyond the limits. For the great irony of the Beautiful Life was that it precluded the creation of new life. As soon as one's cells were renewed, they became sterile. Not a single Beautiful could give birth except through cloning, and, even then, deformities were the norm. There was a horrid cruelty to watching one's ersatz child shrivel and rot like an over-delicate fruit.

Bertrand swore they would discover how to conquer that defect in time. That they would reacquire the ability to produce perfect children through one incubator or another, natural or manufactured.

Helen was not so sure.

It seemed to her nature's revenge for their disobedience to time. Though the Beautiful Life claimed to have escaped time's prison, she suspected all the Beautifuls would be rounded up in the end.

BERTRAND (1)

Helen's questions and answers always reverted to Bertrand. During the dull weeks of quarantine and Mhairi's recovery, he only communicated by hologram. Naturally, prudent reasons for staying away might exist. Yet standing outside her glass door in person would hardly have inconvenienced him.

The moment Helen conceded his power over her, Bertrand's games of control had resumed. The very same ones that drove her to the Museum nine months earlier. Above all, his unsubtle reminders who held all the keys – quite literally, given her situation. Her role in this pantomime was that of penitent lover, begging forgiveness and lamenting the faintest *froideur* on his part. No doubt he expected her to compose letters or sonnets entreating his affection. Preferably circulated in public. After all, he had lost much face when Helen Devereux, paramour to the great Bertrand Du Guesclin for so long, turned her back on him.

She didn't believe his excuse that important business kept him away. Yet his face in the holograms was drawn and tense. As her quarantine dragged on, she suspected he was keeping her prisoner, that she was no longer a carrier of anything more infectious than frustration. He was punishing her like a naughty child confined to its bedroom.

One morning the most senior doctor stopped by, a new diffidence in his voice.

'I'm afraid your sister must remain in isolation a while longer,' he said. 'You, however, are to receive your first proper visitor tomorrow.' He smiled. 'A most important visitor, I must say! Please assure him we are honoured.'

No need to ask her visitor's identity.

After he left, Helen stood by the window, gazing out at an enormous statue of the double helix – the City's proud symbol – in the plaza below. Here in Albion's elegant centre, one might forget the vulgar hum of energy and plasti-steel machine parts in its rim. Forget the drones and raw materials processed to order, the biomedical research and computer-fed experimentation. One might forget the production of novelty food and drink to sate bored, pedantic palates and appetites. Forget, indeed, that the Beautiful Life rested on dull spider webs of technology and industry and settle right down to an eternity of play: *faux* dramas and elaborate games, pleasure parties and trysts, intrigues and mild feuds, narcotics and unreality devices to while away hours, months, years, decades.

Helen sighed, glanced up at the sky. A straggling skein of geese flew overhead. Day by day the skies outside had gained a softer edge. Autumn was coming.

BERTRAND (2)

Bertrand came without warning the next day. Helen looked up from her breakfast to find him in the doorway. For a long moment, they surveyed each other's changes. His face was smooth, youthful as ever. Yet she detected anxieties beneath his customary smile and playfully-raised eyebrows: a new weariness, perhaps even baffled anger.

He tutted sympathetically. 'I see you did not come home a moment too soon. Nine months away and already you grow ... Well, I'll say no more. You have a mirror here, after all.'

'Delighted to see you, too!' she cried.

But Helen knew he was right: without regular treatment, ageing had resumed its inexorable tread.

He took her hands. 'You know I speak only out of love. And you know very well I am delighted to see you.'

Helen squeezed his fingers.

'Thank you,' she murmured, nodding at the adjoining room where Mhairi appeared to be asleep. 'You saved my sister's life.'

'I know,' sighed Bertrand, sinking into a chair beside her. 'One does what one can. By the way, I expect nothing in return.'

He sniffed. Glanced round the room. Taking out his pocket screen he murmured a command.

A small drone entered and began to scan, lights flashing. When Helen tried to speak Bertrand shook his head in warning. His screen glowed. He read the message. A furrow appeared on his smooth forehead.

'It is safe to speak frankly now,' he said.

'Safe?' asked Helen in wonder. 'How could it be otherwise?'

'The drone detected several surveillance devices and blocked their transmissions.' He leaned forward. 'I am spied upon, Helen. Yes, even me. Even here.'

'But who?' She could not believe anyone would dare. Not unless they wished to be expelled from the City for the crime of Discordia.

'Nine months can be a long time, my dear,' he said. 'Absurd as it seems, my position is not what it was, both in Albion and, indeed, all the Cities. There are disputes in the Council. Grave controversies. You should know this, so my enemies do not use you against me.'

'How can anyone dispute with the Chairman of the Council?' cried Helen. 'You are a founder of this place. Of the Alliance of Five Cities. Of the Beautiful Life itself. It would not exist without you. You *are* the City of Albion's natural leader.'

He settled back in his chair.

'Yet some are dissatisfied,' he said, 'once-dependable colleagues and friends. They want more. They are tampering with Faustian matters, Helen! Research that goes far beyond the cell renewal I gave so much to develop. I will say no more. The less you know, the better.'

He examined her again.

'I shall be away for a week or two, my love, visiting other Cities across the world. Seeking support for my position.'

'Is it to do with…' She hesitated. 'This *tampering* you mention?'

'Everything I do now is concerned with that. But when I return my sole concern shall be you.'

He stroked her hands, lingering over an incipient wrinkle. 'I shall keep you safe,' he said. 'Even from time. Our Beautiful Life shall resume stronger and more precious than ever.'

Helen realised – with that sixth sense all possess when watched – Mhairi had woken and was staring at Bertrand through the glass wall dividing the quarantine rooms. A terrible burden of obligation for her sister made Helen lower her head. Thus, she didn't notice the flicker of conspiracy that passed between Dr Mhairi Macdonald and Bertrand Du Guesclin: an unhappy complicity.

She was too busy thinking how Bertrand owned her now. Not in exchange for the Beautiful Life, just her sister's short, ugly one.

TO WALK IN EARLY AUTUMN

Helen took her first walk round the City. She went alone and preferred it that way.

It occurred to her how a visitor from Baytown would marvel at the wide avenues lined with statues gathered from the lost world's museums and galleries. Trees a rarity in this concrete world, their fallen leaves vacuumed by patient drones. Everywhere glass glittered with not a pane cracked. Palaces a dozen times higher than the steeple of Holy Innocents Church

Its people, too, were creatures of another destiny. Not in appearance, limb and face and torso all human, but in their essence. The strolling Beautifuls were a pageant of grace and gaiety.

Helen wandered from plaza to park, skirting marble fountains and hologram displays, on through a shopping district lined with drone-tended boutiques to the towering statue of the double helix at the City's heart.

Every trace of the ancient market town of Huntingdon upon which the City of Albion squatted had been demolished and cleared except for a single structure: a Medieval stone bridge with six arches divided by granite buttresses to guide the onrush of the River Great Ouse. A strange refugee from history, she thought, as symbolic as the enormous monument of the double helix nearby. Both sought to contain the flow and ripple of life, to channel its mindless floods and seasons, its eddies and droughts. Except the analogy of a river did not quite work in Albion. Here the Beautiful Life dammed life's flow in a circular pond – a stagnant pool, she feared. Yet beyond the City's self-defined limits, nature bubbled and frothed with life, always, always new life.

A cool breeze blew a single brown, curling leaf across the concrete. Somehow it had evaded the cleaning drones. She stooped to pick it up and sat on a bench in the shadow of the helix statue.

An automated trambus pulled up. Doors opened. No one got in or out. It glided away on its circular route.

This is home, she thought, *the only one left to me*. Truly, it was a safer home than rowdy, raw Baytown with its reek of sweating humanity, its moist earth and plant scents, its untameable sea. The City was silent in comparison, germless, the Beautiful Life settled long ago. Seasons were of little consequence here.

If Albion is paradise, she thought, perhaps sacrificing the people outside is justified. After all, only a small number could live as Beautifuls. The dead leaf on her palm was designed to be replaced by another, the cycle repeating until evolution made its species obsolete. But here the Beautiful Life had halted evolution. Was sacrificing the primitives natural then? Bertrand believed so. Helen knew some on the Council advocated a thorough cleansing of all ur-humans, that Bertrand was soft-hearted in comparison, arguing every Beautiful had been a primitive once and that to erase the human gene pool was dangerous. Who knew what use they might yet serve? Hence the people outside were to be kept in ignorance and atavism, forced to regress, their numbers strictly limited like animals in a game reserve.

Helen thought for a long hour beneath the towering double helix, the dead leaf a feather on her palm. Beautifuls drifted through the empty square at irregular intervals in no particular hurry. A few unBeautified technicians wearing drab uniforms to denote their status, mourning clothes for their own mortality, rushed zealously to work. Over the years drones had replaced human servants wherever possible, yet a few remained useful, often serving as Deregulators in the wild lands round the City. It had been the idea of Bertrand's great rival on the council, Dr Guy de Prie-Dieu, to plant a chip in their skulls so they might be retired from service conveniently.

Helen watched and waited for nothing new to happen, for the time to pass without urgency or demands. When you could live a thousand years, what was an hour, what a day? Ennui crept back into the veins of her spirit until she felt as dusty as the dead leaf in her hand.

ELOISE DU GUESCLIN

The City provided a hologram news and entertainment service featuring pleasure resorts maintained by each of the Five Cities – paradises one might visit for a requisite number of credits – as well as fashion guidance and specialist programmes on a thousand hobbies to fill long, idle days. And gossip, always lots of gossip. In a world so small, everyone knew a little about everyone else, whether through mutual acquaintance or whispered conversations.

In this way, Helen came across a show that made her fear for Bertrand.

It was cast in the form of a debate. Two experts – the City teemed with experts – were playing at *jeux*, a popular genre. Most *jeux* were frivolous debates: whether wearing last season's fashions confirmed daring individuality or distasteful arrogance; whether one's clones could be prettier than oneself; whether the new table manners proposed by a self-appointed authority when eating fish on the bone were *really* more graceful than those proposed by another. Gay, charming debates, best enjoyed with a glass then replicated at a party.

This particular *jeux*, however, was serious.

It revolved around a moral dilemma. Whether one should design new life forms for one's convenience. As she listened, Helen leaned forward. This was a question close to Bertrand's heart. Was this what he had meant by *tampering*? She noted the audience figure recorded at the bottom of the hologram was huge.

One of the players, a serious young man with a noble mien, proposed the Beautiful Life would be best served by replacing drones with servitors constructed from living tissue, each created to fulfil a particular function. His opponent replied so vaguely – though wittily – that Helen concluded the 'debate' was set up with one outcome in mind.

Still, the hologram contestants in the *jeux* fenced with poise and humour. *Are not drones hideously ugly?* Suggested the stately proposer. *At least they never argue back,* countered his foe, *unlike disappointed lovers. How vulgar it would be to bandy words with a creature one has created! One would never live it down!*

With each sally, a *jeux*-judge awarded favours to one side or the other. It was this judge that reassured Helen.

On an ivory throne sat Bernard's own sister, Eloise Du Guesclin, her almond eyes and fluffy blonde hair exactly as when Helen last met her. She wore a sumptuous silk gown in the style of Marie Antoinette.

At last the contenders knelt before her, awaiting judgement. A foregone conclusion as far as Helen could see. Bertrand's prohibition of new life forms – whatever the technical possibilities – were well-known. As were his fears of gene-infection resulting from reckless experimentation.

The hologram of Eloise's perfect, high cheek-boned face expanded in close up.

'I declare the winner...'

Her voice was faintly shrill with excitement. How she craved attention, thought Helen. Poor little Ellie Gover had been plain, podgy round the face, her complexion pinpricked by eczema, belly inclined to rolls of flab. For her, at least, the Beautiful Life lived up to its name.

'I declare for the proposal!'

Helen wondered if Eloise had got mixed up. The proposal meant the creation of new life forms. Above all, it meant defying Bertrand. The gasp from the virtual audience expressed itself in hologram symbols glowing like fireflies then flying off round the room before fading: shocked faces or floating eyes that blinked in surprise, fans wafting to cool their owners' astonishment.

Helen commanded the hologram to close and stared out of the window of her quarantine room. If Bertrand's own sister publicly undermined him, his position on the Council must be insecure indeed, though Eloise was capable of almost any spiteful caprice. That explained his frantic trips to Albion's sister cities in Europa and Asia, even South America where a single City was sited, a safe distance from the irradiated badlands of the former United States, constantly vigilant the continent's natives did not breed back into a nuisance. His quest for allies was a further sign of weakness; proof his support within Albion was dwindling.

Not for the first time since her return, Helen felt an irrational urge to look upon the Jewel, to stare into its bright blue sapphire for reassurance. It felt far from reach.

ΣIGHT

NOON

How many armies have travelled this earth? Some spilling across arid plains in search of water like a migration of wildebeest. Some a column of termites or a padding wolf pack, canines slavering, yellow eyes intent, noses scenting prey. Some mere men: foolish, persuadable, led by greed or custom or fear.

Big Jacko's army reached the Whitby to Scarborough road at noon. Their up and down progress along hidden, narrow tracks had been slow, scouts fanning out constantly to capture or kill any who might bring word of their approach. Seth among them: he knew the lands near Baytown better than any.

Their caution proved unnecessary. No one around except a few goatherds and shepherds, all easily rounded up. As Stu joked, there'd be no shortage of meat that night. He added with a grin, 'Most of it bitch.'

In the shadow of Biller Howe Dale, the army gathered nearly four hundred strong, its vastness a testament to rewards heaped on its king by the Deregulator in Whitby. Seth sat on a pony next to Big Jacko, swollen with pride. Across his lap, the battery-powered foghorn. In his hand, a lance topped with a bright yellow pennant – the pharaoh's colour – for Queen Morrighan proclaimed that King Jacko's great affinity was with the morning sun. Like that burning orb, he cast forth rays of illumination.

The small group of horsemen were joined by a bearded giant in leather armour, chief of the mercenary Reivers. When he spoke in his thick, guttural tongue hardly any understood.

'This is it,' Jacko told the chief. 'Stick to the plan, and we're smiling.'

Seth stirred with excitement. Was it time? Everyone knew the plan. Three-quarters of the army led by the Boss, foot soldiers mainly, would attack Baytown itself, scattering everyone in the surrounding townland and seizing the village. It was known Big Jacko wanted to keep an eye on the Reivers in case they burned his new kingdom to ash and bones.

The remainder of the troops, mostly mounted, would sweep into Hob Vale, capture the farms there and the old youth hostel at Hob Hole. Most especially, the Hall. The Boss was particular about that. Seth loved how he anticipated everything.

Earlier, as they marched from Fylingdales, the Boss had clapped him on the shoulder.

'Nah then,' he'd said. 'You know how I've worked to make that place me own. You know it better than any of me other boys. I'm trusting you, Seth, to take that house without a broken window or plant pot. With me?'

'Yes, boss!'

'Good.' Big Jacko had grinned. 'And remember, the king always keeps his promises. When you take the Hall, you get to keep your sister safe and your uncle's room, like we agreed. With me?'

'Yes, boss.'

'You're a good boy, Seth.'

As the clans of shaggy, barefoot Reivers took up position behind the wood at Biller Howe Dale, that praise vibrated in Seth's heart. And he was favoured with a final honour. When all Baytown was safe, he was to climb the tower of Holy Innocents Church, where Father had wasted his whole life, stand on its summit and sound the foghorn in triumph.

'Let's go!' roared Big Jacko.

A ragged cheer grew into a swell of voices. Anyone observing the hot, cruel expression of many an unwashed face would have detected a pillager's hunger. Such an observer might have pitied the people of Baytown. Only then did Seth doubt what he had brought upon the heads and hearths of friends, comrades, childhood companions and neighbours – when it was too late.

BESS

Impossible to comprehend the solace of a loyal dog to a troubled man. Not that Michael considered himself troubled exactly. Except, even on a day when summer seemed reluctant to hint at the coming autumn, when deep blue skies without a cloud spread a distant haze over a glinting blue sea and insects hummed drowsily, troubling thoughts occurred. With each one he scratched Bess's head. She panted, wagged her tail in reply.

First up, a nagging certainty of letting down his brother. He had promised poor James to save Seth if he could. That implied trying. Word of Jacko's stay in Whitby then removal to the decaying radar station at Fylingdales had inevitably passed through Baytown. As had his riding out on raids. Wherever Jacko ventured must be far to the west or south; no rumour of it came Baytown's way. It upset Michael to think of peaceful James Pilgrim's son turned brigand.

Perhaps that was why he resisted Tom Higginbottom's suggestion of raising a large posse to drive Big Jacko from the district. Why bother, argued Michael, when their enemy's forces were reduced to a handful. What harm could he realistically inflict on populous Baytown? But Michael knew the real reason he argued for inaction. So long as Seth dwelt nearby, there seemed hope of redemption. He also remembered finding City-made padlocks on the doors of Fylingdales: meddling in City business never ended well.

That sunny midday he sat in the front garden of Hob Hall after a lunch of fresh bread, cheese, tomatoes and onion. Blue lavender and numerous herbs blended to form a sweet, cloying scent. Once more he scratched Bess's head. Her tail wagged obligingly.

They had managed the recent outbreak of plague well, keeping the infection at bay rather than in Bay. Its aftermath was what grieved the whole community.

Every day revealed fresh cause to mourn the loss of Dr Mhairi Macdonald. Though Amar kept her library open in honour of the cranky, benign old woman, and a new conductor had been found for the Baytown Orchestra, none could replicate her medical knowledge.

Bess gazed up at him, scratching fleas with a vigorous back leg.

Michael had put away his smoking things when he heard a drum of hooves. Instantly he was on his feet and rushing indoors. This was no group of farm boys racing their nags down to the beach for a lark. War cries rose above the whinnies and thunder of galloping horses.

ALARM

Michael hared to his room. Habitual doubts vanished in action: grab shotgun and bandolier, sword and scabbard. Out, out, charging past a startled Averil with a single cry of 'Arms! To arms!' Into the farmyard at the rear of the Hall even as the first rider galloped in, sword raised.

Instinct jerked up the shotgun. A billow of sulphurous smoke. The horseman fell back off his rearing mount, stomach torn open.

More were in the yard now. Too many! He ducked into an outbuilding where women cowered with their children then burst through a backdoor into a walled vegetable garden at the side of the Hall. From here he could follow a nettle-choked path to Holy Innocents Church. One little used since Reverend James Pilgrim's death.

No qualms about abandoning Hob Hall. It was lost. What mattered was summoning enough men to regain it.

Reloading as he ran, Michael emerged on the road, almost colliding with a horseman. A dozen raiders milled in the lane, flintlocks, swords, lances and axes to hand.

Too many!

Without pausing to fire he dodged between stamping hooves. Riders turned in surprise. A pistol cracked nearby. Fortunately, the gunman's horse chose that moment to buck. Despite point blank range the bullet whistled by.

Now Michael was in the churchyard, panting as he ran. Another gunshot behind him. Stonework on the porch spouted dust. Then he had burst into the darkness of the church, its air cool and still after the turmoil outside.

Slamming the heavy doors, he rammed home an ancient bolt, frantically piling heavy pews as a barricade. Moments later he was at the back of the church, yanking ropes, one in each hand, jumping up and down like a crazed child.

The first deep, reverberating chime rang out. Another. Another. Discordant bells spread out clashing waves from the tower of Holy Innocents Church, echoing across the fields of Baytown. The traditional warning of enemies to hand, its message simple: *Arms! To arms!*

TO ARMS

Charlie Gudwallah heard the bells and knew them no false alarm. His gut told him, and Charlie harboured great faith in his gut. Within minutes he was strapping on a breastplate made from varnished leather, stuffing single-shot pistols into his belt.

Outside the Puzzle Well Inn, frightened people were gathering from all over the village. Charlie knew folk would be streaming into town from outlying farms and fields where they prepared the harvest. He rushed to the jetty and stared out to sea.

The tide was high, lapping against cliff base and sea wall. Nearly every coble sailing from Baytown – and a number from Scarborough and Whitby, even as far south as Filey – were out that day, drift netting shoals of herring that teemed off the coast. Baytown's strongest out there, hearing the bells and debating whether to haul nets.

'Let off the rocket!' bellowed Charlie. 'Hand out weapons!'

An unnecessary command, the volunteer constables' armoury was already thrown open.

'Form up!' he shouted. 'Get the drum! Form up!'

A tattoo began as the town drummer beat with a will. A few dozen of the militia – young and old, male and female – were marshalled into line by better-trained volunteer constables. With each passing minute, more folk arrived. Baytown had survived Dying after Dying by combining at the Puzzle Well when dire need arose.

One of a dozen scouts sent up the hill rushed back.

'There's fucking hundreds coming!' he muttered.

Charlie's eyes widened. He realised people were looking uneasily for directions where they might flee. No hope of running down the beach with the tide so high. If Baytown had been surrounded, there was no way out.

'Rubbish!' he called back, pointing his long-barrelled rifle at the clouds. It went off with a satisfying noise. A shocked silence fell on the crowd. It crossed Charlie's mind how often he had obeyed senseless, suicidal orders in the Crusades. Now his chance had come to dish out a few of his own.

'After me!' he cried. 'We'll hold whoever's up there as long as we can. Where's that rocket!'

On cue, a loud whoosh of sparks hurled a long plume of smoke over the bay. Charlie prayed it would hasten the fishing fleet back to shore.

'After me!' he shouted again.

With that, sixty armed folk hurried up the hill.

SILENCED (1)

Dang. Dang. Dang. The clashing tocsin of Holy Innocents Church matched by thudding against the church door. Already it bulged. Any moment the bolt must shear from the wood.

He let go of the ropes. After a last few clangs, the bells fell silent. Time to look to his weapons. Two cartridges in the shotgun, only four left in the bandolier. Each must count. He loosened the City-forged sword in its scabbard – his best hope. Nothing fleshy could resist such a blade.

Bangs and thuds continued against the door. Michael realised he felt nauseous. His bladder might release an unbidden stream. After the Crusades, he had sworn to never take another man's life and faithfully kept that oath. Already he'd killed one of the raiders. His bitter, guilty vow mocked him now.

The door gave, crashing against the makeshift barricade of pews he had erected.

Where to fight? Here and risk getting trapped? Outside in the graveyard? Maybe capture a horse. Get away.

A childhood spent exploring the church's secrets saved Michael Pilgrim. He ran to the vestry, bolting the door behind him. In the corner stood a heavy oak table. He dragged it aside to reveal a trapdoor with a rusty iron ring laid between the flagstones. Bracing his legs, he hauled at the ring. No movement! The wood must have swollen. Straining every muscle, he yanked. The trapdoor rose an inch then flew upwards so that he staggered back.

Crashing noises and loud curses indicated his enemies were inside the church, looking round for him, guns ready for the slightest movement, wary of his shotgun. It wouldn't be long before they tried the vestry door, broke it down. Michael went to a low arched door set in the thick stone outer wall. Behind it was a staircase leading up to the church roof. He threw it open so the staircase was visible. With luck, they would waste time exploring the possibility he had hidden up there.

Taking out his lighter, Michael spun the flint-wheel. Guided by its flame, he lowered himself through the trapdoor. His boots soon met a hard, shifting, knobbly surface. Reaching up, he pulled down the trapdoor and ducked. It thudded shut, blowing out the lighter flame.

Conscious what lay beneath his feet, he stared into a darkness thick as water. The mound he stood upon reached almost as high as the ceiling. Frantically he worked the flint wheel. If it failed to spark he was lost. Then the wick caught, a yellow glow spreading to reveal a vaulted catacomb.

He had entered the ancient charnel house of Holy Innocents Church, its echoing space filled with bones from the previous century's carnage. Skull and ribcage, fibula and tibia, pelvis and knucklebone. Skeletons jumbled and sieved by decay. The long fetid cave reeked. Well it might. Hundreds of people's remains mouldered there.

Gasping, Michael crunched over piles of bones, kicking them aside like a child wading through twigs and autumn leaves, his lighter held high to guide his way until he reached a narrow brick staircase. This led up to a square wooden hatch.

He pulled hard. Like the trapdoor in the vestry, this one had swollen with damp and opened with a loud crack. In a fluid movement, Michael was outside, the dark eyes of his shotgun scanning the churchyard.

No bastards here. All looking for him inside.

A woman's persistent scream came from the direction of Hob Hall, reminding him his home was lost – temporarily.

SILENCED (2)

The fearful little mob marched up the hill behind the town drummer. Charlie couldn't help recalling the Grand Old Duke of York. Instead of ten thousand men, he found a dozen volunteer constables waiting for him at the top, clutching various weapons.

Frantic minutes followed as he marshalled everyone with firearms, crossbows and bows to the flanks of the street to provide a crossfire. In the middle – including himself, to lend the line backbone – a pre-prepared barricade manned by impromptu warriors armed with pikes, spears, axes and spiked clubs. It seemed the best they could do.

Still, the bells of Holy Innocents Church pealed the alarm. Abruptly they went quiet. Whoever had been pulling the ropes – and he could guess his name – had been silenced. *Shame's everywhere,* he thought, bitterly.

Charlie Gudwallah was one for convivial gossip rather than fine speeches. It seemed his time for speechifying had come.

'Remember this,' he told Baytown's tiny army of defenders, 'we're what stands between those fuckers out there – whoever they are – and our own folk sheltering round the Puzzle Well. We've got to win time for the lads out at sea to get back.'

He struggled for a finale. 'An' I promise you this! There's a free drink waiting at the Puzzle Well Inn!'

Charlie realised no one was listening. He wheeled to face the road into Baytown. Tramping feet became a column led by a familiar figure. On his head, an outlandish yellow hat with comical earflaps. Around him, a mounted retinue armed from foot to forehead.

If Big Jacko had depended only on his London Boys and local hirelings Charlie might have laughed fit to bust at that daft yellow hat. But hundreds of enemies jostled behind a giant in leather armour on a horse.

Charlie Gudwallah didn't hesitate. Raising his musket, he aimed carefully at Big Jacko. Fired. Pan and muzzle flashed. Smoke puffed. The shot's report echoed. The world seemed to freeze. Slowly, like a girt tree falling, the giant Reiver captain slid off his horse. His crunch on hard earth was heard even by the Baytown men a hundred yards away. They roared as the advancing column of Reivers halted.

'He's the one I aimed at all along!' lied Charlie, reloading joyfully. 'That right big bastard!'

Big Jacko, pale with fury, pointed at the smaller force opposing him. 'Kill those fools!' he shouted, his order lost in the din.

IN A GRAVEYARD

Michael had long considered the world a vast graveyard. With a sounder knowledge of the sciences, he might have said as much of the universe. Now his world shrank to the churchyard of Holy Innocents. He had simple visions of the near future: cripple as many enemies as possible then scarper.

He stole along the side of the church and peeped round a buttress. More horsemen further up the lane. How many? Too many. Twenty, at least, inside and outside Hob Hall. He recognised a few of Mayor Jacko's boys and understood the mischief.

A grim desire to survive consumed him. Oh, they'd find it one thing to gallop like furies into Hob Hall, quite another to hold onto it when the Baytown Militia arrived, hot for vengeance.

He became aware of distant gunshots. So they had attacked Baytown itself, too! No help could be expected soon from that quarter.

Michael Pilgrim sneaked through the nettle-shrouded graveyard, using wonky slabs and mausoleums as cover, to a dry stone wall by the lane. Here a single raider guarded the horses of the men busy ransacking the church.

Slinging his shotgun over his back, he drew his sword. With a prayer for luck, he hopped over the crumbling wall, landing a few yards from the lone Reiver.

'Hey!' warned the man. A youth, not a man. His last warning on earth.

Michael Pilgrim's absurdly sharp sword hacked deep into the youth's head, brains and blood spattering.

Grabbing a horse, Michael swung a leg over the saddle and clattered down the lane towards the old youth hostel at Hob Hole. Perhaps Mister Priest Man could rally some resistance.

Within minutes, a dozen raiders were after him, beating the sides of their horses, digging in cruel spurs.

IN THE END

When it came, it came quickly. For thirty endless minutes, Charlie Gudwallah's forces held off the horde swirling round the entrance to Baytown. A miracle to last that long. But a

mercenary's courage is only partially for hire: few were prepared to sacrifice their lives for Big Jacko. And Charlie's lucky
shot bringing down their leader taught the Reivers to hang
back.

In the end, sheer numbers told. Though the crossfire of
the volunteer constables piled bodies on the road, Big Jacko
ordered gangs of Reivers to outflank the Baytown men. Desperate hand-to-hand fights broke out in the narrow, twisting alleys
of the ancient village. Men bellowed and screamed as they fell.

'Back!' commanded Charlie, fearful of encirclement or a
rout. 'Steady, mind. You lot, get the wounded down first. No
running now. Face the front there! Pikes raised! That's it. Eyes
front!'

Backwards down the hill they shuffled, leaving a dozen dead
and dying. Thrice that number of their enemies sprawled or lay
dying before the barricade or in the winding snickleways.

'Down to the Puzzle Well!' cried Charlie.

To his amazement, they were not pursued. It seemed the
enemy was pausing to lick his wounds. Maybe they had lost
all discipline and were getting down to the vital business of
looting.

By the shore he found a welcome sight: the Baytown fisher-
fleet landing on slender strips of beach revealed by the turning
tide, its numbers swollen by boats from Filey, Scarborough,
Whitby.

Tom Higginbottom shoved through a mob of weeping
children, mothers clutching bairns and babies, men clutching
weapons.

'We're packed down here like herrings in a tray,' he cried,
grabbing Charlie by the arm. 'How many of 'em are there?'

When he learned the size of Jacko's army, Tom surveyed the
chaos of their own forces in despair. At that moment Charlie
glimpsed a desperate plan. A ruthless plan, some might call it, a
plan for the future rather than a lost battle in impossible terrain.

'Them cobles could carry bigger fish than herring,' he said.

Tom Higginbottom looked at him without comprehension. But Charlie knew his meaning and mind. The horror of it was who must be left behind – thrown back to bait the flood of Reivers seeping down the hill. *Shame's everywhere*, thought Charlie, grimly.

HOB HOLE

Michael had a head start. Not least he knew the twists and turns of the lane leading down to Hob Hole through shady coppice and sheep-nibbled pasture. His main hope was in Mister Priest Man defending the wooden footbridge over the stream to the old youth hostel. Whatever else might be said of the visionary cosmic voyager, he knew how to point a blunderbuss in defence of his people.

Michael heard sounds of pursuit; dug his heels into the cantering mare. A stubborn creature, reluctant to gallop without a prick of sharp spurs.

Soon it became obvious his enemies were gaining. Briefly, he considered a firefight. Jump them at point blank range. Take a few down. Maybe drive them back up the lane. Luckily for him, he avoided so suicidal a course. There, through the trees, he glimpsed light glinting on moving water. He was a stone's throw from the footbridge and sanctuary. Round a corner of muddy lane he raced.

Only then did he realise his mistake.

Where was it? The footbridge had gone! Pulled up by the Nuagers when they heard the alarm bells ring out. He glimpsed faces in the windows of the youth hostel, gun barrels and crossbows poking out. Allies, true, but a deep stream swollen by the high tide blocked his way to them. If he attempted to wade over, the Reivers would shoot him in the water like a trapped seal.

Michael slid off the horse and ran for a stony path climbing steeply to the cliff top. At the bottom, he turned, raised his shotgun. The first rider appeared from the direction he'd come.

Bang. A shot meant for horse not rider. The creature stumbled, neighed, reared, its chest bloody. The next raider reined in, unable to get around the kicking, wounded beast, clinging on to his seat for dear life. *Bang*. This time Michael missed.

Snatching cartridges from the bandolier, he reloaded in time to see the first rider – who had jettisoned his wounded mount – rush towards him, sword raised high. *Bang*. A true shot, tearing off a chunk of the man's shoulder, spinning him round until he toppled backwards into the beck. *Bang*. Another horse winged. It leapt in the air. Landed unsteadily. The lane was full of horsemen now. Several bullets whistled past.

He bounded up the steep, narrow path. Hard terrain for a horseman to follow, not impossible, just hard. But he knew they'd want his head for the blood he'd spilt. That alone would goad them on.

Chest heaving, Michael reached the cliff top. Here he paused to load his last two cartridges. He could hear iron-shod hooves on the flinty path he'd taken moments before. Without a doubt, others on foot would be following the horsemen.

Because of the gradient, his first sight of an enemy was a single head then shoulders; two large pistols ready-cocked. Concealed behind a tree, he took aim. Fired. *Click*. A misfire! Percussion cap faulty. He aimed again. *Bang*. His second barrel discharged, and a lead ball smashed into the rider's face, throwing him backwards.

Michael didn't wait to survey his handiwork. Cartridges spent, his last resource was flight. He weaved like a hunted deer along the twisting cliff path, through trees and scrub teetering on the edge. Shouts and hoofbeats pursued him.

Two horsemen cantered into view, pistols raised. Winded, Michael could run no further. He hurled his useless shotgun into a dense bramble patch and drew his sword. A gunshot rang out. Something whistled inches away from his ducking head. Next time he would not be so blessed.

He backed to the cliff edge. Behind him was a bare gash of red earth eroded in winter then washed away by the neap tides.

Wary of his sword, the two riders trotted a little closer, readying their pistols. So close they would not miss. Michael lunged downwards into the little gully in the cliff, seeking cover from their fire. His fingers scrabbled at loose earth; clawed uselessly at the dust and gravel. With a shriek of terror, he lost control. He slid helplessly over the edge of the cliff and fell out of sight.

The two horsemen watched from their mounts, wary of going too near the edge. For several minutes they peered down, muttering to each other. Below waves crashed onto rocks.

A trumpet call made them stir.

'Yah!' called the leader. With that, they rode back the way they had come to claim their share of the loot.

ANOTHER DAY

A ragged volley of muskets and shotguns echoed across the bay from the area round the Puzzle Well. Surely one of the last. Tom Higginbottom had left Charlie with a few dozen volunteers to hold off Big Jacko's final attack while every available coble and skiff loaded up with people. Even with the extra boats, too many had been left behind, stranded on the jetty beside the Puzzle Well Inn. Many more had already fled into the maze of Baytown's courtyards and cottages, seeking a hole to hide in.

Tom pulled at the oars, his eldest son Ben on the bench alongside him, both too numb for talk. An hour was all it had taken to tear asunder the world of Ben's youth and Tom's manhood. Somewhere back on shore was his wife, young Ben's mother – no one could find her before they left, among the last boats to cast off. Tom dreaded how the Reivers might use her, still a comely woman despite four bairns living and two dead.

He stared miserably at the jetty beside the Puzzle Well Inn. No more volleys rang out: Charlie had surrendered or been overwhelmed. The garrulous innkeeper had insisted on leading the rear guard, claiming that as an evacuation by sea was his idea, it would look like a coward's work if he didn't stay.

Half a mile from the beach – the turning tide sped their progress – Tom shipped oars, leaving his coble to ride a gentle swell. With the extra boats from elsewhere on the coast, they'd saved a third of Baytown. And Charlie had made sure the majority were men or women of fighting age. 'We'll survive as we did in the Crusades,' he had murmured, clasping Tom's hand in farewell. 'That's to say, me old pal, for another day.'

When Reivers appeared on the jetty, Tom's face hardened.

'Set the sail,' he ordered, stepping gingerly through people packing his long, flat-bottomed boat. Their collective weight meant they were riding low. The sooner land was touched the better.

'We'll lead the way to Scarborough,' he told Ben. 'The currents'll carry us round Ravenscar right easy today. And we've kin in Scarborough.'

Thus, the little armada limped south, shadowing the long line of cliffs until Baytown was behind and Scarborough Castle on its headland came into view.

FOGHORNS

Bo-o-o-o-m urged the foghorn. *Bo-o-o-o-m.*

Its defiant voice echoed around the beach and cliffs to summon people forth – for reward or woe as Jacko deemed fit; as the Pharaoh of Baytown saw fit. All, all summoned to parade before the new king favoured by the Old Gods and his puissant priestess-queen in her shiny City raincoat, all, all, prisoner or hired man, loyal servant or reluctant slave, summoned by the foghorn.

Darkness had fallen when Big Jacko staged his drunken triumph. Bonfires burned high on the beach, fed by prisoners beaten with club or gun butt if they slacked. For Queen Morrighan had declared that Pharaoh Jacko's victory fires should rival the sun. Gangs of prisoners were tearing down derelict buildings to carry wood to the beach for burning.

The wild drinking and rapine of the afternoon had soured to surliness by evening. Lusts satiated, thirsts slaked. Indeed, precious little remained in Baytown to eat or drink. The harvest was weeks away, and the Reivers were hungry as maggots. Few women and girls were left unviolated by the time darkness fell.

Jacko had promised his Reivers Baytown for a day. And King Jacko kept his promises.

Seated upon a makeshift throne, he accepted homage, yellow crown upon his head. No one found his headgear comical now. Behind him stood queen and courtiers. Reiver clan chiefs stepped forward to receive payment, princely rewards of City clothes and unbreakable tools and power cells, precious objects worthy of terrible risks. Most bowed gratefully, a few were sullen. The casualties that day had exceeded everyone's expectations: over sixty of their men would never return home laden with prizes, Yorkshire soil their home forever.

After the mercenaries came prisoners, a long procession. One by one they were forced to crawl through a narrow hoop set before the Pharaoh's throne. Any whose pride exceeded the hoop's diameter was shot out of hand. After the first two, no one refused to humble themselves. Seth watched familiar figures crawling on their bellies with averted eyes: Charlie Gudwallah, shoulder bandaged, scalp still bleeding from a sword gash; Amar, his handsome face mottled by purple bruises; Armitage the Blacksmith glowering at his daughter Miriam who served Baytown's new queen in the role of lady's maid; Mister Priest Man, top hat stubbornly still on his head even as he wriggled through the hoop.

Bo-o-o-o-m proclaimed the foghorn. King Jacko's reign had commenced. *Bo-o-o-o-m*.

ΠΙΠΣ

PILLBOX

The cliffs of Baytown were mere layers of sediment, layers of time. Time had not stopped for Michael Pilgrim either, clinging to the cliff side a hundred feet up.

When he fled a sure death from the horsemen's pistols, slipping and scrabbling at loose dirt, over the edge of the void with a shriek, he anticipated a long fall terminating in darkness. Yet any local fond of beachcombing knew a narrow ledge ran beneath the overhang where Big Jacko's men trapped him, its presence a relic from another war. Long ago a sturdy concrete fortification had been built into the cliff to deter invasion from a nation no longer in existence. While the earth around it eroded and slid into the sea, the pillbox endured.

Michael landed on its roof, dropped his sword, teetered for a moment then hugged the cliff wall concealing him from his enemies above.

Fearful hours followed. First, he witnessed the Baytown fishing fleet's evacuation from the beach. Then Big Jacko's triumph as twilight became night. Michael cowered behind the crumbling pillbox wall. What cruel fun they would take if they spotted him. The foghorn's boom chilled his heart. Bonfires cast lurid flickers over the procession crawling through Pharaoh Jacko's narrow hoop. Around midnight, he listened helplessly as a gang of Reivers took their pleasure with a protesting, crying girl at the cliff-foot. Was that girl Averil? He had no way of knowing.

Dawn cast a red glow on the pillbox. Exhausted, hungry, parched, Michael attempted an ascent. The bare cliff above his head seemed an impossible barrier. Any moment a handhold might loosen, a foot shy free of a fickle cranny. He stared always upward, refused to look down. Behind him, he heard gulls, sounds of the sea. Panic seized him halfway up. He clung for interminable minutes struggling to breathe evenly, knowing he must advance or perish. Then muscles unclenched and with a desperate scramble he reached the top, hauling himself over the cliff's lip to lie panting. Nearby a pile of horse manure buzzed with flies.

As light gathered, Michael retrieved his empty shotgun from the brambles where he'd tossed it. Then he hurried towards Ravenscar, away from Baytown. At a stream he drank and drank iron-flavoured water, scrubbing dried blood from his hands and face.

Mid-morning found him a good distance south, in a dark, nettle-filled farmhouse with a half-burned roof. Michael cleared a nest behind the nettles and slept, his weariness alike to despair.

RIVEN TARMAC

He shivered as he awoke to darkness. Hours yet before daybreak. Rain pattered on what remained of the farmhouse roof, and his nostrils filled with the earthy, acrid aroma of wet nettles.

How, he marvelled, had Big Jacko gathered so large a force? To hire that many men involved unimaginable costs – in food alone if nothing else. Last night's foghorn-serenaded triumph offered clues. The Reivers were paid with City goods. No doubt others would receive land and bonded serfs. Old, old ways to persuade men to kill. As ever, the Deregulator lay behind it, one way or another, humble Will Birch punishing the community that gave him birth.

Michael did not care to imagine the scenes in Hob Hall. He curled in a ball for warmth, sick with helpless rage.

One decision was already made, to travel to York and seek help from the Modified Man. The trick was getting there alive.

Before leaving, Michael found a mould-eaten plastic bucket in the farmhouse's kitchen, attaching it to his bandolier as a pannier. Nearly twenty hours since he last ate, he needed to forage hard on the way.

The season favoured him as he trekked down a main road, its tarmac riven by tree roots. Blackberries and hazelnuts went into the bucket, along with mushrooms for toasting and a plump hedgehog he spitted over a fire of dead twigs without delay. Gnawing its fatty innards triggered an attack of stomach acid. Salty mustard would have made it more palatable, but he ate every scrap.

A hard day's tramp brought him to a familiar crossroads as darkness and drizzle came on: Thornton-le-Dale, the deserted settlement with its barricade of rusty vehicles where he'd fired warning shots at Johnny Sawdon. Long ago, it seemed. A few miles east lay Pickering and friends, food, warmth, shelter. But he could go no further that day.

Limping to the barricade Michael detected faint scents of wood smoke and charred meat on the breeze. He touched the hilt of his sword. At that instant, a heavy hemp net flew from the darkness and tangled his arms. Within moments, clutching hands surrounded him. Fists pummelled, and he felt himself pushed to the ground.

MEAT ON T'HOOF

Trussed like a capon, weapons taken, Michael Pilgrim was shoved down a dark lane. A half-moon revealed his captors. The last people he expected, *floggers*, recognisable by their long black robes and red City crosses.

The smell of roasting meat intensified. They arrived at a large camp of smoky, wetwood fires dotted round a single leather tent.

The penitents slept on blankets beneath makeshift awnings and the bare stars.

Few paid attention as he was led to the tent. There, on a plastic folding chair of some antiquity, lolled the floggers' Master, a plump, hairless man, his yellow eyes veined and dilated. Eyes that glistened in the firelight. The eyes of a man far gone on intoxicants.

Without a word, Michael's captors handed his shotgun and sword to their leader. Upon drawing the plasti-steel blade, the chief flogger hissed excitedly.

'City magic! How does a beggar carry a sword like this?'

Michael shook his shoulders free from restraining hands.

'With honour, sir!' he said. 'I won it in the Crusades for saving a captain's life. Perhaps you should use it to cut me free. It's what the City would want.'

The Master's brow bunched. His strange, bleary eyes narrowed with guile. 'Blasphemy for one like you to possess City magic! Do you think I do not see the mark you wear?'

He pointed at the **F** branded on Michael's cheek. The floggers made the sign of a **C** over their hearts.

'Put him with t'other meat,' commanded the Master, hefting his new sword in wonder.

They took him to a handcart away from the Master's tent. Here a thin, pale figure cowered. Michael was surprised to see he wore a begrimed flogger's robe: an apostate, perhaps, or transgressor of their strict code. Maybe an ally.

'Please, masters!' Michael called. 'At least loosen my arms.'

After a muttered conference, rusty manacles connected by eighteen inches of chain were clamped round his wrists. The chain itself ran through a bracket on the handcart's shafts. No one spoke as the manacles were fitted. He was to learn the floggers distrusted talk as smacking of thought. And thought led to disobedience to the City. A gloomy silence lay over the entire camp. Michael estimated nearly a hundred of them round the smoky fires. Exhaustion numbed his sorrow.

After much grinning and squinty-eyed inspection, his fellow prisoner spoke in a sly taunting voice, 'Reckon they'll roast a fine heifer like thee 'fore they get round to me. I'm too stringy for good eating.'

Michael was all attention. 'Eating?'

'Aye. Meat on t'hoof! That's what tha's become. That and a packhoss to pull this 'ere cart.'

Michael detected the nasal accents of South Yorkshire.

'Cannibals?' he asked. 'I thought you floggers considered yourselves good men. Scourging yourselves so the Old Gods and the City keep off the plague. Isn't that your story?'

His companion sniffed. 'Mebbe it were like that in days of t'Big Dying. Now us whips are softest calf's leather, more for ticklin' than scourgin', if tha knows what I mean.'

'Never tried it,' admitted Michael.

'Aye?' The bony man in a filthy robe leaned forward. 'It's more a pleasure than pain, believe me.'

'So why are you missing out on the fun? Why are you chained up here like me?'

For a long, sullen while there was no reply.

'Meat on t'hoof,' muttered his companion, rolling over to sleep on the damp grass. 'That's all y'are now, mister.'

TOWARDS HELL AND HULL

Over the next week, Michael Pilgrim came to know his fellow prisoner all too well. Nothing like hauling a heavy handcart over muddy, rutted paths to reveal a man's foibles. First off, Gil – Michael never learned his surname – pulled as lazily as possible, expecting the new 'packhoss' to take the strain.

'Tha's such a big, strong bugger compared to me!' whined Gil when Michael pointed out the problem.

Weary miles through woodland and steep-sided valleys. Streams feeding meres constantly impeded their way. Miles of whispering bulrushes where beavers built and birds called by day. Startled frogs and snakes fled paths churned by the flog-gers' sandals. Gil called the midges worse than nagging women.

Constantly, Michael brooded on escape. Every delay strength-ened Big Jacko's grip on Baytown. Loathing for the self-styled Pharaoh who had uprooted Michael's entire existence obsessed him. Part of him – mentored by the Crusades to be cold and pitiless – could not wait to start hacking away with his sword. He fantasised executions where a snivelling King Jacko begged and pleaded.

Michael's better angel implored him to emulate Grandfather's tolerance and kindness towards an enemy. Reverend Oliver Pilgrim would have striven for a just peace and reconciliation rather than more killing.

Gil seemed to sense Michael's inner turmoil as they pulled the cart.

'Tha's afraid, Pilgrim!' he jeered. 'Nought but a babby for all your brawn.'

The object of this scorn struggled hard not to wring the little man's neck.

Despite his annoying ways, Gil let slip information. Michael learned the floggers' true relationship with the City: that they travelled from place to place spying for forbidden technology. Any transgressors were reported to the relevant Deregulator whose districts their pilgrimage passed through. In return, they received food, clothes and – their real reward – what Gil called *sweeties*, something he claimed to miss terribly. Each evening the floggers abased themselves before the Master and were granted one or two sugar-coated capsules: addictive intoxi-cants, Michael surmised from glazed eyes round campfires and slow, dreary speeches.

That long week the floggers trudged between villages and hamlets in the wetlands of East Yorkshire, scourging themselves in return for gifts of food. Most folk were wary of offending the holy men. At Beverley, they received a different welcome. The people fired warning shots, forcing the pilgrimage to retreat.

'Can't blame 'em,' conceded Gil. 'Last time we called at Beverley, t'Maister took a sweetie too many an' kidnapped a boy to hand round. He likes what he likes, tha knows.' Gil's manner suggested he shared the taste. 'Anyhow, it ended in a grand ol' barney an' we left on t'double. A couple of us was strung up outside Beverley Minster like pheasants.'

Gil laughed. 'We got us own back though. Went straight to t'Deregulator in Hull an' told him they was building a radio transmitter in Beverley Minster. Hee! Hee! Next day a drone blew up the whole place as a warning.'

Indeed word of the ancient church's destruction had reached Baytown. No one had guessed the floggers' spite lay behind it. Michael was beginning to see why his grandfather had initiated a strict policy of driving all floggers from Baytown.

A REUNION

The floggers approached Hull from the coast, crossing water-logged fields reverting to salt marsh as dykes and drainage systems failed. Michael pulled the cart balefully, head lowered.

Hull appeared through the mist on a rainy afternoon as a jagged horizon of burned and bombed buildings. The brief civil war that followed the first Great Dying had been especially unkind to Hull for reasons no one remembered. Apart from a Deregulator's compound constructed to the same specifications as the concrete fortress in Whitby, only hermits and outcasts favoured the lost city. Folk thereabouts had relocated a few miles west, a mile inland from the broken Humber Bridge, naming their settlement New Hull. Here the floggers planned to stage a great ceremony to appease the City of Albion.

'Why's tha looking at me like I shat in thy breakfast?' demanded Gil.

Michael said nothing. His jaws moved rhythmically, mas-ticating the coarse bread of lentils and barley that constituted his ration – half of what Gil received. When his fellow prisoner turned away, Michael reached out and snatched a fair share.

Discovering the theft drove the little man to his feet, spraying useless threats. Michael chewed stolidly: never had bread tasted sweeter.

Today was to be an easy day. No more travel for a while, yet he detected unaccustomed purpose among the drugged, apathetic floggers.

Michael examined the settlement of New Hull on its hill, the site chosen to escape flooding. Rising sea levels had made the villagers wary of the wide, tidal river. A fort of wood and salvaged stone had been erected on a man-made mound. He guessed New Hull must be ruled by a feudal lord. Perhaps that was the future: reversion. He recalled Big Jacko boasting of plans to build a castle round the nucleus of Hob Hall and new houses by the Museum. Were any still alive in Baytown to thwart those plans? Charlie, Tom, Amar, Priest Man? All killed or crippled by now, most likely.

The floggers had camped away from the village, beside the Humber Bridge or what remained of that imposing structure. A central chunk had been bombed long ago and blocked the river's flow. Rusting cables trailed like monstrous dead ivy.

By now Gil had forgotten his stolen bread sufficiently to leer. 'Lookin' forward to tonight, Pilgrim?' Michael regretted revealing his name and home.

'Should I?'

Gil chuckled with an edge of hysteria.

Afternoon came. Scores of folk from the surrounding lands approached the long, crumbling road-ramp leading up to the mighty bridge. Even with its span fallen it dominated the river, hundreds of feet high. Trees with laden leaves sighed in a wind blowing in from the North Sea. Gulls and terns cried on the estuary, and Michael longed for home.

How strange to be so lost! A despised slave, no other word applied. Except perhaps dinner.

In this gloomy reverie, he became aware of a young, handsome woman with hennaed hair before him. At first, he did not recognise her, despite exploring her pert body in Scarborough nigh on a year before. Then memories struck him hard: of revelling in her mouth and neck and breasts and secret places. He recalled the girl saying that she was from Hull. Evidently, she'd returned home after Scarborough. She was more pale and tired than when he had won her favours with a dead dog.

For long moments they examined one another. To have fallen so low shamed him thoroughly and his instinct was to pretend he did not know her. But he had been brought up with fastidious manners and nodded respectfully as he might to any lady.

'Hello,' he said. 'A pleasure.'

'Hiya.'

Both glanced sideways. She played with her long hair. He suspected – perhaps wishful thinking – her eyes showed concern.

'I never expected to meet you like this,' he said, apologetically. 'A temporary reverse, I assure you.'

He wondered if his talk was too fancy for her taste. What did he know of the girl, after all? That she had excited him. That she'd reciprocated a hungry passion. It wasn't much.

'Aye,' she said.

Both became aware Gil was interested.

Michael waved her close. His breath must smell vile. 'Please, will you help me?' he murmured in her ear. 'Please let me say how you can help me.'

'I'll tell on 'ee, Pilgrim!' warned Gil. 'No whis'prin'!'

The girl – whose name he had never learned – bent her ear to his mouth. The scent of her hair stirred him.

Whatever Michael said, Gil never heard, for a toot of trumpet announced the arrival of New Hull's lord from his makeshift castle. The ceremony was to begin.

The girl stepped away from Michael. Reaching out, she touched the **F** on his cheek.

'P'raps I'll help,' she whispered, so close he felt the warmth of her breath on his cheek. 'First, you must tell me your name. And your home, so I'll know where to find you.'

As soon as he uttered the words, she vanished into the swelling crowd.

THE MORTIFIED MEN

Gil flapped his bony hands with excitement.

'Tha'll see, Pilgrim! Tha'll see it now! Even that pilchard t'Maister means business for this one!'

'Why exactly are you chained to this cart?' asked Michael, and not for the first time. On each occasion, Gil had uttered curses in reply. Now he said, 'Cos I tried to become t'Maister! Lucky for you I'm not. I'd show *you* a whipping, Pilgrim, one you'd never forget.'

Michael had witnessed a few desultory scourgings over the last week in isolated hamlets and villages. None had involved more than a few of the floggers. Brutal rites aimed at aweing ignorant peasants rather than supplicating the City. This coming ceremony was intended to display the floggers' full power.

A fair had gathered in the hazy afternoon, folk walking or riding in carts from all over the district: even from across the Humber, its far shore littered with flooded factories and oil refineries, Lincolnshire folk arriving in flat-bottomed trading boats.

The enormous twin towers of the suspension bridge dwarfed the crowd; concrete titan legs embedded deep in the river mud. The section of bridge between them may have collapsed, forming a tangle of steel and concrete at low tide, but the enormous supporting towers stood firm. These monuments inspired the floggers' faith that afternoon: t'Maister had promised much blood would be shed in exchange for a miraculous favour from the City.

First, the cowled figures formed a circle of a hundred. As Michael watched from the handcart, Gil grew frantic beside him, moaning, 'It in't fair, I tell thee! I should be among 'em! I should be t'Maister!'

'Shut up!' muttered Michael, scanning the crowd for the girl from Scarborough. No sign of her. Perhaps she'd thought better of helping him.

For a long while, the circle of penitents faced inward, faces hidden beneath their cowls. Then t'Maister strode round the outside of the circle, swishing a three-tailed scourge attached to a wooden handle. Gil might claim the floggers' whips merely tickled, but t'Maister's looked painful enough. Knots had been tied at the end of the tails, studded with small pieces of flint.

As he paced the circle, t'Maister struck his followers' backs with a resounding thwack. Anyone who flinched got an extra blow. Gradually the crowd's mood changed from amusement to intense silence. At last t'Maister's restless pacing ceased.

Raising his hands to the clouds he cast back his hood, intoning a prayer Michael was glad his grandfather and brother could not hear, a perverted mockery of their Lord's Prayer:

> *Our City that art Heaven,*
> *Right feared be thy name.*
> *Thy kingdom's come and we obey.*
> *Punish any man that don't worship thee,*
> *Give 'em plague and daily woes,*
> *Make 'em starve that break thy laws*
> *And deliver us from drones.*
> *For thou art the power and glory.*
> *Drink our blood forever and ever,*
> *Eat our flesh as thy daily bread.*
> *Amen! And so say all of us!*

Gil mouthed the words as they were recited, glazed eyes staring south towards the City of Albion. A mindless exultation was forming in the weedy little man, lending him power and purpose.

'Oh, great City!' appealed t'Maister. 'Oh, Sons of the Gods! In return for the blood we shed for you, bless the harvests of the folk gathered to worship you today! Mend the great bridge over the river, we pray!'

At this, the floggers made the sign of a **C** over their hearts, calling out special entreaties. To Michael's infinite disgust many in the crowd followed suit. Could they not see, here of all places, before the remnants of an engineering marvel that once mastered a mighty force of nature, how human beings were better than this? Better than slaves to the City? That given a chance they could mend all the bridges that were broken.

Beside him, Gil's eyes rolled. In his fervour, he twitched and pinched himself.

The penitents stripped off their robes to expose meagre, naked bodies, hurling the tatty clothes into the centre of the circle. Four of the women, their dugs hanging like the small, pigskin bagpipes they played, set off a wail akin to screeching souls in hell.

Michael watched the circle of floggers rotate clockwise, chanting their version of the Lord's Prayer. Scourges and whips beat bare backs.

'Hear us!' bellowed t'Maister, thrashing his own back and staring ecstatically in the direction of the City. 'Drink our blood! Eat the bread of our flesh! Save us from plague!'

Thin, bloody lines were appearing on a few backs where skin had broken. Gil was right. They meant business this time. Gil himself pummelled his chest with bony fists, longing for a proper scourge.

Many in the crowd wept or cried out, their words drowned by the blaring, ceaseless bagpipes. A few turned away, frowning. Some rushed forward to lick droplets of lucky blood that had dripped onto the trampled grass. A few rubbed rags on the flog-gers' bloody wounds, daring their lash to gather a precious elixir for anointing the sick or doorposts to deter devils and witches.

At this climax, when all eyes were on the frenzied whipping, Michael felt a sharp poke in his side. He turned to find the girl from Scarborough beside him. She dropped something solid at Michael's feet. A flash of hazel eyes met his. A brush of long hair. Then she had gone.

Michael knelt as though in supplication to the City, dis-creetly sliding the object into his ankle length boot. No one noticed, least of all Gil, who had taken to banging his forehead against the handcart.

The object felt cold, lumpy against Michael's ankle. It was a short, sharp farrier's knife with a bone handle, the kind used for prying obstinate stones from a horse's hoof. Perfect for what he had in mind.

CUTTING LOOSE

As darkness gathered, the pious ceremony beside the bridge turned to feasting. Elation and relief – along with ale, poteen, cider – set the assembled folk ring-dancing. A young pig roasted on a spit and wooden bowls of vegetable stew were passed round. Michael was grateful for a portion. He would need all his strength that night.

A flogger slipped Gil a blue, sugar-coated pill which he gulped triumphantly.

'See that, Pilgrim!' he chortled. 'I got me a sweetie!' He leered in the dancing firelight. 'Enjoy tonight, Pilgrim! Tha'll get yours soon enough.'

Gil lapsed into a stupor, one shared by most of the exhausted penitents. Many lay face down for the cool night air to dry their weeping wounds. Extra sweeties had been issued to dull the pain.

Towards midnight the crowd of locals drifted away. Michael had hoped the girl from Scarborough would approach him: he wished to thank her properly and learn her name. But she did not show herself. Perhaps she judged it too dangerous.

Michael watched closely as t'Maister retired to his tent with a teenage boy. A sea-breeze picked up, agitating trees into long rustles and whispers. Leaves fluttered down.

Silence settled on the camp apart from snores and whimpered dreams. It surprised Michael no guard was set. Perhaps the floggers believed a grateful City protected them. He leant over Gil, who was grunting rhythmically in his sleep.

Hey!' he whispered. 'You awake?'

The grunting became a contented sigh. Michael did not care to speculate what murky pleasures inhabited Gil's slumbering brain.

Michael knew it was prudent to eliminate the little man while he slept; the thought had tormented him while he made his plans. If the disgraced flogger woke to find his fellow slave gone, the alarm would be raised instantly. A simple procedure to take the sharp knife and stick it into his weedy heart. Somehow Michael could not.

With the tip of the farrier's knife, he worked at the padlock securing his manacles, a crude lock with a sizable lever hidden in the mechanism. Gently, gently he waggled the knife tip. The girl from Scarborough had chosen the tool well. *Click.* The hasp of the padlock gave a hair's breadth. More patient waggling, another click. This time the manacle opened.

He was free of the hated handcart! Michael turned to discover Gil staring up at him, mouth agape, gathering breath before he raised the alarm. Clamping his hand over the little man's mouth, Michael slammed the bottom of the knife's bone handle onto his forehead. Once. Twice. Gil twitched. Mewed. Sagged. Went very still.

Now Michael was gasping. *Stupid fucker,* he moaned inwardly, *why did you have to wake up?* Shock and misery wasted precious minutes as he stared at the corpse. Another murder, would it ever stop? No point lamenting Gil he told himself as though waking from a bad dream, every moment threatened discovery.

Stripping the dead flogger of his hooded robe, Michael pulled it over his clothes. Fresh, warm blood from Gil's forehead made the cowl sticky. *Stupid fucker*, his feverish mind repeated, and Michael knew he meant himself.

In the Crusades, he had learned that killing one man makes the next easier. Perhaps that was why he took up an iron hammer used to mend the handcart's wheels. With a face concealed by Gil's cowl, he walked straight over to t'Maister's tent. That charlatan must not be allowed to steal his sword.

Michael prayed the sweetie-stuffed Maister slept deeply. For both their sakes.

No one called out as he stepped around prone bodies, his dark figure lit dimly by the embers of dying campfires. Don't fear, he assured himself, don't fear. He was just a loyal flogger after somewhere to piss.

Outside t'Maister's tent he listened. A snuffle within sounded like sleep. The entrance flap was untied and stirred in the wind. Hammer in one hand, knife in the other, Michael ducked inside.

He feared two sleeping bodies in there – for t'Maister had taken a boy to bed with him – but Michael's luck had changed. Whatever they'd got up to was over. No sign of the lad, just a single white body half-covered by acrid blankets.

Creeping closer, he saw a dull glint of teeth as t'Maister's breath whinnied. Michael's eyes adjusted to the dark. Then he panicked. Surely, the man was waking, just like Gil had! Without pausing to think he smacked the hammer square on t'Maister's forehead. He stuffed his sleeve into the open mouth so it could not call for help. Prepared to use the knife. But there was no struggle, the hammer blow had finished the job. *Stupid fucker*, his soul moaned.

With shaking hands, Michael produced a treasure the floggers had failed to discover. Taking out his lighter, he spun the flint wheel. Its dim light revealed t'Maister's corpse staring into space, mouth hanging open stupidly, and there, on top of a wooden chest, his sword, bandolier and shotgun.

Gathering his possessions took an eternity; longer still to snatch up a sack and shove in a blanket, loaf of bread and bottle. He killed the lighter. No shouts of alarm. His nose wrinkled. The tent stank of the dead man's dried sweat.

Gingerly, sword in hand, he opened the flap. A dozen floggers slept soundly round a nearby fire. Once through them, he could escape into the night. Only then did Michael realise he had lingered in the tent too long.

On the far side of the camp, several very awake floggers were crowded round the handcart, talking to something pale. Gil! The blows to his forehead had not killed him after all.

Michael did not hesitate. He stepped out of the small tent and hurried in the opposite direction to the handcart. A voice cried out in protest as he trod on an arm. Then he was free of the camp and masked by deep shadow, crawling up the four-lane road-ramp and onto the bridge proper, concealed by the rusty hulks of lorries and cars.

Even as he scurried, angry bellowing rose from the flogger's encampment. A flight of ancient concrete steps led down to the muddy shore where he vanished into scrub and undergrowth and friendly darkness.

ΤΣΠ

SOME KIND OF GAME

Mhairi's recovery proved rapid – suspiciously so. Within a day of Bertrand's visit, she rose from her bed, impatient to escape quarantine. The hermetically sealed door hissed; Helen hurried in.

'Look at you!' she cried, embracing her sister. 'The picture of health!'

A claim belied by arms and legs thin as famine, a sallow complexion and pinched face.

'Alive at least,' said Mhairi, 'thanks to you.'

'Not me. Bertrand arranged the airbulance, everything really.'

Dr Macdonald sat stiffly on the hospital bed. She peered out the window at the towering statue of the double helix.

'You should assume he has *motives*,' she warned, 'though I'll try not to offend him by appearing ungracious. What worries me is the price he will demand from you, Helen.'

'Never mind that.'

Helen flapped a hand as though at a troublesome fly.

'Bertrand is always playing some kind of game,' said Mhairi.

'My, you *have* recovered!'

It seemed likely their conversation was being monitored. She would hate Bertrand to feel insulted after his generosity.

'I'm very grateful to him,' Helen said, warmly. 'As I'm sure you are.'

Mhairi watched her intently. A sly note entered her voice. 'What should puzzle us all,' she said, 'is why he rescinded my banishment. Now *that* must have taken some string-pulling. Has he mentioned … anything to you? No? I just wondered. All the more strange then.'

'Perhaps he's changed his mind about you,' said Helen. 'We all change.'

Both knew the last thing Bertrand appreciated was change.

The next afternoon Mhairi insisted they go for a walk in the sunshine. Nothing could have been more welcome after weeks trapped indoors.

Still feeble, Mhairi moved slowly, her arm looped through Helen's. Yet her sharp eyes examined each face they passed. Helen got the impression she expected to meet someone she knew or was hoping to. Not unlikely, even though three decades had elapsed since her banishment to Baytown for denouncing the Beautiful Life. And Mhairi was conspicuous: the sheer fact of her withered skin and grey hair caused shudders of disgust among some of the strollers.

If not for her evidently Beautiful companion and protector, it was probable a security squad would have been summoned. But Helen was recognised by nearly every Beautiful they passed, many of whom bowed or curtsied. To be the official paramour of Bertrand Du Guesclin was no small thing in the goldfish bowl of the Five Cities.

'Oh, look!' said Helen. 'They've finished it.'

It was a three-sided pyramid rising a precise one hundred and forty-four metres, an allusion to the City's immutable population. The towering monument celebrated the ultimate sacrifice possible for a Beautiful. During the Crusades, three Beautifuls from Albion had perished in the campaign of Locust culling, largely due to equipment malfunctions. Their individual heroism was celebrated on each side of the glass pyramid, holograms of their deeds and smiling faces playing day and night.

Mhairi and Helen craned their necks to observe the apex on which a pigeon perched.

'I take it there is no monument to the people they slaughtered,' said Mhairi, loudly.

'One must not say that here,' whispered Helen, 'even if one thinks it. Besides, would you want hordes of settlers migrating into Europa?'

'Yes, actually I would,' said Mhairi, 'There's plenty of room. Their genes could mingle with the other people who survived the epidemics, and all would be stronger for it.'

Still, Helen looked round nervously. 'I do feel sorry for the poor people caught up in that dreadful Crusade,' she said. 'Take Michael Pilgrim and his friends...'

She stopped in confusion. Since returning to the City, she had barely remembered him or the other Baytown folk. Her apparent indifference came as an unwelcome surprise. Yet she reasoned one can forget even the oldest friends. And although she did count him a good friend, he could be no more than that. If anything, she missed Averil Pilgrim's guileless enthusiasm more. The girl had fanned the few lingering embers of Helen's own youthfulness when they worked together in the Museum. And Baytown's fields and woods would be donning their autumn colours and birds gathering before their long journeys south. The sea and beach would smell salty with fogs, and to walk on the shingle as it crunched beneath her boots would be to feel especially alive and free. Helen set the thought aside. For Mhairi's sake, she must give up all longings for Baytown.

'I'm thirsty,' declared the older woman. 'Let's go to a café I've heard about.'

'Oh?' said Helen in surprise. 'Who told you about it?'

'One of the nurses,' said Mhairi. 'Or a doctor. I forget. It's near this monument. And I have a question for you.'

They soon found the place and sat on the terrace amidst a few languid couples. As before, Helen and Mhairi attracted plenty of notice.

'Do you intend to remain in the City?' asked Mhairi once the service-drone had taken their order.

Helen saw no point pretending, her sister was always shrewd. 'I believe the moment I called upon Bertrand's assistance, my "little rebellion", as he no doubt considers it, came to an abrupt end. I suppose I have no choice but to stay now.'

Mhairi sipped her coffee. The first she had tasted in a long while. 'Even if my banishment is forgotten, I still mean to return home as soon as I'm stronger,' she said. 'And home means Baytown. Do you know, I wouldn't be surprised if our benefactor anticipated me wanting to leave Albion, and might even have dreamed up a scheme for turning it to his advantage. Even this conversation may be part of his game.' Again she examined Helen with a peculiar intensity, as though trying to read her thoughts.

'He foresees a lot of things,' conceded Helen. The prospect of staying in Albion seemed doubly lonely without Mhairi.

Absorbed by this thought, Helen barely noticed a stranger in the overalls of a technician bump into her sister. Something tiny and white caught the corner of her eye. A tightly folded square of paper! Then the man had gone. Mhairi sniffed, a fierce gleam in her eyes.

Helen remained frozen. Her sister pocketed the paper so awkwardly half the café must have noticed.

No one leapt up to arrest them. Indeed, there was only a tiny police force in the City. Dissent and crime were as rare as ugly Beautifuls, sure routes to banishment and a painfully brief lifetime back among the ur-humans.

Mhairi's smile broadened. 'Lovely coffee!' she said. 'Almost worth catching the plague to taste it again. *N'est-ce-pas?*'

Helen recalled her sister's comment about games and wondered who exactly was playing whom – and why.

WHY

'What are you doing?' hissed Helen, as they left the café. She steered Mhairi to a small park where a fountain bubbled, lit from below by alternating colours of the spectrum. No one around to overhear, at least, no one visible.

'I'm enjoying myself for a change,' replied Mhairi. 'Do you disapprove?'

'You know what I mean! That man in the technician's uniform passed you a note. And without a trace of subtlety. Do you imagine it wasn't noticed by the people around us?'

Mhairi settled on a bench near the multi-coloured fountain. 'Perhaps that was the idea.'

Helen perched nervously beside her.

'Do you want to read the note he gave me?' asked Mhairi.

Unfolding it took a moment: on both sides, the paper was blank, not a trace of writing.

'Is there a message hidden here?' asked Helen.

'No. It contains no secret message.'

'Then I don't understand. Why?'

'Ah, why,' said Mhairi, settling back. 'If you listen, I will tell you. I think we may safely assume we are not monitored here. At least by the people I fear. Up to now, they must have no idea I might trouble them. Let's take the risk anyway.'

Ten minutes later Helen sat in silence.

'So you see,' concluded Mhairi, 'if I am caught, Bertrand will disclaim any knowledge of my 'plot'. He has made that clear. Besides, who would think to blame him? I, on the other hand, am a known troublemaker. The worst he could be accused of is naivety in curing me and allowing me back into the City. I'm sure you'll agree his plan is perfect. He gets what he wants, including you.' Mhairi's voice hardened. 'And so do I.'

Helen struggled to comprehend.

'Can this laboratory you speak of really be so bad?' she said. 'How is it different from other facilities experimenting with the Beautiful Life?'

'That is a good question.' Mhairi looked into the bubbling fountain. 'I was foolish not to foresee this day. Bertrand also blames himself. But it is logical, perfectly logical. Why stop at renewing existing cells and organs to ensure one is forever young? Why limit yourself when the means exists to design new life forms, new creatures? To be, in effect, like God on the day of creation.'

'I still don't see how they benefit. Not properly,' said Helen. 'Haven't they got everything they could ever want?'

Her confusion was genuine. That something so wrong lurked in the shiny, cleansed City of Albion. The Beautiful Life itself seemed natural as a plump goose compared to the things her sister feared.

'I'm going with you,' said Helen.

Mhairi smiled and took her hand. 'Thank you, but no. It will be dangerous. As for myself, I near the end of my time. You have years ahead, probably centuries.'

'I am going with you!' cried Helen.

Now Mhairi grew stern. 'Didn't you hear? Even Bertrand is afraid to move openly against these people. They are without scruples of any meaningful kind. They make Bertrand look benign. Yes, I never expected to say it, but Bertrand is a beacon of integrity compared to them. If they capture us, they have the power to inflict worse punishments than death.' She shivered. 'I have met one person they modified. A fine, brave man made to appear loathsome as a kind of cruel joke.'

'That decides it,' said Helen, 'you need me.'

The coloured lights in the fountain pulsed. A flock of birds passed overhead, migrating south, driven by autumn. A scattering of dark dots across a pale sky.

MEANS TO AN END

They walked the streets until dusk. Mhairi judged it unwise to return to the quarantine rooms. Few people passed: the City's scale dwarfed its limited population. Drones took humanity's place – whirring on wheels or caterpillar tracks or mechanical legs – attentive slaves no one noticed. Except it seemed they were about to become obsolete, down to the last circuit and bolt.

Lamps glowed bright even before the sun faded. Mhairi led Helen to a block of apartments for humble technicians rather than Beautifuls. At the entrance she spoke a code. Glass doors swished.

'How did you know that code?' asked Helen. The answer was obvious: Bertrand. He must have contacted Mhairi while Helen slept in the room next door, persuading her to take risks he dared not countenance himself. Mhairi had always been reckless. Helen brightened at the thought she could protect her sister at long last.

They took a lift to the tenth floor, meeting no one. It opened onto a spotlessly clean corridor. Plastic doors lined both walls at exactly regular intervals. Mhairi read the apartment numbers then chose a door. Another code; its lock clicked open.

The apartment beyond consisted of a large rectangle with minimal furniture. Arches led to a kitchenette and bathroom. Helen slumped on a sofa; she was suddenly irritable, hungry.

'It's not too late to go back,' said Mhairi, watching her.

Since their conversation at the coloured fountain, neither had said much.

Helen flapped a hand at the room. 'Do you remember how sumptuous my quarters were when I lived with Bertrand? A palace, I suppose you'd call it. And the irony? All those rooms and gardens made me claustrophobic. His rambling palace became a choked forest that stretched on and on without a clearing in sight.' She sighed. 'Yet I have no doubt the people fretting and pacing in apartments like this would be utterly envious of my dark forest.'

Mhairi sat heavily on the bed. 'As Charlie Gudwallah might put it,' she said, rubbing her back and putting on a broad, Baytown accent, '*shame's everywhere. As, my dear, is irony.* I'd give a lot to be in the Puzzle Well Inn right now.'

They found Bertrand's gifts in an empty wardrobe. Food bars and a heavy rucksack containing a metal box with security-pad;

a sheet of paper with more codes; a mini-screen; a stubby handgun; a key card for a dronecar.

'Everything we need for a party!' said Helen.

'Just the means to an end,' said Mhairi, gravely. 'Probably our own.'

GHOSTS IN THE NIGHT

It did not take long to cross the City's circular core and enter its outer ring of factories, warehouses, agri-businesses. Night brought thick clouds, steady rain. Mhairi and Helen sat in the front seats of the driverless car, peering through oily trickles on the windscreen: the functional buildings around them lurid and distorted beneath the street lamps.

Mhairi was consulting the mini-screen Bertrand had given them, checking how the little handgun worked.

'I'd imagine you have to point it and pull the trigger,' said Helen, helpfully.

Still, Mhairi had nothing to say. She was all business.

'Are we nearly there?' asked Helen.

'Yes.' Mhairi turned her attention to the heavy steel case and security-pad.

The drone car halted at a level crossing. Warning lights pulsed on the monorail track. On either side of the road, behind high electric fences, were holding areas for livestock: sheep to the left, shepherded by a vigilant drone. Blue voltage flashed as a wayward ram broke from the flock. It leapt back to join the others. On the other side of the road, clearly visible through the wire fence, more drones were selecting cattle for slaughter: scanning, discharging tasers, scooping up the inert bodies. A desperate lowing and mooing rose from the distressed herd in their concrete pens.

Mhairi turned to Helen. 'It could as easily be humans as cattle,' she said. 'We must succeed tonight, you know.'

'I'm afraid,' whispered Helen.

'Good. You should be.'

An unmanned freight train rolled past and the warning lights faded.

Their car resumed its journey, soon arriving at a large, unfenced expanse of tarmac and concrete between long rectangular sheds – forcing chambers for vegetables and organic matter.

'Stay on the road,' Mhairi instructed the car. 'In that parking space.'

She muttered a complex sequence of numbers and words into the screen and waited. Colours and symbols flashed. Nothing moved among the scattered buildings, not even a drone. No technicians would be working this late. A sigh of satisfaction escaped Mhairi.

'Bertrand's codes worked,' she said. 'The security systems – while apparently functioning as normal – have developed a blindness towards us. We are invisible to them. We can come and go like ghosts in the night.'

A troubling analogy, thought Helen, for ghosts are already dead.

CODES

They stepped out of the car. Rain fell constantly, touching the night with the noise of waters.

'Let's go,' said Mhairi, consulting the screen.

Helen noticed the pistol butt jutting from her pocket. Overhead a large airliner rumbled as it approached a docking bay on the far side of the City, fresh in from Mitopia in the dark heart of Europa or perhaps Han City off the coast of China; maybe from Mughalia in the lush island once called Sri Lanka or Neo Rio on the Brazilian coast. With such small populations little trade in raw materials was necessary between the cities of the world; nor was there the slightest competition for resources. Indeed, the whole human population – if one counted Beautifuls alone as human, and they did – numbered a precise half a million bodies, no more, no less, spread across every continent.

The two women hurried to a long hangar painted with bio-hazard warnings. Reaching into the rucksack containing the steel box, Mhairi produced two transparent breathing masks.

'Put the mask on,' she said. 'We'll only need them in this shed.'

'What are they growing in there?' asked Helen.

'Life. What else can you grow?'

Mhairi activated her mini-screen to enter a code, and two high metal doors slid open to reveal an echoing space illuminated by banks of UV panels. Specks drifted out into the night air. The shed was hazy with a cloud of mushroom spores like stars or dust motes circling in space. Beneath the UV panels were racks of grotesquely swollen fungi: mottled toadstools a metre across or simply dough-like mounds, grey, cancerous.

'They process it into animal feed,' explained Mhairi. 'You need not look so disturbed, it's quite harmless. We need masks because the spores stick in one's throat.'

'I see,' said Helen. It was her job to carry the heavy rucksack.

Mhairi studied the screen. 'This way.'

As they left the entrance, the heavy steel doors slid shut. It felt like a long walk between the glowing banks of fungi trays. A drone emptied a heap of fungi into a hopper, but the machine paid no attention as they passed.

'We near the moment of truth,' said Mhairi. 'If Bertrand's codes fail us now…' She hesitated. 'Well, I wouldn't be surprised if we ended up as fertiliser for the fungi.'

They approached a large set of reinforced plasti-steel doors. Helen noticed a dozen camera eyes scanning. She gripped her sister's arm.

'Keep going,' muttered Mhairi.

She held up the screen and approached a security-pad beside the blast doors. Lights flashed. Suddenly – so that Helen cried out in fear – the doors swished open. A ramp descended into darkness.

'Perhaps you should wait here,' said Mhairi. 'Down there… Well, I'm expecting a few horrors.'

'No,' whispered Helen, 'let us go together.'

They started down the ramp.

'Wait!' Mhairi's voice rang out in warning.

Before them were two security drones: more like fully-armed battle drones to Helen's eyes. Each eight feet tall on limb-like caterpillar tracks. Multiple arms jutted to carry weapons: cannons, rocket launchers, napalm throwers. Pincers for all manner of grisly work.

The drones activated. Green lights pulsed on their plasti-steel bodies.

'Don't move,' said Mhairi, raising the mini-screen.

Helen's flesh prickled. They were being scanned. And very thoroughly. Instinct urged her to turn and flee. For long moments the women waited. Helen felt Mhairi relax slowly beside her.

'They see us but don't see us,' she said. 'I think it's safe to step around them.'

'Are you sure?' Helen's squeak echoed in the concrete tunnel.

'No.'

Mhairi took her hand, leading Helen to a narrow gap between the drones. One grab with a pincer and they would be snipped like cotton threads. They sidled through. Still, the drones scanned them.

'Calmly now,' said Mhairi.

They passed down to the lowest level, a hundred metres beneath the earth's surface. Neither could know that up above, a fancy, gilded aircar was circling the cloudy shed where fungi swelled, popped and sowed clouds of noxious spores.

THE FINAL CODE

Several more doors and an airlock obeyed Bertrand's deactivating codes. Another pair of security drones confronted them: these were armed with grabbing arms and net guns in addition to pincers. As before, the terrible machines scanned and tolerated their existence. Helen could not help dreading a sudden change of mind.

The drones guarded a final pair of doors. Biohazard warning symbols were everywhere.

'Do you wish to stay outside?' asked Mhairi, softly. 'I think you should.'

Helen shivered. 'Please don't leave me alone with those soulless monsters.' She nodded at the drones.

'You realise only the most powerful people could assemble weapons like those for private use,' said Mhairi. 'What lies beyond those doors is sure to be impressive. Why else guard one's treasure with fierce dragons?'

'Will there be people in there?' asked Helen.

Mhairi shrugged. Pulled out the handgun. 'We've been assured otherwise. And Bertrand has been proved right so far. His sources of information are clearly impeccable.'

'Then why does he need us,' asked Helen, 'if he already knows everything?'

'He needs someone to blame if his plan goes wrong.'

The hurt on Helen's face made her sister smile sadly. 'Don't worry, it's me he means to sacrifice, not you. I'm sure he would be appalled to learn you've come along. Let's finish this and be gone.'

'I wish we'd never come here,' moaned Helen.

'All my life had been leading me to this end,' said Mhairi.

Presenting the screen activated a final code. Doors hissed open, releasing a sterile aroma.

HORRORS

Mhairi led the way inside. They found themselves at the rim of a wide, circular hall lit by feeble ceiling lights. As they entered, light-strips brightened to reveal open-plan workstations and meeting spaces; banks of consoles and a relaxation area. In the centre, a slowly revolving sculpture of the double helix cast in pure gold, three feet high, shining as light caught blue gems. Helen remembered the Jewel revolving in the Baytown Museum, the Jewel designed as a talisman against mortality.

'Are we...'

Mhairi silenced her with a finger raised to her lips. She edged into the large room, pistol half-raised. Her eyes darted. Nothing moved. Not even the drones stationed in alcoves set into the walls. Pleasant, polite drones: the kind without weapons to tear off your arms.

'I want to see what these people are up to,' said Mhairi.

They approached a sealed door. A small window revealed a corridor beyond. Mhairi scanned the security-pad with her screen. Codes glowed. With a pneumatic sigh, the door slid open.

At first, Helen wondered if they had entered a storage area. Lights activated as they stepped into the corridor, revealing yet more doors, a dozen on each side like the entrances to cells, each door flanked by windows and consoles.

'What is this place?' Helen whispered.

'Eden,' said Mhairi. 'Or a minor Big Bang. Or Hell. Maybe even Heaven. Take your pick.'

Still, Helen did not understand. Later she would marvel at her innocence. Hadn't her life revolved around the double helix and its grotesque possibilities for decades when she lived with Bertrand? This corridor of doors – like a passageway from a dream – had always been waiting.

Mhairi stepped over to a grey window. Touched a button. The glass cleared, revealing a curious sight. Helen blinked in puzzlement then cried out. Even Mhairi flinched.

The creature within sat forlornly at a low table. Its face had been sculpted to lack expression. It had been granted two spindly legs and two large, attentive brown eyes. Four arms ended in long-fingered hands. Quite naked, it lacked genitalia. Just an anus for faeces and a stumpy gland to discharge urine. As they watched, its fingers moved with astonishing speed, unpicking threads and fibres from a short strip of rough, oakum rope. It paused. Again the fingers whirled, fast as a concert pianist's. Within moments it had rewoven a section of the long fibres.

Mhairi's face grew cold. 'Such dexterity could be useful in some contexts,' she conceded.

'But why?' said Helen, unable to take her eyes off the creature.

'It is an alternative to a drone,' said Mhairi. 'Is that so hard to understand? Let's look at another.'

She went to the next cell. Activated the window. Both stepped back instinctively.

The cell inside was flooded. Three human-shaped creatures swam leisurely. Helen's hand flew to her mouth. The creatures – she couldn't call them people – possessed gills and flippers where their feet should be. One swam to the window and stared out. What did it see? Something strange, Helen guessed, much as she did. Something unnatural. It had been created to be its own version of natural. She reached out. The window went grey.

'I see now,' she said.

But Mhairi wanted more. Marching up the corridor, she activated windows. In each room bizarre humanoid creatures were revealed: pigmies designed to move on four legs, clearly counterparts to pet dogs; others with swollen glands to produce essences for harvest; some heavily muscular with scaly skin and hands, useful as warriors; others, if the size of their penises were a guide, for sexual purposes. All stared out at Mhairi and Helen with wide, inscrutable eyes. Stupid eyes. Clearly, intelligence was not deemed desirable. But Helen caught glints in some of the faces. Thoughts behind the immobile skin. Once these creatures started to learn – as all life learns, must learn if it is to endure the world of change around it – who could guess how they would evolve beyond their creators' intentions? Perhaps those blank faces would develop muscles to convey thoughts and feelings. The tongues in those mouths shape words of their own creation.

'These appear to be some of the more finished products,' said Mhairi. 'I imagine there have been plenty that didn't work out.' She licked her lips. 'We may assume those unfortunates fed the fungi above. Recycling, you might call it.'

Helen realised she was shaking. 'I must see more!' she cried. 'Are we to set them free? Is that why we came?'

'In a sense,' said Mhairi. 'Let's get it over with.'

They returned to the wide, circular room and Mhairi descended a flight of steps to a half-concealed workstation in a recess. A mini-fusion generator hummed nearby.

'The rucksack,' she commanded, brusquely.

Helen realised it had been on her back all along. Now she felt its weight. Slipping her arms from the straps, she passed the bag over. Mhairi took out the steel box and console. Again she muttered complex codes. A long warning bleep. In the silence that followed a red light flashed rhythmically then faded.

'It's done,' she said. 'Help me, Helen.'

They hid the box behind the fusion generator where even a close scan would be confused by the energies it produced.

'Three hours,' said Mhairi. 'Enough to get away if we move quickly.'

'Is it what I think?' asked Helen.

'If you're thinking of a small fusion bomb, yes.'

They headed back for the entrance. The instant Helen lifted the screen to activate the security-pad, its high doors slid open.

APHERCOTROPISM

They gaped at one another. If the stubby gun hadn't already been in Mhairi's hand, all might have gone differently. But she jerked it up. Commanded in a firm voice.

'Step forward. Don't give me a reason to use this.'

The couple framed by the doorway hesitated. Mhairi took careful aim.

'No need for that,' spluttered the young man in a shiny lilac suit. He had obviously just left a party. His shoes were long and curled raffishly at the toes, his sash a glowing purple. In an affectation of individuality, his eyes were different colours: one brown, the other aquamarine. Helen recognised him at once. Indeed, he had sometimes dined at Bertrand's mansion: Guy de Prie-Dieu, as he styled himself, once just plain Dr Guy Price. A geneticist like Bertrand and a co-founder of the City.

Wearing a silk ball gown worthy of Cinderella, Eloise Du Guesclin leant on his arm.

'Good lord!' said Mhairi. 'If it isn't Ellie Gover, too! Do come in.'

She waved the handgun, and the splendid couple entered. Guy de Prie-Dieu was visibly nervous – understandably: he had demanded Mhairi's execution when she protested against the way primitives were being persecuted all those years ago. Only Bertrand's personal intervention had reduced her sentence to exile. Eloise, however, seemed blearily jaunty.

'I can smell Bertrand behind this,' she said, ignoring Mhairi and addressing Guy. 'It will be interesting to find out why he sent them here. To spy, I imagine.' Her eyes were glazed, pupils dilated. She spoke with too much vivacity, like a child excited by its game of make-believe. Eloise peered at Helen. 'I'm surprised he sent *you*. He was always so damned protective of you.'

'Bertrand doesn't know I'm here,' said Helen.

Eloise shrugged. '*C'est pas grave*, in any case. Now do run along!' She tittered. 'Back to those savages you find so adorable.'

'Actually, I have a few questions first,' said Mhairi. She levelled the pistol at Guy, who flinched. 'An impressive concoction of body parts you've assembled here, Dr Price. What do you plan to do with them?'

The scientist flexed his fingers.

'Oh, do tell,' drawled Eloise. 'It hardly matters now. What was that word you taught me, Guy? Apher … cot…'

'Aphercotropism,' he said.

'It means,' said Eloise, reciting like a clever child, 'the response an organism makes as it grows to overcome obstacles in its way. *There!*' She flounced triumphantly. 'I remembered!'

Mhairi glowered. 'Are those poor creatures your *response* to obstacles?'

'One of them,' said Eloise.

'Don't you think they have souls?' asked Helen. 'Feelings?'

Questions dismissed with the wave of an elegantly be-ringed hand. 'One might ask the same question of sheep,' said Eloise. 'Do you know, Helen, when I fought in the Crusades I first imagined this phase of the Beautiful Life. It was so dull out there, one had far too much time to think. Of course, the drones work well enough, we all know that. But I found *living* servants so much more fun. And I mean *fun*, Helen.'

She giggled like a naughty girl.

'I thought to myself then,' continued Eloise, in her high, innocent voice. 'How much more fun my pet primitive would be if he had been designed specially for the purpose. When I mentioned it to Guy here – oh, we do share *tastes*, don't we, darling?'

He smiled thinly in reply.

'Anyway, Guy told me about this astonishing place. He's been working away for years down here.'

Again Eloise giggled. Covered her pert mouth.

'Of course, we'll have to get rid of Bertrand now.' Her eyes widened. '*Tant pis!* He'll never countenance apher ... cot ... Whatever we want to do.'

'Which means what exactly?' asked Mhairi. Her gun still pointed. 'Whatever do you want to do?'

WHATEVER FOREVER

'Isn't it obvious?' gushed Eloise. 'We're on a whole new Crusade! The greatest in all the world's history. To repopulate this land with beings we have perfected. *Creatures* – yes, let's use your word, though I prefer *angels* – able to transport an entire mountain with their bare hands, stone by stone, if that's our whim. And you can be sure we'll design them to be ever so grateful for the life we give them.' Her dilated eyes opened wide. 'Do you know, I've always fancied being worshipped as a goddess.'

'Too late, my love,' said Guy de Prie-Dieu. 'You are my goddess already!'

She simpered winsomely, beaming at him.

Then Helen understood. A startled flood of comprehension. Terrible, terrible boredom had spawned this laboratory. Guy and his chums must have grown the first creature to flatter their own cleverness. Can do, will do. They probably never meant to make another. Then the bug bit. Competition set in between them. Oh, she could guess it all! Knew how the higher Beautifuls thought. One new life form after another, all to make empty days meaningful, to mock nature's limits as teenagers defy strict parents in the name of finding themselves.

So much for the scientists. What of heedless, thoughtless Eloise? That, too, seemed clear. All her life she had been in Bertrand's shadow, the Crusades her attempt to win a name. But so one-sided a conflict brought little glory, and here was her revenge.

Helen saw another reason Eloise referred to the creatures in their cells as angels. Perhaps she saw in them the children she could never have. Down here, in this underground cauldron, she could cook up as many as she wished.

What fun to fill the world with doting slaves! Parading armies, pageants, choirs ten thousand strong to hymn one's name! Aphercotropism to overcome the sameness and predictability of days and years then decades and – why ever not? – centuries then millennia stretching ahead. On and on until there was nothing new to do or feel that had not been done or felt endless times before. Until death itself, hitherto the great enemy, no longer seemed quite as frightening.

Helen shook her head. Not in anger or disgust but sorrow. 'You're as lost as the rest of us,' she said. 'Just as much to be pitied in the end.'

Mhairi was less understanding. Sheer contempt twisted her lined, weathered face.

'I have one question, Dr Guy Price,' she said. 'Where do you get the genetic material to modify? Don't pretend you grew those poor monsters without seeds.'

The smooth-cheeked scientist stirred. Held up a finger.

'Ah, the moot point!' he said. 'Do you know, I'd rather not say.'

'Don't be a silly darling!' Eloise rolled her eyes. 'What difference will it make if she knows? We harvest primitives, stupid! How else? Nice healthy ones. There.'

Guy yawned.

'Enough talk,' he said. He'd always been a man of few words. 'Security!'

Doors slid open. A battle drone rolled into the room, weapons raised. Helen shrieked in horror. Mhairi, however, did not lower the pistol.

'Drop the gun,' said Guy, 'and I'll let your sister go. Otherwise ... Well, you can guess, I'm sure.'

Mhairi glanced sideways at Helen. Her pistol barrel shook. Against such a drone it was a bow and arrow.

'Do I have your word on that?' she said, her voice quavering.

'Why not,' said Guy. 'You mean nothing to me.'

'You promise?'

'I promise.'

Still, Mhairi hesitated. 'Why should I believe you?'

'Because contrary to what you believe, Dr Macdonald, I am a civilised person.'

This argument swayed her. All her life Mhairi had believed in the existence of civilised people. With a crump, the pistol fell to the carpet. Guy smiled at Eloise. He turned to the drone. 'Do kill the fools, for goodness sake!'

The drone swivelled. Aimed stubby barrels at the intruders. Scanned.

'Get rid of them now,' repeated Guy, impatiently.

But the drone detected nothing to kill.

Eloise turned to Guy in surprise. 'What...? Oh, you are a naughty boy! This is one of your little jokes, isn't it?'

Nevertheless, she produced a small handgun from her evening bag, in case the joke turned sour.

A small hard voice interrupted her. It was directed at the drone.

'Kill those two instead!'

The crisp command belonged to Helen Devereux. She pointed at Guy de Prie-Dieu and Eloise Du Guesclin. 'That one and that one.'

Instantly steel arms flicked out: claws seized Guy's neck. His head flew in the air with a gush of blood. Eloise's scream echoed around the cave-like room. *Bang. Bang. Bang.* Shot after shot ricocheted wildly as Eloise discharged her pistol. Then the drone had her gun arm. Pruned it from her body. A further blow caved in Eloise's sculpted face. She crumpled in a heap of flesh and bones.

The drone deactivated. Helen stared at the mangled corpses in horror. She turned to her sister. 'Mhairi, we must...!'

But Mhairi lay on the thick carpet, blood mushrooming from her coat, breath rattling, eyes bulging. Eloise's frantic shots had not been in vain.

Helen rushed to kneel beside her. A thin spray of blood blew out with her sister's last breath. She twitched. Went still forever.

NIGHT RAIN

Rain still fell when Helen stumbled outside. She had left Mhairi's body in the laboratory. In a few hours, it would be turned to ash by the fusion bomb.

She walked with slow, heavy steps to the drone car parked by the road. Her mind numb, gut sickened. Any moment she expected to see Mhairi rushing after her. Not the Mhairi who had grown old while Helen stayed young. Just a little girl who always scraped her knee, whose tears were dried by her big sister. Helen was that big sister. And she had failed to protect her in the end.

The drone car rolled through brightly lit streets. Always the night rain fell. Helen wondered if it fell on Baytown, too, its thirsty fields and muddy streets, ancient becks flowing by circuitous routes into the salt sea. Always the night rain must fall until the world ended. Yet Mhairi would neither see nor hear nor taste nor feel another drop. The night rain's song was her little sister's elegy. And Helen must listen, unloved, alone.

DON'T LEAVE ME

She pushed open the door of the quarantine room. The lights were off, but a yellow glow from the window lay across the carpet. Then she saw him in an armchair, staring out at the enormous sculpture of the double helix.

'Where have you been?' asked Bertrand.

His voice was strange, strained.

'Do you really not know?'

He swivelled the chair to face her.

'I fear you've done a foolish thing, Helen,' he said. 'So foolish I could not anticipate it.'

Helen sat heavily on the bed. She felt drained of hope, defeated. 'Just one foolish thing?' she said. 'There seem to have been many in my life.'

They watched one another in silence.

'Now I am going to do another,' she said.

He leaned forward in the armchair. 'What is that?'

'I am going to pay a debt to Mhairi.'

'Where is she?' His question was brittle. 'I was monitoring her then the signal stopped.'

'You gave her codes and a screen,' said Helen.

'Of course. All purchased at a ridiculous cost. Let me add, she, too, is happy to pay a price.'

'Was happy,' said Helen.

He looked at her sharply.

'She was clutching your screen, Bertrand, when I watched her die.'

The armchair creaked as he rose. Stepped over to the window. His silhouette was framed by the double helix.

'Don't worry,' said Helen, 'the bomb is in place. It will explode in an hour.'

He stiffened. 'Who killed her, Helen?'

'Your sister. She, in turn, was killed by a drone. Those were marvellous codes you provided, Bertrand.'

'Eloise dead? Rubbish! She was truly there?'

'High as a lark! Or a vulture. With her dear friend and lover, Dr Guy de Prie-Dieu, no less. I think you know that.'

'And Guy?'

'Dead, too.'

He came to the bed where she sat and perched beside her. For a long while, both stared out of the window. He stirred and placed his hand on hers.

'I arrived back from Mitopia and hurried straight here,' he said. 'I had a foreboding something had happened to you.'

'Then you were right.'

'And I will make up for it as best I can.'

Helen squeezed his hand. 'How old we've grown, Bertrand. Wouldn't it be wonderful to always start afresh each day? But that can never be, can it?' She cleared her throat. 'I've decided to pay a debt to Mhairi. To the past I should have shared with her.'

'So you say.'

'I've decided to return to the Museum and maintain her library there. And to never come back.'

'Then you shall die there.' His voice was suddenly harsh. 'You shall age rapidly. And die!'

'Yes.'

He wrung her hand. In the quarter-light, she saw tears glisten on his smooth, boyish cheeks, heard him choke.

'Don't leave me,' he whispered. 'I need you, Helen, more than ever since Eloise turned against me … You are the only person on this earth who understands me. Please don't leave me alone.'

She withdrew her trapped hand. Not brusquely, with infinite patience.

'You'll forget me in time, Bertrand. And you have so much time ahead of you.'

He sniffed. 'That's what I fear, Helen. The years alone! It's so hard to love again. Sometimes I grow afraid of the Beautiful Life.'

'Then come with me,' she said. 'With your medical knowledge, think of the good you could do. And the sea is beautiful, Bertrand. We could watch its tides come and go together.'

He laughed. Something of his usual manner returned. Helen knew then she had lost him.

'You don't ask much, do you?' he said, peevishly. 'Just my life. It seems a strange kind of love to want me to die alongside you.'

'It is the only kind we're allowed,' said Helen, 'the best we can hope for.'

Bertrand rose. His assurance was back. More strained than usual but back in control.

'Oh, you'll come begging me to save you,' he said, 'when your face wrinkles like a rotting carpet. Your breasts wither into sagging bags. When your breath disgusts your own mouth. Oh, you'll beg for the Beautiful Life then.'

Helen also rose. She began to pack what few possessions she had brought from Baytown.

'At least deliver me back to the Museum,' she said. 'After that, I shall never ask a single thing of you.'

'Very well, I'll arrange it. It would be best for you to be far away when that bomb goes off, in any case,' he said. 'And I anticipate needing to leave the City for a while myself. But you'll beg for my help in time. You'll plead and plead. And don't think I'll let you live like a spoiled princess among the primitives like I did before. That charade is over. If I'm to be miserable and live with danger, so shall you. You'll see!'

TO BAYTOWN

Bertrand kept his promise. The aircar collected Helen from the roof of the building where she'd been quarantined. As it descended, she sniffed: the rain had stopped. A cool, fresh-scented breeze blew in from the countryside.

Her last vision of the City of Albion as the drone-piloted craft sped north was a dome of light that dwindled and dimmed. England fell away beneath her. She slumped in the padded seat and wept.

Half an hour later the aircar slanted towards the Museum. Though it should be in darkness, Helen was surprised to see pinpricks of fire burning in the overgrown car park. Down swooped the aircraft, revealing a small encampment of tents and picketed horses; the dark figures of men round their campfires.

'Don't land!' she ordered the machine. 'Not here.'

Warning lights flashed in the cockpit. A voice informed her they would be landing shortly. Helen half-rose; repeated her command.

'Not here! Not here, I say!'

But the aircar had instructions that did not include obeying its passenger. With a whine, it touched down outside the Museum entrance. Side-doors rose like a bird lifting its wings.

Helen made a dash: reached the entry-pad of the steel-shuttered building and spoke the code that would deactivate all security systems. The lock bleeped back defiantly. She tried again. The code had been changed! A perverse revenge of Bertrand's. She was Curator of the Baytown Museum no more.

A rough hand hauled her around and as it did so the aircar shot skywards. Helen faced a young man in a dark uniform.

'You're Seth, aren't you?' she said, in relief. 'Seth Pilgrim.'

He whistled in wonder. A dozen men with straggly beards and diverse weapons formed a semi-circle behind the youth.

'Can you take me to your uncle?' she asked. 'Where is Michael? Is he at Hob Hall?'

She needed to tell him what had happened to Mhairi; more urgently, she wanted his protection. For long, uncomfortable moments she felt the men's eyes upon her. Seth Pilgrim seemed about to say something but thought better of it.

'This way, me ladyship, I reckon the Boss would like a word.' He flashed Helen a grin. 'You'll find things changed in Baytown now.' Again he considered his words. 'An' you won't find me Uncle Michael here at all.'

TALE THREE

SUMMER SEEDS, AUTUMN HARVESTS

ΘΠΣ

---◦✧◦---

THE JUSTICE OF PHARAOH JACKO

Charlie Gudwallah shivered in the charnel house of Holy Innocents Church. He was not alone: Mister Priest Man shared his prison, along with a dozen others bold or stupid enough to defy their new king. There was plenty of room for more. The thousands of bones stored in the vaulted chamber had been removed by the prisoners and piled in the graveyard. Skeletons that must have known Charlie's grandparents when they ran the village store before the Great Dying.

Gradually prisoners were taken away, their manacles knocked open by a blacksmith. What fate befell them Charlie never learned. His gaolers, none of them Baytown men, ignored his questions except for an occasional kick or cuff. Once a day, sufficient food to prevent starvation was delivered in a communal basin, along with water. No other comforts came the prisoners' way.

In the end, only Mister Priest Man and Charlie remained. From glimpses of daylight when guards brought their ration, Charlie realised autumn was advancing in Baytown. That the harvest season, always a time of weary labour, must be nearing its end.

'The fields'll be stubble now,' he said to Mister Priest Man, 'and the swallows gathering. Important time for the Puzzle. That's when we collect or barter the bruised apples and pears for cider and brandy. By the barrel-load, mind. Me and the kids go round all the apple trees in what was once people's back gardens. It's amazing what still grows there. And we pick black-berries for jams or wine, buckets and buckets of 'em! Wheat, too, as much as we can afford. "Yon sack of wheat," I tell the missus, "contains enough beer and bread to feed a *multitude*."' Charlie chuckled. 'Fancy words like that always make her flap me with a dishcloth. I'd give a lot to be dodging that wet cloth right now.' He grew silent for a while. 'They better not have touched her, Priest Man,' he said, 'or the kids, bless 'em.'

Mister Priest Man rarely interrupted, and Charlie was glad of that. He'd always loved to talk. After he made it back from the Crusades, talking helped keep at bay memories with a bitter taste.

But all times end and so did their captivity. Charlie and Priest Man were led out into the churchyard and around the building to the porch, where bored-looking men stood guard. The place had been stripped bare and whitewashed. Only a few of the pews were left, altar and crosses all gone, although the carved pulpit for sermons remained, no doubt so the new king could browbeat his subjects.

Pharaoh Jacko sat on a wooden armchair at the end, hard-faced men around him. A few Reivers from up north and plenty of others Charlie didn't recognise. All armed.

No one spoke as the Pharaoh of Baytown inspected his prisoners.

'You've lost weight, fat man,' he told Charlie. 'Not getting enough of your own ale, eh? That might just be 'cos *we're* drinking it.'

His followers chuckled or smiled.

'I never rush to kill a man,' said King Jacko. 'Maybe I'm too soft. It's been said of me. But I say, you never know when some-one'll turn out useful. Take you, Priest Man, are you going to be useful?'

The filthy, scarecrow priest glanced round the church.

'There's a mighty power in this place,' he said. 'None should underestimate it.'

Jacko grinned. 'Yeah, that power is me.' He turned to the prison warders. 'Take Mister Holy Man away, boys, and give him a kicking he'll remember. Then let him go. Pharaoh Jacko's justice won't be so gentle next time.'

His orders were promptly followed, leaving Charlie alone, weighed down by chains.

'Now you're a different case,' said Jacko, regretfully. 'You, I can't let live. See these gents here?' He indicated the Reivers. 'You shot their chief, and they want you to pay for it. Slowly, mind.'

Jacko turned to the shaggy warriors in their coarse woollen cloaks and furs. 'He's all yours.'

How long can it take a man to die? In Charlie Gudwallah's case, long. First, they stripped and whipped him through the winding streets and alleys of Baytown so all might see. Many a customer and neighbour hid their faces or wept at the sight. Some people contrive to be liked by almost everyone, possibly because they feel a need to be liked; such was Charlie.

Ropes were tied around his ankles, and he was lowered headfirst into the Puzzle Well, emerging half-drowned and sobbing. Now the rope was tied to a horse, riders dragging him over the pebbly beach while he screamed for mercy. None was on offer. Instead, his bleeding body was bolted into a metal cage the size of a large coffin and hung from the tower of Holy Innocents Church. Some said it took him five days to die. Others said three.

HARVEST

Within days of Big Jacko's conquest, Miriam Armitage became the mistress of Hawsker Manor. All Baytown and a large area beyond belonged to the Pharaoh, and he made his policy plain: those he favoured would gain; those who displeased him could expect eviction, starvation or a swift end. Charlie Gudwallah's fate served as warning enough.

Meanwhile, the harvest was gathered in drowsy sunshine.

Miriam didn't care to think about stupid old Charlie, she had worries closer to home. Stu had acquired a new sternness since assuming his title, Lord of Hawsker Manor. Miriam thought it sounded very well indeed, though it frightened her somehow. A big man with big land. Not that she disapproved of him getting *a little* hoity-toity. She was determined to encourage the dignity he'd need if their son were to rule after his daddy.

'A lord has to be cold and distant and proud, Stu,' she chided when he smiled too much, 'or they'll not fear him. None should dare contradict you.'

Except his wife; and Miriam trusted she was his wife though no ceremony had blessed them. At night they giggled secretly about their sudden elevation, and she was determined not to let him down.

Along with the derelict and deserted village of High Hawsker, Stu controlled several farms, crofts, and the old caravan site by the cliffs at Hawsker Bottoms where a fishing clan dwelt. Plenty of folk to obey him – and a dozen soldiers to persuade those who didn't.

Miriam rarely stirred from the farmhouse that had been renamed Lord's Manor. For one thing, her womb swelled so heavy with the boy inside that she feared disturbing his rest by travelling. Then there was the job of supervising her household: not many servants, it was true, two maids and a housekeeper, all doubling up as farm labourers when needed. But new boots take time to break. Besides, Miriam was a *lady* now. Lord Stu's lady.

Three weeks after they took possession of Hawsker, long-anticipated visitors called. A grudged visit as soon became clear. Miriam expected a little stiffness from her parents – she was well-aware how Father hated Jacko and hoped he had sense not to show it. What she didn't expect were signs of fear. They stood nervously in her new living room, its furniture fresh-waxed and polished by the servants, its plastic antiques on proud display.

'Sit, won't you?' she said, sharper than intended, more order than invitation.

They perched on the edge of their seats to sip the warm ale she provided; both declined the honey-cakes and cold meats served by the housekeeper.

'We only came to see if you've changed,' announced her father, with sudden bitterness.

'And have I?' asked Miriam, resting a hand on her swollen belly and glancing at Stu. 'Have *we*?'

Her mother dabbed an eye with a handkerchief.

'Aye,' said her father. His subsequent silence spoke a thousand harsh words. They left a few minutes later and never came back.

After her parents, no one visited in a friendly way, at least, none of her friends from the old days, just the other London boys King Jacko had also made lords of a manor. Stu joked *they* only came to see if his land was better than theirs.

Perhaps loneliness explained why she asked for a riding pony when the Pharaoh's tithe was announced. So she could ride out with Stu on the king's business. Maybe she determined to face down the hostility surrounding them. Oh, Miriam read *that* alright in the eyes of Stu's tenants and crofters, in the insolent way her own servants replied to her.

Stu soon found occasion to flog a crofter for refusing outright to mend his master's fences and Miriam whispered, 'Fine him a ewe as well; that'll bother him more than the flogging.' It gave her a fearful glow when he followed her advice. Proof she *was* the Lady of Hawsker.

Emboldened, she warned, 'I know these people better than you, Stu. They'll do anything to cheat the Pharaoh of his proper tithe. Then you'll look worse in his eyes than the other lords.'

Stu had to concede it likely. He always understood horses better than humans.

'They'll not fool me so easily, my love,' she said.

The Lord of Hawsker rode out with his lady and men. A large, bullock-drawn cart followed to collect the Pharaoh's taxes. Collect it they did. Miriam proved canny at sniffing out hiding places and evasions, pits or false ceilings in barns, secret stores in the woods. Little got past her. One disappointed farmer snarled at her, 'Whoop it up while you may, Miriam Armitage. Them that's gone away will be back before long!'

After Stu's men finished beating him with musket butts, the farmer was unfit for more farming for a while. Or chewing the grain he'd hidden because he lacked teeth. Miriam could not watch. But no one quarrelled with Lord Stu after that. Sacks and vegetables formed a neat pile in the cart: lentils, peas and beans, and sacks of potatoes; smoked hams and balls of wool, tallow candles and rolls of leather, salted fish and casks of apple brandy; clucking chickens with trussed legs. The storehouses of Hawsker Manor filled with plenty.

The Pharaoh's Tithe was itemised carefully by Miriam in a little book sent from Hob Hall.

'You're amazin',' declared Stu, cuddling her in bed one night. Her husband struggled with his letters other than *S*, *T* and *U*. October winds rattled the big farmhouse's eaves as Miriam clung to him. Baby was growing day by day. A pleasant picture entered her mind, their son riding through fields of high corn, larks singing and flitting overhead. Stu's corn, then their son's corn, then their grandson's, on and on forever.

THE DEREGULATOR

Then the weather changed. Clouds amassed over the long curve of the bay and rain slanted. A small procession of men rode out from Hob Hall for Whitby, led by King Jacko. No crown on his shaven head that day, no fanfare or fawning. The horsemen took paths slick and sticky with mud. Behind his boss, on a new dappled mare, trotted Seth Pilgrim.

Words were few among the men as they descended the winding streets of Whitby. The air tinged with a faint fluorescence, a constant shimmer of rain. Beyond the town, beneath slate clouds, the sea stretched grey and dull.

Seth craned his neck to peer upwards. High on the West Cliff stood the Deregulator's compound. He thought the building beautiful in its power, bleak and impregnable.

'We going up there, boss?' he asked.

Big Jacko grinned without mirth. 'Not this time. Wait here boys,' he commanded. 'Seth, you come with me.'

He led the way across a rickety swing bridge then up a short hill to a feral park. Within the tangle of trees and thorny shrubs stood a mansion, once the municipal art gallery and museum.

'Here, boss?' asked Seth. It seemed a strange place for a rendezvous with the most powerful man in North Yorkshire.

'Yeah, round the back.'

Big Jacko led the way to an open door, pistol in hand beneath his waterproof poncho. A pair of doves clattered over the trees at their approach.

A short corridor led to a large hall. The entire floor was covered with broken display cases, jumbled objects – a Victorian teacup, a model sailing boat, a Bakelite telephone. Moss colonised anywhere damp. The skylights above were green with algae. Seth switched on his torch.

At that moment a voice spoke from the shadows.

'You, boy, turn off the light. I told you to come alone, Jacko.'

Seth's torch wobbled; Jacko's meaty hand shoved it down.

'Off,' he muttered to Seth. 'Very sorry, sir!'

A sniff from the dark corner. Seth detected a silhouette and recognised the pedantic voice: it belonged to the Deregulator of Whitby, William Birch. Seth had the distinct feeling a gun was pointing at them from the shadows.

'No matter if he hears what I have to say, I suppose,' said the voice. 'I have a simple message, Jacko.'

'Thank you, your honour,' said Jacko. 'Er, why did you want to meet me in a place like this, sir?'

'Discretion, Jacko,' replied Birch. 'You see, the situation has changed.'

A pause. Was that nervousness in the Deregulator's voice?

319

'You need to know we require no more *materials* from you,' said the dark figure. 'No more collections or payments. Our arrangement is over. The situation has changed.'

A note of pleading entered Jacko's voice. 'Not 'tween me and you, Mr Birch, surely. Think how far back we go, London and afterwards. I've come to…' He laughed self-deprecatingly. 'Rely on your generosity, sir. What with power cells and City stuff. It's how I pay my men.'

'I told you, you're on your own now.'

There was a rustle of mice or rats in the rubbish-strewn museum.

'One thing, however, makes you still useful to me,' said the Deregulator. 'It seems a City lady who was recently stripped of her citizenship – I mean the Curator of the Baytown Museum – has vanished. I have received indirect queries about her. Do you know anything of her whereabouts?'

Jacko's eyes widened in surprise. 'Haven't heard of that lady since she flew off with Dr Macdonald.'

Will Birch's silhouette brooded. 'I would pay well for that information. Meanwhile, off you go.'

Seth sensed his boss's anger building.

'I can't do that, Mr Birch,' he broke out, hoarsely.

'Why not?'

'I can't help thinking you have as much to lose as me, with respect, Mr Birch, sir.'

Abruptly, Big Jacko's own City-made torch cast its beam, revealing the short, plump figure of Will Birch, blinking in the light. He held an absurdly large handgun and wore body armour and a helmet.

'Go while you can,' said the Deregulator, raising his gun. 'If it's any comfort to you, Jacko, I did mean to eliminate you. But I'm not a bad man, whatever I may have been forced to do. I even respect you on some levels.' He grimaced. 'I'd keep an eye on Pickering and Malton if I were you. Oh, and York. That advice is my last gift to you, Jacko, that and letting you live. Go! Enjoy the kingdom I gave you. Perhaps you should call it *Birchland* in my honour.'

Jacko stiffened as though he would reach for his own weapon then subsided. The Pharaoh of Baytown strode proudly from the ruined museum into the rain.

AVERIL'S AUTUMN

That autumn was one of painful growth for Averil Pilgrim. Days drifting with danger and disillusion amidst the piled leaves and unexpected goodness to remind her of spring, winter's inevitable reward, and of summer, green and branching.

Seth made it clear her survival depended on his goodwill. To certain powerful people, the only safe Pilgrim (excluding himself, naturally) was a dead one. So he became the worst kind of stranger. Someone loved who was now feared and distrusted. Someone once pitied, now despised. Kin no longer kindred.

But it wasn't Averil's nature to crumble. Had she not braved the plague that finished Dr Macdonald and driven away Helen Devereux? She saw how the orphans of Hob Hall and folk given a home there by her father were fast on their way to serfdom, and for the sake of her family's honour – a dangerous vanity – she resolved on decency. Or her conception of it. That meant resistance of a passive sort.

Not long after Jacko's interview with the Deregulator, his partner in greatness wandered into the kitchen of Hob Hall with her two brawny handmaids. A year earlier, before her sudden rise, Madame Morrighan had courted Averil Pilgrim.

'I see one of me servants has a stiff spine,' remarked the Queen in her musical, dreamy brogue, a voice belied by eyes hard as bullets.

Taking the hint, her two maids hurried over to Averil and thrust her into a kneeling position.

'Hope can be the strongest thing, can it not?' mused the Queen. Her glance took in the other servants, still predominately loyal to the Pilgrims. 'Some stiff-backed girls would do well to remember their uncle is dead. That he flew over the cliff like a bird without wings and that all his Crusader pals have gone the same way. Nothing to hope for there, I think.'

She took up a pestle and mortar on the table. The kitchen was still and attentive. A smouldering log crackled in the stove. Queen Morrighan ground idly at the herbs in the mortar, releasing a scent of rosemary.

'I know two cures for a stiff spine,' she said.

The girl glanced up.

'The first cure,' said Queen Morrighan, 'might seem awful strange to a fine lady o' the manor like Averil Pilgrim. The second is the whip. We'll start with the first, shall we?'

Averil tasted her medicine early the next morning.

THE LABOURS OF AVERIL PILGRIM

Rough hands dragged the girl from her warm bed above the stables. Averil's bedroom in the Hall had been requisitioned on the day Jacko moved in, now she shared with a dozen other servants.

Outside she found Queen Morrighan, her white face a mask as usual. On either side waited her two handmaids, grim as their mistress.

'Show her,' commanded the Pharaoh's wife.

One woman produced a leather riding crop and the other a gnarled stick of thorn wood.

'Remember my cures,' said Queen Morrighan, 'work or whip.'

The last words she deigned to utter on the matter, for Averil's humbling was assigned to her serving women. A lucky thing for the girl. Neither woman was soft of hand or heart, but they were lazy.

As autumn turned to winter, Averil undertook the labours devised for her. Their purpose was plain, to break the last remaining Pilgrim's spirit for the edification of Baytown. Week after week, she toiled from dawn until daylight dwindled. Tasks designed to humiliate without evoking too much pity.

Most proved a question of endurance, the kind every peasant learns without anyone's sympathy. For days on end, she was forced into the fields, rain and wind whipping in from a turbulent sea. Her task, when she wasn't digging or weeding or collecting bucket loads of stones, was to scare off birds lest they devour seeds sown in the autumn. At first, she shooed away the gulls and crows, only to watch them settle a dozen yards off. Then one afternoon, dripping from a downpour, she heard boots squelch in the mud behind her. There stood Amar.

They seldom met these days. He, like her, toiled inordinate hours, managing the Pharaoh's farm as once he had for the Pilgrims, though then with far more leisure and infinitely more respect. Averil flushed with shame at the scarecrow she'd become.

'Brought you this,' he said, looking out for spies. Amar handed her a catapult he had devised that sprayed handfuls of pebbles. 'And this. I tried it on the beach. Scares the hell out gulls.'

He produced a wooden rattle and urged her to try. She rattled away furiously, creating a noise like a frenzied machine gun. A parliament of rooks and unkindness of ravens scattered, cawing and protesting.

'I like it,' she said, solemnly.

Not long afterwards, Averil was ordered to serve the chief stockman, a flood-survivor housed by Reverend James Pilgrim.

'I've been given orders about you,' he confided. His clear, watery blue eyes examined her as he might one of his lambs or foals. His name was Matlock.

First came herding cattle with an instruction from on high to 'feed t'bull' in his paddock. This stirred sleepy Matlock to the comment. 'We'll see how that goes on.'

Twice a day she fed Bottle the Dexter bull under Matlock's wary eye. Otherwise, she was ordered out into the fields to 'guard' the livestock, a labour as useful as scaring gulls. Still,

Averil preferred it to the atmosphere in Hob Hall. She came to know each goat, cow and sheep individually, as well as the swine feeding on fallen acorns in the wood. It amused her to give them names half-remembered from Shakespeare or the other books Father and Uncle Michael had encouraged her to read.

Often Averil considered running away to join the band of rebels who were said to have settled down the coast. But what if she got there and found no friendly Tom Higginbottom? Besides, her duty lay here among her own folk. She resolved to outlast Big Jacko and his Queen.

Then Matlock received another instruction and shook his head. 'They want you to lead Bottle round t'yard to show how good you are with him.' He frowned. 'It's my fault, Averil, I told *her* that t'beast ate out your hand, placid as a lambkin.' Unexpectedly, the grizzled man brightened.

'Aye!' he declared.

But he would explain no more.

The bull, though far from the most aggressive of its kind, had a variable temper. Above all, Matlock had warned her to never enter his pen or put herself in a position where it might butt her. Now she was ordered to thread a rope through Bottle's nose ring and lead him around the yard like a puppy.

Averil barely slept before the morning of this feat. The entire household had been summoned to watch and, she suspected, laugh and jeer as she fled hither and thither to avoid a trampling. But when Bottle's paddock door swung open and she led the bull out, pulling him by a stick attached to the ring in his nose, the beast was fierce as a kitten. She toured the yard to shouts of approval from the Hob Hall orphans and other retainers. Even Big Jacko's boys joined in. Others muttered the Pilgrim girl must have magical powers for, see, she'd bewitched the bull – a story that had gone round Baytown twice by nightfall. Queen Morrighan merely glowered.

Once Bottle was safely in his pen, Matlock whispered in Averil's ear.

'Slipped a little something in his feed this morning. Thought I'd overdone it and that he'd keel right over. But don't fret, lass, he'll be mardier than ever by t'afternoon.'

Next day, blustery and cold, Averil was transferred back to the yard where an eye could be kept on her. Here she was ordered to muck out the stables and byres. An arm and back-aching task. It seemed Queen Morrighan's prediction about broken spines might come true. Dozens of beasts – horse, human, cattle and swine – deposited their dung in the environs of the yard. The air stank of sweet decay and ammonia. By the end of her first week, she reeked the same way; mud, straw, shit and slurry caked her clothes.

It might have been the stables that broke her spirit in the end. Except one cold afternoon, when her breath steamed and bones protested, she heard a commotion by the farmyard gates. Amar was working beside her, having finished his own tasks early in order to help. Both looked up from their whispered conversation and lowered their shovels.

Outside the gate, they found a small, thin man in a cowl and robe, leading scores of gaunt, crazy-eyed folk with scourges in their belts. The little man knelt in the mud before Pharaoh Jacko and his wife, motioning his followers to do the same.

'Maister!' he cried. 'Ah've come to thee for justice! Aye, and revenge! Where's that Michael Pilgrim? He owes us a life!'

The mass of floggers muttered in angry agreement.

'You are too late,' replied Queen Morrighan, loftily. 'He died three months ago.'

The Master of the floggers looked confused. 'Mistress,' he cried, 'that can't be reet!'

A garbled tale followed, overheard by dozens of witnesses. A tale Pharaoh Jacko might have preferred to keep quiet. For it transpired Michael Pilgrim was very far from dead. He had become an armed fugitive as dangerous as ever, rumoured to be travelling the region in search of allies and vengeance.

Averil gasped with joy, instinctively clutching Amar's hand. Alive! That meant Uncle Michael would surely return. She shot a triumphant glance at Queen Morrighan and found the older woman's peculiar black eyes boring into her own. This time Averil did not flinch. She smiled, curtsied, and returned to shovelling shit in the stables, whistling as she worked.

TWO ⊙

---✵---

POWER

Seth almost forgot what it was like to be sober at midnight, to not nurse a hangover at noon. He had plenty of girls, too, though never the ones he really wanted. In fact, Seth wasn't always sure it was the girls he wanted. His bed-companions seemed more afraid than excited, but they kept him warm when December gales rattled the windows of Uncle Michael's room.

Seth's first intention had been to remove every last book from the old library of Hob Hall, cleanse all trace of his uncle. So many books: histories, novels, poetry, atlases, biographies, like a cosmopolitan crowd. He burned a whole wall's worth for warmth until a realisation occurred. What made him useful to Jacko was not his strength or prowess with arms; ironically, it was the very education he despised.

There was no denying Jacko felt a superstitious awe for what he called 'proper book-learning' or what Seth termed 'shite'. Thus the books seemed suddenly valuable, and he even glanced through volumes for titbits of information to tickle the Pharaoh's interest. Sometimes he looked into the topic of pyramids and thought of haunted Fylingdales on the moor and its dangerous prisoner.

Jacko held court in Holy Innocents Church. The neglected building had been repaired, scrubbed and cleared of anything pertaining to religion until it seemed bare to Seth. But he was glad of the change.

Where the altar once stood, Big Jacko placed his throne. Here, one bright December morning, he waved Seth over to a vacant stool at his feet.

'My boy,' began Jacko, his eyes softened by a pipe of stuff, 'do you ever think about power?'

Seth nodded. He didn't dare reveal his exact longings.

'What is power?' mused the Pharaoh. 'A habit, that's all. Listen…' He motioned Seth closer. 'There's them that always asks questions, never satisfied with what they're told. They want their own truths to believe in. The kind of person your grandfather was, Seth, or your uncle, stubborn bastards with power they get from trying to do right by everyone – specially their own conscience. An' that's what makes 'em dummies. They always end up losers against men like me.'

Seth listened closely.

'Then there's them who suck up to power 'cos it's easier that way. Smart, ain't it? Thinking's hard work, so they let others do it for 'em. It niggles, and it rubs, but some people want nothing better, like bitches after a whipping, watching you with big eyes.'

He sniffed. '*Yessers*, I call 'em. One way or another they always think, *Yes sir, this is it, this is the only way it can be, the way I've been told it has to be, the way it'll always be.* Yessers is what we like best. Get me?'

Big Jacko's eyes assessed the length of the stripped church.

'Then there's people like me, Seth, maybe you one day. We understand power better than anyone. Like, that it's our due to tell sheep where to nibble and how much to have. Like, that swords and words are the same, just ways to get what we want. All that matters is what we want.' His voice took on an aggrieved tone. 'What's so wrong with that? Dummies and yessers want things, and so do we. We're only different 'cos we get 'em.'

Big Jacko frowned, and Seth sensed a change of mood.

'You've heard them stories about Michael Pilgrim stirring up an alliance against me, haven't you?' asked the Pharaoh.

All winter, traders and spies (often one and the same) had brought rumours concerning Michael Pilgrim. That he was riding around North Yorkshire with a small band of followers to raise an army that, come spring, would cast the false Pharaoh into the sea. They dubbed themselves the 'Free Folk', much to the scorn and ire of Jacko and his court.

'I heard them stories, boss,' said Seth. 'My uncle was always crazy. But he means to fight.'

Big Jacko nodded. 'Can't blame him for that,' he said, 'it's only what I'd do in his place. Know what, Seth? I'm going to put a price on your uncle's head. A price that'll get me what I want.'

Seth's turn to nod. 'He's dangerous to you, boss.'

Had he really said that? Had he condemned his own uncle to be assassinated by bullet or blade? It seemed he had. A gulp of sorrow burst in his soul. Images swirled of days when Uncle Michael had been an undoubted friend. He could make no sense of how they had arrived here, Father's church converted to this throne room, everything he had been nurtured to respect lost. For long moments he grieved. Then a native hardness banished those feelings. He glimpsed a new knowledge of his own.

'We're as powerful as we make others weak,' he said, solemnly.

Seth knew that had to include his uncle.

Big Jacko belched a breakfast of lamb's kidneys.

'Next spring I'm going to turn the people of Malton and Pick'ring into *yessers*,' he said. 'In the spring they'll learn who's Pharaoh. Get me?'

Seth nodded.

'That's why I want you to write some letters for me offering a reward for Michael Pilgrim's head. A big reward.'

Seth hesitated. Wasn't there a last plea he should make for his father's brother?

'Yes, boss,' he said.

FYLINGDALES

Winter winds blew cold over Fylingdales Moor. Bare thorns and reeds stirred beside muddy pools. Nature never sleeps entirely but grows by abiding. Clouds blew overhead, and few noticed or cared.

It occurred to Helen Devereux every tyrant needs a place of exile and imprisonment. The Russian Tsars chose Siberia; French monarchs built the Bastille; a diminutive Austrian with a toothbrush moustache diverted his enemies into camps from which they emerged as ashes.

So much for history. Big Jacko, Pharaoh Jacko, selected Fylingdales on the edge of his new domain...

Months earlier, after Bertrand's aircar ejected Helen outside the Baytown Museum, she had been hustled straight to Holy Innocents Church where Jacko met her in the nave. It was then, in her agitation, that she blundered.

Blinded by self-pity and hysteria at Mhairi's death, disorientated by her exile from the City and abrupt dismissal as Curator, she didn't think how Mayor Jacko came to sit in the church or wear such a strange yellow hat. Words gushed as she wrung her hands.

'Mayor Jacko,' she sobbed, 'I must go straight to Hob Hall! I must see Michael Pilgrim!' Later she marvelled at her own theatricality, as though she was playing the role of naïve, innocent heroine in a melodrama. 'I must tell you, I am no longer the Curator of the Museum.' Suddenly she had felt dizzy. It had been hours since her last food or drink. 'I must see my friends at Hob Hall ... I'm banished from the City.'

At that moment the night's horrors had overwhelmed her – Guy de Prie-Dieu's hideous laboratory and Eloise du Guesclin torn limb from limb by a drone, then clutching Mhairi's lifeless corpse, pleading for her sister to live – she fainted in a heap.

Helen had awoken to darkness. Trying to move arms and legs revealed she was trussed and gagged. Panic turned to numb terror. Where was she? It soon became obvious she was in a covered wagon on a nightmare, bruising journey.

At Fylingdales she had been released. Michael Pilgrim's nephew, Seth, watched her curiously, as though he wanted something from her.

'Lock her up,' he ordered the gaolers. 'Put her with the others, but make sure she's warm and well fed.'

The 'others' she was thrust among had turned out to be disparate and desperate: Tom Higginbottom's wife and a dozen farmers and fishermen deemed dangerous by the new king of Baytown. She learned of Jacko's sneak attack and victory but little more, just that the prisoners had been herded to Fylingdales within days of the battle.

As weeks passed, more prisoners arrived, bringing tales of tithes and beatings, executions and confiscations of land as farms were turned into manors for the Pharaoh's men.

Days of darkness; nights the same. Her only clock the drip, drip of moisture working its way down to her subterranean prison.

Helen came to learn the limits of darkness. How one compensates. They were locked beneath the radar station in an echoing concrete basement full of diesel generators, their only light provided by guards bringing a cauldron of watery porridge for breakfast and thin vegetable soup for dinner. Some days there was bread. Occasionally shreds of gristle in the soup. After the meal, the guards left, and darkness reasserted itself.

Once a day they were taken outside for exercise. That precious half-hour kept Helen sane. She blinked at daylight until her eyes adjusted, drinking air untainted by the stench of her fellow prisoners' bodies and waste – indeed her own – as she surveyed the bleak moor. Too soon she was driven back down below.

THREE

---※---

POWER (2)

The pillars on which a king's power rests have two legs and arms, not to mention a brain. His feasts and fighting, fealty and fun, all depend on people. As the first snowdrops peeked from the cold soil, word spread from Hob Hall of a second tithe. Not this time to satisfy the King's table and storehouses but to feed him with labour. In short, to create a caste of 'bonders' or serfs. Each community or family must choose men and women capable of heavy work and send them to Hob Hall on the appointed day.

When Amar told Averil, she paused in spooning up the soup he had stolen for her. Her handsome young face had gained a bruised, defiant air, yet she was healthy enough. Enforced exercise on Queen Morrighan's behalf kept her lean, and Amar made sure adequate rations from the Pharaoh's personal store came her way.

'The people are to queue outside the hall and have their names recorded,' he told her. 'But there's more. I believe Jacko wants to use them to construct a new castle and village named after himself.'

'They are to be slaves,' said Averil, bitterly.

'Yes.'

'But we have always been free folk in Bay! Not a bonder among us. We were always proud of that and looked down on folk who kept slaves as savages, primitives.'

Amar went to the door. No one was spying on them.

'Your brother is the one compiling the list of names and settling old scores, I'm told.'

Averil's face fell at this news.

'He scarcely seems my brother at all.'

Reaching out, Amar took her hand. Dirt engrained its pores and blackened her nails; the skin was hard, thick. He kissed her bony knuckles. She did not resist.

'Then his loss is great,' he said.

THE TABLES OF THE MONEY CHANGERS

Averil's outrage simmered and grew as the tithe ceremony approached. Right across Baytown and the lands subject to Pharaoh Jacko folk fretted and disputed as to who should be chosen. Countless reasons were found to nominate a neighbour or his son; others declared stoutly they'd have nowt to do with it. Many more stayed silent in the hope no one would notice they existed.

Time hurried on regardless, and signs of spring multiplied: buds on twigs and branches, subtle shifts of light in the sky. A day arrived when the lanes and tracks leading to Hob Hall filled with people coming to register. Few looked happy. Perhaps that was why King Jacko and Queen Morrighan stayed well out of view, their place occupied by a little-loved figure among Baytown folk.

Seth Pilgrim lolled behind long tables set up in the front garden of the Hall. To the side stood a brazier in which branding irons smouldered. Guards were everywhere, especially floggers twitching their whips, led by their new chief, Maister Gil.

Murmuring swelled into a low buzz as people gathered.

'Bring up the first manor,' ordered Seth.

The first manor turned out to be Hawsker. With an unreadable expression, Lord Stu waved forward the dozen chosen from his estate to be branded as bonders. A frightened youth was pushed to Seth's table and stated his name. Soldiers led him to the brazier and pressed his hand onto an anvil, palm flat against the metal. With quick efficiency, a branding iron hissed on the bare skin of the bonder's forearm. Screams broke the silence. When the youth was taken away, a J for Jacko marked his arm.

A shocked pause while Seth consulted his list: it was one thing branding a sheep or cow, quite another a man.

'No!' cried a shrill, female voice.

A girl not yet twenty hurried over to the branding table. Averil Pilgrim's name flew around the assembled crowd. Washed and combed, she wore clean, respectable clothes.

Perhaps some corner of her mind remembered Reverend James Pilgrim's dull homilies about righteous anger and the tables of the money changers. How his Saviour had overturned stalls for selling doves in the Temple. Maybe she saw, as her brother failed to see, that it was Seth himself who would be hated most for this day's work.

'This is not right!' she cried, quivering. 'Baytown folk have never been bonders!'

Hundreds of eyes surveyed the girl and found her anger infectious. She faced the waiting crowd alone, looking for support until a voice called out.

'Aye! The lass is right! I'm heading home.'

'Bugger this!' shouted another.

'It's Michael's niece! A Pilgrim! A Pilgrim, I say!'

'Heed the girl!' roared a dishevelled figure.

This last thundering voice was familiar to everyone in Baytown: Mister Priest Man, top hat held aloft to reveal his shiny bald crown. 'I'll no more of this Pharaoh feller,' he bellowed, 'nor shall the Nuagers!'

The crowd caught his fever. Shouts. Gesticulations. Rage held in check for months by stick or fist or gun barrel bubbled free. Suddenly people were hurrying from Hob Hall in all directions, parents dragging or carrying children, old folk led as swiftly as they could walk.

A misguided cavalryman fired two pistols in the air for order and panic set in. Now people fled for their lives. Not least Mister Priest Man and his Nuager followers, a sizable group, charging through a line of floggers who lashed out blindly with their whips. Horsemen gathered in the lane, and infantry formed up to repel attacks on the Pharaoh's Palace. But no one had a mind to attack Hob Hall, escape was all the people of Baytown wanted.

Within minutes, only Big Jacko's men and a smoking brazier remained of the ceremony. That and a young female prisoner dragged away to the cells beneath Holy Innocents Church.

THE JUSTICE OF PHARAOH JACKO (2)

'So what am I to do with you?' asked King Jacko.

Averil stood before him, head lowered, hands bound.

Beside him on a smaller chair sat Queen Morrighan. For once the pale woman's face had lost its composure. When she spoke yellow teeth were revealed.

'She should join her uncle's comrade in his cage. *That* is what the Heron Goddess wishes.'

Jacko's court in Holy Innocents Church waited expectantly. Several dozen of the Pharaoh's intimates had gathered there, all fully armed, including many of their women. The rebellion had caught everyone by surprise and stirred frissons of alarm. Worse, it had triggered yet more of the population fleeing into Dalby Forest, including Mister Priest Man and his many Nuagers. Crucial sources of labour that the manors depended on, especially if their lords were called away to campaign. Seth Pilgrim hovered miserably by a pillar.

'Let's get this straight,' said Jacko to his queen. 'You mean she should join him *in* the cage? What, with Charlie-boy still there?'

To be trapped with the putrefying innkeeper in a space marginally larger than a coffin was a grim punishment indeed. A cursory knowledge of human nature suggested that – sufficiently maddened by starvation – the girl might find him irresistible.

Queen Morrighan nodded. 'It's what the Heron Goddess wants.'

The king glared at her.

'Pharaoh Jacko decides his own justice,' he said, his voice gravelly, 'and he don't need no other counsel. Neither from god nor man.'

This first public sign of division between king and queen made a few courtiers shuffle nervously. Queen Morrighan flushed, pink patches appearing on her white cheeks.

'But maybe your Heron Goddess has a point,' brooded Jacko. 'Them Pilgrims have caused me a world of trouble. Nothing wrong with making an example for all to see, is there?'

Queen Morrighan settled back with a slight smile.

The girl's gaze remained on the ground, and Big Jacko's attention strayed to Seth Pilgrim. The youth fidgeted then stepped forward.

'Boss,' said Seth. In his distress, he clenched and unclenched his fists. 'I know she done wrong, boss, I know she deserves to be made an example of. I know all that.'

His voice wobbled. Yet he threw back his shoulders to meet the Pharaoh's eye.

'But she's my sister, boss! All the family I've got left. And we're twins, do you know how that feels?'

Big Jacko's expression gave no clues.

'And I promised to save her,' continued Seth, 'I promised her.'

The Pharaoh nodded slowly. For a long time, he considered.

'I had a sister too when I was a kid,' he said. 'Wish she could see me sat here now.'

Queen Morrighan looked at her husband in surprise.

'You're a good boy, Seth,' said Jacko, 'like a son to me. You're right to stand up for your sister.'

With a jarring scrape, his throne went back.

'Do you fuckers hear that?' he roared, his head lowered like a bull's. 'Seven of me own sons got blown up by them City cunts! Seven! And God knows how many daughters. Did you know that?' His voice echoed around the bare walls of Holy Innocents Church. 'They was just kids! Kids!' He slapped his chest. 'Only Jacko feels that pain! Just me!'

He sat back heavily in his chair. His rage blew itself out as suddenly as it had arisen. A calculating gleam entered his eyes.

'Well then, Seth, you agree she needs punishing,' he said. 'So what's it to be?'

The young man's eyes darted around the room. Fell on the flogger, Maister Gil, scourge in hand.

'Him, boss,' he said, pointing.

Big Jacko nodded.

They tied her to a handcart, her wrists bound so arms and legs were spread. The same cart she had used to transport dung.

Gil, his eyes shiny from a blue sweetie, paced the straw and manure littered farmyard, cracking his three-thong whip. The yard was full of people summoned to watch.

With a rough jerk, he tore aside her linen blouse to reveal a soft white back and the tops of round buttocks. This seemed to stimulate him. Impatiently, he ripped off the remainder of her clothes. At once he set about his work, singing the floggers' hymn in a high, ecstatic voice, gasping for breath between each line.

Punish any man that don't worship thee!
Give 'em plague and daily woes!
Make 'em starve that break thy laws!
And deliver us from drones!

Averil's cries and pleading remained unanswered; the lashing only ceased when King Jacko ordered that Gil should be dragged away before he killed the girl. By then she had fainted, a lattice of bloody lines written across her back, ready for banishment to the cells of Fylingdales.

As Amar watched helplessly, his thoughts fled across miles of deserted forest and moor to York, Malton and Pickering, to the coast where other Baytown refugees licked their wounds and prepared to fight. Only war could free Averil now: when spring made roads passable, it must come.

FOUR

THE ARMIES OF PHARAOH JACKO

Seth Pilgrim cantered along the verge of a pitted road. His mare snorted and tossed her mane. Reining in, he examined the long, straggling column.

The Whitby to Pickering road was full of soldiers, horses, wagons driven by Pharaoh Jacko's reluctant conscripts bearing provisions and tents. Wild-haired doxies hitched rides amidst the baggage, anticipating more profitable rides come evening.

Dust drifted in gritty clouds from hundreds of tramping feet and hooves. The Pharaoh's spring campaign had started late: already blossom was thinning on cherry and apple trees, and the first fledgelings were flown on winds of May. Roads were dry, and a cloud of gritty tilth blew their way from an ancient municipal tip so that folk covered their mouths and noses with neckerchiefs.

No matter if they marched later than intended, thought Seth, the huge army filled him with pride and awe. From all over the North they'd come, men with weapons to match their ambitions, drawn like wasps to a honeypot by tales of Big Jacko's largesse when he first conquered Baytown. Far more than City goods were on offer this time: Pharaoh Jacko promised land, the cream of prosperous districts well recovered from the Great Dying. Orchards, wheat fields, cattle, horses, slaves. Yes, Pickering, Malton and York would have new masters soon, lords who paid tribute to their Pharaoh.

Onward marched the army. Big Jacko's boys formed the Royal Guard, leading companies of mercenaries and conscripts. Reivers in large numbers from the borders of Jockland scenting a little prosperity. Small bands from Cumberland and Lake Country led toBaytown by tinkers' rumours, carrying motley weapons and precious little spare fat; likely lads with a taste for adventure. Even a contingent of Scallies from beyond the hills way out west, sharp-eyed jokers, their accents as strange to Seth's ears as the barefoot Jocks' grumbling and mumbling.

So many appetites to satisfy! Sometimes it worried him. He alone knew what others couldn't guess: that the Deregulator in Whitby was no longer supplying City products. What would happen when the war was over and the Pharaoh's allies demanded payment? Yet the Boss seemed unconcerned. He had shown Seth a dog-eared tourist guide to York and explained that city would be his capital. The gloriousness of it swept aside Seth's fears. Of course! Did not Jacko's vision match his own secret dreams?

Just then he became aware of a faint humming overhead. A drone! His horse shied at the noise. All along the column men dived for cover in ditches and bushes. Shielding his eyes with a hand, he stared up at the swooping, circling craft. Seth recognised it as a kind used regularly by the Deregulator of Whitby, and his heart leapt. Could it be so? That the Deregulator had decided to help his old partner after all? One drone would be enough to wipe out their enemies in less time than it takes to scour a doorstep. Seth noticed Jacko staring up with evident hope and longing.

As if hearing their thoughts, the machine drifted south towards Pickering and the so-called Free Folk o' the North. The Pharaoh's army also marched south across the moors. An imposing ridge rose in the distance: the Heights of Horcum.

THE HEIGHTS OF HORCUM

Soon the same drone circled above a company of soldiers dug into the rugged hillside. Like the Pharaoh's men they cowered and covered their heads. Only two stood upright, apparently unconcerned. Both knew from past experience that if the drone wanted them dead, they would be cinders.

'Can Jacko have the City on his side?' asked Michael Pilgrim in despair.

The creature beside him – it might be stretching a point to call him entirely human – twitched his miniature elephant trunk of a nose.

'I predict otherwise,' said the Modified Man.

'Then why spy on us?'

'To observe is not to intervene,' sniffed the Modified Man. 'Truth is, Michael Pilgrim, unflattering as you might find it, the City of Albion does not care a straw if you primitives slaughter one another.' He leered. 'We're all here on sufferance as far as *they* are concerned.'

Still, Michael gazed up, fearful the drone would dive and attack.

'Alternatively,' said the Modified Man, 'there may be other explanations. It puzzles me that Pharaoh Jacko's petty empire hasn't attracted *a little* deregulation. Perhaps our dear friends in the City of Albion are distracted by some internal dispute, thus allowing their man in Whitby to sit on his hands as he sees fit. You told me that you believe Jacko has an arrangement with the Deregulator there … Ah, look, you worry yourself in vain! This time, at least.'

The drone had turned in the direction of Whitby and soon vanished from sight. All attention returned to the column of soldiers drawing closer across the bleak moor.

'Here they come like ants,' opined Mister Priest Man, joining Michael and the Modified Man now that the skies were clear. He mimed mandibles with finger and thumb. 'Ants a-scurrying with their little jaws a-gnashing. Yet faeries and sprites won't bless 'em, I can assure you of that.'

They were stood on a rock overlooking lands broken by a single ribbon of road. Around them, comrades old and new, captains from Malton, Pickering and many a settlement east, west and south. Stranger allies, too: the Modified Man had bought a large squad of grim followers, men and women who obeyed his commands without question. At the head of all, one appointed General-Elect by popular demand: Michael Pilgrim.

He followed Mister Priest Man's pointing finger through his binoculars. From the high ridge, the length of the column was clearly visible, though obscured by dust clouds.

'There's thousands of the buggers!' cried a young man promoted to war-leader by neighbours and kin near Kirkham, mainly because he captained their handball team.

Michael focused his binoculars and made notches in a stick with his dagger for several minutes. 'No more than twelve hundred,' he concluded, 'maybe fourteen…'

He met his officers' eyes. 'But as I've said before, numbers are only an advantage if you can deploy.'

Dangerous months had hardened his native dreaminess. The **F** branded on his cheek had grown stark, defiant. He wore a century-old bulletproof vest emblazoned with the legend *POLICE* and ancient bullet holes. Blue armbands marked him as part of the alliance named the Free Folk – though definitions of what qualified as freedom varied considerably among them. One thing united the little army, an abiding distaste for Pharaoh Jacko's rule.

'We should ride back to Pickering,' declared the Modified Man.

Michael shook his head.

'No, we'll fight here then fall back in good order.'

The other officers watched intently. Michael knew this moment would define his leadership – and whether they fought as a united force.

'The bulk of our army is in Pickering!' protested the Modified Man in his peevish, phlegmy voice. The miniature elephant's trunk quivered.

What he said was true. Even as they debated, over two hundred men were training in Pickering Castle and fortifying the town. Less than a hundred had ridden out to the Heights of Horcum to delay Jacko's horde.

'Numbers are only an advantage if you can deploy,' repeated Michael. 'We fight.'

THE LAND'S LIE

Over the course of his life, Michael Pilgrim had passed the Hole of Horcum several times. On each occasion he had thought, *A few determined men could give a much larger force a bloody nose in this vale.* The land's lie was perfect.

First, your enemies struggle up a steep, curving track from Saltergate Moor to the Heights of Horcum. Up there only a narrow passage existed between the dense thickets of Dalby Forest and the Hole itself, a deep bowl scooped from the land during the last Ice Age. Woodland provided shooters cover on one side of the road; on the other a near-cliff for your foes to tumble down – perfect.

Michael supervised as they dug in on the ridge overlooking the moor. Their horses (every man had a mount, an essential part of his plan) cropped under the trees, well-guarded and picketed.

He focused his binoculars. Big Jacko's army was close now, tramping slowly as the gradient rose towards Horcum, Reivers at the head, a wild lot who confused cruelty with strength. Michael had heard how Charlie Gudwallah suffered at their hands.

'Stay out of sight until my signal,' he urged his untested soldiers. Farmers and shepherds, blacksmiths and cobblers, farriers and tailors, scarcely warriors at all, despite weeks of frantic drilling. Weeks when spring celebrated its victory over winter with peach and apple blossom.

Yet even as he had taught his makeshift army how to kill, Michael had brooded over broken promises: that he would study war no more, that he was done with killing.

Did sour irony fill his mouth as he urged peaceable shepherds, 'No mercy, friends! Dead or crippled is all they deserve.'

Sadly for him, it did.

THE BATTLE OF HORCUM (1)

Seth knew the enemy was on the ridge, amidst gorse and scrub and boulders. Pharaoh Jacko had conferred with his commanders, granting the Reivers first blood-honour. A dubious prize to Seth's mind. Advancing up the steep, rutted road while God alone knew what shit poured down on you.

'The hill's yours, boss,' bowed the Reiver-Captain, who proudly wore plastic boots and shiny, water-resistant clothes – his City wages from last year's campaign. Perhaps he hoped to earn a waterproof hat to complete the outfit.

Bo-o-o-o-m sounded the foghorn. The army of Pharaoh Jacko cheered, banging spear and pike butts on the ground.

Seth shielded his eyes with a hand, staring up at the Heights of Horcum. A cloudless blue sky framed the silhouettes of saplings, maybe men. With a jangle of armour and weapons the Reivers advanced.

Up on the hill, Michael Pilgrim called out, 'Wait! Wait!'

He noted the speed of the column, its density, how they had neglected to put out a protective line of skirmishers. Then he loaded his gun with a cartridge containing lead ball.

Up the road they came with no sense of urgency he could discern. How many? Three hundred in the first regiment, at least, and this was just the vanguard of the Pharaoh's army. In their hands a medley of weapons: spears, flintlocks, axes, long swords, a few crossbows.

'Wait!' he ordered again. 'Keep low!' Anxious faces were bobbing up from their cover in the gorse.

The enemy could have no real idea of the Free Companies' strength. An element of surprise he wished to preserve.

Tramp, tramp of their feet, halfway up now, nothing to stop them it seemed. The first ranks passed a pole driven into the road-side as a marker, and Michael jumped on a rock, aimed his shotgun.

'Now!' he shouted.

An unnecessary command. All around men rose from their cover and fired. A ragged volley boomed, drowning out the furious battle cries of the men below. Smoke billowed then was whipped away by the breeze.

Michael had already reloaded and was taking aim. Yes, a score down, and many more wounded. A devastating volley with them packed together. A few stray bullets whipped past the men on the ridge. Wasted powder. Wild shots. And a man firing was a man not charging.

Still, the Reivers pushed up the hill, disordered by the rocky terrain, reaching an abrupt bend in the road as it followed the shape of the ridge. Once this corner had been turned the column halted. For the way forward was blocked.

Down in the road bullets smacked into flesh with a solid, sickening thump. Arrows and crossbow bolts curved down, piercing shoulders and upturned faces.

The Reiver-Captain in his plastic suit and breastplate fashioned from a fan oven door squinted up at the barricade of tree trunks and green branches. His enemies skulked behind it, shooting with feverish haste, almost within reach. On one side of the barricade, the Hole of Horcum fell steeply: a drop he didn't fancy. That left one direction.

'At 'em, laddies!' he roared.

Guns crashed as they charged the last yards to the barrier. Men fell all around, but the Captain was preserved. Hadn't he been blessed with luck at his birth? The warlocks of his clan had guaranteed him a ripe old age: charms hung round his neck to assure it.

Now his men were mounting the barricade, jeering in triumph as the cowardly Yorkies fled like hares up the road towards a corner of dense woodland. As the Reiver-Captain waved on his men, thirty, forty on the barricade, he became aware of something hissing like an adder beneath the wood ... a trail of smoke ... burning powder ... a fuse.

The barricade exploded, hurling men and branches and leaves into the air, igniting oil and brushwood laid there purposefully.

On the spur of the hill, the Modified Man tittered, trunk-like nose wobbling. The cause of his mirth visible through gushing clouds of smoke: crushed, torn bodies and screeching men; some stared at stumps before they expired.

'Science, Pilgrim!' he crowed. 'I told you to trust in science!'

Still, the Free Folk on the hill fired, adding to the din. But Michael knew the Reivers could not retreat, the sheer numbers of men pushing up from Saltergate Moor must force them to climb round the remains of the barricade.

'Back to the horses!' he shouted, blowing a whistle. 'Back! Back!'

Other officers heard and blew whistles of their own. The Modified Man – who an hour earlier had sulked that they were not riding back to Pickering – had the temerity to argue. 'Why?' he squeaked. 'Look at them, Pilgrim! My ruse worked! They're defeated. My explosion did it for them.'

Michael noticed a slender figure nearby, her face covered by a mask: Scheherazade! Michael grabbed her arm.

'Get your master away from here if you want him to live! Go! Go!'

With desperate haste, he herded his men into the woods where the horses waited. Even as they mounted, it became clear the Pharaoh's men had overrun their position on the ridge.

'We'll wait here as long as we can,' he ordered. 'Use the time to reload, friends, we'll not leave a single man to their mercies if possible.'

When the last of the Free Folk arrived, he ordered them down the churned up tarmac highway to Pickering. Of the eighty or so who rode out that morning only three of the horses lacked a rider. All around him young men boasted of their exploits; others were subdued, abashed by their first taste of war.

Michael found Mister Priest Man riding alongside. The Nuager's face streaked with smoke beneath his top hat.

'I told you the sprites and faeries wouldn't bless Jacko,' said Priest Man. 'How many ants did we squash? How many beetles?'

Michael remembered the long, remorseless column of Pharaoh Jacko's army.

'Not enough,' he said.

THE BATTLE OF HORCUM (2)

Seth delayed ascending the corpse-littered slope that the Pickers had defended so stoutly. Smoke rose still from behind the spur of the hill. His ears rang with the explosion that had echoed around moor and vale.

A single prisoner had been discovered cowering behind a rock, too frightened to flee. Otherwise just a couple of corpses. Bad luck for the coward: even now the Royal Guard were questioning him. Seth could hear the youth pleading and the thud of boots.

He cantered over to a group of baggage wagons. 'You!' He pointed his riding crop at the conscripts from Baytown holding the reins. Farmers and fishermen he'd known since boyhood. 'Get ready to move off!'

They stared back with sullen eyes.

'I want those wagons on top of yon hill,' he drawled. 'Hear me?'

'You found the nerve to go up there yet, Seth Pilgrim?' called a voice behind him. 'Brave warrior, as you are.'

Seth wheeled his horse to identify the voice's source. Dozens of blank faces surrounded him. A few whores perching on the wagons tittered.

'Mind you do as I say,' he said, spurring away towards the hill.

Almost at once he came upon bodies. The dead were no strangers to anyone of his generation. But the corpses on the steep road fascinated and repelled him.

Dismounting, he led his horse to the pile of twisted bodies awaiting shallow graves. Lead balls had torn open stomachs, spilt out flesh and pale grey organs. A few men on the roadside gasped or sobbed, awaiting help.

As he rounded the hill and came upon the still smouldering barricade, Seth's horse shied. Something soft beneath its hoof frightened the beast: a blackened hand and arm, severed by the explosion. Its owner was nowhere to be seen, no doubt one of the bodies being carried away to the burial pit.

At the top, he found Stu with a large band of horsemen. His friend was Captain of the Pharaoh's Cavalry now.

'What's happening, Stu?' he asked.

'They've headed that way.' Stu pointed down the road towards Pickering.

Seth had visited the town with his father and mother in better times, travelling in a large party from Baytown to trade in the market square and cement important friendships. He had felt proud to be a Pilgrim then.

'The Pickers have proper slowed us down,' grumbled Stu. 'I told the boss we should scout ahead, but he said he didn't want to lose no horse in an ambush. Instead, he got this.' Stu gestured at the carnage on the hill. 'We won't reach Pickerin' before nightfall now. Nowhere near.'

Seth looked out at the Hole of Horcum, its wide hollow created by unimaginable forces. And nearby, the trees of Dalby Forest were watchful, outnumbering the Pharaoh's army ten thousand times over, mocking their strength, their courage. He hated this place.

Seth cantered off in search of his leader and reassurance.

A KIND OF TRUTH

Seth wasn't the only Pilgrim in need of reassurance.

After stabling his horse, Michael Pilgrim pushed through excited crowds in Pickering Market square discussing the battle. His blackened hands stank of sulphurous powder, likewise his soul.

Pickering was occupied by hastily drilling men-at-arms. Pikes, swords and crude firearms were visible everywhere, bales of fodder for horses and mounds of the resulting dung. There was the air of a grand medieval fair in the ancient town, except that sensible folk expected neither profit nor pleasure from the next few days. Most feared to lose what little they had wrung from life, for reports of Pharaoh Jacko's rapacious style had preceded his army.

Michael gulped a pot of ale someone thrust at him. Then his eye fell on worn stone steps leading up to the town's parish church. Afraid the men he led would see his trembling hands, Michael hurried through the graveyard into the church.

The last century had been relatively kind to St Peter's and St Paul's – a kindness Michael could not find for himself. Sinking on an overturned stone font, he rubbed at the black stains on his hands.

After today, where were his intentions to live better?

Tears pricked his eyes. The helpless self-pity of all who have done deep wrongs that they believe define themselves.

Yet there he sat, architect of an ambush that had maimed and killed scores of mother's sons. Not easy deaths either. You're good at this, Michael Pilgrim, he jeered in his soul. Don't pretend otherwise.

Late afternoon sunshine slanted through the stained glass windows of the church. A few coloured panes showed signs of recent repair. Believers had clung on here until recently, but now, like his dear, hapless brother, they were gone forever. He longed for a little peace and usefulness on this earth, a wife to give him children and the possibility of love. That was *his* faith. And he needed no God for it.

Sighing, Michael left his shotgun and sword by the font and paced the central nave. The soft glow through the windows illuminated frescoes painted half a millennium earlier, their colours fading but discernible.

Across an archway, scenes of Hell, scarlet devils and the souls of sinners writhing. Opposite it another arch: St George astride a warhorse in his knight's armour, thrusting a lance through the dragon's jaws. The dying monster's clawed legs waved like a puppy's; its tail wrapped feebly round one of the horse's forelegs.

Michael remembered the mummers acting out St George's victory on the beach of Hob Hole and a voice crying:

'I am that mickle mighty George! Look upon me
Thou serpent-creature that leads folk astray!
Look at this sword!'

The serpent in his gut twisted. Was he St George or the Dragon?

For a long while, Michael sat on the stone altar steps of the decaying church. Slowly, afternoon light shifted along walls and floor. A rueful blankness softened his doubts.

Then, as all thoughts long-prepared grow finally articulate, Michael Pilgrim glimpsed a kind of truth. He was neither St George nor Dragon, hero nor villain. In this mouldering architecture of belief, he understood the duty before him. Not to *preserve, preserve, preserve* as Grandfather had taught; it was too late for pining – and whining – over all they had lost.

At last, he understood his struggle with Pharaoh Jacko as bigger than both of them, a crusade worthy of the name. To build something new and good from the wreckage and debris his species left behind. Wit and reason might drive the work; kindness and patience and always faith in mankind.

A word favoured by his grandfather came to mind: *civilisation.*

He spoke it aloud, the precise syllables echoing defiantly round bare rafters. The word, so long weighed down by mourning, quickened Michael Pilgrim's heart. He felt breath deepen and accepted another paradox: that when Pharaoh Jacko's army arrived in Pickering, only the worst savagery might secure civilisation.

With a final glance at St George, Michael retrieved his weapons and headed for Pickering Castle and a council of war.

WILL O' THE WISP

On the same day Pharaoh Jacko's army fought the self-styled Free Folk of North Yorkshire, another force was on the move. If that is, squelching through marshes counted as moving. The boots and legs sucked by East Yorkshire's peaty mires belonged to feet accustomed to firmer ground.

'Are we lost again?' muttered Tom Higginbottom. A pointless question, they were blatantly lost. Even turning back would be a slog; churning feet had only made the fen path boggier. It seemed all East Yorkshire had reverted to swamp, and no one knew a quick way around.

The column led by Tom Higginbottom consisted of Baytown refugees and other folk from coastal districts with common cause against Big Jacko. Weapons and gunpowder had been readied, bands of volunteers drilled. Two hundred with nought to lose and homes to regain, a force capable of tipping the scales – if only they could join their allies in Pickering.

Tom Higginbottom, however, was learning that some prefer to blot out misfortune than face it head-on.

'*Dementia,*' giggled ex-Corporal Baxter, high on stuff carried all the way from Scarborough, a town that had grown a mite too hot for the former Crusader. Hence his decision to join the Baytown refugees.

'Dementia?' Tom never hid his scorn when it came to Baxter. 'Is that it?'

Baxter sniggered. 'Don't blame me.'

'Look,' said Higginbottom, 'you're the one who swore this road would take us to York. And from there it's only a short day's march to Pickering. Now we'll be too late to matter!'

Baxter blinked at the angry fisherman. 'It must have led there once, guy,' he reasoned. 'All roads lead everywhere if you follow 'em long enough.'

The grumbling column retraced its steps. So large a body of soldiers could not help but attract attention – and fear. Villagers who rarely saw a stranger other than tinkers or wandering entertainers hid until they had passed.

Their new route took them to the outskirts of Hull, a vast, silent grave of concrete and brick that stretched for miles in the sunshine. Midges swarmed round pools in bomb craters, and a haze filled the horizon. Tom had a notion motorways would lead from the port, highways too formidable to succumb to swamp; if not clear roads, maybe they could follow railway tracks north.

Every hour of delay tightened his despair and fear. His whole family's future depended on this march; on the refugees tramping along the shore of the Humber, joining a dual carriageway still silted by winter floods.

As the mighty Humber Bridge drew near, many in the company grew afraid, a few tearful, lamenting how far they had fallen from the glory of their ancestors.

Sunset: the west alight with low fires. Tom shielded his eyes. Something glinted on the road ahead like a will o' the wisp. He made out a slender figure on a shaggy pony, a young woman, the glint coming from a highly-polished hubcap hung around her neck. Gold and silver ornaments were sewn into her purple coat.

The girl trotted closer, and he became aware of a hand tugging his sleeve.

'I've seen her before,' whispered Baxter.

'Aye?'

'She lived in Scarborough for a while,' said Baxter. 'Came there with a man who disappeared. She waited round for him then left. She can look after herself.' His manner suggested personal experience. He licked his lips.

'Aye?'

The girl waved at a wooden fort on an earthen hill a mile or so from the bridge. When she spoke, her accent was strange to Baytown ears.

'My brother's lord of yon fort,' she said. 'He might help you.'

'If you want to help us, lass,' said Tom, 'you'll show us the quickest road to Pickering. Even then it won't be quick enough.'

'I've a question first,' she said, touching a dog fur entwined round the polished hubcap across her chest like a charm. 'About a feller from Bay.'

When Tom and Baxter heard the man's name and her interest in him – and her brother's concern, for understandable family reasons – each reacted their own way.

'Blow me,' muttered Tom.

'*Dementia*,' breathed Baxter.

GOOD

Pickering was a plum worth picking. A ring of prosperous farms and hamlets surrounded the market town, soil well planted and fallowed, woods coppiced and maintained, herds pastured and wormed. Hence Pharaoh Jacko's army made slow progress south. The lure of booty melted away large sections of the column. Threats, promises and cajoling were required to reassemble them. By then, plumes of smoke rose for miles around.

Two days wasted in this way, with the bulk of the army camped around a manor house two miles north of the town. Pharaoh Jacko fumed impotently. Others, like Stu, reckoned it days not wasted at all.

Scouts led by him rode a slow circuit of the town, discovering numerous streets blocked by demolished buildings – in effect a city wall constructed of rubble. A sure sign, too, of the defenders' determination.

If the Pharaoh's men stormed the mounds of bricks and slates and glass, what then? More barriers of shattered houses waited. Seth detected his uncle's cunning behind it all, for everyone knew Michael Pilgrim served as the Pickers' general.

Big Jacko and his commanders listened gravely to Stu's report as twilight fell. None fancied another Horcum.

'They're sly as foxes,' opined the new Reiver-Captain, successor to one dismembered by the Modified Man's exploding barricade. 'They prefer nipping at us to straight fighting.'

Pharaoh Jacko occupied his favourite throne, transported there in the wagon train. No indication of his thoughts reached his brown eyes.

'We could siege 'em,' pondered a red-bearded Jock. 'Starve 'em out. Fuckin' Tykes! Aye, I cannae see wha' else will answer.'

Everyone guessed the Jock-Captain's intention. Raze the district while its defenders were trapped in the town then return to Jockland with as much plunder as they – and any slaves they took – could carry.

Seth kept quiet. It was Stu who spoke out as Captain of the Pharaoh's Horse.

'No need for that,' he said, jauntily. 'Because them Pickers are chicken, they've left a back way half open so they can scarper to Malton if their walls get busted. The only barrier's a few cars. Get through that, and you're into the market square. That's right in the centre of the town.'

Big Jacko's eyelids fluttered.

'You sure, Stu?'

The tousle-haired young man nodded. 'Rode up real close myself, boss. They took a few pot shots, but I could see they think we're too dumb to come at 'em from behind.'

'Good,' said Pharaoh Jacko. Now his cold gaze moved from face to face. All but the Jock-Captain glanced aside. 'Good.'

FIVΣ

———◦✛◦———

PICKERING CASTLE (1)

Dawn cast tints of pink and copper over Pickering Castle's tumbled stones and walls. Built by Norman invaders then conquered by neglect, that May dawning granted the place fresh life. The walls were intact enough to serve as a dubious defence, its ditches still deep enough to slow attackers. And so the Free Companies used it as their armoury, parade ground and headquarters.

Within the circuit of the walls rose a steep-sided mound of earth topped by ruins and protected by a dry moat. Upon this little hill stood Michael Pilgrim and his officers. Before them paraded a sizable army, six companies of fifty or sixty, each with different coloured armbands and a flag, trained and drilled by their general. Reluctant soldiers eager to return to their perpetual war against hunger in farms and steadings.

Looking down on them, Michael felt no glow to match the sunrise. What discipline they had acquired might melt at the first test. Then all would be lost: Pickering, Malton, the entire North. Then civilisation would be a notion mocking him to his grave.

The Modified Man, who stood beside him, stirred.

'It is customary for a general to address his troops before battle,' he wheezed, trunk-nose dripping. Mornings were never a good time for the Modified Man's sinuses.

'Aye,' broke in Mister Priest Man, 'I heard a flutter of wings last night, Pilgrim, the Faery o' the Vale visiting us. Sow a little of her luck on those frightened lads down there.'

Expectant faces gazed up at them, and Michael Pilgrim shrugged. When he spoke his voice echoed around the castle walls.

'Friends! I'll not talk long. Soon all of us must take up the position we've been given. And not a one of us must budge from it. Not one of us! Only when ordered to do so. Our plan depends on that, friends! It's a good plan. A blessed plan.' (Here he shot Mister Priest Man a glance and was met with an approving nod). 'I say, it will bring us victory!'

He paused. Was that the sound of marching feet? For a wild moment he thought Tom Higginbottom had arrived with the reinforcements they wanted so badly. But it was only an echo, a projection of his hopes, maybe a mockery.

Michael knew he should say more, encourage them to die for their own cause. His grandfather came to mind, Reverend Oliver Pilgrim making him learn speeches from Shakespeare, including *Richard the Third*, and a jumbled version emerged:

'Friends, if you fight bravely today you'll sleep without fear for years to come. If you show no mercy to those who deserve none, you can be merciful the rest of your days. If you kill a man today, think: "That man could be the one stealing all I've built in this world. The man spoiling my wife and daughter!" If you fight well, I say, wives and children and grandchildren will call you their hero and protector. Aye, all the days of your life!'

He drew his razor-edged City sword. His officer's sword.

'For civilisation!' he roared.

Though precious few of the soldiers before him knew what the word meant they understood a sword. Cheers erupted, drums and rattles sounded, trumpeters blew a cacophony of defiance.

The Modified Man leered. 'Looks like King Jacko might have a rival for his throne,' he snuffled. 'Shame he outnumbers us four to one. Or was it five?'

BATTLE

Pharaoh Jacko made no speeches that dawn other than to curse his commanders for slowness. Seth reckoned the boss should be happy it took so long to form up: to him their army seemed the greatest parade on earth. Today's battle would tear the region open like a loaf of fresh bread.

They marched from Kingthorpe Manor down the Whitby Road to Pickering. No foghorn yet, Big Jacko told Seth to stay close and sound the attack when ordered.

During the night a barricade had been thrown up by the Pickers to block the road. As the front ranks of the column approached, puffs of smoke became bangs, whizzes and cracks. Seth reined in alongside Big Jacko. Although a few of their men had fallen from the guns and arrows discharged by the Pickers behind their pathetic barrier, none of the enemy hung around. Down the hill or into the maze of collapsed buildings they fled, back into the town.

Pharaoh Jacko watched impatiently as cars and bits of wood were pulled aside.

'Don't seem many of 'em, boss,' said Stu. 'There weren't that many at Horcum either.'

Jacko said nothing. Never had he looked more like a king, splendid on his battle horse, padded with armour and weapons.

'Shall I sound the foghorn?' asked Seth.

'Not yet,' said Jacko. 'When I say.'

Seth felt a stir of jealousy as Jacko gripped Stu's elbow.

'Ride down there and see if that little way in you told me about is still wide open.'

Moments later scores of cavalry were clattering down the hill, ahead of the column.

On one side of the Whitby Road, high mounds of bricks and masonry blocked all entry points into town: a pathless, tangled maze where Pickers could be seen lurking. Easy to see their game. Numbers would count for little fighting house to house. But the Pharaoh wasn't a fool.

'Keep straight on,' he ordered his commanders. 'We'll enter Pick'ring through its backside!'

The march increased its pace. Arrows and pot shots from the west side of the road took down more men until skirmishers were sent out and the Pickers turned chicken yet again, melting out of sight into the ruins.

Within minutes, the column reached a large roundabout athwart a crossroads. More bullets fell upon the vast army. More skirmishers charged out and drove back bands of Pickers, both sides firing pistols and muskets at close range. Seth kept low in his saddle, itching to sound the foghorn.

Stu and his cavalry galloped back to join their Pharaoh.

'It's just as it was last night down here, boss.' His horse bucked slightly as a bullet whined past. 'Just a barricade leading to the Market Place so they can escape easily.'

'I reckon they've already withdrawn the bulk of their army to Malton,' said Seth, eager to be heard. 'That's where the big battle will be, not here.'

Big Jacko nodded, lifted his tall, yellow Pharaoh's crown and bellowed in a voice deep as a bass drum.

'This is it, boys! I want to own this town by midday!'

Seth pressed a button. The foghorn sounded long and loud. *Bo-o-o-o-m. Bo-o-o-o-m.* Its mournful voice echoed off walls and roofs and lampposts that had shed no light for generations.

Answering roars came from the Pharaoh's legions. Weapons waved, mouths opened wide. Then the companies at the front were trotting after Stu's cavalry, heading for the market square.

Seth didn't give Pickering an hour, let alone until midday.

THE MARKET PLACE

Michael watched as the Pharaoh's horsemen pulled aside the low barrier of burned out cars. The men he'd ordered to defend it were already fleeing into the Market Place, firing panicked shots as they retreated. So far so good.

His plan's first critical test was coming. If the Free Companies' discipline broke in the next ten minutes, all was over. If only Tom Higginbottom had come! Michael knew he could have relied on Tom and the Baytown refugees to hold firm.

'They're here!' cried a young lad with a pea-green armband, brandishing a halberd. 'Fuckin' 'ell! Look!'

A surging mass of warriors, poor men from irradiated Geordieland, want and hunger their birthright. Many barefoot – and more comfortable that way – with crude weapons and armour. A few armed with muskets, blunderbusses, long-barrelled pistols. Crossbowmen, too, plenty of those. With so many pushing their front ranks into the square he didn't fear their firearms. Hand-to-hand fighting was the danger as they massed in the Market Place.

Every exit had been deliberately blocked with demolished buildings save one: a wide, steep road to the ruins of Pickering Castle on its hill. A road called, appropriately enough, Castlegate. Michael knew he had moments to get the two companies he led into position. If Jacko sent in his cavalry before that, his precious plan would unwind.

'Quick! Quick!' he ordered, shoving men into place. 'Azure Company, there! That's it, pikes! Shooters at the back and in between. That's it! Come on, you Pea Greens!'

Lines of pikes and halberds levelled, scores of gun barrels raised.

Bo-o-o-o-m came Big Jacko's foghorn from somewhere out of sight, a sound Michael loathed. It reminded him of clinging to a cliff as all Baytown crawled through a hoop before the new Pharaoh's throne. A harsh fury gripped him.

'Ready, friends!' he cried, cocking his shotgun and pacing before the ranks. 'Remember, we only retreat when I say. Slowly and in good order. Step by step.'

Ranks of frightened faces greeted him. White knuckles gripped the shafts of polearms. Unsteady hands hefted guns.

'They'll buy a bad bargain in Pickering Market today, friends!' he cried.

Men and lads chuckled hysterically at his feeble wit. Then something happened that Michael never expected, a voice at the back – wheezy, rheumatic, was it the Modified Man? – squeaked: 'A Pilgrim! A Pilgrim!' Another joined him. Another. Then both companies were chanting, their courage waxing with each shout: *A Pilgrim! A Pilgrim!*

BLOOD

In any fight, silent moments occur. Two male robins cheeping and fanning breast feathers to win a mate will pause, black, pitiless eyes glinting before sharp beaks stab. Stags, too, will assess a rival's strength before lowering horns. So it was in Pickering Market.

The column of shaggy-haired Reivers halted in the centre of the square. They saw a phalanx of lowered spear points, gun barrels like hollow eyes, flags waving.

'Fire!' cried a voice from within the pikemen.

A rolling volley at short range. Muzzles flashed. Sulphurous smoke billowed. Half the front rank of the Pharaoh's column fell, chests ripped open, limbs shattered. Others staggered back, blood welling through fingers vainly trying to staunch a wound.

Then the seething mass of Big Jacko's column made a disorganised dash across the square. One intention: to get close and hack a way through the Picker ranks.

The fight for Pickering Market had begun.

Michael Pilgrim fired. Snatched fresh cartridges from his bandolier. Fed his shotgun. Aimed. Fired again. The acrid smoke made him gasp, spit. Despite the haze, one thing was clear: the warriors with their swords and axes and discharged pistols were forming a wall of dead or twitching bodies in front of the Free Companies.

Don't be fooled, he urged himself, *stay with the plan*. A hundred were sure to be overrun by a thousand in the end; he knew that. The plan anticipated that.

A gust thinned the smoke. The enemy were regrouping on the other side of the square, preparing a final, decisive charge. Now was the time. Taking out a whistle he blew three sharp blasts. Other whistles answered. His officers had heard.

'Step by step, friends!' he urged. Numbed and in shock from the intensity of the last few minutes, the smoke-blackened ranks of the Free Companies retreated up the wide street of Castlegate. Soon they had left the smoke behind. Their equipment rattled as they hurried. No hordes pursued them. Not yet.

He pushed through to the front and straightened the line. Tired, nervous eyes met his own.

'Well done, lads!' he cried. 'Well done! They'll rue their bargain at our market today! Reload as we step backwards. That's it! Breathe deep! Keep moving back!'

His glance fell on the Modified Man clutching a multibarrelled pistol of his own manufacture. One of many fancy weapons he had brought to Pickering, eager to try out.

'What are you doing here?' hissed Michael Pilgrim. 'Get the fuck back to the castle!'

To his surprise, the freakish mutant obeyed, taking his bodyguards with him.

Back they stepped up the hill towards the castle. All the houses were sealed off, every side road blocked with rubble. Castlegate had become a funnel, its spout discharging at the top of the street outside Pickering Castle and into this funnel poured the Pharaoh's army. Like the Free Companies they pursued, there was nowhere to go but uphill.

'Far enough!' ordered Michael Pilgrim. By now they were two-thirds of the way up Castlegate. 'Close the ranks! Pikes, have your pistols ready this time.'

A hurried clatter of weapons. Those without firearms – and most of the Free soldiers carried a crude gun of some kind – held the pikes and halberds of others. A few men shook convulsively, amazed to have survived so long. The enemy had lost all vestiges of humanity. Animals to be put down without mercy.

Lumps of living flesh to transmute into dead flesh. Michael sensed his men's mood. It had got that way in the Crusades, too.

'This time we kill, friends!' he fumed, pacing in front of the ranks. 'But remember, retreat only upon the signal. Remember the plan, friends!'

The front ranks of Pharaoh Jacko's endless column marched through the rapidly dispersing fug of gunpowder smoke at the foot of the hill. Michael recognised a new determination in his enemies to match the Free Companies' own – corpse for corpse.

A PILGRIM

Seth heard a faint chant of voices calling his name and thought, momentarily, it was for him. He met Pharaoh Jacko's startled glance. The big man chuckled.

'Good,' he said, 'I need your uncle's head.'

Within the town, all hell broke loose. Seth guessed the noise came from the market square, crashing volleys, a din of shouting. No way to see what was happening with hundreds of troops milling between.

'Stu!' ordered Big Jacko. 'Cut a way through that lot an' tell me what's going on.'

Seth bit back jealousy. Stu! Always Stu! With a spur of his big horseman's boots and a dozen big-boned cavalrymen in his train, Stu waved the flat of his sword to clear a path through the foot soldiers queuing to enter the square. Soon the riders vanished round a corner. Still, the guns spoke. A fog of powder smoke settled on that end of the town. Its acrid, rotten egg taste made Seth spit.

He didn't doubt imminent victory. So few against so many!

Unexpectedly the gunfire dwindled into stray shots. Fell silent. Stu appeared, his sword sheathed.

'We've got 'em on the run, boss,' he said. 'Those Jocks and Reivers are earning their pay today. You'll see.'

Pharaoh Jacko led his mounted bodyguard and officers into the square, raggedy soldiers stepping aside to let them pass. There, as the smoke cleared, Seth stared down in surprise. The ground was thick with contorted lumps, many still alive, shrieking and calling for their mother or for help or water. His horse shied as it stepped gingerly round corpses to the entrance to Castlegate. Only a handful of the dead wore the coloured armbands of the Pickers.

The Pharaoh o' the North looked round incuriously.

'Stu was right again,' he said, after taking a report from the new Reiver-Captain. 'Sounds like there's not many of 'em. The rest must have scarpered. Probably back to Malton.'

He produced a hand-drawn map of the town from a pouch at his belt, the fruit of well-rewarded spies in the guise of tinkers. His wide forehead furrowed as he traced the shapes of charcoal lines with a finger. Seth was called over to help.

'The road they're taking leads up to the Castle, boss,' said the youth. 'It's just a ruin.' He spoke quickly so Stu couldn't beat him to it. 'Half its walls are down. I went there when I was a kid.' (And, Christ, hadn't Uncle Michael bored him back then with his history lectures). 'It's not a real fortress no more.'

Big Jacko nodded slowly and pointed at the entrance to Castlegate.

'Form 'em up,' he said.

Minutes passed as the mighty column of his army re-gathered. This time the Jocks rather than mauled Reivers took the lead.

CASTLEGATE

Michael Pilgrim had never been a patient fisherman. Odd, he was patient in most things. As he watched the mob of Jocks advance up the hill, trumpets blaring, axes, swords and flint-locks waving, he reacted wildly.

'Fire low!' he urged, aiming his own shotgun to cripple.

Crash went the volley. The pitiless routine resumed. Muzzles flashing and spewing spurts of smoke. The stench of powder. Fumble. Reload. Crash. A second volley.

One thing kept Michael from firing and killing until they were overwhelmed.

'The plan!' he shouted. 'Shooters back! Back! At the double! Pikes slowly now! Match my pace! Steady over there! That's it, friends!'

A critical moment. Trusty captains from Pickering and Malton led half their companies in a mad pelt to the top of the lane near the castle entrance. The rest, pikes and halberds levelled, retreated backwards in a crab-like shuffle, their pace set by a slow drumbeat.

Michael Pilgrim turned every few seconds to assess the enemy. As he'd expected, the two volleys in the narrow funnel of Castlegate had halted them. But they were holding their ranks. Not long before they advanced once more.

When the Free pikemen joined the shooters at the top of the hill, he paused.

'Into the castle everyone! Go! Go!'

The work of Azure and Pea Green Companies was almost done. One last twitch of the lure remained before the fish bit…

A mad scramble as they ran down and up ditches, friendly hands from within the broken castle walls pulling them into its doubtful protection.

Michael ran across a wide grassy space to the mound of earth at the heart of the castle, surrounded by a ditch lined with sharp wooden stakes. Heads poked up behind hastily rebuilt walls. Two more companies lurked in Pickering Castle, mostly hidden.

At the top of the mound, he drank deeply from a bucket of water, his chest heaving. Mister Priest Man watched, the holy man's eyes glittering.

'The Faery o' the Vale's still helping, Pilgrim! See!'

Indeed, the entire plan had worked so far. Big Jacko's army was massing outside the ineffectual castle walls, preparing to annihilate a trapped, exhausted enemy they believed to number no more than a hundred. Michael hurriedly re-filled his bandolier from a bag of cartridges.

'Bless her faery socks!' he cried. 'I might even give the old girl a kiss.'

The Nuager did not smile back. 'That wouldn't be wise,' he said. 'Mortal may not breed with immortal folk.'

Bo-o-o-o-m went the foghorn below. The Pharaoh's army was commencing its attack.

PICKERING CASTLE (2)

An egg-shaped circuit of ancient stone walls, low and uneven at the castle's front, the rest too high to climb without ladders: such was Pickering Castle. The Pharaoh's army prepared to pour into this enclosed space through its vulnerable front door. Confident in numbers, blood up, they gave no thought to what waited within.

The keep's high mound rose in the centre of the grassy oval, providing lots of masonry for cover, as well as fresh-built walls concealing a hundred men ordered to lie flat. Deep ditches before the keep were full of sharpened stakes, dividing the castle in two, a killing zone designed by wily Normans who knew well how to snare attackers.

Pharaoh Jacko surveyed his army. The Jocks and Reivers were raging. Too many would already never go home: brothers, uncles, friends from boyhood. He knew that lust for vengeance, how it flared then guttered. A wise general uses such wildfires. Others, perhaps wiser still, feared flames can burn the hand that tries to control them…

'Boss!' urged Stu, 'I don't like this. It's too easy. If we go in there, we'll be trapped.'

Pharaoh Jacko's eyes widened to show their whites.

'It don't feel right,' said Stu. 'At least let me ride round the castle walls and see what's what before we go in.'

Jacko wavered. Seth, envious of his comrade, cried out: 'It's just a pile of old stones in there, boss! They're the ones that are trapped. If we hang back, they'll escape out the back.'

The Pharaoh of the North laughed. He had come too far for this moment. So far! Besides, how could he keep in check the wild bloodlust of the men who followed him? Why should he?

'Finish the fuckers!' he roared, drawing scimitar and pistol. 'No pris'ners! Hear that, boys! I want the head of everyone in this town!'

His cry spread like an inferno. Soon it became a chant. *Take their heads! No prisoners!*

'Sound it, Seth!' he ordered, with quiet satisfaction. 'Crank her real loud!'

Bo-o-o-o-m. Bo-o-o-o-m. War cries joined the foghorn's voice, oaths and curses. Pharaoh Jacko's army surged madly forward, indifferent to crashing volleys as they stormed into the ditch before the castle entrance. Fallen men were trampled like grass.

'Yaah!' bellowed Big Jacko. For the Pickers had turned chicken again! Abandoning the walls, fleeing into the ruins of the castle.

Nothing stops a tide, thought Seth, as he watched crowds of men flow through the gatehouse and over the low outer walls. Nothing except a cliff.

PLANS

Within minutes of storming the walls, hundreds of men were packed inside the enclosed inner half of the castle's circumference, all sense of their officers lost in the crush. Behind them yet more shoved and strained to gain entry. The bedlam of their combined war-cries drowned out reason.

Michael turned to a lad crouching beside him on the crown of the keep's steep-sided mound. 'Send her up.'

The boy touched a large rocket with a match, and up it whooshed, exploding with a bang of sparks and smoke.

For a long moment, the struggling mass of soldiers below glanced up at the rocket. Then hundreds of flashes blinded them. Muskets, blunderbusses, pistols, rifles crashing and barking as the hidden Free Companies discharged their weapons. They could hardly miss at such range – nor did they.

No need for orders now. All that mattered: fire, reload, fire.

Michael barely noticed the Modified Man beside him, supervising a catapult he had devised to hurl grenades trailing spitting fuses into the mob below.

Crump. Crump. The grenades blew smoking holes in the packed ranks. Holes that filled rapidly. Those outside were still pushing in, unaware of the slaughter.

'Ha!' squeaked the Modified Man, readying another of his inventions. A dozen long steel pipes salvaged from a factory, fused together then mounted on a frame. Each tube loaded with powder, lead shot, sharp-edged stones.

Mucus dripped excitedly from his trunk as he lit fuses. Flame whooshed. More men perished below.

For shocked minutes the Pharaoh's army reeled, panicked, died. But these were fighting men to the bone; soon groups rallied and charged the hated Pickers. Fierce hand-to-hand struggles ended swiftly as Jock or Reiver was shot at point blank range or speared on a pike or halberd.

Up on the mound, Michael turned to the lad beside him.

'Fire the second rocket!'

Up it went. Now for the plan's finale. Though two hundred of the Free Folk fought in the castle, the remainder waited at its rear. Their moment had come.

Then Michael was firing again, gladdened to see the vast army of the Pharaoh in desperate retreat. Piles of corpses and wounded littered the turf, staining the summer grass black.

TRAPS

Seth's mare pawed the ground. Smoke formed a choking fog. Worse was the fog of noise: a constant smash of guns and thud of explosions. He could not imagine what was happening in the castle. Worse, far worse, he realised that the army was leaderless, out of control, its officers buried in a scrambling, elbowing mass of men. One half trapped within the walls, the other half outside.

'Boss!' shouted Stu. 'Boss! We got to pull back. It's a trap, like I said! Sound the retreat, boss.'

Pharaoh Jacko seemed unable to comprehend so sudden a reversal.

'Boss, we can still save the army,' urged Stu. 'Get 'em back down to the market square!'

Big Jacko stirred.

'Hit it, Seth,' he called. 'Do what Stu says.'

Short, anxious blares burst from the foghorn as Seth worked the button, praying its power wouldn't give out. The tuba-like voice throbbed a message of alarm through the din of guns.

Meanwhile, Big Jacko and his officers chivvied the first frightened group of soldiers from the castle walls, directing them back down the hill. Stu galloped the same way to rally the retreating men when they got there.

A second rocket rose from the castle and exploded.

'It's a signal!' muttered Seth, though no one was listening.

The rocket's message soon became clear. Round the side of the castle marched the remaining two companies of the Free Folk. These were men mostly without firearms, drilled to stay in close order with pike and halberd levelled.

'Fuck!' screeched Seth. 'Boss!'

The Pickers' collective cheer became a roar as they advanced. What might have been a semi-orderly retreat to the market square became a rout. Pikes pierced fleeing men. Anyone who stumbled or tried to fight back were hacked or stabbed. Still, the Pickers pushed forward until most of Big Jacko's army had fled after their Pharaoh into the town. The remainder were trapped in Pickering Castle.

Lucky for Seth's peace of mind he never witnessed the massacre. How fear infected placid men with senseless cruelty and bloodlust. How the piles of corpses mounted like haystacks in autumn and ditches grew muddy with blood.

SIX

DIE AND LEARN

As the midday sun rose over Pickering, there was a hurried council of war in the Black Bull Inn adjoining the square.

Seth stood with a dozen others in the taproom, facing the Pharaoh's throne – a hand-made wooden settle with a message carved in curly letters on its back: *A right warm welcome to ye!* A sullen, angry gathering. All knew Jacko's conquest tottered in the balance and that his decisions that morning had cost hundreds of lives.

'Well, boys,' he said, palms flat on his meaty thighs, legs spread apart, 'guess we underestimated 'em. Simple as. But that won't happen no more. How many have we got ready to fight?'

One by one the commanders reported. Seth was surprised how many had survived. But it is no easy business to kill a man. There were still enough, more than enough.

'And the Pickers, Stu?' brooded Big Jacko. 'How many do we reckon they've got?'

'Can't have started out with more than three hundred from what prisoners say.' Stu shrugged. 'And we've killed a portion of 'em, boss. Not as many as we'd like, but a good few.' Again he shrugged. 'You live an' learn, boss, that's what you always tell us.'

A white-toothed grin split Jacko's face. 'Yeah,' he growled. 'Live an' learn. What do you think we should do next, Stu?'

'Do? What they did to us. Tempt 'em down here, on our terms this time. Then give the fuckers payback.'

'What if they're not tempted?'

Stu considered. 'Either they march off to Malton, in which case we've won. Or they risk fighting, and we damn well make sure we do win. Either way, they lose, boss. All we have to do is wait.'

Big Jacko nodded. Seth felt confidence growing in the room.

'You're a smart boy, Stu,' declared the Pharaoh. He snorted. 'Live an' learn? Nah! Those Pickers are going to *die* an' learn.'

NOT OVER

'So there it is,' concluded the scout up in Pickering Castle, 'not over yet.'

Miraculously Pharaoh Jacko had rallied his army, that was plain. Michael sat at a table in the old chapel of the castle with the other officers: Mister Priest Man and the Modified Man – the latter apparently dozing – and six company commanders. Everyone exhausted to varying degrees and wary of what must come next.

'Well then,' began Michael Pilgrim in his role as General-Elect, 'we did better than any dreamed possible.'

Better if you discounted all conscience, he thought.

Abruptly the Modified Man woke with a twitch. '*Better* isn't good enough, Pilgrim!' he squeaked. 'Break them. Kill them. Drive them back to the atavistic hovels and sties where they belong, I say!'

Muttering round the table. For a start, only their general knew what *atavistic* meant – or thought he did.

'We haven't won yet,' agreed Michael, his tone reasonable, 'but you're right. What matters is finishing this. And we have a simple choice. Continue the battle while they are damaged and reeling from so many losses. Alternatively, withdraw and fight another day, in which case they'll probably burn Pickering to the ground. Either way, they won't take us for granted again.'

The officers considered his words. Half the army was desperate to return to their farms and the plantings that would prevent famine. Delay might result in desertions when they were already poorly outnumbered.

'How do you propose we win?' demanded the Modified Man, adding with a sneer, '*General?*'

Michael settled back in his chair. Sniffed. Whatever they had done to the Modified Man in Albion had been ruinous to his odour.

'By doing exactly what they want us to.'

'Which is?'

'Give them a chance for revenge.'

The stone chapel of Pickering Castle absorbed their talk, as it had voices and words beyond count for half a millennium.

'How do you propose to do that?' squeaked the Modified Man. 'I'm all ears.'

Beside him, Mister Priest Man scratched troublesome armpits. 'Offer a sacrifice to the toadstools, eh, Pilgrim?' he said. 'They drink blood, yer know, like men sup ale. How else do they have red spots?'

The Modified Man's dripping nose-trunk twitched at such nonsense. 'Savage!'

Michael Pilgrim, however, listened gravely to the Nuager. 'You might be onto something there, Priest Man,' he said. 'You certainly might.'

Half an hour later, the six companies – Pea Green, Azure, Marigold, Lilac, Buff and Grey – paraded in Pickering Castle. According to the roll call, their ranks were thinned but far from disastrously.

'So, friends,' concluded Michael Pilgrim, addressing them from the mound of the keep, 'we risk losing all we have won today by delay. Let's finish this, here and now. Then get back to our fields and crops. Who is with me?'

Loud cheers echoed off the derelict walls and corpses tossed into moat and ditch.

Three of the companies marched out of the castle's back gate into scrubland woods, the opposite direction to the Pharaoh's army waiting in the Market Place.

Three companies comprised of volunteers watched them depart. Baytown folk in the main, including Mister Priest Man and his Nuagers. Big Jacko's ambitions threatened the whole region, yet these felt a particular need for victory.

'Many a toadstool to sacrifice down there,' said the priest.

Michael checked the hammers of his shotgun and supply of cartridges.

SACRIFICE

Time sped and slowed when the firing started, and Seth's bowels felt distinctly loose. Bullets skipped and whistled and whined. Pretending to calm his nervous mare kept his mind off what was happening on the far side of the vast square. The Pickers were pushing wagons padded with sandbags, turning the wagons sideways to use as cover instead of charging into the dense horseshoe of men blocking their route.

Flights of arrows from the Pharaoh's men and a final ragged volley of muskets ended in a long *bo-o-o-o-m* from the foghorn. Not for retreat this time. There would be no more unwieldy, uncontrollable charges into traps where superior numbers were a hindrance rather than advantage.

'Just the Jocks attack!' shouted Pharaoh Jacko. 'Everyone else stays back! Give 'em plenty of room, boys!'

Seth ducked instinctively as the warriors drew long swords and dirks. They rushed at the feeble barricade, indifferent as dozens fell to the Pickers' volley.

Black bats flew over the desperate melee in the entrance of the square. Black bats with tails of smoke. *Crump. Crump.* Men howled, blinded by shrapnel, their faces and hands torn open. Still, grenades arched over. Some sprayed flaming oil that turned the Jocks' clothes into burning flags.

Seth became aware of shouting at the end of the market, currently blocked with piles of masonry from a burned-out ruin of a supermarket.

A flank attack, exactly as Stu had foreseen. But the Pickers would gain no advantage of surprise this time.

'Stu,' called Pharaoh Jacko from his big horse, 'sort 'em out.'

The cavalry needed no encouragement. A wave of Pickers was pushing back the Reivers placed on the tall heap of bricks and cars blocking the road. Stu tooted a hunter's horn.

Seth knew it was time. All fear left him. He felt a rush of exultation as his horse picked up speed. Then they were among the Pickers. He slashed his sword feverishly at dodging figures. One lunged to grab his reins, and he discharged his pistol into the man's face. Blood and bone and brains sprayed.

Again the hunter's horn. The cavalry were retreating! Had the Pickers won, after all? No, Stu knew his business, the charge had won time to assemble a phalanx of Reivers to stop the Pickers from getting further into the square. Their ranks opened to let the horsemen through.

Seth whooped. Got one! Blew off his face like bursting a pumpkin! Bang! That fuckwit wouldn't grab *his* reins no more!

They cantered back to the Pharaoh who was beaming. Another attempt at flanking – this time from the direction of the church – had been anticipated and halted. The Pickers had played their last trick. Now all they could do was fight and die.

Seth wondered if it was worth reloading his pistol. The enemy were being pushed back on three sides, outnumbered and weary. Soon they'd start throwing down weapons and begging for mercy. Then the fun would start. Seth remembered how slowly the Reivers had killed Charlie Gudwallah. Instinctively he moved his horse closer to Big Jacko and decided to reload his pistol after all.

SACRIFICE (2)

It had always been a desperate endeavour. More hope than plan, Michael Pilgrim saw that now, even as he discharged his last cartridges into the mass of warriors clambering over their broken barricade. They should have retreated to Malton while they still could. Too late.

Already Castlegate was clogged with bodies bearing coloured armbands, the bravest of the Free Folk.

Slinging the empty shotgun across his back with a practised movement, he drew his sword. The dull, plasti-steel City blade, his noble reward for butchering unarmed women, children and men enfeebled by famine. A Jock's small round shield lay at his feet, and he seized the buckler with his free hand then leapt into the melee.

Reason left him. All sense of moderation. Up, down, back, forth, his arms worked like a dancer wheeling and lunging to connect with other dancers. Except his partners fell back with dying screams and severed limbs. Gashes appeared on his arms. His bullet-proof vest bearing the legend POLICE took a slug that knocked him over backwards. Still, he kept hold of the sword, stunned while comrades parried and stabbed around him, his chest a throb of agony.

Not long now, he thought, must get up. The coloured armbands would take flight soon. A third already dead, maybe more. Most of all he dreaded capture and the torture that would follow. Must get up. And strong hands did indeed haul him to his feet.

He blinked through his pain at the wild warrior who had hold of him. For a moment he didn't recognise the bearded face inches from his own.

'Priest Man,' he gasped. 'Save yourself. It's over.'

Too weak to run, Michael knew that. The bullet stopped by his POLICE vest had winded him utterly. But the Nuager was laughing; behind him, the Modified Man was crowing about the success of his grenades.

'The Faery o' the Vale brought us a gift, Pilgrim!' chortled Priest Man.

As Michael's breathing steadied, he followed Priest Man's pointing finger. Disbelief became tears trickling down his blackened face.

REFUGEES

Tom Higginbottom had never thought highly of Pickering folk. Opinions he shared liberally with Corporal Baxter who trudged alongside, a faraway look in his ratty brown eyes for once unrelated to *stuff* ingested, snorted or smoked.

'You listening?' asked Tom, suspiciously.

'Don't get much choice,' muttered his comrade.

'Well, you bloody well should,' grumbled Tom, 'you might learn something for a change. Yonder plume of smoke is coming from Pickering itself unless I'm much mistaken.'

'Didn't like the way *she* left us in Malton,' Baxter said for the twentieth time.

'I told you,' said Tom, 'there was no need for her to lead us here by the collar. She promised to get us from Hull to Malton dead quick and by heck that she did.'

She being the mysterious girl who hailed them beside the Humber Bridge. Tom had no doubt their journey would have taken days longer if the girl and her brother hadn't guided them to York via a shortcut through Beverley. A happy route, as it turned out, because scores of Beverley folk who heard the hated floggers were in alliance with Big Jacko decided to join the Baytown refugees. At York, more swelled their ranks, stripping the populous city in response to an urgent summons from their fabled leader, the Modified Man.

'Don't mess with the Modified Man,' Baxter had advised Tom.

'Why's that then?'

'Because he isn't what he's meant to be.'

Tom had worked that out for himself.

After a quick rest in York, they had marched north once more, reaching Malton at midnight of the previous day. There *she* and her brother had ridden off, giving Tom a message and a tiny parcel wrapped in cloth.

'Give these to Michael Pilgrim,' she'd said with a searching look. 'Tell him this: the rest is his to choose.'

With that, she turned back towards the Humber and Hull.

The column – swollen yet further by a few score armed folk from Malton, including brawny Aggie Brown, who had been patrolling the area for raiders and flaying alive any foolish enough to surrender – set off before first light and arrived at Pickering early in the afternoon, only to find smoke rising from the town and a rumble of gunfire.

'We're not too late then,' said Tom. 'Pass round an order, Baxter.' He frowned down at his comrade who was blinking and fidgeting. 'On second thoughts, I'll do it.'

Hundreds of men and women prepared weapons and snatched a dry meal. Then they marched towards the town at double pace.

No drums beat or horns heralded their advance. Aggie Brown, who knew Pickering well, rode out with other mounted soldiers to find the enemy. When she came clomping back on her massive carthorse, Tom's eyes gleamed at her tale.

'Well, I'll be damned. Remember the kind of days we used to have in the Crusades, Aggie? You know, when everyone got together like.'

Oh, she remembered, her sly, ugly look showed that clearly enough. And, come to think of it, Tom had heard stories of how she took it upon herself to abattoir the livestock on her large farm – cows, swine, poultry and sheep – the lot. Not every Crusader carried a burden of guilt.

'Might be one of those days again, Aggie,' he said. 'Don't you think?'

A woman of few words, she stared with disturbing intensity in the direction of Pickering.

CONQUEST'S END

Without trickery or ruses to help them the Pickers were turning out ordinary warriors. Already they were being pushed back against walls and rubble, small groups surrounded by men with no thought of mercy. The fight was to the death now. Its aftermath would be conquest, new owners of farms and livestock and women and land.

'Lord o' the North!' Seth cried, as Pharaoh Jacko rode up. Others took up the call.

'We're not finished yet, boys!' shouted Jacko. 'When they start to run, that's when we ride 'em into the ground!'

Not long, not long, thought Seth, checking his pistols for the tenth time. Through drifting gun smoke, he peered at the struggle round Castlegate until a voice interrupted him.

'What the fuck!'

Seth followed Stu's gaze to the rear of the square. Guards had been posted there, now they were scattering like panicked pigeons.

'Where you goin'?' roared the Captain of the Pharaoh's Horse, reaching down to grab a fleeing man.

The man glanced back fearfully the way he'd come, towards the roundabout leading out of town – or into town, depending on your direction of travel. ... Then Seth got it.

'Boss!' he shouted, yanking his charger's reins in a circle. 'Look!'

Big Jacko turned slowly. His face gradually changed expression: astonishment, wonder then horror. Had they not suffered enough surprises for one day? Victory turning into massacre in Pickering Castle. Relentless casualties from the moment they entered this dismal town – a place Big Jacko fully intended to reduce to ash once the battle was won. Now this.

Into the square marched a column of pikemen and shooters in good order. Seth recognised their leader at once: Tom Higginbottom! Beside him his son, young Ben, and with them every Baytown refugee capable of bearing arms. Here, exactly where they shouldn't be.

'Line up! Line up!'

Stu was calling, marshalling his cavalry for a charge. Their best hope. Sweep the newcomers out of the market square before they could deploy.

Crash. The volley knocked a dozen lads from their saddles. Other bullets struck the horses themselves. Everywhere beasts bucked and reared.

'Charge!' shouted Stu. No one was ready.

Crash. The second volley as deadly as the first; riderless horses galloped away from the bristling pikes. Seth discharged his pistol without aiming.

The third volley broke Pharaoh Jacko's cavalry. They dashed in all directions, seeking a way out of the market square and the panic spread, infecting the foot soldiers hacking or stabbing at the Pickers. One by one, then in wild groups, Reivers and Jocks ran towards exits from the square, ways deliberately blocked with rubble and demolished buildings.

Now the pikes were advancing slowly, pausing every ten yards for the shooters to reload and fire. The much-reduced Free Companies found fresh heart and fought with cruel determination, cutting down enemies who minutes earlier had threatened to overwhelm them. Thus, the Baytown refugees commenced a massacre to rival the one planned for themselves. There was no virtue or justice to it, none at all, just bare, brutal power.

As Michael Pilgrim averted his gaze from the grim scenes in the square, he seemed to hear Charlie Gudwallah's voice, its exact music already fading in his memory, saying as he poured out drinks in the Puzzle Well Inn, *Shame's everywhere, Michael, shame's everywhere.*

SΣVΣΠ

—◆—

FYLINGDALES MOOR

Evenings in late May could fall bleak on Fylingdales Moor. Sunset driven over the land by low gusts; rain spatters on thorn tree and heather. In the dusk-light, the radar station's buildings hunched like malevolent shadows. Little wonder sensible travellers hurried past Fylingdales, a more haunted spot hard to imagine. But not all travellers were sensible.

'Do you think he saw us?' whispered Tom Higginbottom.

He referred to the silhouette of a man pacing the flat roof of the radar pyramid, high above the moor.

'No signs,' replied Michael Pilgrim.

Four figures crouched behind a large concrete administration block half a mile from the pyramid. Tom and Michael, faces blackened with ashes; Aggie Brown armed with four pistols and several butcher's knives; and a new recruit, Murphy, recently a gaoler serving Big Jacko at Fylingdales. He had been allowed no weapons.

'The entrance to the tunnel is there,' muttered Murphy, indicating concrete steps leading down to a basement beneath the sagging administrative block. Pungent ferns and lichen filled the narrow stairwell. 'I found it but didn't tell no one. They won't expect us popping up like moles.'

'Better not,' said Aggie – a speech two words longer than most of her utterances. To underline her meaning, she half-drew a razor-sharp knife honed on the throats of numerous heifers and sheep.

'No need for that, Aggie, I'm sure,' said Michael.

Murphy was frightened enough already.

The ex-gaoler had come forward as soon as Michael and the other victors from Pickering rode into Baytown. That had been yesterday, all celebrations cut short by the discovery Averil Pilgrim and Helen Devereux were beneath Fylingdales, along with Tom's wife and other malcontents against Big Jacko's rule. Potential hostages rather than mere prisoners.

Murphy reported only half a dozen men loyal to the defeated Pharaoh were in Fylingdales, along with his queen and her serving women.

'There's kids, too,' he said, 'the Queen's brats and one other, a baby.' He paused. 'And someone close to you, boss,' he'd added, reluctantly. 'Your nephew.'

'Seth?' asked Michael. 'So he wasn't killed in the fighting.'

Less complicated all round if he had been.

Murphy had another tale to tell: of a tunnel, a dark, unstable, dank way in and out of the pyramid, but one he alone had discovered, being a man fond of caves and potholes.

'I'll show you, boss,' he'd promised, 'if you'll pardon me for any wrongs I might have done against your kin.'

A deal Michael accepted reluctantly. His gut distrusted Murphy.

Yet there they were, crouching as twilight settled on Fylingdales Moor, preparing to follow the turncoat's lead. Twenty heavily armed men hid in outbuildings at the edge of the radar station, ready to rush forward, but Michael acknowledged they had placed themselves in Murphy's grubby hands.

'Well then,' he said, by way of command.

Murphy descended the concrete steps into the basement and vanished from view.

TUNNELS

The maze of communication tunnels beneath the base was intended for safe passage during an attack. A hundred and fifty years after their construction they were safe as quicksand.

'You sure this is the way?' demanded Tom.

Water dripped, and the concrete passage reeked of earth, mould, stenches reminiscent of shallow graves. Occasionally their torch beams revealed side rooms storing rusty machines of doubtful purpose. One chamber contained three skeletons spongy with algae laid out on plastic tables.

'There's nowt valuable on 'em,' Murphy advised.

How deep were they underground? Michael couldn't tell. He recognised the sound of running water and turned to their guide.

'What's that?'

Murphy grew shifty. 'Wasn't here before,' he said. 'I dunno.'

'How long is it since you last took these tunnels?'

A year, it turned out. Much changes in a year.

'We go either forward or back,' pointed out Tom.

On they crept, torch beams scanning the ground ahead, the air rank and ticklish. The noise of dripping water intensified.

'Wasn't like this last time,' said Murphy, clearly rattled.

'Are we lost?' asked Michael.

'Nay.'

'Should we go back?'

'Nay.'

'Then on?'

'I s'pose so, boss.'

Michael didn't like the turncoat's habit of addressing him as he had once Big Jacko. Now did not seem the time to mention it.

'Well then,' he said.

The descending tunnel levelled out. All halted, peering up at the ceiling for signs of collapse. Further on their suspicions were justified. The roof had caved in and an underground stream – the source of the noise – formed a small waterfall that was clearly behind the landslip. Their torch beams reflected muddy, bubbling water. Only a narrow way through remained, low and irregular in shape.

'I swear this is new!' said Murphy, beginning to panic.

Michael understood the man's fear: how Big Jacko would have punished such a failure. He laid a hand on Murphy's arm.

'I believe you. It's okay.'

Murphy's breath came in gasps. His eye fell on Aggie Brown. Her hand had crept to the hilt of her butcher's knife.

'Can you scout through yon hole and see if the way ahead is clear?' asked Michael.

'Aye,' said Murphy, 'I will.'

With that, Murphy crawled into the hole, his torch raised so as not to get it wet. A few minutes later he called out.

'It's good, boss! Through to the other side in no time and the tunnel's sound.'

Michael made as though to follow, but Aggie stopped him with a raised palm and wriggled through first. Michael then Tom Higginbottom followed. And that caused the mischief. Both were big, broad men, not least Tom. His foot caught the earthen wall of the gap, and it began to cave in. A sudden rumble then billowing soil covered his legs.

Lucky for him friends waited on the other side to haul him out. A minute later they stood in the concrete tunnel, gasping as they examined the blocked way behind them.

There had better not be another collapse ahead of us, thought Michael, or we'll be here forever.

'Not far now,' breathed Murphy. 'Best to show dim lights if we can.'

THE COURT OF PHARAOH JACKO

Rooms and offices once humming with devices filled the central radar pyramid. Here uniformed technicians had scanned the heavens for satellites, cosmic debris, intercontinental ballistic missiles. All gone, washed away by forgotten tides. Only the satellites kept circling the earth, unheeded in a vacuum.

Averil Pilgrim knelt on the floor alongside Helen Devereux, their hands bound by thick plastic cable torn from the radar equipment. Despite aching hunger, she watched the comings and goings around her closely. Not many courtiers were left: Queen Morrighan, of course, and her bruiser-women, the same who had tormented Averil after Baytown fell. And Miriam Armitage fussing over her baby son day and night. So much for the women.

Averil counted only six fighting men besides their leader, one of whom, like Miriam, refused to acknowledge her existence. Early on she had made the mistake of whispering Seth's name when he passed, but Queen Morrighan heard and a sound slapping followed. Her brother had fidgeted and frowned as she grovelled beneath the pale woman's blows.

Oh, Averil knew that surly look on his face! The same confusion and consuming rage he had felt most of his life. Father had provoked it constantly, as had Uncle Michael, and now, amidst the tatters of his faith in new, stronger gods, that look was back.

Hours passed miserably in the bare, dusty rooms, Pharaoh Jacko stiff on a plastic chair, bloodshot eyes staring into space. Sometimes he raged at followers no longer alive, accusing them of cowardice and treachery. Then all lowered their eyes, cringing as he paced like a caged tiger, his meaty hands restless. Other times he boasted of a deliverance he expected any moment and his cleverness in keeping back a bargaining chip worth all of Baytown ten times over. 'No one beats Big Jacko in the end,' he said. And Averil half believed him.

By her side slumped Helen Devereux. The girl reached out her bound hands to squeeze the older woman's cold fingers. The ravages of the prison on Helen's perfect beauty shocked Averil; time had coarsened her ivory skin and sagged her cheeks so swiftly, tiny wrinkles appearing on her neck and forehead, even her elegant hands. It was as though a curse lay on the City woman, like a mermaid taken from the sea to shrivel upon land.

As night fell, Miriam's husband strode into the room. His thick leather coat smelt of rain and his boots were soaked.

'Good news, boss,' he said.

Big Jacko's brooding gaze lifted to meet his lieutenant's.

'The Deregulator talked to Seth about a trade,' reported Stu, 'through some kind of speaking wall in his compound. We didn't get to meet him face to face. But Seth did good, boss. The Deregulator said he was going to come here in person to collect her. That was a couple of hours ago. Might already be on his way.'

No reaction from the big man.

'Where is Seth?' asked Jacko. 'Has he come back with you?'

'His horse took a stone in its hoof near Sleights,' said Stu. 'He thought you needed the news real quick, so I left him walking his horse back here. He'll be along.'

Big Jacko rose impatiently. His glance fell on Queen Morrighan and her women.

'You think I ain't going to get what I want, don't you?' His fists balled. 'You ungrateful fuckers think Jacko hasn't seen the look in your eyes. Big Jacko sees everything!'

His rage subsided. Queen Morrighan glanced fearfully at the shuttered windows. Thrusting a pistol and scimitar in his belt, Jacko walked to the door.

'We'll wait for him on the roof, Stu,' he said. 'Nothing like greeting a guest nicely, eh?'

With a quick nod at Miriam clutching their baby, Stu followed his boss out.

DIM LIGHTS

Aggie led the way. One hand held a torch swaddled with muslin, the other her knife. Murphy sidled behind, aware Tom kept a close eye on him.

'You'll see, boss,' he breathed in Michael's ear. 'They've fitted new doors, so it's impossible for prisoners to get out. Don't mean we can't get in though.'

Murphy waved at Aggie to halt. The air was suddenly different, the stink of damp less intense.

'Nearly there,' he said. In the ghostly light of Aggie's torch, he looked haggard. Again Michael smelt betrayal. No help for it.

Murphy took them to a steel door at the tunnel's end and pointed to say, *down yonder*.

A general readying of weapons followed. Michael wore his bulletproof vest complete with bullet holes, the word POLICE obscured by ashes and dirt.

Murphy pushed gently at the rusty door, its creak loud enough to stir Fylingdales' numerous ghosts – or guards. Tom reacted to the noise by pushing it aside and ducking through, sword in hand, turning his torch to full beam so he might blind any ambushers. A long, bare corridor greeted them, stretching into darkness. Tom doused the light.

Murphy found himself thrust in front as a human shield.

'How far?' whispered Michael.

'Couple of corners, I swear.'

Once more they used the glow-worm of Aggie's torch for illumination. With each corner, the air grew fresher. Finally, a light showed at the end of the corridor.

Murphy nodded eagerly and pointed. But Aggie was already padding towards the light, a knife in each hand. Tom followed warily.

Wait here, Michael motioned to Murphy, his own sword ready.

A minute passed. Then Tom was at the end of the corridor, waving.

Could it be so easy? Michael counted nigh on twenty folk gathered in the guardroom before the long, concrete bunker that had served as their prison. As for the gaoler, no cause to worry about him. Aggie had cut his throat as he slept in his bunk.

'Now we can't question him,' hissed Michael, angrily.

She answered with a cruel smirk. Some dreamed different dreams about the Crusades, learned different lessons. Still, she was an ally, and Aggie Brown was better on your side than not.

The prisoners clung to each other, emaciated and pale as mushrooms. Many bore lesions and scabs, all were clearly starved. Not much prospect of them fighting despite there being plenty of weapons left in the guardroom. Michael watched Tom Higginbottom's wife sob in her husband's arms – tears of grief and comfort, fear and hope. Of Averil, no sign. Beth Higginbottom said she was upstairs with the Pharaoh's queen, a special hostage.

'Helen Devereux? The City woman?' asked Michael.

Tom's wife revealed she had been taken with Averil.

'Let's find them both,' he said. 'Then get out of here.' He shot a suspicious look at Aggie Brown. 'See those handcuffs on the shelf, Aggie? They're an alternative to killing everyone we meet. Pass them round. If we can take prisoners, we will. Murphy, show us the way to the front entrance.'

The turncoat picked up a short-handled halberd from a peg and led them to a flight of concrete stairs.

THE TESTAMENT OF JACKO

From the flat roof of the radar pyramid, Jacko stared up at the half-moon. Drizzle fell, and a low wind sighed over the moor. Stu waited besides him, listening in silence as his master spoke.

'Those fuckers let me down,' growled the big man. 'I ain't going to forget it neither. When we're back on our feet, Stu, I'm going to take an army up north and make 'em pay. Reivers, Jocks, they'll shake at the name of Jacko!' He struck his chest then his voice softened.

'They're out there now, scattered across the North. They believed in Jacko and his luck. Bad luck all round.' He paused, pondered. 'Ever wonder about luck, Stu? What it is. Why it comes one man's way and not another's. Luck's like a hope turned real. It's where everything in the world comes together to work your way. The crazy thing is most men don't even know when they're lucky. Not a bleedin' clue! Me, I know I'm lucky. Why? Because Jacko was born to be king, he can't help it. *That's* how he's lucky. Because Jacko sees what other men don't even guess. *That's* how he's lucky. Because Jacko…'

He frowned.

'Maybe I ain't so lucky,' he said, troubled eyes scouring the skies towards Whitby. 'Every day I think of me kids I lost in London. Every day! It makes me want to make the whole world pay. But the world is too big, Stu, we're made for what it wants, not the other way round…'

Again he seemed to consider.

'They say a man makes his own luck. So is what happened me own fault? Losing what I had in London then here? I bet you're thinking, *How can Jacko be lucky when he's just lost a battle and ain't even got a home?* Well, Stu, I'll tell yer, Jacko's lucky 'cos he never says die. Never says never. To the death, that's Jacko's motto, to the death!'

Then, arms straight by his side, eyes upturned to the gibbous moon, Big Jacko began to croon softly, his voice an echo of the wind playing the dark, dank moor, a favourite song learned from his mother when he was not yet five, before she vanished one night, and he never learned why, a song that had seen him through a lifetime's calamities and triumphs: *I'm forever blowin' bubbles, pretty bubbles in the air…*

Stu listened until the first verse ended and his leader turned to him with sudden gentleness.

'Now go and get us both a drink, son. I'm thirsty, and the Deregulator will come soon.'

'Sure, boss.' said Stu, relieved to be allowed to go. 'Drink comin' up.'

TO THE DEATH

No one barred the rescuers' way up from the dungeon beneath the radar station, up through stairwells bordering a lift shaft, their weapons ready. The released prisoners followed a little behind, hobbling and supporting one another.

'There,' muttered Murphy into Michael's ear, pointing up a flight of stairs at a metal door askew on its hinges. 'Beyond there's a room, a kind of big lobby. The pyramid's right above it. You'll find double doors there that take you out onto the moor.'

Michael recollected the steel blast doors set in walls three feet deep.

'Okay.'

'At the back of the big room,' continued Murphy, 'are other places where that bitch – the Queen – will be with her women. And most likely your kin, Averil.'

'Jacko?'

His question soft as breathing.

'Could be anywhere.'

Murphy was shaking again, hands unsteady on the halberd. Michael met Tom and Aggie's eyes and came to a decision. Sheathing his sword, he unslung the shotgun from his back and waved them to follow, a finger on his lips. 'Only shoot if I do,' he mouthed.

Up the last stairs, they padded. Adrenaline drove them forward, cold and fast.

Tom Higginbottom peered through the doorway. Pale electric light cast a beam on his face. He held up three fingers to his comrades. Voices could be heard clearly.

Is the boss up there now?

A London accent.

Yeah, with Stu.

A third voice broke in, also a Londoner.

Stu said the boss has a plan.

He's always got a fuckin' plan.

Tom rose, set his boot against the door. With a fluid movement, he thrust it fully open and dodged through, stubby musket levelled.

Michael darted after, his gun barrel seeking targets, Aggie close behind with her two pistols. He took in the scene at a glance.

The lobby was wide, lift shaft on one side, doorways lining the walls. By the big steel blast doors, three men sat at a table, a pack of cards scattered across its surface. All gaped at the intruders.

'Still as stones!' Tom ordered, his musket shouldered.

A command already obeyed. One man's arm was in a sling. The other two carried no weapons but knives. Swords, spears and a dozen muskets were propped against a wall.

'On the floor. All of you. Quiet!'

Three gun barrels pointed. The guards scrambled.

'Make a noise, and you're...'

Then Michael almost screamed with frustration. Big-thighed Aggie had landed on a guard's back, yanked his hair and was threatening to saw his exposed throat with her knife. Perhaps she expected terror to make them compliant. Instead, the youngest panicked, bellowing instinctively, 'Fuckin' 'ell! Help! Help!'

Tom was the first to react. The barrel of his gun thrust into the young guard's mouth while Michael drew his sword to settle matters silently.

'Quiet everyone!' he advised. 'Quiet!'

The guard's shout faded to an echo.

For a long moment, all stood panting. Aggie's knife was still poised over the guard's throat. She, at least, seemed to be enjoying herself. Or just about to.

'Aggie Brown,' said Michael, calmly and firmly, 'lower the knife. Thank you. Now please go and fetch the folk we came here to free. Get the prisoners out onto the moor. We've got people out there watching...'

At that precise moment a large, burly shape clattered down a flight of stairs and into the room, leather coat flapping, a long-barrelled pistol in his belt. He gawped at visitors he had clearly not imagined possible: reached for the gun.

Time blurred. Michael watched the pistol swing in his direction, jerking up his sword as an instinctive shield. A flash. Simultaneously the blade disintegrated, the precious City blade that cost his honour and happiness, scattering into a thousand plasti-steel fragments like sand cast to the four winds. He heard a second gunshot beside him even as he stared in amazement at the hilt in his hand, aware the sword had just saved his life, deflecting a bullet meant for his head. When Michael Pilgrim looked up the man in the leather coat was staggering back, clutching his chest.

Tom Higginbottom's musket smoked as he reloaded.

Then Aggie was stuffing a knife in his hand, her face greedy as she muttered, 'Do him, Michael. Finish him off.'

The wounded man fell on his back, gasping and twitching. Michael stepped over. Close up his enemy seemed very young, little older than Seth.

'Where's Jacko?' asked Michael, kneeling beside the lad's head.

The young man's eyes rolled upwards, and Michael understood.

Moments later he had borrowed a long butcher's knife from Aggie and all her pistols. His shotgun and bandolier he entrusted to Tom.

'Find Averil and Helen,' he said, 'and get the people outside. No more shooting unless it's necessary. Do you hear me, Aggie Brown?'

His command echoed in the cold room.

'I'll not have my niece's life sacrificed for a little revenge, do you hear me?'

Aggie nodded. Blood from the gaoler whose throat she had cut still daubed her cheek. *Civilisation*, thought Michael Pilgrim, bitterly, *all for civilisation*.

He entered the stairwell from which the leather-clad youth had emerged.

ΣIGHT

---❖---

THE KINGDOMS OF THE WORLD

The pyramid of Fylingdales was not hollow. Rooms formed a labyrinth several storeys high within thick outer walls that were riveted with hundreds of plate-sized radar nodules. Cracked screens and electrical devices littered corridors commuted by beetles. Workstations that once scanned the cosmos surveyed mounds of trash. In several rooms, skulls and bones, mildew that had been clothing, belt buckles, phones, keys.

Michael mounted the stairwell, pistol cocked, torch in his free hand. Somewhere nearby was the one man whose death might bring peace. *One in, one out,* Charlie Gudwallah had been fond of saying. So be it, thought Michael, him or me.

Slowly he climbed through the pyramid's dark heart. Every so often he switched off the torch and listened: strange echoes and vibrations in the sepulchral structure. His heart beat painfully. Jacko had every advantage in this windowless maze. Even now he might be waiting behind a doorway, ready to pop out and blast Michael at point-blank range. Surely, he had heard the pistol shot and Tom's reply.

The stairwell climbed, giving onto landings and corridors. He struggled to relax the tightness of his throat. An urge to call out gripped him, to challenge the man in the shadows, command him to step into the light. Gingerly he ascended, keeping low. So slow and cautious was his progress that it came as a surprise when he reached the topmost storey and glimpsed night sky through a doorway.

The roof! Still, no sign of Jacko. Perhaps he was hiding in a corridor or room below, waiting for intruders to pass on the stairs.

Knife in one hand, pistol in the other, Michael crept up the last four concrete steps and looked out across the flat, rectangular roof of the pyramid. With a rapid motion, he slid outside.

Drizzle fell across Fylingdales Moor. A pale half-moon showed through a gap in the clouds then was obscured. Light enough for Michael Pilgrim to see a dark shape raising a pistol and respond in kind. Raindrops glistened on Big Jacko's bald forehead and cheeks.

Neither spoke. Both had pistols aimed. At such a range it would be hard to miss.

'I'm glad it's you,' said the Pharaoh.

No anger or hate in his deep voice.

'It should never have come so far,' said Michael. 'You wanted too much.'

'Maybe.'

They assessed each other, calculating when to shoot. Whoever fired first must expect an instant return.

Big Jacko stirred. 'Ain't a man's desires what makes him who he is?' he asked. 'I always wanted everything, even when I was a kid. Only, no one gave me nothing, so I took it instead.'

'That's over,' said Michael. 'Lay down your gun. I promise you a fair trial with a jury where you can state your reasons. I can't do more.'

Jacko seemed to consider this offer.

'Can't do that,' he said. 'I need the City woman.'

With that, he fired. Michael's finger jerked instinctively. Two bright flashes and puffs of acrid smoke a moment apart. Something nicked his ear, making him cry out. When he glanced up, the moon had appeared through scattering clouds to reveal Jacko tottering back, his left shoulder smashed by Michael's bullet.

The big man lost his balance and toppled over the rim of the pyramid, clutching the low guard rail with his uninjured hand, hanging on lest he roll down the steep slope and crash to unyielding earth. He roared like a beast in panic and pain. His feet scrabbled for a toe-hold on the metal radar nodules, slippery with rain.

Michael stepped over. Blood ran down his neck, hot, sticky, his ear buzzing and throbbing. He stared down at Jacko. The wounded man cried out again, an animal roar of fear.

This was the time to finish it, he thought, stamp on Jacko's hand until he let go. But as he looked down his glance fell on the protective vest he wore bearing the word *POLICE*. He had deliberately concealed the white letters with dirt and ash. Now the rain was washing it clean, *POLICE* faint but distinct. The word reminded him of his grandfather Reverend Oliver Pilgrim. The old man's numerous ideals had been easy to confuse with weakness. He seemed to hear his grandfather's voice quoting Shakespeare, both for delight and instruction, *'"The quality of mercy is not strained," Michael, remember that! "It droppeth as the gentle rain from heaven … it blesseth him that gives and him that takes…" Always remember that, Michael. Preserve, preserve, preserve.'*

He felt the rain on his weary face that was branded **F** for Felon – it might as easily have been for *fool*, weren't all born to that? Wasn't the world an orchestra of fools scraping discordantly at their own rhapsodies, their own lark songs? He felt tears trickle down his face to join the rain. Relief made him choke back sobs. An ache in his spirit that had never lifted since the Crusades loosened its grip.

Michael Pilgrim reached down to grab the Pharaoh by the scruff of the neck. With a heave, he dragged him back up, the heavy man's legs and uninjured hand finding purchase. At the top, he lay gasping, his broken shoulder leaking blood.

Running feet made Michael turn: Tom Higginbottom.

'We've got 'em all!' crowed the fisherman. 'Not even a fight! Averil's safe. Aggie's got the Queen guarded. Never seen anyone looking so angry and frightened all at the same time. It's over.'

Tom walked to where Jacko lay gasping.

'Do you get to kill him or me?' he asked.

Michael reached out to hold Tom's arm.

'Enough killing.'

'But the bastard deserves nothing less!' protested Tom, shaking free. 'Think of Charlie.'

Again Michael's hand closed around his friend's arm. 'What do we deserve, Tom? You and me and Aggie? And Baxter? Even Charlie? All of us who came back? What do we deserve?'

The night rain fell gently on guilty and innocent alike, blurring the world with watery shadows.

Tom sighed. 'I'm tired,' he said. 'I've had enough.'

HELEN

They locked the prisoners in the same basement gaol Big Jacko had used for his enemies: the wounded Pharaoh and his queen and her two children; Stu propped upon Miriam Armitage who also held their baby, defiant, protective tears on her cheeks; the remaining guards and serving women. Such a small royal court, in the end, marched at gunpoint into the pyramid's bowels. A steel plate door clanged behind them: bolts shot home.

Helen Devereux did not stay to watch. She floated upon a swirling cloud of joy, fear, but mostly disbelief that half a year's dark nightmare could be so suddenly over. Perhaps their liberation was yet another cruel game designed by Queen Morrighan; any minute, Jacko would resume his power. Averil kept close, blankets draping their shoulders as the pyramid filled with friendly voices.

Nearly a score of armed men and women milled around, including a strange-looking creature Helen vaguely remembered from City rumours. Its trunk-like nose offered the clue to his identity: a notorious rebel against the Beautiful Life.

He – or it – shuffled over, examining her through piggy pink eyes. When he spoke, it was with a wheezy squeak. The smell of his breath disgusted her.

'What strange changes,' he leered. 'It seems the City is a disease that kills all when its magic fades. All are punished, one way or another. They turned me into a monster, as you see, but you, my lovely, are rotting from within like a cankerous rose. Ha!'

Helen shrank back. He shuffled forward. Was he mad?

'Teach your former lover *that*,' he said, shrilly. 'Time will not be denied, I assure you. Nature will not be denied.'

A bulky figure stepped between them. She blinked up at Michael Pilgrim. How battered he looked. Ear bandaged, cheek branded, scars on his hands. The faint air of dreamy shyness she had found touching and boyish when they first met conquered by hard vigilance.

The Modified Man flapped his hands in disgust.

'Just remarking, Pilgrim, that even as I…' He began to cough. A racking agony subsiding into gasps. 'Even as … I…' he spluttered, 'can feel my end coming fast.' He peered hungrily into Helen's face as though divining signs. 'City youth is fool's gold!' he squealed.

Michael steered Helen aside to a bubbling cauldron originally meant for the royal party; the soup it held consisted of onions and carrots, plain oats and barley. A faint smile touched his lips, though she couldn't guess the irony behind it.

'Some for the lady,' he called, waving over a youth Helen recognised as Tom Higginbottom's son, Ben.

Michael watched gravely as she gulped the scalding broth. He seemed in no hurry to talk.

'Is the Museum open again?' she asked.

'I don't know. I hardly spent two hours in Hob Hall before riding out here.'

'You saved my life,' she said. 'And that of all the others.'

He shrugged. 'I didn't do it alone. People never manage much alone.'

Tom Higginbottom came running in through the open blast doors.

'We've got company,' he said. 'The very worst kind.'

THE DEREGULATOR OF WHITBY

Silently, the aircar descended. The rain had stopped.

Some of the small crowd in the echoing bunker hurried outside, readying weapons. Not that muskets or swords were effective against the drone currently stomping from a ramp at the rear of the vehicle. A drone that usually guarded the Deregulator's compound in Whitby. It walked on Tyrannosaurus legs, its weapons swivelling as sensors mapped potential zones of resistance. Then it halted, cannons and napalm-throwers primed.

'Everyone lay your guns and swords on the ground very slowly,' called out Michael Pilgrim. 'Do it now!'

The aircar hummed, and red lights on its side flashed. Another door opened, and a ramp slid down. A man appeared, back-lit by the bright cabin. He carried a weapon capable of blasting holes in the pyramid's concrete walls. Plasti-steel armour protected him, along with a see-through helmet and face mask. His features were familiar to anyone of a certain age from Baytown. As a boy, he had been humble Will Birch.

'Michael Pilgrim,' said the Deregulator of Whitby.

His voice boomed round the moor, amplified by the helmet's loudspeakers.

'Come closer.'

Michael did as instructed. He realised a few others had also stepped forward, so he did not go alone: at their head, the Modified Man and, though he waved her back, Helen Devereux.

The battle drone adjusted its position to accommodate these extra targets.

'I see you have the very person I want, Pilgrim,' said Will Birch. 'No! *Two* people I want. Assuming you classify one of them that way.'

The Modified Man's nose twitched.

Birch glanced around. 'Where is Jacko? Have you killed him? I expected Jacko to trade her, not you.'

Overhead clouds were dispersing rapidly to reveal a clear, starlit night. Even the wind's moan had died away.

'Jacko is dead,' said Michael, 'as are all his people.'

He could only pray the Deregulator did not search the pyramid. It wouldn't take long to find the basement-prison.

Will Birch pursed plump lips. Accompanied by the war drone his assurance was complete. Perhaps it gratified old insecurities to petrify former schoolmates.

'It doesn't matter about Jacko.' He wagged a reproving finger. 'You've turned out quite the killer, Pilgrim! Your dear-departed grandfather would be horrified. Bloodbaths in Baytown and Pickering and now yet more homicide. Do you remember the old man's sermons about the sanctity of human life?'

His booming voice faded.

'I remember,' said Michael.

'Now, Pilgrim, get everyone outside. Quickly, I say.' He indicated the drone. 'Or I'll ask my friend to help.'

For frantic minutes the Baytown folk assembled on the trampled grass before the blast doors. Satisfied, Birch turned to Helen and the Modified Man. 'You two, into the aircar.'

Michael stepped back. Resistance did not occur to him. If the Deregulator chose, he could slaughter everyone present with a single command to the drone and a few squeezes of his finger. Impotence gripped him, sickening, debasing, all he had ever known when confronted with the City's power. With those feelings came self-contempt. Yes, he was a coward still with all a coward's fears. Michael hung his head and for a horrible moment felt exactly as he had when serving in the Crusades.

Then an unexpected voice spoke out. It belonged to Helen Devereux.

HELEN (2)

'I'm not coming with you.'

She drew a knife, one used by a queen for sacrifices to bring luck and extend life. Helen had picked it up, scabbard and all, when her enemy was disarmed. Somehow the malicious and unkind always seemed to triumph in this world, but whatever happened, there would be no more days and nights of horror in a dark gaol for her. Queen Morrighan's knife would see to that…

Helen held the tip to her left breast. Pressed its point close. Mhairi would have known where and how to end her life in an instant. The thought of her sister gave Helen courage.

Out on the moor, crickets chirped. Will Birch hesitated.

'Oh, come now, Miss Devereux, please spare me your theatricals.'

Helen stared back at him. Did not speak. She remembered playing her violin with Mhairi in the old chapel on the cliff, how Harry the tomcat had rubbed against her legs. She had told Mhairi that she would no longer live in fear, that she could yet do some good in the world. And her little sister had trusted her…

'Come along,' chided the Deregulator. 'There is someone important who believes you are dead. Someone who might even turn a blind eye to certain, ah hum, transgressions of mine if you were delivered to him safe and sound. I have to say, Jacko did a wonderful job of keeping your existence secret.'

Helen barely listened. She could feel the knife pricking into the soft skin of her breast. A City knife, she guessed, one of Big Jacko's rewards for providing the young flesh turned into monsters by Dr Guy de Prie-Dieu. Crimes Mhairi had sacrificed her life to end…

'Do let's be civilised about this,' continued the Deregulator. 'It is unwise to disappoint an important man like Blair Gover.'

Now Helen stirred.

'Blair Gover, is it? What has happened to Bertrand Du Guesclin?'

'After you vanished and were assumed dead, he reverted to his original name,' said Birch. 'He has put out a bulletin urging a return to what he terms *gravitas* in Albion.'

A smile crept over her pale lips.

'I'm not coming with you.'

'Really?' Will Birch pointed his gun. 'Then I promise to kill these primitives, two at a time, until you see sense. It is merely my duty.'

Even amidst her fear, a bleak loathing hardened in Helen's soul.

'The moment you fire,' she said, 'this knife goes in. Then you can explain it to Dr Gover. I won't care either way.'

The barrel of Will Birch's gun swept the terrified crowd. Helen could sense his calculations.

'Very well,' he said, stiffly, 'I shall content myself with informing Dr Gover where he may find you. But tonight is just tonight. You see those savages, those Pilgrims, you have grown so fond of? Rest assured I'll do my duty, sooner or later.'

Helen did not doubt him for an instant. The tip of the knife wavered. Wasn't she always beaten in the end?

A coughing, wheezy chuckle made Helen steady her hand.

'I'll go instead of her,' called out the Modified Man. 'I'm valuable to you as well. The despised rebel, eh? My capture's worth something to you, especially when you report Miss Devereux's location to your masters.'

Birch's expression was hard to read behind the glass shield across his face. His voice echoed through the amplifier like a giant's.

'Why not,' he said, icily. 'I'll settle for you.' He glanced at Helen and bowed.

The queer creature limped towards the aircar, following Birch up the ramp. Simultaneously the battle drone wheeled and stomped back to the rear doors of the craft. Before entering the aircar, the Modified Man turned and showed to Michael Pilgrim what looked like the top of a metal canister, before jamming it back into his pocket.

'Farewell, Pilgrim,' called the hideous creature. 'Remember, their arrogance will destroy them one day. If I were you, I'd start running. *Now!*'

With that warning, he limped into the aircar, and the ramp rose behind him.

NOW!

'Run!' roared Michael Pilgrim in his best parade ground bawl. 'Run for your lives!'

Lucky for them the Deregulator had gathered every available primitive in Fylingdales outside its blast doors.

'Go!' he bellowed, pausing only to pick up his shotgun.

The aircar engines hummed. Like panicked sheep, the people fled across the moor. Those too weak to run were carried or dragged.

'Faster!' he urged.

People screamed as they tumbled and scrabbled through the heather and thorn bushes and saplings. The aircar was rising now, its lights flashing, engines whining. Up it angled until it hovered a hundred feet over the pyramid, revolving to face towards Whitby.

'Take cover!' cried Michael. Then he hurled himself onto the ground and prayed.

A blinding flash tore the night apart. The boom and shock waves of an explosion. In an instant, the aircar buckled, engulfed by fire. Ponderously it fell, crashing into the pyramid, crushing concrete and steel, walls collapsing as a second explosion – far bigger than the first – lit the night, gouging a hole out of the building. With a rumble, the pyramid subsided into a mound of dust and concrete and plaster.

At long last, the Modified Man had found a use for the City bomb Michael had traded to feed his family in the hungry winter.

Tom Higginbottom seized his shoulder. Lurid flames turned their faces red as devils'.

'Jacko!'

Michael understood. Deep beneath that mountain of debris, the Pharaoh and his followers would be forever imprisoned in his tomb.

'They'll get to eating each other down there before long,' predicted Tom. 'Unless they suffocate first.'

No time for speculation. That must come later. Picking themselves up, the fugitives hurried for the cover of Dalby Forest. Sure as eggshells, the City would be sending drones out to investigate the explosion. No one fancied being around when they arrived.

SETH PILGRIM

A mile away across the moor, on the Whitby to Pickering road, Seth Pilgrim gripped his mare's reins as she bucked and pulled, terrified by the explosion and fireball engulfing Fylingdales. He had witnessed the aircar take flight and the Baytown folk scatter before it blew to pieces.

'Father,' he muttered in his panic, 'Mother.'

Tears stung his eyes. Grief fastened like leeches on a young heart coarsened by Big Jacko's service. Seth glimpsed what was lost to him. What had just begun. Abandoned by mischance to a world without friends or home or purpose.

Did he blame himself? Mourn the choices that exiled him from Hob Hall, from a community and life little loved? Only the bleak moor beneath a half moon and glittering stars bore witness.

Seth Pilgrim led his limping horse away into the night. Before the drones arrived, he had long vanished.

EPILOGUE

PILGRIM TALƐ

—————✣—————

When Helen Devereux returned to the old chapel once occupied by Dr Mhairi Macdonald, a guardian spirit greeted her: Harry the tomcat, fat on his summer of mice and unwary birds. For the first time in decades, catching her own food became a challenge for the pampered City woman.

Within days, Helen offered her services as musical director of the Baytown Orchestra and established a school for the village children, insisting only that they brought slates (plenty of those on ruined roofs) for writing practice and made modest payments of food so their teacher did not starve. A bad time to open a school with harvest nigh, but Michael Pilgrim led the way, sending over the orphans of Hob Hall for a lesson each morning; human nature decreed that a community which regarded him with grateful awe should follow suit.

One day Helen and Michael met to discuss the school outside the Museum, the building still locked and guarded by steel shutters and electric shocks whenever door or window was touched.

'A shame the Museum remains dark and closed,' she said. 'It would be perfect for my school, and the orchestra could rehearse here. Baytown needs a proper public building. I could live here, too; Mhairi's old chapel will never be a proper home for me. If nothing else, the roof is falling in. I found a collapse of tiles and plaster this morning.'

She chose not to mention that living alone amidst scurrying rats frightened her. Helen realised he was watching her as though making up his mind to say something.

'For some time,' he began in his cautious way, 'I've wondered – and so has Averil – whether it would be better for you to move into Hob Hall. We've no end of spare rooms.' He laughed apologetically. 'It's a humble place, we know, after what you're used to.'

Her eyes wrinkled in surprise.

'And we thought – Mister Priest Man agrees – your school should move to Holy Innocents Church. And Dr Macdonald's library could go there, as well. So you see, you would be a curator once more. Only of living knowledge and minds.'

Helen's heart leapt at so strong a mark of Baytown's acceptance. She knew Mhairi would have approved with every layer of her soul.

'Thank you,' said Helen. 'The Museum would be a better place for a proper school, but your plan is good and kind and sensible, as always. I accept gratefully. As long as Harry the cat may come with me.'

'That he can,' said Michael, grinning as he puffed at his pipe. 'Though he'll have to get acquainted with my Bess.'

Bess had been kept safe by Amar during Big Jacko's tenure as lord of Hob Hall. The faithful sheepdog nearly shook off her tail with wagging and burst her lungs barking when her master finally rode home.

While they talked outside the Museum, a small red light glowed above the door. Neither noticed. Yet a strange thing occurred the next day. The new Deregulator of Whitby flew in with drones and uniformed technicians to strip the Museum of forbidden technology – screens and machines, all loaded into cargo holds and borne back to the City of Albion. Only furniture and the exhibits remained.

A simple message was left with Averil and Amar, who dared to enquire what was happening.

'Tell Helen Devereux,' said the new Deregulator, very slowly and loudly as one might address a brace of half-wits, 'that a true friend gives this building and all its exhibits over to her sole care.' The uniformed woman frowned at them disapprovingly. '*True friend*. Understand?'

Luckily they did and hurried to find Helen in the church where she was teaching the rudiments of the alphabet using slates and chalk.

That same evening she clasped the precious Jewel in her hands once more, delighting in its perfection and beauty. Yet she did not doubt the identity of her anonymous *true friend* or that Dr Blair Gover had made his final gift to her – including averting retribution upon Baytown for a certain explosion over Fylingdales. Neither did it escape her notice that by returning the Museum to her possession, he had prevented the possibility of her moving into Hob Hall. As Mhairi once pointed out about Blair – or Bertrand or whatever he chose to call himself in a few hundred years' time – he never tired of his games.

Every morsel of birth feeds the Earth's appetite for death. The harvest in Baytown that year was bumper.

From dawn until dusk folk laboured in the fields to mow and stack and store. All available hands, weak and strong alike, played their part. Helen learned the meaning of calluses and sunburn.

Big Jacko's depredations had stripped the district's larders, and the new mayor declared a communal storehouse would be established for orphans, cripples, widows and old folk. Larks trilled, and insects buzzed. Hot days were scented with summer.

At last, the harvest was home, just in time for the autumn equinox. A bloated pink and ivory moon lit Baytown that night, casting eerie sheens over sea and stubbly field and rooftop. The Nuagers led by Mister Priest Man offered sacrifices of fruit to gods old and new, not least the Faery o' the Vale and her retinue of mischievous hobs.

A fair gathered on the Commons above Baytown. All afternoon, wagons decorated with evergreens and flowers rolled into town to prepare a moonlit banquet. Tugs of war and feats of strength were performed on the grass. Folk feasted on piles of fresh loaves and a fat sow roasted whole. Fish were fried and potatoes baked. Blackberry pies sweetened with honey stained many a child's cheeks and mouth. Ale and hoarded wine flowed from jugs.

True, a shadow flitted high above the gathering in the form of a spydrone. Only the most vigilant noticed it. The trill and twitter of larks in the fields masked the faint hum of its engines.

'We'll have them buggers one day,' muttered Tom Higginbottom to Michael Pilgrim as they gazed up, hands shielding their eyes.

'Maybe,' said Michael, recalling the Modified Man's parting words: *Remember their arrogance will destroy them one day.*

As the moon rose, dancing commenced that would last until dawn. Prominent among the couples was one set to wed at Christmas, Averil and Amar. Older folk rediscovered their dancing legs, too, Tom and Beth Higginbottom capering with more determination than grace. Their son, Ben, stood at the side, mourning someone buried beneath a hillock of concrete on Fylingdales Moor, his lost, beloved Miriam Armitage. Travellers on the moor reported ghostly voices wailing in grief from the ruins at night, unless it was the wind. Young Ben hated to think of Miriam trapped for eternity in the dark basement of the pyramid and with such companions. But soon enough a girl from Hawsker took pity on him and dragged him willy-nilly into the circle of dancers.

Helen watched it all with melancholy joy. If only Mhairi were beside her, perhaps she would feel less detached. Yet she was treated with honour and given a seat among the Pilgrims of Hob Hall. There she witnessed a harvest no one anticipated.

A small party trotted into Baytown on ponies hung with ribbons and garlands. Strangers with strange accents from Hull welcomed to the feast and led to greet the Mayor. Among them, a tall, comely young woman wearing a purple dress glittering with gold and silver from the lost days – wedding rings, sovereigns, gold watches without time. Her hennaed hair glossy and thick, piled into a bun held in place by an ornately carved whalebone comb. In her arms, she carried a child also dressed in finery. A boy around one year of age. Helen watched curiously as the young woman approached Michael Pilgrim.

Mutual blushes confirmed the nature of their prior acquaintance. Both developed an interest in straightening their party clothes.

'I've brought you a gift,' she said.

Raising soft, arch eyes to meet his own, she offered the child, proud appeal in her glance.

'I thought he should know you,' she said. 'See! He has your eyes.'

Blue eyes. Pilgrim eyes.

Then Helen understood – and felt very old, very rueful. She realised the hour was already late and that she should return to her bed in the Museum. Quietly, she left as Michael Pilgrim gingerly took the boy and held him up high to witness and be witnessed by the moon, marvelling at his face and perfect little hands and the precious warmth of his breath, acknowledging his son to the red harvest moon.

ΛCKПOWLΣDGΣMΣПTS

I would like to thank the following people for supporting this book:

Everyone at Cloud Lodge Books for their creativity, encouragement and professionalism.

Paul Osborne for providing the initial spark for **Pilgrim Tale** over a few beers one rainy night in York.

Flight Lieutenant Rick Weeks for arranging an unforgettable visit to RAF Fylingdales.

A big thank you to the 'early readers' whose suggestions and comments proved invaluable: Sara Bowland, Jane Collins, Richard Gray, Bob Horne, Dori Murgatroyd, Anna Perrett and Craig Smith.

Last, but never least, Ruth Murgatroyd, for her gift of close reading when dystopia was far from her cup of tea. I hope the raspberry cordial sweetened the brew...

ABOUT THE AUTHOR

Tim Murgatroyd was brought up in Yorkshire. He read English at Hertford College, Oxford University and now lives with his family in York. He is the author of several novels of historical fiction and a poetry series. Pilgrim Tale is the first book in his Pilgrim Trilogy.

RΣΛD MORΣ

---◊◊◊---

Chapter One from

Pilgrim Lost
Book Two in the Pilgrim Trilogy

SPRIΠG

ΘΠΣ

SETH PILGRIM

That winter a fire was visible from the Cumbrian hills, a lone flare rising from the old nuclear power station at Sellafield on the coast. The Maister of Floggers Gil stared long and hard, night after night. Distant flames rose high then died to a sickly glow between shore and sea that finally went dark.

'I reckon there'll be plenty of changelings for boiling an' grinding,' he predicted. And the two Mistresses agreed.

Even then, Seth Pilgrim knew which bonder would be driven into the briar-tangled woods and ordered not to return empty-handed. Who must risk the same sickness as bud and beast and bird's egg. It felt like his due.

THE SICKNESS

The early spring was dank. Out west by the Irish Sea, far from Baytown and all Seth had ever known as a lad, four years had passed.

Now he stood in the rain at the edge of woods from which poked chimneys, cooling towers, steel cranes draped with ivy, huge concrete rectangles, the remains of the nuclear plant. Few in Cumbria came here by choice. The sickness – invisible as airborne plague spores – caused vomiting, cancers, deformed babies to expose on cold hillsides.

He glanced back at the knot of armed men watching from a nearby hill. Prominent among them, Maister Gil, scourge in belt. They would camp up there until he returned and maybe reward him with extra gruel and oat bread if he got lucky.

Seth waded into the shallow River Calder running like a winding road through the many square miles of the overgrown site. Shackled ankles joined by an iron chain made him hobble. On his back hung sacks to gather the harvest.

The water was icy, but Seth had grown accustomed to cold – what field-bonder was not? As he followed the gravel streambed, alder and willow cloaked him. Choruses of birdsong echoed in the stirring woods. He glimpsed bluebells, purple-pink orchids, dog violets and pink campion. An odd sensation stole up from his heart, one he had almost forgotten: freedom. Those bastards on the hill could not see him here and dared not follow.

He waded past the remains of a concrete weir and recalled why no one dared. Even on the outskirts of Sellafield, the sickness lay strong.

But for now he was free.

For a moment, the old Seth Pilgrim of Baytown days flared.

'Screw you!' he cried, his racing heartbeat a wild fantasy of power – cutting Maister Gil's throat like a squealing sheep's, oh yes, then turning on the Mistresses like this and this.

HARVESTING

They had given him a notched, rusty knife and hempen net to capture prey. Seth perched beneath a willow on the riverbank, reluctant to enter the pathless maze of thickets and buildings. Once in that lot, he'd be lost. For a while he sat, watching rain putter across the grey stream, sharpening the knife on a whetstone. He was hungry as always. But only madmen foraged in Sellafield, except perhaps for fish swimming down from the high fells and lakes of the mountains. Clean soil up there. Clean waters. Clean air.

Sighing, he wrapped grass around his ankle shackles so they would not chafe or clank. Stealth was needed – and sharp eyes.

Half a mile from the river, Seth feared never finding a way out again. Birds chirruped excitedly as they squabbled and mated, but he saw none worthy of his net. Last summer's briars still bore thorns to snag his raggedy clothes. The woods clogged with underbrush, roots and tendrils beneath the canopy. At last, he found a peculiar fungus sporting odd, noxious horns. Then, by a scummy pond, he came upon a frog with two heads. Into his sack they went.

Warm in the wood, unnaturally so. Again he grew fearful and clutched the knife. What if rumours of monsters dwelling around the power station were true? Of cursed survivors of the original plagues who could never die, famished for living flesh. Scarcely a soul among the folk he dwelt doubted such stories. Dark, dark the forests and shadows and secret places. Hell is hot, taught the Mistresses. Hell is hot.

Seth sometimes remembered, even in his distress – like noticing a glow worm on a moonless night when clouds choke the wan light of the stars – science lessons delivered by Father and Uncle Michael in the old library at Hob Hall. Both had been great ones for condemning superstition as a prison house for mankind. 'Humanity will never recover what it has lost through superstition,' Uncle Michael had taught his nephew and Seth's twin Averil, and a dozen other kids bent over slates and chalk…

Slowly, his breath steadied; he pushed deeper into the woods towards the heat's source.

THE CORE

Seth stumbled upon a smoke-blackened cooling tower beside scorched walls and the remains of a collapsed roof. Whatever conflagration Maister Gil watched from the hills that winter had raged here. Something mysterious had caused the blaze, but now it was cold, the soot and tar of its burning sticky with rain. Poison and sickness spread far and wide with the billowing smoke.

As Seth emerged from the trees, he encountered a hidden glen before the buildings, a car park sprouting grass. At his approach, a small knot of deer scattered, their hooves clattering as they vanished among the trees.

All except one.

A fawn – a few weeks old, still not weaned from its mother's teats – tried to follow its herd. Four legs it had, another two hanging limp and useless like bizarre tails from its lumpy spine.

Seth assessed the changeling hungrily. Deformities were common enough when the wind chose certain directions, and among humans too, but this was perfect. Exactly what the Mistresses found useful. Yet for all his natural disgust at the limping creature, it stirred feelings he could not explain. Perhaps it was the extra set of splayed teeth and moist gums protruding from its forehead. Or the pitiful little legs hanging from its back.

He hobbled over and pushed it to the ground.

Lucky for once, he told himself, the fawn meant extra food for sure.

He slumped on the grass-tussocked tarmac, the foal beside him. Its soft brown eyes stared up. It did not struggle.

Then Seth looked around and, for all his weariness of spirit, noticed things.

First, the ivy scaling up the burned cooling tower, leaves and stems a defiant green. No holding back life's climb towards the sun. He realised the rain no longer irritated his face and hands. It cleansed him. Droplets gathered on the back of his branded right hand, lingered on his face that had forgotten how to smile.

He noticed a few early bees drifting between clumps of pale yellow primrose, flies buzzing over a pile of deer dung, red butterflies. He noticed the raindrops on his cheek had been joined by something barely recalled: something salty, precious, his eyes' own creation. Something he dared never show before the Mistresses or their people because weakness provoked bullying, taunting. Yet tears had rediscovered him. He could not say why.

Memories flashed across Seth Pilgrim's mind like sunlight across a rippling stream, too quick to grasp. One clearest of all, among lost hopes and dreams, before defeat and years of wretched slavery crushed them, one by one. A fantasy of himself in the fabulous City of Albion, beloved and feared by all, master of drones and fabulous aircars…

Then it faded. Once more he slumped on rotting tarmac before a burned-out relic of mankind's lost dominions and powers. The rain quickened.

He positioned the panting fawn for the knife. Slitting its throat would be a mercy to them both. God knew it was ugly, crippled, weak. The fawn could only hobble, not run, shackled by fate instead of chains.

Wearily, Seth readied the blade. Deep in a heart corrupted by cruelties – too many for someone his age, too gross to face down except in foul dreams – he recalled another knife in his hand, another act of sacrifice, how he had … Oh, he could not bear to think of it now…Old Marley, the hapless tramp, known since he was a small boy, the vagrant his Father fed and clothed out of charity each Christmas…

'No!'

His cry died amidst rain dripping from branches. Wind soughing in the trees.

Shackles clanking, Seth rose and put the knife in his rope belt.

'Run along, ugly,' he told the fawn, helping it with a boot up the backside so the changeling's extra limbs quivered comically.

Seth Pilgrim's face resumed its customary absence of expression. He'd pay for this small mercy. Maybe with Maister Gil's whip, maybe worse.

THE COVEN IN THE HILLS

The coven and its bonders occupied a hamlet of stone farmbuildings on a hillside six miles inland from Sellafield. From this lofty point, you could see the Isle of Man on a clear day. Turn east, and the high peaks of Seatallan, Great Gable and Scafell Pike rose.

It was still raining when the horsemen led by Maister Gil plodded up the track to Fell Hall. Behind them shuffled an exhausted Seth Pilgrim.

He was in great disfavour with Maister Gil for failing to gather enough changelings. When boiled by the Mistresses into magic oils stained bright with plant juices, they fetched good barter from credulous farmers all over Lake Country, even as far south as Lancaster.

Seth knew Maister Gil too well. The bony little man was out of love with the entire world. Since the Great Dyings reduced humanity to a thin scrape across the surface of the earth, everyone might be called disappointed. Yet few vented their frustrations quite like Gil. Five years earlier he had led a band of floggers as their Maister, a petty king of sorts. Now floggers were outlawed after the defeat of Pharaoh Jacko at the Battle of Pickering – a slaughter Gil only narrowly survived – and the establishment of the Commonwealth of the North exiled him to the wild Cumbrian hills.

On the way, he and a handful of loyal followers had captured other fugitives from Pharaoh Jacko's fall, Seth Pilgrim included, promptly branding them as bonders. Gil's destination had been old allies, the Mistresses of Fell Hall, where he joined their coven.

It came as little surprise to Seth that dragging him in chains across bog, rigg and beck would not appease Gil. Once dismounted, he changed into his old Maister's robe and cowl and beat Seth with a three-tailed scourge. As he worked, Maister Gil chanted the old flogger's hymn, perhaps in a spirit of nostalgia, perhaps to cheer himself up:

> Our City that art Heaven,
> Right feared be thy name.
> Thy kingdom's come and we obey.
> Punish any man that don't worship thee,
> Give 'em plague and daily woes,
> Make 'em starve that break thy laws
> And deliver us from drones.
> For thou art the power and glory.
> Drink our blood forever and ever,
> Eat our flesh as thy daily bread.
> Amen! And so say all of us!

The punishment might have been worse, but Gil and his comrades were sodden by a night camped in the rain and soon drifted off to warm themselves with mulled ale by the fire.

AMONG BEASTS

Seth slept in a low stone byre and stable that was bolted on the outside each night. Few comforts came his way, each guarded jealously. There were his blanket and various ragged clothes of fur and homespun castoffs sewn together. A decent pair of clogs. A secret stash of wooden wedges carved over long winter nights that comforted him when he felt most abused. And stray, impractical reminders of yearnings finer than an empty belly: a plastic toy aeroplane from the Before Days; a gold cylinder with a sliding lid containing a stick of dried out, rose-red paint he discovered when scavenging a car. Each carried meanings to him. What they might be, he shared with no one.

His companions in the gloom of the byre were shaggy hill ponies, cattle, and a brace of two-legged beasts of burden less free than the other farm animals. Like Seth, they wore ankle shackles. Not that they could run far even without chains, all the bonders were agreed on that. Farmers in neighbouring vales feared spells and curses from the Mistresses of Fell Hall; most would gladly help hunt down runaways in return for a blessing on their ewes or oat fields.

It was clear that Seth's fellow bonders enjoyed lighter labours than him. Maister Gil never forgave the lad's glory days as right-hand man to Pharaoh Jacko. And he never ceased blaming Seth's uncle Michael Pilgrim for outlawing the bands of floggers who once ranged from settlement to settlement with impunity.

'Them were grand days,' he reminisced in his cups one night when Seth was forced to serve supper to his betters. 'The City was friend to us wandering folk for many a year.' His eye fell on Seth, and his face darkened. 'I should've strangled that bastard Pilgrim in his sleep when I had the chance. And I will yet.'

Seth said nothing, his face blank. But he listened. As the two Mistresses were fond of saying, knowledge is power.

'Tinkers are telling,' Gil resumed to his companions, 'the Deregulators are losing interest in the doings of us little folk.' His voice took on a whine of complaint. 'I heard they even closed down their holy compounds in Hull and Scouseton. Places they've been deregulating for a hundred years! And some say they're taking their mighty drones back to the City, them that kept us rightly downtrodden.'

Maybe so. But drones could still be heard at night, jet engines roaring like dragons over Lake Country. There was even wild talk of magical City creatures out east, not so much changelings, as strangelings…

After his beating, Seth lay on his front in the byre while the animals shuffled and his fellow bonders snored. New thoughts stirred. The fire in Sellafield might be a sign, like freeing the changeling fawn. The City was abandoning its Deregulators' compounds up and down the coast. Perhaps the all-powerful City was in trouble. Perhaps it needed new servants – new men for a new time whom it would generously reward. Slowly, as dawn bled light through the roof slates, Seth conceived of a future beyond Fell Hall. He recollected his store of carefully carved wooden wedges and made plans.

PLOUGHING

Rain horizontal as he ploughed the lower slopes of the hill. Seth and two ponies up to their fetlocks in mud made pungent by liberal doses of manure. The Mistresses loved their spuds, and Gil, who played the role of bailiff and farm manager at Fell Hall – often badly – had ordered Seth out for a final cross-plough. Wrong weather with the soil waterlogged, but Seth knew better than to argue.

'Whoa there!' he called as the ploughshares sawn from an old duraplastic car bonnet snagged in the mire. 'Steady!'

Plumes of breath from the hot horses, tails swishing at flies drawn by their sweat. On the hill above, the dark shapes of the farm and smoke rising. Low clouds obscured all points of the horizon.

Should I run now, wondered Seth, on such a day as this?

Daily the urge tormented him. He could unshackle his ankles with the hammer and pointy chisel he had hidden, release the ponies from the plough and gallop until they were winded and broken then run, run until he dropped. Surely that would be far enough away.

But Seth knew he must be patient.

Almost at once, his patience was rewarded. On a neighbouring track, he saw a party of folk approaching. Most were prosperous by the look of their woollen clothes; even their servants wore shoes. A man with a breastplate fashioned from an oven door rode at the head, pistol in belt, leading two women on a farm cart that jolted and tilted over the stony way. The servants followed on foot, driving a fat ewe.

Seth bowed as they passed. He recognised the man as the Lord of Erringdale, a firm supporter of the Fell Hall Coven. On the cart sat a bonny young girl alongside an older, hard-faced woman with a swollen stomach. Seth guessed the story, a pregnancy not going well. The woman's anxious old goat of a husband bringing her to the Mistresses to set matters right with a good old, plain, honest mass.

In the rear of the cart, Seth noticed a large ale barrel as payment for the rites. His heart quickened. A mass followed by a barrel that size could only end one way – and offer his chance for escape.